The MORTAL ENGINES series

"Superbly imagined"
The Times

"Marvellous ... utterly captivating in its imaginative
scope and energy. The only flaw I can see is the
difficulty of putting it down between chapters."
Daily Telegraph

"Reeve is the only writer in the field who is producing
work that is genuinely inventive and transforming"
Guardian

"Phenomenal... violent and romantic, action-packed
and contemplative, funny and frightening"
Sunday Times

"One of the most inventive and ambitious
children's novel sequences of recent years"
Nicolette Jones

"A magnificent story and one of the most
compelling I have read so far this year"
Bookseller

"Reeves writes with confidence and power. He is not only a
master of visceral excitement, but at every turn, surprises,
entertains and makes his readers think... Unmissable"
Book For Keeps

By Philip Reeve

Mortal Engines

Predator's Gold

Infernal Devices

A Darkling Plain

Fever Crumb

❁

Here Lies Arthur

❁

In the BUSTER BAYLISS series:

Night of the Living Veg

The Big Freeze

Day of the Hamster

Custardfinger

❁

Larklight

Starcross

Mothstorm

PHILIP REEVE

A DARKLING PLAIN

SCHOLASTIC

Scholastic Children's Books
An imprint of Scholastic Ltd
Euston House, 24 Eversholt Street
London, NW1 1DB, UK
Registered office: Westfield Road, Southam
Warwickshire, CV47 0RA
SCHOLASTIC and associated logos are trademarks and/or registered
trademarks of Scholastic Inc.

First published by Scholastic Ltd, 2006
This edition published by Scholastic Ltd, 2009

Copyright © Philip Reeve, 2006
Cover illustration copyright © David Wyatt, 2009
The rights of Philip Reeve and David Wyatt to be identified as
the author and illustrator of this work have been asserted by them.

ISBN 9781407110943

A CIP catalogue record for this book is available from the British Library.

Printed by CPI Bookmarque, Croydon, CR0 4TD
Papers used by Scholastic Children's Books are made
from wood grown in sustainable forests.

1 3 5 7 9 10 8 6 4 2

This is a work of fiction. Names, characters, places, incidents and dialogues are
products of the author's imagination or are used fictitiously. Any resemblance
to actual people, living or dead, events or locales is entirely coincidental.

www.scholastic.co.uk/zone

CONTENTS

PART FOUR

For Sarah
(as always)

For Kirsty and Holly
(of course)

And for
Sam, Tom and Edward
(eventually)

Ah, love, let us be true
To one another! for the world, which seems
To lie before us like a land of dreams,
So various, so beautiful, so new,
Hath really neither joy, nor love, nor light,
Nor certitude, nor peace, nor help for pain;
And we are here as on a darkling plain
Swept with confus'd alarms of struggle and flight,
Where ignorant armies clash by night.

Matthew Arnold, *Dover Beach*

ACKNOWLEDGEMENTS

A Darkling Plain and its three predecessors would have been quite different kettles of fish without the inspiration, advice and encouragement which their author has received from Brian Mitchell, Leon Robinson, Liz Cross, Mike Grant and Gavin Wilson. Gigantic thank yous are also due to my editors, Kirsten Stansfield, Holly Skeet and Katy Moran, and to everyone at Scholastic who has worked so hard to make the *Mortal Engines* quartet a success. For help with a couple of details in the present volume I am indebted to Alison Janzen, and to my father, Michael Reeve, who seems to know *everything*. And thanks, finally, to Nick and Kjartan, who let me take their names in vain.

Philip Reeve
Dartmoor, 2006

PART ONE

1

SUPER-GNATS OVER ZAGWA

Theo had been climbing since dawn; first on the steep roads and paths and sheep-tracks behind the city, then across slopes of shifting scree, and up at last on to the bare mountainside, keeping where he could to corries and crevices where the blue shadows pooled. The sun was high overhead by the time he reached the summit. He paused there a while to drink water and catch his breath. Around him the mountains quivered behind veils of heat-haze rising from the warm rocks.

Carefully, carefully, Theo edged his way on to a narrow spur that jutted out from the mountain-top. On either side of him sheer cliffs dropped for thousands of feet to a tumble of spiky rocks; trees; white rivers. A stone, dislodged, fell silently, end over end, for ever. Ahead, Theo could see nothing but the naked sky. He stood upright, took a deep breath, sprinted the last few yards to the edge of the rock, and jumped.

Over and over he went, down and down, dazed by the flicker of mountain and sky, mountain and sky. The echoes of his first cry bounded away into silence and he could hear nothing but his quick-beating heart and the rush of the air past his ears. Tumbling on the wind, he emerged from the crag's shadow into sunlight, and glimpsed below him – far below – his home, the static city of Zagwa. From up here the copper domes and painted houses looked like toys; airships coming and going from the harbour were wind-blown petals, the river winding through its gorge a silver thread.

Theo watched it all fondly till it was hidden from him by a shoulder of the mountains. There had been a time when he had thought that he would never return to Zagwa. In the Green Storm training camp they had taught him that his love for home and family was a luxury; something that he must forget if he were to play his part in the war for a world made green again. Later, as a captive slave on the raft-city of Brighton, he had dreamed of home, but he had thought that his family would not want him back; they were old fashioned Anti-Tractionists, and he imagined that by running away to join the Storm he had made himself an outcast for ever. Yet here he was, back among his own African hills; it was his time in the north that seemed to him now like a dream.

And it was all Wren's doing, he thought as he fell. Wren; that odd, brave, funny girl whom he had met in Brighton, his fellow slave. "Go home to your mother and father," she had told him, after they escaped together. "They still love you, and they'll welcome you, I'm sure." And she had been right.

A startled bird shot past on Theo's left, reminding him that he was in mid-air above a lot of unfriendly-looking rocks, and descending fast. He opened the great kite that was strapped to his back and let out a whoop of triumph as the wings jerked him upwards and his dizzy plunge turned to a graceful, soaring flight. The roar of the wind rushing past him died away, replaced by gentler sounds; the whisper of the broad panels of silicon-silk, the creak of rigging and bamboo struts.

When he was younger Theo had often brought his kite up here, testing his courage on the winds and thermals. Lots of young Zagwans did it. Since his return from the north, six months ago, he had sometimes looked enviously at their bright wings hanging against the mountains, but he had never dared to join them. His time away had changed him too much; he felt older than the other boys his age, yet shy of them, ashamed of the things he had been; a Tumbler-bomb pilot, and a prisoner, and a slave. But this morning the other cloud-riders were all at the citadel to see the foreigners. Theo, knowing that he would have the sky to himself, had woken up longing to fly again.

He slid down the wind like a hawk, watching his shadow swim across the sunlit buttresses of the mountain. Real hawks, hanging beneath him in the glassy air, veered away with sharp mews of surprise and indignation as he soared past, a lean black boy beneath a sky-blue wing invading their element.

Theo looped-the-loop and wished that Wren could see him. But Wren was far away, travelling the Bird Roads in her father's airship. After they escaped from Cloud 9, the mayor of Brighton's airborne palace, and reached the Traction City of Kom Ombo, she had helped Theo find a berth aboard a south-bound freighter. On the quay, while the airship was making ready to depart, they had said goodbye, and he had kissed her. And although Theo had kissed other girls, some much prettier than Wren, Wren's kiss had stayed with him; his mind kept going back to it at unexpected moments like this. When he kissed her all the laughter and the wry irony had gone out of her and she had become shivery and serious and so quiet, as if she were listening hard for something he could not hear. For a moment he had wanted to tell her that he loved her, and ask her to come with him, or offer to stay – but

Wren had been so worried about her dad, who had suffered some sort of seizure, and so angry at her mum, who had abandoned them and fallen with Cloud 9 into the desert, that he would have felt he was taking advantage of her. His last memory of her was of looking back as his ship pulled away into the sky and seeing her waving, growing smaller and smaller until she was gone.

Six months ago! Already half a year... It was definitely time he stopped thinking about her.

So for a little while he thought of nothing, just swooped and banked on the playful air, swinging westward with a mountain between him and Zagwa; a green mountain where rags and flags of mist streamed from the canopy of the cloud-forest.

Half a year. The world had changed a lot in that time. Sudden, shuddering changes like the shifting of tectonic plates, as tensions that had been building all through the long years of the Green Storm's war were suddenly released. For a start, the Stalker Fang was gone. There was a new leader in the Jade Pagoda now, General Naga, who had a reputation as a hard man. His first act as leader had been to reverse the *Traktionstadtsgesellschaft*'s advance on the Rustwater Marshes, and smash the Slavic cities which had been nibbling for years at the Storm's northern borders. But then, to the astonishment of the world, he had called off his air-fleets, and made a truce with the Traction Cities. There were rumours from the Green Storm's lands about political prisoners being released and harsh laws repealed; even talk that Naga planned to disband the Storm and re-establish the old Anti-Traction League. Now he had sent a delegation to hold talks with the Queen and Council of Zagwa – a delegation led by his own wife, Lady Naga.

It was this which had driven Theo to rise at dawn and bring his old kite up into the high places above the city. The talks were beginning today, and his father and mother and sisters had all gone to the citadel to see if they could catch a glimpse of the foreigners. They were excited, and full of hope. Zagwa had withdrawn from the Anti-Traction League when the Green Storm took power, appalled by their doctrine of total war and their armies of reanimated corpses. But now (so Theo's father had heard), General Naga was proposing a formal peace with the barbarian cities, and there were even hints that he was prepared to dismantle the Storm's Stalkers. If he did, Zagwa and the other African statics might be able to join again in the defence of the world's green places. Theo's father was keen for his wife and children to be at the citadel for this historic moment, and anyway, he wanted to have a look at Lady Naga, whom he had heard was very young and beautiful.

But Theo had seen all he ever wished to of the Green Storm, and he did not trust anything Naga or his envoys said. So, while the rest of Zagwa crowded into the citadel gardens, he swooped and soared on the golden air, and thought of Wren.

And then, below him, he saw movement where nothing should be moving; nothing except birds, and these were too big to be birds. They were rising out of the white mist above the cloud-forest, two tiny airships, envelopes painted in wasp-stripes of yellow and black. Their small gondolas and streamlined engine pods were instantly familiar to Theo, who had been made to memorize the silhouettes of enemy ships during his Green Storm training. These were Cosgrove Super-Gnats, which the cities of the *Traktionstadtsgesellschaft* used as fighter-bombers.

But what were they doing here? Theo had never heard of the *Traktionstadts* sending ships into Africa, let alone as far south as Zagwa.

And then he thought, *They are here because of the talks*. Those rockets which he could see shining like knives in the racks under their gondolas would soon be lancing down into the citadel, where Naga's wife was; where the Queen was. Where Theo's family were.

He was going to have to stop them.

It was strange, how calm he felt about it. A few moments ago he had been quite at peace, enjoying the sunlight and the clear air, and now he was probably about to die, and yet it all seemed quite natural; another part of the morning, like the wind and the sunlight. He tipped his kite and dropped towards the second of the Super-Gnats. The aviators had not seen him yet. The Gnats were two-man ships, and he doubted they were keeping much of a watch. The kite took him closer and closer, until he could see the paint flaking from the ship's engine pod cowlings. The big steering fins were emblazoned with the symbol of the *Traktionstadtsgesellschaft;* a wheeled and armoured fist. Theo found himself almost admiring the daring of these aviators, who had flown so deep into Anti-Tractionist territory in their unmistakeable ships.

He kicked the kite backwards and stalled in mid-air, the way he had learned to do when he was younger, riding the thermals above Liemba Lake with his school-friends. This time, though, he came down not into water but on to the hard, curved top of the airship's envelope. The noise of his landing seemed horribly loud, but he told himself the men down in the gondola would have heard nothing over the bellowing of their big engines. He freed himself from the straps of his kite, and tried to tuck it beneath the ratlines which stretched across the surface of the envelope, but the wind caught it and he had to let go to stop himself being pulled away with it. He clung to the ratlines and watched helplessly as it went tumbling astern.

Theo had lost his only means of escape, but before he could worry about it a hatch popped open beside him, and a leather-helmeted head poked out and stared at him through tinted flying-goggles. So someone had heard him after all. He threw himself forward, and he and the aviator tumbled together through the hatch and down a short companionway, landing heavily on a metal walkway between two of the airship's gas-cells. Theo scrambled up, but the aviator lay unmoving, stunned. She was a woman; Thai or Laotian by the look of her. Theo had never heard of easterners fighting for the *Traktionstadts*. Yet here she was, in one of their ships and one of their uniforms, flying towards Zagwa with full racks of rockets.

It was a mystery, but Theo hadn't time to ponder it. He gagged the aviatrix with her own scarf, then took her knife from her belt and cut a length of rope from the netting around the gas-cells, which he used to bind her hands to the walkway handrail. She woke while he was tying the last knots and started to struggle, glaring out angrily at him through her cracked goggles.

He left her writhing there and hurried along the catwalk to another ladder, climbing down between the shadows of the gas-cells. Engine noise boomed around him, quickly drowning out the muffled curses from above. As he dropped into the gondola the light from the windows dazzled him. He blinked, and saw the pilot standing at the controls, his back to Theo.

"What was it?" the man asked, in Airsperanto. (Airsperanto? It was the common language of the sky, but Theo had thought the *Traktionstadts* used German. . .)

"A bird?" asked the man, doing something to his controls, and turned. He was another easterner. Theo pushed him against a bulkhead and showed him the knife.

Outside, the city was coming into view beyond a spur of the mountains. The crew of the leading Super-Gnat, with no idea of what was happening aboard her sister-ship, angled her vanes and started to swing towards the Citadel.

Forcing the pilot down into his seat, Theo groped for the controls of the radio set. It was identical to the radio he'd had in the cabin of his Tumbler-bomb during his time with the Storm. He shouted into the microphone, "Zagwa! Zagwa! You're under attack! Two airships! I'm in the one behind!" he added hastily, as puffballs of anti-aircraft fire began to burst in the sky all around him, and shrapnel rattled against the armoured gondola and crazed the window-glass.

The pilot chose that moment to try and fight, lurching out of his chair and butting Theo bullishly in the ribs. Theo dropped the microphone, and the pilot grabbed his knife-hand. They struggled for control of the knife, until suddenly there was blood everywhere, and Theo looked and saw that it was his own. The pilot stabbed him again, and he shouted out in anger and fear and pain, trying to twist the blade away. Staring at his opponent's furious, clenched face, he did not even notice the leading airship vanish in a sheet of saffron flame. The shock wave came as a surprise, shattering all the windows of the gondola at once, and then the debris was slamming and jarring against the envelope. A torn-off propeller blade sheared through the gondola like a scythe. The pilot went whirling out through the immense gash where the side wall had been, leaving Theo with an after-image of his wide, disbelieving eyes.

Theo stumbled to the radio set and snatched up the dangling microphone. He didn't know if it still worked, but he shouted into it anyway, until exhaustion and terror and loss of blood overcame him. The last thing he heard, as he slipped down on to the deck, were voices telling him that help was on its way. Twin plumes of smoke were rising from the citadel. Above them, blue as damselflies, the airships of the Zagwan Flying Corps were climbing into the golden sky.

2
MATTERS OF THE HEART

From: Wren Natsworthy
AMV Jenny Haniver
Peripatetiapolis
24th April, 1026 TE

Dear Theo,
I hope life in Zagwa is not too dull? In case it is, I
thought I should sit down and write you a proper
letter to tell you all that I have been doing. It
seems hard to believe that it's been so long . . . it
seems like only yesterday – Brighton, and Cloud
9, and Mum. . .

Soon after you left for Zagwa, Professor
Pennyroyal left us too; he has friends in other
cities, and he's gone to stay with some of them –
or sponge off them, I suppose, because he didn't
bring anything with him out of the wreck of Cloud
9, only his clothes, and they were too outlandish
to fetch much at the Kom Ombo bazaar. I felt
almost sorry for him. He was a help, getting us to
Kom Ombo and then blustering at those hospital
doctors until they looked after Dad for free. But
he will be all right, I think (Pennyroyal, I mean).
He told me he is planning to write a new book,
all about the battle at Brighton. He promised
me that he won't lie, especially about you or me,
but I expect it was one of those promises he
will forget the instant he sits down at his
typewriter.

Dad is all right, too. Those Kom Ombo doctors gave him some green pills to take, which help his pains a bit, and he hasn't had any attacks since that awful night on Cloud 9. But he seems awfully old, somehow, and awfully sad. It's Mum, of course. He really loved her, despite what she was like. To be without her, not even knowing if she's alive or dead, upsets him terribly, tho' he tries to be brave.

I thought that once he was well enough he would want to take me straight home to Anchorage-in-Vineland, but he hasn't suggested it. So we have been travelling the Bird Roads ever since, seeing a little of the world and doing a little trading – antiques and Old-Tech mostly, but harmless stuff, not like that awful Tin Book! We've done quite well – well enough to get the ship a fresh coat of paint and have her engines overhauled. We've changed her name back to Jenny Haniver, which is what she was called before Prof Pennyroyal stole her from Mum and Dad all those years ago. We wondered at first if it would be dangerous, but I don't think anyone remembers any more that that was the name of the Stalker Fang's old ship, and if they do, they don't much care.

Have you heard about the truce? (I always thought General Naga was a good sort. When we were captured by the Storm at Cloud 9 his soldiers were very inclined to prod me with their guns, and Naga stopped them doing it. It's nice to know that the new leader of the Storm takes a firm stand on prodding.) Anyway, everyone is very excited about the truce, and hoping the war is over, and I hope so too.

I am getting quite used to life as an air-trader. You would think me ever so much changed if you could see me. I've had my hair cut in the latest style, sort of lopsided, so that it comes down below my chin on one side but only to ear-level on the other. I don't want to sound vain, but it looks <u>extremely</u> sophisticated, even if it does make me feel sometimes as if I'm standing on a slope. Also I have new boots, tall ones, and a leather coat, not one of those long ones that Daddy and the other old-style aviators wear, but a tunic, with a red silk lining and pointy bits at the bottom called tappets or lappets or something. And at this moment I am sitting in a café behind the air-harbour here in Peripatetiapolis, feeling every inch the aviatrix, and just enjoying being aboard a city. I could never really imagine what real cities were like, growing up in sleepy old Anchorage as I did, but now I spend half my time aboard them I find I love them – all the people, and the bustle, and the way the engines make the pavements throb as if the whole of Peripatetiapolis is a great, living animal. I am waiting for Dad, who has gone up to the higher tiers to see if the Peripatetiapolitan doctors can find some better pills than the ones the Kom Ombo lot prescribed. (He didn't want to go, of course, but I talked him into it in the end!) And sitting here, I got thinking about you, the way I do quite often, and I thought. . .

It wouldn't do, Wren decided. She scrumpled the page and lobbed it into a nearby bin. She was getting to be quite a good shot. This must be the twentieth letter she'd written to Theo, and so far she'd not mailed any of them. She had sent a card at Christmas, because although Theo wasn't very religious he lived in a Christian city and probably celebrated all their strange old festivals, but all she had written was *Happy Xmas* and a few lines of news about herself and Dad.

The trouble was, Theo had probably forgotten her by now. And even if he did remember her, he was hardly likely to be interested in her clothes, or her haircut, or the rest of it. And that bit about how much she liked city life would probably shock him, for he was an Anti-Tractionist through and through and could be rather prim. . .

But she could not forget him. How brave he had been, on Cloud 9. And that goodbye kiss, on the Kom Ombo air-quay, amid all those oily ropes and heaped-up sky-train couplings and shouting stevedores and roaring engines. Wren had never kissed anyone before. She hadn't known quite how you went about it; she wasn't sure where her nose was meant to go; when their teeth banged together she was afraid that she was doing it all wrong. Theo had laughed, and said it was a funny business, this kissing, and she said she thought she might get the hang of it with a little more practice, but by then the captain of his airship was hollering "All aboard that's coming aboard!" and starting to disengage his docking clamps, and there had been no time. . .

And that had been six months ago. Theo had written once – a letter which reached Wren in January at a shabby air-caravanserai in the Tannhäusers – to tell her that he had made it home safely and been welcomed by

15

his family "like the prodigal son" (whatever that meant).
But Wren had never managed to compose a reply.

"Bother!" she said, and ordered another coffee.

Tom Natsworthy, Wren's father, had faced death many
times, and been in all sorts of frightening situations, but
he had never felt any fear quite so cold as this.

He was lying, quite naked, on a chilly metal table
in the consulting-room of a heart-specialist on
Peripatetiapolis's second tier. Above him a machine with
a long and many-jointed hydraulic neck twisted its metal
head from side to side, examining him with a quizzical
air. Tom was pretty sure that those green, glowing lenses
at its business end were taken from a Stalker. He
supposed that Stalker parts were easy to come by these
days, and that he should be glad that all the years of
war had at least spawned a few good things; new
medical techniques, and diagnostic machines like this.
But when the blunt steel head dipped close to his torso,
and he heard the machinery grating and whirring inside
those shining eyes, all he could think of was the old
Stalker Shrike, who had chased him and Hester across
the Out-Country in the year London died.

When it was all over, and Dr Chernowyth switched off
his machine and came out of his little lead-walled booth,
he could tell Tom nothing that Tom had not already
guessed. There was a weakness in his heart. It had been
caused by the bullet which Pennyroyal had shot him
with, all those years ago in Anchorage. It was growing
worse, and one day it would kill him. He had a year or
two left, maybe five, no more.

The doctor pursed his lips and shook his head and told him to take things easy, but Tom just laughed. How could you take things easy, in the air-trade? The only way he could take things easy would be if he went home to Anchorage-in-Vineland, but after what he had learned about Hester he could never go back. He had nothing to be ashamed of – *he* had not betrayed the ice city to Arkangel's Huntsmen, or murdered anyone among its snowy streets – but he felt ashamed for his wife's sake, and foolish for having lived so long with her, never suspecting the lies she had told him.

Anyway, Wren would never forgive him if he took her home now. She had the same longing for adventure that Tom himself had had at her age. She was enjoying life on the Bird Roads, and she had the makings of a fine aviatrix. He would stay with her, flying and trading, teaching her the ways of the sky and doing his best to keep her out of trouble, and when Lady Death came to take him to the Sunless Country he would leave Wren the *Jenny Haniver* and she would be able to choose whichever life she wanted for herself; the peace of Vineland or the freedom of the skies. The news from the east sounded hopeful. If this truce held there would soon be all sorts of opportunities for trade.

When he left Dr Chernowyth's office Tom felt better at once. Out here, beneath the evening sky, it seemed impossible that he was going to die. The city rocked gently as it rumbled northward up the rocky western shoreline of the Great Hunting Ground. Out upon the silver, sunset-shining sea a fishing town was keeping pace with it beneath a cloud of gulls. Tom watched for a while from an observation platform, then rode an elevator back to base-tier and strolled through the busy market behind the air-harbour, remembering his first visit to this city, with Hester and Anna Fang, twenty years before. He had bought Hester a red scarf at one of these stalls, to save her having to keep hiding her scarred face with her hand. . .

But he did not want to think about Hester. When he started thinking about her he always ended up remembering the way they had parted, and what she had done made him so angry that his heart would pound and twist inside him. He could not afford to think of Hester any more.

He began to walk towards the harbour, rehearsing in his mind the things he would tell Wren about his visit to the doctor. ("Nothing to worry about. Not even worth operating. . .") Passing Pondicherry's Old-Tech Auction Rooms he stopped to let a crowd of traders spill out, and thought he recognized one of them, a woman of about his own age, rather pretty. It looked as if she had been successful at the auction, for she was carrying a big, heavy package. She didn't see Tom, and he walked on trying to remember her name and where he had met her. Katie, wasn't it? No, Clytie, that was it. Clytie Potts.

He stopped, and turned, and stared. It *couldn't* have been Clytie. Clytie had been a Historian, a year above him in the Guild when London was destroyed. She had been killed by MEDUSA along with all the rest of his city. She just *couldn't* be walking about in Peripatetiapolis. His memories were playing games with him.

But it had looked so like her!

He took a few steps back the way he had come. The woman was going quickly up a stairway to the level where the airships berthed. "Clytie!" Tom shouted, and her face turned towards him. It *was* her, he was suddenly certain of it, and he laughed aloud with happiness and surprise and called again, "Clytie! It's me! Tom Natsworthy!"

A group of traders barged past him, blocking his view of her. When he could see again she was gone. He started hurrying towards the stairs, ignoring the little warning pains in his chest. He tried to imagine how Clytie had survived MEDUSA. Had she been outside the city when it was destroyed? He had heard of other Londoners who had escaped the blast, but they had all been members of the Merchants' Guild, far off on foreign cities when it happened. At Rogues' Roost Hester had encountered that horrible Engineer Popjoy; but he had been in the Deep Gut when MEDUSA went off. . .

He pushed his way up the crowded stair and saw Clytie hurrying away from him between the long-stay docking pans. He could hardly blame her, after the way he'd yelled at her. He must have been too far away for her to recognize him, and she'd mistaken him for some kind of loony, or a rival trader angry that she'd outbid him in the auction rooms. He trotted after her, eager to explain himself, and saw her run quickly up another stairway on to Pan Seven where a small, streamlined airship was berthed. He paused at the foot of the stairs just long enough to read the details chalked on the board there and learn that the ship was the *Archaeopteryx*, registered in Airhaven and commanded by Cruwys Morchard. Then, careful not to run, or shout, or do anything else that might alarm a lady air-trader, he climbed after her. Of course, with her Guild training, Clytie Potts would have had no trouble finding a place aboard an Old-Tech trader. No doubt this Captain

Morchard had taken her on as an expert buyer, and that was why she had been at the auction house.

He paused to catch his breath at the top of the stairs, his heart hammering fiercely. The *Archaeopteryx* towered over him in the twilight. She was camouflaged, her gondola and the undersides of her envelope and engine pods sky-blue, the upper parts done in a dazzle-pattern of greens and browns and greys. At the foot of her gangplank two crewmen were waiting in a pool of pale electric light. They looked rough and shabby, like Out-Country scavengers. As Clytie approached them Tom heard one man call out, "You get 'em all right, then?"

"I did," replied Clytie, nodding to the package she was carrying. The other man came forward to help her with it, then saw Tom coming up behind her. Clytie must have noticed his expression change, and turned to see why.

"Clytie?" said Tom. "It's me, Tom Natsworthy. Apprentice Third Class, from the Guild of Historians. From London. I know you probably don't recognize me. It's been ... what? ... nearly twenty years! And you must have thought I was dead. . ."

At first he felt sure that she *had* recognized him, and that she was happy to see him, but then her look changed; she took a step backwards, away from him, and glanced towards the men by the gangplank. One of them – a tall, gaunt man with a shaven head – put a hand to his sword and Tom heard him say, "This fellow bothering you, Miss Morchard?"

"It's all right, Lurpak," said Clytie, motioning for him to stay where he was. She came a little closer to Tom and said pleasantly, "I'm sorry, sir. I fear you have mistaken me for some other lady. I am Cruwys Morchard, mistress of this ship. I don't know anyone from London."

"But you. . ." Tom started to say. He studied her face, embarrassed and confused. He was *sure* she was Clytie Potts. She had put on a little weight, just as he had himself, and her hair, which had been dark, was dusted with silver now, as if cobwebs had settled on it, but her face was the same . . . except that the space between her eyebrows, where Clytie Potts had rather proudly worn the tattooed blue eye of the Guild of Historians, was blank.

Tom began to doubt himself. It had been twenty years, after all. Perhaps he was wrong. He said, "I'm sorry, but you look so like her. . ."

"Don't mention it," she said, with a charming smile. "I have one of those faces. I am always being mistook for somebody."

"You look so like her," said Tom again, half-hopefully, as if she might suddenly change her mind and remember that she *was* Clytie Potts, after all.

She bowed to him and turned away. Her men eyed Tom as they helped her up the gangplank with her package. There was nothing more to say, so he said "Sorry" again and turned away himself, blushing hotly as he made his way off the pan. He started across the harbour towards his own ship's berth, and had not gone more than twenty paces when he heard the *Archaeopteryx*'s engines rumbling to life behind him. He watched her rise into the evening sky, gathering speed quickly as she cleared the city's airspace and flew away towards the east.

Which was curious, because Tom was certain that signboard beside her pan had said she would be in Peripatetiapolis for two more days. . .

3
THE MYSTERIOUS MISS MORCHARD

"I am sure it was her!" Tom said, over supper that night at the Jolly Dirigible. "She was older, of course, and the Guild-mark wasn't on her brow, which threw me a little, but tattoos can be removed, can't they?"

Wren said, "Don't get agitated, Dad. . ."

"I'm not agitated; only intrigued! If it is Clytie, how come she is still alive? And why did she not admit who she was?"

He did not sleep much that night, and Wren lay awake too, in her little cabin up inside the *Jenny*'s envelope, listening to him pad along the passageway from the stern cabin and clatter as quietly as he could in the galley, making himself one of those three-in-the-morning cups of tea.

At first she was worried about him. She hadn't quite believed his version of what the heart-doctor had said, and she felt quite certain that he should not be staying awake all night and fretting about mystery aviatrices. But gradually she started to wonder if his encounter with the woman might not have been a good thing after all. Talking about her at supper, he had seemed more alive than Wren had seen him for months; the listlessness which had settled over him when Mum left had vanished, and he had been his old self again, full of questions and theories. Wren couldn't tell if it was the mystery that appealed to him, or the thought of a connection with his lost home city, or if he simply had the hots for Clytie Potts; but whichever it was, might it not do him good to have something other than Mum to think about?

At breakfast next morning she said, "We should investigate. Find out more about this self-styled Cruwys Morchard."

"How?" asked her father. "The *Archaeopteryx* will be a hundred miles away by now."

"You said she bought something at the auction rooms," said Wren. "We could start there."

※ ◈ ※ ◈ ※

Mr Pondicherry, who was a large, shiny sort of gentleman, seemed to grow even larger and shinier when he looked up from his account-books to see Tom Natsworthy and daughter entering his little den. The *Jenny Haniver* had sold several valuable pieces through Pondicherry's Old-Tech Auction Rooms that season. "Mr Natsworthy!" he chuckled. "Miss Natsworthy! How good to see you!" He stood up to greet them, and pushed back a great deal of silver-embroidered sleeve to reveal a plump brown hand, which Tom shook. "You are both well, I hope? The Gods of the Sky are kind to you? What do you have for me today?"

"Only questions, I'm afraid," Tom confessed. "I was wondering what you could tell me about a freelance archaeologist called Cruwys Morchard. She made a purchase here yesterday. . ."

"The lady from the *Archaeopteryx*?" mused Mr Pondicherry. "Yes, yes; I know her well, but I'm afraid I cannot share such information. . ."

"Of course," said Tom, and, "Sorry, sorry."

Wren, who had half-expected this, took out of her jacket pocket a little bundle of cloth, which she set down upon the blotter on Mr Pondicherry's desk. The auctioneer purred like a cat as he unwrapped it. Inside lay a tiny, flattened envelope of silvery metal, inset with minute oblong tiles on which faint numbers still showed.

"An Ancient mobile telephone," said Wren. "We bought it last month, from a scavenger who didn't even know what it was. Dad was planning to sell it privately, but I'm sure he'd be happy to go through Pondicherry's if. . ."

"Wren!" said her father, startled by her cunning.

Mr Pondicherry had put his head down close to the relic and screwed a jeweller's glass into his eye. "Oh, pretty!" he said. "So beautifully preserved! And the trade in trinkets like this is definitely picking up now that peace is breaking out. They say General Naga hasn't time to fight battles any more, now that he's found himself a lovely young wife. Almost as lovely as Cruwys Morchard. . ." He looked at Tom and winked, one eye made huge by the glass. "Very well. Just between ourselves, Ms Morchard was indeed here yesterday. She brought a job-lot of Kliest Coils."

"What on earth would she want with those?" wondered Tom.

"Who knows?" Mr Pondicherry beamed and spread his hands wide, as if to say, *Once I have my percentage, what do I care what my customers do with the rubbish they buy?* "They are of no earthly use. Trade goods, I suppose. That is Ms Morchard's profession. An Old-Tech trader, and a good one, I believe. Been on the Bird Roads since she was just a slip of a girl."

"Has she ever mentioned anything about where she comes from?" Wren asked eagerly.

Mr Pondicherry thought for a moment. "Her ship is registered in Airhaven," he said.

"Oh, we know that. I mean, do you know where she grew up? Where she was trained? You see, we think she comes from London."

The auctioneer smiled at her indulgently, and winked again at Tom as he slipped the old telephone into a side-drawer of his bureau. "Ah, Mr N, what romantical notions these young ladies do have! Really, Miss Wren! *Nobody* comes from London!"

Afterwards they took coffee on a balcony café and looked out eastward across the endless plains of the Great Hunting Ground. It was one of those warm, golden days of spring. A haze of green filled the massive ruts and track-marks that passing cities had scored across the land below, and the sky was full of swerving swifts. Away in the east a mining town was gnawing at a line of hills which had somehow been overlooked until now.

"The strange thing is," said Tom thoughtfully, "I'm sure I've heard that name before. I wish I could remember where. *Cruwys Morchard.* I suppose it was on the Bird Roads, in the old days. . ." He poured Wren more coffee. "You must think me very silly, to let myself be so affected by it. It's just that the thought of another Historian, still alive after all these years. . ."

He couldn't explain. Lately he had been thinking more and more about his early years in the London Museum. It made him sad to think that when he died the memory of the place would die with him. If there really were another Historian alive, someone who had grown up among the same dusty galleries and beeswax-smelling corridors as him, who had snoozed through old Arkengarth's lectures, and listened to Chudleigh Pomeroy grumbling about the building's feeble shock-absorbers, then the responsibility of remembering it all would be lifted from him; the echoes of those things would linger in other memories, even after he was gone.

"What I don't understand," said Wren, "is why she won't admit it. Surely it would be a selling point, in an Old-Tech trader, to say they came from London and were trained by the Historians' Guild."

Tom shrugged. "I always kept quiet about it, when your mother and I were trading. London was unpopular in those years. What the Guild of Engineers had done upset the whole balance of the world. Scared a lot of cities, and led to the rise of the Green Storm. I suppose that's why Clytie took another name. The Pottses are a famous London family; they've been producing aldermen and Heads of Guild since Quirke's time. Clytie's grandfather, old Pisistratus Potts, was Lord Mayor for years and years. If you want to pretend you're not a Londoner it wouldn't be a good idea to go around with a name like Clytie Potts."

"And what about those things she bought at Pondicherry's?" Wren wondered.

"Kliest Coils?"

"I've never heard of them."

"There's no reason why you would have," her father said. "They come from the Electric Empire, which thrived in these parts before the rise of the Blue Metal Culture, around 10,000 BT."

"What are they for?"

"Nobody knows," said Tom. "Zanussi Kliest, the London Historian who first studied them, claimed they were meant to focus some sort of electro-magnetic energy, but no one has ever worked out a practical use for them. The Electric Empire seems to have been a sort of technological cul-de-sac."

"These coils aren't valuable, then?"

"Only as curios. They're quite pretty."

"So what's Clytie Potts going to do with them?" asked Wren.

Tom shrugged again. "She must have a buyer, I suppose. Maybe she knows a collector."

"We should go after her," said Wren.

"Where to? I asked at the harbour-office last night. The *Archaeopteryx* didn't leave any details of her destination."

"She'll be heading east," said Wren, with the confidence of someone who had been studying the air-trade for a whole season and felt she had its measure. "Everybody is going east now that the truce seems to be holding, and we should too. Even if we don't find Clytie Potts there will be good trading, and I'd love to see the central Hunting Ground. We could go to Airhaven. The Registration Bureau there must have some more details about Cruwys so-called Morchard and her ship."

Tom finished his coffee and said, "I'd been thinking you might want to go south this spring. Your friend Theo is still in Zagwa, isn't he? I expect we could get permission to land there. . ."

"Oh, I hadn't really thought about that," said Wren casually, and blushed bright red.

"I liked Theo," Tom went on. "He's a good lad. Kind and well-mannered. Handsome, too. . ."

"Daddy!" said Wren sternly, warning him not to tease.

Then she relented, sighed, and took his hand. "Look, the reason Theo has such good manners is that he's really posh. His family are rich, and they live in a city that was part of a great civilization when our ancestors were still wearing animal skins and squabbling over scraps in the ruins of Europe. Why would Theo be interested in me?"

"He'd be a fool if he isn't," said her father, "and he didn't strike me as a fool."

Wren gave an exasperated sigh. Why couldn't Dad understand? Theo was in his own city, surrounded by lots of girls far prettier than her. His family might have married him off by now, and even if they hadn't, he was sure to have forgotten all about Wren. That kiss, which had meant so much to her, had probably meant nothing at all to Theo. So she did not want to make a fool of herself by chasing off to Zagwa, knocking on his door and expecting him to pick up where they'd left off.

She said, "Let's go east, Dad. Let's go and find Clytie Potts."

4

LADY NAGA

Theo, who had been adrift for days on slow tides of pain and anaesthetic, came to the surface at last in a clean, white room in Zagwa Hospital. Through veils of mosquito-netting and smudged memories he could see an open window, and evening sunlight on the mountains. His mother and father and his sisters Miriam and Kaelo were gathered around his bed, and as he gradually recovered his senses Theo realized that his wounds must have been very grave indeed, for instead of teasing him and telling him how silly he looked lying there all bruised and bandaged, his sisters seemed inclined to cry, and kiss him. "Thank God, thank God," his mother kept saying, and his father, leaning over him, said, "You're going to be all right, Theo. But it was touch and go for a while."

"The knife," said Theo, remembering, touching his stomach, which was wrapped in clean, crisp bandages. "The rockets. . . They hit the citadel!"

"They exploded quite harmlessly in the gardens," his father assured him. "Nobody was hurt. Nobody but you. You were badly wounded, Theo, and you lost a lot of blood. When our aviators brought you in, the doctors were ready to give you up for dead. But the ambassador heard of your plight – the Storm's ambassador, Lady Naga – and she came and worked on you herself. She used to be some sort of surgeon before her marriage. She certainly knows a thing or two about a person's insides. That is a claim to fame, eh, Theo? You have been healed by General Naga's wife!"

"So you saved her life, and she saved yours," said Miriam.

"She will be delighted to hear that you are on the mend!" said Mrs Ngoni. "She was very impressed by your bravery, and takes a great interest in you." She pointed proudly to a mass of flowers in a corner of Theo's hospital room, sent by Lady Naga. "She came to see me herself, to tell me how well the operation had gone." She beamed, clearly rather taken with the visitor from Shan Guo. "Lady Naga is a very good person, Theo."

"If she is so good, what is she doing in the Green Storm?" asked Theo.

"An accident of fate," his father suggested. "Really, Theo, you would like her. Shall I send word to the citadel to tell her that you are better? I am sure she will want to come and talk to you. . ."

Theo shook his head and said that he did not feel strong enough. He was happy that he had been able to stop the barbarians, and grateful to Lady Naga for saving his life, but he felt awkward at finding himself in debt to a member of the Green Storm.

He was allowed home the next day. In the weeks that followed, as he grew slowly stronger, he tried not to think about Lady Naga, although his parents often spoke about her. Indeed, all Zagwa was talking about Lady Naga. Everyone had heard how she had taken off her fine clothes and put on a doctor's smock to save the life of young Theo Ngoni, and as the weeks went by there were other stories about her, how she had visited the ancient cathedral-church which had been hollowed out of the living rock of Mount Zagwa in the Dark Centuries, and prayed there with the bishop himself. Everyone seemed to think that this was a good sign, except Theo. He suspected it was all just another Green Storm trick.

Two of the Queen's councillors came to ask him about his memories of the airship he had boarded. They told him that the aviatrix he had captured was being questioned, but would not co-operate. They congratulated him on his bravery. Theo said, "I wasn't being brave. I had no choice." But secretly he felt proud, and very pleased that everyone in Zagwa would think of him as a hero now instead of only remembering that he had once run away to join the Storm. "I'm glad I was able to stop those townies before they hurt anyone," he told the councillors. The councillors exchanged odd, thoughtful looks when he said that, and the younger of the two seemed about to say something, but the older one stopped him; they left soon afterwards.

Outside his parents' house, Zagwa baked in the sun. The city was not quite so magnificent when you saw it from ground level; the buildings were shabby; bright paint peeling off the walls, roofs sagging. Weeds grew through cracked pavements. Even the domes of the citadel were streaked with verdigris. Zagwa's great days were a thousand years behind it; the mighty empire it used to rule had been laid waste by hungry cities. In the shade of the umbrella tree across the street men gathered in the afternoons to talk angrily about the latest news of townie atrocities from the north. Maybe some of the young ones would grow so angry that one day they would go off to join the Storm, just as Theo had. Theo

watched them from the window sometimes, and tried to
remember being that sure of things, but he couldn't.

One afternoon, almost a month after the air attack, he
was reading in the garden room when his father and
mother brought a visitor to see him. Theo barely looked
up from his book when they entered, for he had grown
used to visits from his many aunts and uncles, all
embarrassingly keen to see his scars and remind him
what a tearaway he'd been when he was three, or
introduce him to the pretty daughters of their friends. It
was not until his mother said, "Theo, my dear, you
remember Air Marshal Khora?" that he realized this visit
was different.

Khora was one of Africa's finest aviators, and the
commander of the Zagwan Flying Corps. He was a tall
man, and handsome still, though he was nearing fifty
and his hair was turning white. He wore ceremonial
armour, and around his shoulders hung the traditional
cloak of the Queen's bodyguard; yellow with patterns of
black dots, representing the skin of a mythical creature
called a leopard. He bowed low to Theo, greeting him
like an equal, and small, inconsequential things were
said which Theo was far too overcome to remember.
Khora had been his hero since he was a little boy. When
he was nine he had whiled away a whole rainy season
making a model of Khora's flagship, the air-destroyer
Mwene Mutapa, with a little inch-high Khora standing
on the stern-gallery. It was such a surprise to see him
here, actual size, in the familiar surroundings of home
that it took Theo several moments to notice that he had

not come alone. Behind him stood two servant-girls, foreigners dressed in robes of rain-coloured silk, and behind them, in plainer clothes, another woman, very short and slight, whom Theo knew from photographs in the Zagwan news-sheets.

"Theo," said Air Marshal Khora, "I have brought Lady Naga to meet you."

Theo knew that he ought to say, "I don't want to; I don't want anything to do with her or her people," but he was still tongue-tied in Khora's presence, and anyway, as the ambassador came towards him and he saw her delicate face and the heavy black spectacles (which she had not been wearing in those news-photographs) he discovered that he knew her.

"You were on Cloud 9!" he blurted out, startling Khora and the servant-girls, who had been expecting some more formal greeting. "The night the Storm came! You're Dr Zero! You were with Naga and. . ."

"And I am still with Naga," the woman replied, with a faint, puzzled smile. She was young, and quite pretty in a boyish way. Her hair, which had been short and green when Theo first met her, was longer now, and black. The neck of her linen tunic was open and in the hollow of her throat hung a cheap tin cross which she must have bought from one of the stalls outside the cathedral. She reached up to touch it as she said, "So you were with us aboard Cloud 9 last year, Mr Ngoni? I'm afraid I don't remember. . ."

Theo nodded eagerly. "I was with Wren. You took us away from the Stalker Fang and asked Wren about the Tin Book. . ." His voice trailed off. He had just remembered the uniform she had been wearing that night. "She used to be some sort of surgeon," his father had said, but that had only been half true; she had been a surgeon-mechanic; a builder of Stalkers for the Green Storm's dreaded Resurrection Corps.

"That was you?" she asked, still smiling. "I'm so sorry. So much happened that night, and so much has happened since... How is your wound? Healing?"

"It is better," said Theo bravely.

Khora laughed, and said, "The young heal quickly! I was wounded myself once, at Batmunkh Gompa, back in the year '07. A damned Londoner stuck his sword through my lung. It still hurts me sometimes."

"Theo, my boy," his father said, "why don't you show Lady Naga the gardens?"

Awkwardly, Theo indicated the open door, and Lady Naga followed him outside with her girls trailing at a respectful distance. Glancing behind him, he saw Khora deep in conversation with his parents, and his sisters watching and giggling. They were probably wondering which of the ambassador's servants he would fall in love with, Theo realized. Both girls were very beautiful. One was Han or Shan Guonese; the other must have come from somewhere in the south of India; her skin was as dark as Theo's, and her eyes, which met his as he stared at her, were the blackest he had ever seen.

He looked away quickly, and tried to cover his confusion by pointing out the path which led to his favourite part of the garden, the terrace overlooking the gorge. The shadowed walk was overhung by trees heavy with orange flowers, and Lady Naga stooped to pick up one that had fallen on the path, and turned it in her hands as they walked on. Watching her, Theo noticed that her small fingers were dappled with patches of bleached skin and tea-coloured stains. "Chemicals," she explained, seeing that he had noticed. "I worked for a long time with the Resurrection Corps. The chemicals we used. . ."

Theo wondered how many dead soldiers she had Stalkerized, and how six short months could have turned a shy little officer from the Resurrection Corps into the wife of the leader of the Storm. As if she guessed his thoughts, Lady Naga looked up at him and said, "It was me who killed the Stalker Fang that night. I rebuilt another old Stalker, Mr Shrike, and set him to attack her. General Naga was impressed. He seemed to think I'd been very brave. And I suppose he felt I needed protection, for there are a lot of people in the Storm who worshipped her, and would be glad to see me dead. And – well, you know how sentimental soldiers can be. At any rate, he took good care of me on the voyage home to Tienjing, and when we had got there, and he was secure in the leadership, he asked me to marry him."

Theo nodded. It was embarrassing, to be talking about such private things with her. He had seen Naga; a fierce warrior who clanked around inside a motorized metal exoskeleton to compensate for his lost right arm and crippled legs. He could not imagine that Dr Zero had been in love with him. It must have been fear, or lust for power, that had made her say yes.

"The General must miss you," was all he could think of to say.

"I think he does," said Lady Naga. "But he is a good man, and he really wants peace. He wants to see friendship restored between Zagwa and the Storm. I persuaded him that I should be the one to talk to your leaders. He thought I would be safer here. There are still elements of the Storm who hate Naga for trying to end their war, and hate me for destroying their old leader and letting Naga take over power. He thought that by flying halfway around the world I might escape them for a while. It seems he was wrong about that. . ."

Theo wondered what she meant. But at that moment they reached the edge of the trees; the sunlit terrace opened before them, and for a few minutes Lady Naga could say nothing but "Oh!" and "Ah!" and "What a magnificent view!"

It *was* magnificent. Even Theo, who had known it all his life, felt awestruck sometimes when he stood on this terrace and looked over the balustrade. The steep sides of Zagwa gorge dropped sheer to the aquamarine curve of the river far below and the mountains rose above, thick green cloud-forest giving way to snow, soaring up and up towards the dazzling sky where greater mountains hung; giant storm-clouds, white and ice-blue in the sunlight. A few wind-riders were hanging on the thermals overhead, reminding Theo of his own flight, and the kite he'd lost. It occurred to him that Lady Naga had not yet thanked him for saving her from the townie air-strike. He had thought that was what she had come here for.

"Whatever made you want to leave all this and join the Green Storm?" she asked.

Theo shrugged awkwardly, unhappy at being reminded of his time as a flying bomb. "It's all under threat," he said. "The Flying Corps do their best to defend our borders, but every year more and more of our farmlands and forests are eaten. The cities of the desert move south, and bring the desert with them. I had listened so long to my father and my friends talking about it, and I just wanted to be *doing* something. I thought the Green Storm had the answer. I was younger then. You think things are simple when you're young."

Lady Naga smiled quietly. "How old are you, Theo?"

"Now? I'm nearly seventeen. Oh, be careful!" he cried, for the dark servant-girl, apparently quite fearless and as taken as her mistress with the view, had leaned far out over the crumbly balustrade to look down. "Careful!" Theo shouted. "It's very old! It may give way!"

The girl paid him no attention at all, but the other servant said softly, "Rohini," and reached out to gently pull her back. Her black eyes gazed at Theo, startled and confused.

"Rohini cannot hear you," explained Lady Naga. "She is a deaf-mute, the poor thing. She came to me as a slave; a wedding gift from Naga's oldest friend, General Dzhu. Of course, I do not hold with slavery, so she has her freedom now, but she has chosen to stay with me. She is a good girl. . ."

The girl Rohini bowed to Theo, thanking him for saving her, or apologizing for putting herself in danger. "It's all right," he said, "it doesn't matter. . ." and then remembered that she couldn't hear and tried to mime it, which made both girls laugh. They were as bad as his sisters, Theo thought, but he didn't really mind.

Just then, down a stairway from the upper level of the gardens, came Air Marshal Khora, with Theo's parents. All three looked very solemn. Khora shot Lady Naga a look which seemed to mean something, though Theo could not guess what. The two servant-girls stopped laughing at Theo and took themselves quickly away to the other end of the terrace. Some of the house-servants appeared with folding tables, chairs, iced red tea, and honey-biscuits. Mrs Ngoni fussed about arranging seats and sending up to the house for a parasol, for she imagined that an ivory-coloured person like Lady Naga could very easily catch sunstroke, and did not want it happening in *her* garden.

"Now," said Khora, when all was done. "To business, Theo. I have a job in mind for you. It may be dangerous, it should be interesting, and it might be of supreme importance both to Zagwa and the world. Of course, you must not accept it unless you truly want it; you have already served Zagwa well and no one will think the worse of you if you turn it down."

"What is it?" asked Theo. He glanced at his parents. His father looked proud, his mother worried. "What do you want me to do?"

Instead of answering directly, Khora stood up and went to the balustrade, looking out across the bright gorge. "Theo," he said, "when you boarded that barbarian airship, did you notice anything unusual about her crew?"

Theo was not sure what he meant. "They were easterners," he said at last. "I remember thinking that I had never heard of easterners fighting for the *Traktionstadtsgesellschaft.* . ."

"Nor have I," said Khora. "Nor has anyone. That aviatrix you captured claims that she and her comrades were mercenaries from the raft-city of Perfume Harbour, in the pay of one of the German cities. She has papers that seem to prove that, and we found a letter of marque signed by the mayor of Panzerstadt Koblenz in the wreckage of the other airship. We cannot prove that they are forgeries. And yet it doesn't quite ring true. Some of their equipment was surprising, too. . ."

"The radio set on the ship I boarded. . ." Theo remembered. "It was a Green Storm model. . ."

Khora returned to his seat, leaned closer to Theo, and spoke quite softly. "I think what you foiled was not an attack on Zagwa by barbarians but an attempt by elements inside the Green Storm to assassinate Lady Naga."

"Why?" Theo started to say, and then remembered what Lady Naga had been telling him. "Because of what she did to the Stalker Fang?"

"Because they hate me," said Lady Naga.

"It is not just that," said Khora. "Lady Naga is too modest to say so, but the recent moves towards peace have largely been due to her influence. General Naga adores her, and does everything she asks."

("I try to guide him," said Lady Naga, blushing.)

"But of course there are others in the Storm who cannot bear the idea of making peace with the Traction Cities," Khora went on. "It would serve them very well if Lady Naga were to be killed, and it would serve them even better if she were to be killed by Tractionists. Naga would hardly push for peace with people he thought had murdered his beloved bride.

"That is why they went to all the trouble of disguising their attack as the work of the *Traktionstadts*. But now that their plan has failed, who knows what they will try next? She is safe while she is here, but they may attack her ship on its way back to Tienjing. They will be watching for her on the Bird Roads east of Zagwa, waiting for another chance to strike.

"So we have decided," he said, "to play a little trick on

Lady Naga's enemies. The talks are supposed to last another week, but between ourselves the talking is all but done. Lady Naga has convinced us of her husband's good intentions, and we have agreed to help him. A few days from now an unremarkable merchant airship will leave Zagwa air-harbour and fly north-west across the sand-sea to Tibesti Static, then north again towards the heights of Akheggar. But somewhere over the desert it will change course and make for Shan Guo. Lady Naga will be aboard it, incognito, with one or two of her people to keep her company. No one will expect her to travel by such a route, on such a ship, and by the time her own ship takes off, after the official conclusion of the talks, she will already have been delivered safe to her husband in Tienjing."

("You talk about me as if I were a parcel," complained Lady Naga, embarrassed at being the cause of so much trouble.)

"The ship Lady Naga travels on should have an African captain," said Khora. "If our enemies heard that a ship commanded by easterners had left Zagwa they might smoke our plan, but with a Zagwan in charge she will appear nothing more than a local trader. Of course, it will have to be someone who has proved his courage and his loyalty, and who can perhaps speak a little Airsperanto."

"Me?" said Theo, catching his drift at last. He looked at Lady Naga, then his parents, and saw that they were all waiting for his answer. His father sat frozen with a honey-biscuit halfway to his mouth, and as Theo watched it slowly came in half and the lower part dropped stickily into Father's lap. "You want me to go?" he said. He felt frightened and excited. To fly north again, to see the world, to be entrusted with such an important mission. . . He looked around him at the pleasant house, the steep sunlit gardens, then back to the grave faces of his parents. He had defied them once, running away to join the Green Storm's war. Surely they would not let him leave again?

"Father?" he asked nervously. "Ma?"

"The choice is yours, Theo," said his father, putting one arm around his wife's shoulders. "You've proved more than capable of looking after yourself, and we know you've been restless, cooped up here, longing to return to the sky."

"Like a caged bird," said his mother.

"We will miss you if you go, and fear for you, and pray as we did before for your safe return, but we will not stop you from going, if that is what you want," his father said. "It is a great honour that the Air Marshal has chosen you."

"You do not have to decide now," said Khora kindly. "The ship does not depart until Tuesday, in the dark of the moon. Think on it tonight, and talk with your mother and father, and let me know your decision in the morning."

But it did not take as long as Khora had expected for Theo to make his decision. Lady Naga had saved his life, and despite all he had been through in the past year, the urge for adventure was still strong in him. And he could not help wondering whether, on the Bird Roads of the north, he might meet Wren Natsworthy again.

On Tuesday night, in the dark of the moon, Theo walked at the Air Marshal's side across Zagwa air-harbour, which stood on a low plateau outside the city walls. In a well-lit hangar Lady Naga's cruiser *Plum Blossom Spring* sat in splendour. She was the loveliest airship that Theo had ever seen, but he barely glanced at her; his attention was fixed on the ship which sat waiting for him on an unlit pan at the very edge of the harbour. She was not a remarkable ship – in fact she had been chosen because she was so *un*remarkable – but Theo could see at once that she was well-built. A sturdy little Achebe 1040 with tapered engine pods and long, graceful steering-fins. Such ships were used all over Africa as freighters and transports, and this one had clearly had a long life, during which she had grown rather grubby and tattered, but she was Theo's first command, and he was convinced that she was a better ship than even the *Plum Blossom Spring*. Her name was *Nzimu*.

Theo had already made his goodbyes, and so, it seemed, had Lady Naga, for she was waiting for him at the foot of the *Nzimu*'s boarding-ladder with just two other people; a young officer who had swapped his Green Storm uniform for the shapeless robes of a trader, and the deaf-mute servant-girl, Rohini. Khora explained that the other girl, Zhou Li, would be staying behind in Zagwa to wear her mistress's clothes and stand in for her at next week's official banquet. She was taller than Lady Naga, and Han rather than Aleutian, but they were enough alike that if any spies were watching they might be fooled into thinking the ambassador was still in Zagwa.

"Theo," said Lady Naga, taking his hands in greeting as he stopped in front of the *Nzimu*, "You remember Rohini, don't you? And this is Captain Rasputra, who insists on coming as my bodyguard."

"She's a precious cargo," said Rasputra, a white smile flashing at Theo out of his black spade of beard. "I promised Naga I'd not let her out of my sight."

"It will be just the four of us," Lady Naga said.

"When you refuel at Tibesti," Khora said, "let everyone believe that Lady Naga and the captain are your passengers, and Rohini is your wife."

"Right," said Theo, glancing at the beautiful servant-girl and feeling glad that his sisters were not here to giggle.

Captain Rasputra said, "The wind is rising."

Lady Naga turned to Khora. "You have a beautiful country, Air Marshal. I hope to return one day, when peace has come back to the world."

"I hope that day will be soon," said Khora, returning her bow. The breeze fluttered their cloaks. As Khora straightened he said, "Lady Naga, I owe you special thanks for ridding us of the Stalker Fang. I knew Anna Fang in life, and I loved her. The thought of that unholy thing walking about with her face. . ."

"I know," said Lady Naga. "I know how it feels. My own brother. . . But you must not fear for Anna Fang. She is at peace." She looked past him at Theo, and stretched out her small hand to him again. "Theo. Shall we go aboard?"

5

A BOY AND HIS STALKER

Fishcake hurried down a side-alley deep in the under-tiers of Cairo. There were a lot of people about, even at this late hour, but that did not worry him. He was only ten years old, and little more than waist-high to most of the passers-by. They barely noticed him as he wove his way between them, clutching his bag of stolen Old-Tech under his robes. From time to time he paused among the knots of men who gathered to argue and haggle in front of stalls heaped high with scraps of machinery. They loved to argue, down here in the Lower Souk, and if Fishcake timed it right and waited till the debate had reached its height they never saw his skinny white hand dart out to snatch a piece of circuitry or a fragment of dented armour.

When he had what he needed he stopped at a food-stall and stole a sticky pastry, which he ate on the move as he scurried down the long maze of ladderways and stairs and 'tween-tier maintenance catwalks that led down eventually into Cairo's drains. The city was rumbling across rough country towards the shores of the Middle Sea, and the fetid spillways of its storm-drain system rang with the squeal and grumble of the vast axles turning. It was mostly shadows down there, except where spokes of red light from furnaces and refineries splayed down through the gratings. The stench, the noise, the fumes would have been too much for most people to bear, but for Fishcake this was home. He felt safe in the city's noisy belly, where almost no one came.

He checked all the same to make sure he had not been followed before he prised open a grating in the wall of the main drain and threw his heavy bag through the hole, then slithered after it.

It was dark in the little side-chamber he dropped into. Dark and dry. A hundred years before, Cairo had gone hunting far to the south, in lands where the rains came hard and frequently. It had needed its network of storm-drains then, but since it returned to the desert they had been sealed off and forgotten. In the Lower Souk Fishcake sometimes heard men saying that the drains were haunted by djinni and evil ghosts, and it always made him smile, because they were right.

He picked up his bag and started wading through the moraine of greasy food-wrappers and empty water bottles on the chamber floor. Near the back of the chamber, where light flickered in fitfully through another grating, something moved.

"Fishcake?" whispered a voice.

"Hello Anna," said Fishcake. He was glad it was her. He switched on his lamp, a stolen argon-globe fed by power that he leeched from a cable upstairs. His Stalker was propped in a corner. She had unsheathed her claws when she heard him coming and the long blades were still bared, raised in front of her blind bronze face. Fishcake felt what he always felt when he came home to her; pride, and loathing, and a sort of love. Pride because he had built her himself, cobbling her together from the pieces of her smashed body that he had rescued from the desert. Loathing because she had not turned out as well as he had hoped. Her armour, which must once have been so smooth and silvery, was dull and dented as an old bucket, scabbed with solder and riveted-on patches which he'd made by stamping soup tins flat. And although he had never seen a Stalker in action, he was sure her joints and bearings were not supposed to grate like that each time she moved. . .

As for the love, well, everybody needs to love someone, and the Stalker was all that Fishcake had. She had saved him in the desert, told him what to do, told him how to rebuild her. She was a strange companion, and scary sometimes, but it was better than being alone.

"I found some couplings," said Fishcake, emptying out his bag in the corner of the chamber where he kept his stolen tools. The chamber rocked and shuddered with the movements of the city. Light spiked through the gratings, shining on the Stalker's unchanging face, her comforting bronze smile. "I'll put you together again soon," Fishcake promised. "Tonight. . ."

"Thank you, Fishcake. Thank you for taking care of me."

"That's all right."

Fishcake had learned that his Stalker was really two people. One was the Stalker Fang, a stern, merciless being who had ordered the Green Storm about for years and now ordered Fishcake instead. But from time to time she would jerk and quiver and go silent for a moment, and when she spoke again she would be Anna, who was much gentler, and a bit bewildered.

At first Fishcake had thought that Anna was just the result of a short-circuit inside the Stalker's complicated brain, but over the months he had come to understand that there was more to her than that. Anna remembered all sorts of things that had happened long ago, and she liked to talk about people and places that Fishcake had never heard of. A lot of her stories made no sense; they were just lists of disconnected images and names, like random pieces from a hundred mixed-up jigsaws. Sometimes she just made sobbing noises, or begged Fishcake to kill her, which he did not know how to do, and wouldn't have done even if he had, in case she turned back into the Stalker Fang while he was doing it and killed him instead. But he liked Anna. He was glad it was Anna tonight.

He found her legs, stacked in a corner beneath some newspapers. He had rebuilt them months ago, and he was quite pleased with them, even though the bottom part of the right one and the right foot were missing and he had had to use an old metal table leg instead. He had never managed to attach them to the rest of his Stalker, because he couldn't find the right couplings, but tonight in the Souk he had struck lucky at last. It was because of this truce out east; traders were arriving in Cairo from all sorts of places that had been war-zones until quite recently, from the territory of the *Traktionstadts-gesellschaft* and the battlefields of the Altai Shan. (There was no shortage of smashed Stalker-bits in the Altai Shan.)

Fishcake drank some water and set to work. He said, "We'll soon be away from here."

"You have found an airship?" whispered the Stalker. She sounded eager. (One thing that the Stalker Fang and Anna parts of her had in common was that they both kept nagging at Fishcake to finish the repairs and take them away to a place called Shan Guo. The Stalker Fang had something important to do there. Anna just wanted to go home.) "I had an airship of my own once," she whispered. "The *Jenny Haniver*. I built her myself, secretly, in Arkangel, stole parts from Stilton's salvage-yards and flew away. . ."

"Not an airship," said Fishcake, who was tired of that story. "How do you expect us to nick an airship? The air-yards are three tiers up; it's too dangerous."

"But we cannot walk to Shan Guo. It will take too long."

Fishcake placed a leg in position and busied himself connecting wires and flexes. "We won't have to walk," he said. "I picked up some news in the Lower Souk today. Guess where Cairo's heading? Brighton. We're going to park beside the seaside and trade with Brighton. Boats and things will go across. And I reckon there's still limpets in Brighton. We could get to Shan Guo easy in a limpet."

"Eyes," whispered his Stalker. She turned her face to him, showing him the smashed lenses of her eyes. "I will need to see, if we are to reach Shan Guo. You will find me new eyes."

Her voice had changed. It was still a whisper, but it was harsher and hissier and Fishcake knew that he was in the presence of the Stalker Fang. He kept his nerve. "Sorry. No eyes. I can't find none anywhere. Maybe in Brighton, eh? Maybe I'll find some Stalkers' eyes in Brighton?"

But he had a feeling he wouldn't. In fact, several of the stalls he frequented in the Lower Souk had Stalkers' eyes for sale; big glass jars full of them, like gobstoppers. Fishcake had decided very early on that he would not be stealing any for his Stalker. He wasn't stupid. He knew that she was stronger and faster and cleverer than him.

But as long as she was blind, she would need to stick with her little Fishcake.

"Maybe in Brighton," he told her again, and set to work on the other leg.

6
RAIN-COLOURED SILK

The *Nzimu* flew nor'-nor'-west all night. By dawn she was cruising in calm air above a seemingly endless desert. Theo, whose nerves had been on edge as he guided his little ship over the mountains north of Zagwa, soon started to feel rather bored. Everything was running smoothly. The ambassador stayed in her cabin, high in the envelope. Her pretty servant came down the companionway in a rustle of rain-coloured silk from time to time to stare at the view from the gondola windows. Once or twice that day he turned and found her watching him. Each time, her dark eyes darted quickly away from his, seeming suddenly very interested in the ducting above the main control station, or the flickering altimeter needles.

There was something familiar about her, and it nagged at Theo through the long, dull hours of northing. Was it Wren whom she reminded him of? But she was much prettier than Wren. . .

Captain Rasputra, meanwhile, turned out to be friendly, competent, polite and perfectly sure that he could fly Lady Naga home to Tienjing without any help from Theo Ngoni. "Look, my dear fellow," he said, when he came down to relieve Theo that evening, "let us sort ourselves out. I'm an aviator with twelve years' experience in General Naga's own squadron. You, on the other hand, are what? An amateur. A failed Tumbler-pilot. I don't mean to be unkind, but you are commander of this tub for official purposes only, so that we may maintain the fiction that she is a Zagwan vessel on a trading voyage. For *practical* purposes, while we are up here in the blue, I think you had better leave things to me, eh?"

Before he turned in that evening, Theo climbed on to the top of the envelope and stood in the wind on the tiny lookout platform there, watching for trouble. He saw none; nothing but a few small desert townlets on the move, dragging their long wakes of dust behind them, too busy with their own concerns to pay attention to a passing airship. The air was empty too, except for a distant sky-train heading south, its long chain of envelopes gleaming like an amber necklace in the sun.

Theo sighed, almost wishing that air-pirates or assassins would attack, so that he could prove his usefulness to Lady Naga and Captain Rasputra. He imagined himself doing something heroic again (conveniently forgetting how frightened he had been aboard that Super-Gnat) and word of it spreading along the Bird Roads until it reached Wren. But when he tried to picture her he found that the only face he could call to mind was that of the servant Rohini.

Alone in her cabin in the stern of the *Nzimu*'s envelope, Oenone Zero, Lady Naga, knelt and bowed her head and made a steeple of her stained hands and started to say her prayers. She did not expect God to answer her, because she did not believe he worked like that. But she had felt his presence very clearly, ever since that night on Cloud 9 when she had thought she was about to die. He gave her strength, and comfort, and courage. It seemed to Oenone that the least she could offer him in return were her prayers.

And so she gave thanks for her time in Zagwa, for the kindness of the Queen and Bishop and of Air Marshal Khora. She gave thanks for the bravery of Theo Ngoni, and prayed that he would come to no harm on this furtive voyage. And there she became distracted by a rather unspiritual thought. What a pity it was that her husband could not have been as young and handsome as Theo. . .

She opened her eyes and looked at the portrait of Naga which she kept beside her bunk; his maimed body strapped into mechanized battle-armour, his battered, ochre face screwed into the awkward smile of someone who has had no practice smiling. Whenever she saw it she wondered what it could be that made such a man love her.

She did not love him. She was just grateful for his protection, and glad that the leadership of the Green Storm had passed into the hands of a decent man. That was why she had been unable to say no when he asked her to be his wife. "Of course," she'd said, and a feeling of numb astonishment had settled over her, which did not lift until she was dressed in her red bridal gown and standing on tiptoe to kiss her new husband in front of a vast assembly of officers and priests and bridesmaids and a nervous Christian vicar, flown in at considerable expense from some static in the Western Archipelago to give Oenone's new god's blessing to the marriage. . .

A gentle knocking broke in upon her memories. The cabin door opened and Rohini came in, shy and silent as ever. Oenone sat down at her portable dressing table and unpinned her hair so that the girl could brush it. In the lamplight the ends of her hair shone faintly auburn; a reminder that some of her long-ago ancestors had probably been Americans who fled to the remote Aleutian islands after the Sixty Minute War. Yet another reason for the Green Storm's hardliners to despise her. . .

She tried to forget them and enjoy the gentle touch of Rohini's hands and the soft, sleepy shushing of the hairbrush. She was glad that the girl had volunteered to come with her on this voyage. Rohini was so much quieter and sweeter than her other servants, who all seemed slightly resentful when Oenone tried to treat them like equals. Rohini was the only one who seemed genuinely fond of her, and appeared to appreciate the kindness that Oenone showed her.

So it came as a horrible surprise when Rohini dropped the brush, looped the rain-coloured belt of her robes around Oenone's throat and, pulling it tight, hissed in a voice Oenone had never heard, "We know what you did, you miserable city-lover! We know how you destroyed our beloved leader, and seduced that fool Naga! Now you will see what the true Storm does to traitors. . ."

Something had woken Theo, and he could not get back to sleep. It was cold in his cabin; his bunk was uncomfortable; he missed his home very much. He turned on the lamp and looked at his wristwatch, but there were several hours to go before he was supposed to relieve Rasputra at the helm. He groaned and turned the light out and snuggled under his scratchy blankets, trying vainly to sleep again.

But as he lay there, he slowly became convinced that his ship had altered course. The sound of the wind against the envelope had changed in some subtle way. He had learned to pay attention to such details during his time aboard the carriers of the Tumbler Corps, where any unexplained course-change might mean that the unit was going into battle. The *Nzimu* had not been due to alter her heading before she sighted the Tibesti Mountains, and Theo had not expected that to happen before sunrise.

What was going on? He imagined a flock of barbarian flying-machines closing in from windward, or a pirate cutter rising from some lair among the dunes. Just like Rasputra to try and outrun them without even telling him! He rolled off his bunk and started pulling on his boots and coat, the only items he had taken off when he turned in.

Halfway down the central companion-ladder he glimpsed Rohini on the walkway below him, heading aft towards Lady Naga's cabin. He was about to call out and ask her what had happened when he remembered that she would not hear him. Besides, he did not want to alarm her over what might be an innocent course correction. Not until he'd talked to Rasputra.

He waited until she had gone past, then slid down the last few sections of ladder and dropped into the gondola. "What's happening?" he asked.

But Captain Rasputra could not tell him, because someone had cut Captain Rasputra's throat so deeply and so expertly that he had died before anything more than a look of mild surprise could register on his pleasant face.

"Captain Rasputra?" said Theo. A movement at his side made him jump, but it was just his own reflection in a window, wide-eyed and stupid. He stared at himself.

Who had done this? Was there an intruder aboard the *Nzimu*? Had some assassin boarded his ship the same way he'd boarded those Super-Gnats over Zagwa? But no; the smell of blood, the horror of finding himself alone with a dead man in this glass-walled place, reminded him vividly of things he and Wren had seen on Cloud 9. He knew now why Rohini seemed so familiar.

He tugged down a fire-axe from a hook on the wall and forced himself back to the ladder and up. As he ran along the walkway to the door of Lady Naga's cabin he heard someone inside say something about traitors. There was a scuffling and a noise of things falling and rolling. Theo shouted to give himself courage, and swung his axe at the lock on the door. It came apart under the first blow and the door swung open.

Inside, amid a tangle of bedding from the overturned bunk and a rolling glitter of vials and bottles from the dressing table knelt Lady Naga, scrabbling with both hands at the belt which Rohini was using to strangle her. Rohini's look of triumph faded only slightly when she looked round to see Theo standing in the shattered doorway.

"Can't you just *knock*?" she asked crossly.

"Cynthia Twite," said Theo.

"Surprise!" the girl replied, with a smile.

Lady Naga made a horrible gurgling noise, like the last of the bathwater heading down the plughole. Theo took a step forward and waved the axe, but he was too gentle to use it, and he knew Cynthia knew it. Remembering the girl's vanity he said, "You look different. . ."

It worked. Tiring of Lady Naga for the moment, Cynthia gave the silk belt one last, sharp tug and let go.

Her victim pitched forward and lay face down, unmoving. "Good, isn't it?" asked Cynthia, indicating her own black hair, which had been blonde when Theo saw her last, and her brown skin, which had been fair. She smiled as if Theo had paid her a gallant compliment. It was her only weakness as a secret agent. She was so delighted by her own cleverness that she could never resist telling her victims how she had tricked them.

Theo hoped that if he could keep her talking long enough, some helpful god might slip an idea into his brain.

"The hair and skin were easy," Cynthia was saying. "The eyes were the real trick. I'm wearing little Old-Tech things called 'Contract Lenses'." She touched a finger to one eye and blinked. When she took her hand away the eye was its old cornflower blue, gazing incongruously at Theo out of her dark face. "If you were any good," she said, "you'd have tried to hit me then. But I see you're still a coward. I'm rather looking forward to killing you, Theo Ngoni. That's why I was saving you till last."

"Please," gasped Lady Naga, heaving about on the deck like something half drowned. "Don't hurt him. . ."

Cynthia stamped on her. "We're *talking*!"

"Cynthia," shouted Theo. "Why are you doing this?"

Cynthia took another step closer, fixing him with her odd-coloured eyes. "This Aleutian bitch betrayed our leader so that Naga could seize power. Do you really think those of us who loved the Stalker Fang would let her get away with it?"

"But why here?" cried Theo helplessly. "Why now? You're part of her household; you could have killed her in Tienjing. . . Killed Naga too."

Cynthia sighed sharply, exasperated by his innocence. "We don't want Naga *dead*," she explained. "That would only mean civil war, and more distraction from the real business of killing townies. We just want to make him give up this truce. If you hadn't interfered when I called our ships in at Zagwa it would be over already. But I'm patient. In a few minutes this old rust-bucket will go down in flames. Rohini will be the only survivor, and she'll tell Naga how Zagwa betrayed us to the townies and the townies shot us down. That ought to put the mockers on any alliance between Naga and your lot. As for the townies, well, he's hardly going to sit down and talk peace when he hears what they did to his pretty little wifelet. The guns will begin firing again. Our mistress will reward us when she returns to Tienjing!"

"You mean Fang? But she's dead!"

Cynthia smiled eerily. "She was *always* dead, African. That is why she can never be killed. She is waiting for us to end this treacherous talk of truces and conditions. Then she will return, and lead us to total victory!"

"You're mad!" said Theo.

"Oh, that's rich, coming from somebody who goes around smashing down doors with a dirty great axe," said Cynthia, and with no more warning than that she swung her foot up and drove him backwards with a kick, snatching the heavy fire-axe from his hands as he went sprawling through the open doorway and tumbled down the companionway to the level below.

A grated walkway hit him hard in the face and he lay there for a moment tasting blood in his mouth and listening for the sound of Cynthia coming after him. He heard her footsteps pacing along the walkway overhead, and saw her shadow moving against the flank of the gas-cell up there. He dragged himself into a crawlspace. After a moment the footsteps stopped. "Theo?" Cynthia called down. "Don't think I'm going to come looking for you. I was looking forward to killing you, but I really can't be bothered to play hide-and-seek. It won't make any difference anyway. There's a bomb under the central gas-cell, set to explode at midnight. So I'm going to take one of your silly Zagwan kites and beetle off now; I've arranged to meet some friends of mine in the desert shortly. Toodle-oo!"

The footsteps started again, and grew quieter as she climbed away from him. Theo guessed she was making for the emergency exit in the flank of the envelope. Just inside it was a locker where half a dozen kites were stored, workaday versions of the one he'd flown in Zagwa. He waited, and heard the hatch open, the sounds inside the envelope changing as the wind rushed in. Quickly, he scrambled along a lateral support to a place where a glastic porthole had been riveted into the skin of the envelope. Out in the starlight, far away, a black bat-wing showed for a moment against the silver waves of the desert.

What about the other kites? Knowing Cynthia, she would have destroyed them. But maybe the delay that Theo had caused might have left her no time to deal with them. He glanced at his watch, and saw with relief that there were still eight minutes to go before midnight. Ignoring the pain in his chest and side he started climbing towards the kite-locker. Even if he had not known where it was he would have been able to find it by tracing the source of the cold wind howling in through the open escape hatch. Sure enough, the locker was empty; Cynthia had bundled the spare kites out through the hatch before she took flight herself. But when Theo stuck his head out he saw one kite caught in the ratlines only a few yards from the hatch, and it was easy for him to reach out and drag it back aboard.

Breathing hard, he started to strap himself into the kite. Then he remembered Lady Naga. The kite was big, and she was small; Theo was sure it would carry both of them. But was she even still alive? He glanced quickly at his watch. The climb to the kite locker had not taken nearly as long as he'd thought. He had to try and save Lady Naga. He had promised.

He left the kite by the locker and flung himself back down the steep companionways to her cabin. She was lying where he had left her, but she started whimpering and trying to drag herself away when she heard him come in, imagining that he was Cynthia.

"It's all right," he told her, kneeling down beside her and rolling her over.

"Rohini," she croaked.

"She's gone," said Theo, trying to help her to her feet. "She was never Rohini anyway. Her name's Cynthia Twite; she was part of the Stalker Fang's private spy ring."

"Twite?" Lady Naga frowned and groaned. Thinking seemed to hurt. "No, she was a white girl, the Stalker's agent on Cloud 9. . . Naga took her home aboard the *Requiem Vortex*, but she vanished when we reached Shan Guo. . . Oh, Theo, I have to get home. If I don't, she or her friends will tell Naga that the townies killed me, and the peace will fail. . ."

"Don't try to talk," said Theo, worried that she would injure herself still further by forcing all these words up her poor, bruised throat. "I'll get you home, I promise. But first we have to get off this ship." He checked his wristwatch. "There's a b –" he said, and stopped.

It was still eight minutes to midnight.

The fall down the stairs, he thought. *My watch is broken. . .*

He had just time to remember his father saying, "I don't know why you youngsters wear these gimcrack bracelet watches. A pocket watch is more distinguished, and far, far more reliable," before the explosion tore his ship apart beneath him.

7

BRIGHTON ROCKS

Brighton had taken a turn for the worse since Wren and Theo left. The flying palace of Cloud 9 was gone, and it had taken most of the city's ruling elite with it. Brighton was ruled now by the Lost Boys. Dragged aboard as captives by the Shkin Corporation, they had escaped from their pens on the night of the Green Storm raid and quickly made themselves at home, setting up their own small kingdoms among the smart white streets of Queen's Park and Montpelier and the dank labyrinths of the Laines, gathering private armies of beggars and rebel slaves about them. They fought amongst themselves, or formed shaky alliances which could be broken over a stolen pair of shoes or a covetous glance at a pretty slave-girl. You could never tell what a Lost Boy would do next. They were vicious and sentimental, greedy and generous. A lot of them were mad. By night their followers fought running battles on the litter-strewn promenades, avenging botched wire-deals and imagined insults.

Yet Brighton was still a popular holiday spot. Its upper-class visitors had all deserted it (the luxury hotels were in ruins, or had been converted into strongholds by Lost Boys) and no more happy families came aboard to fill the cheaper guest-houses and frolic in the Sea Pool, but there was a certain sort of person – well-off artists from the comfortable middle-tiers of cities which the war had never touched, and spoilt young men who fancied a little adventuring before they settled into the careers their parents had bought them – who thought the new Brighton edgy and exciting. They were thrilled to rub shoulders in the clubs and bars with real criminals and mutineers; they loved it when some Lost Boy and his entourage came swaggering into the restaurant they were eating in; they thought the slicks of sewage lapping against the promenades, the raucous, never-ending music and the dead bodies heaved overboard at dawn were signs that Brighton was somehow more real than the cities they had come from. Some of them were robbed during their stay, all of them were fleeced, and a few were found down alleyways in Mole's Combe and White Orc with their pockets emptied and their throats cut, but the survivors would go home to Milan and Peripatetiapolis and St Jean Les Quatre-Mille Chevaux and bore their friends and relatives for years to come with stories of their holiday in Brighton.

There were some like that among the passengers of the launch that set off from the beach where Cairo was parked, but most had darker reasons for visiting Brighton. They were drug-dealers out to push wire and hashish, or thieves, or gun-runners, or shifty-looking men who had heard that in Brighton these days you could buy *anything*. And up at the bows, drenched in the spray that crashed over the gunwales every time the launch shoved its blunt nose through a wave, Fishcake stood staring at the approaching resort and wishing he had stayed safe ashore.

In his hidey-hole aboard Cairo it had been an easy thing to please his Stalker by promising to steal her a limpet, but now that the rusty flanks of Brighton were rising above the swell ahead he was starting to have serious doubts. He kept remembering that his fellow Lost Boys saw him as a traitor. The last time he encountered any of them they had made it plain that they wanted to kill him in a number of inventive ways, and he had been forced to jump overboard and take his chances in the surf. He had assumed that the Brighton authorities would have rounded them up by now, but listening to his fellow passengers talk it seemed that he'd been wrong; the Lost Boys *were* the Brighton authorities.

The launch swung across Brighton's decaying stern, past dirty paddle-wheels and derelict promenades and a district called Plage Ultime where a whole row of limpets was stabled on a dirty metal quay. A girl standing nearby, a traveller from some rich city, said to her boyfriend, "Ugh! Those horrible machines! Like great big spiders!"

"Lost Boy submarines!" the boy said. "You can buy pleasure trips aboard them and see the city from beneath. And that's not all they're used for. Lost Boys are still pirates at heart. I've heard stories of little towns that have crossed Brighton's path and never been seen again. . ."

"Ugh!" said the girl again, but she looked delighted at the thought of boarding a city where real, live pirates lived.

Fishcake did not share her enthusiasm. Returning seemed less and less like a good idea.

The launch entered a channel of calm, filthy water between the central hull and the outrigger district of Kemptown. Abandoned pleasure-piers arched overhead, their corroded gantries sending down a rain of rust-flakes as Brighton shifted on the swell. The voices of the launch crew echoed across the narrowing gap to dockers waiting on the mooring stair. Smells of oil and brine. A dead cat bobbed in a mat of drifting scum. The launch backed its engines, and the other passengers began to gather their bags and pat their clothes, checking that wallets and money-belts were still secure, but Fishcake just turned up his collar and tugged down the peak of his greasy cap and wished that he could stay aboard the launch and let it take him back to Cairo.

His Stalker, who was standing silently beside him, wrapped in the long, hooded robe that he had stolen for her from the Lower Souk, seemed to sense his fear. Her steel fingers closed gently on his arm, and she whispered, "There is nothing to be afraid of. I am with you."

She was Anna today. He took her hand in his and held it tight and felt a little braver. He did not even worry too much when a gust of wind snatched his cap off and sent it whirling up into the sunlight.

Two tiers above, in a fortified hotel on Ocean Boulevard, a Lost Boy named Brittlestar jerked round to stare as the lost cap went whirling past his window.

"What was that?" he demanded.

His friends and bodyguards fingered the weapons in their belts and said they didn't know. One of his slaves said she thought it was just a hat.

"Just a hat?" hissed Brittlestar. "Nothing is *just* anything! It *meant* something! Where did it come from? Whose was it?"

The bodyguards, friends and slaves swapped weary glances. Brittlestar was growing increasingly paranoid, and sometimes at night he woke the whole gang as he thrashed around in his sleep and screamed about Grimsby and somebody called Uncle. The bodyguards and friends were starting to think it might soon be time to pitch him overboard and offer their services to some less sensitive Lost Boy like Krill or Baitball.

Brittlestar, the hem of his silk dressing gown swooshing behind him over the expensive carpets, went rushing to the room where he kept his screens. All the Lost Boys had screens, and all had crab-cameras which they sent sneaking about Brighton to spy on other Lost Boys. Everyone had grown quite used to the scraping of the machines' metal feet inside the city's ventilation shafts, and the echoey, rattling fights which broke out when two rival cameras met. Sometimes at dawn the pavements beneath air-vents were littered with torn-off metal legs and shattered lenses, the debris of desperate battles that had raged through the shafts all night.

"*Everything* means something!" Brittlestar assured his followers, as they gathered in the doorway to watch him grapple with the screen-controls. "You say it's a hat, I say it's a sign. It could be a message from Uncle!" Brittlestar had been dreaming a great deal about Uncle lately. Uncle kept whispering to him. He had come to believe that the old man was still alive, and would soon punish his Lost Boys for letting themselves be captured by Brighton.

But it was not Uncle he saw when he trained one of his cameras on the group of visitors disembarking at the Kemptown Stair. He wasn't sure who he was seeing at first, only that there was something familiar about the little boy leading the cripple in the black robe. Then one of his slaves, a woman named Monica Weems, who had once worked for the Shkin Corporation and had a better memory for faces than Brittlestar, suddenly pointed at the screen and said, "Look! Look, master! It's little Fishcake!"

Little Fishcake hurried his Stalker along litter-strewn pavements under the colonnades at the city's edge, past boarded-up cafés and looted amusement arcades, out at last into the metallic sunlight of Plage Ultime. *To The Beach*, said a stencilled sign on a white wall, and Fishcake and his Stalker followed where it pointed, past abandoned hotels and empty swimming pools, past the gigantic housings of the resort's Mitchell & Nixon engines, down to the hard where the limpets waited.

There was a chain-link fence around the hard, and a padlock on the gate, but fences and padlocks meant nothing to the Stalker. She snapped the lock and Fishcake pushed the gate open and ran among the limpets, feeling a strange nostalgia for the old days in Grimsby. Their armoured cabs and crook-kneed legs, patched with barnacles and gull-droppings, gave the limpets the appearance of enormous, prehistoric crabs. Fishcake knew them all; the *Sea Louse* and the *Thermoclyne Girl*, the *Hagfish 2* and the *Finny Denizen*, but he settled on the smallest, sleekest, newest one, the *Spider Baby*. It stood closer to the water than the rest, and had a board propped against its foreleg offering pleasure trips beneath the city, so he hoped it might already be fuelled.

He looked for his Stalker, but he had left her behind. Poor thing, stomping along on that table leg, she couldn't keep up with him! He started to walk back through the zigzag shadows under the limpets, calling out, "Anna! Come here! I need you to open the hatch!"

With a howl of electric engines two bugs came speeding out of the streets beneath the engine-housings and through the open gate on to the limpet-hard. They were driving much too fast, and both were overloaded, with men and boys packed into their small cabins and standing on the roofs and running boards. Fishcake, noticing the swords and flare-pistols and harpoon-guns that they were waving at him, turned to run, but the only way out was through the gate, which the men spilling from the bugs quickly pushed shut. Whimpering, Fishcake veered towards the sea, but the Drys were all around him, and with them, staring at him, was a boy he knew; a tall, thin, highly-strung, red-headed boy named –

"Brittlestar," said Brittlestar. "Remember me? 'Cos I remember you, Fishcake." He was carrying a spear-gun. "You're the sneak, ain't you? The one as told Shkin where Grimsby lay? Don't think I've forgot. We none of us have, we Lost Boys. Maybe when I show 'em that I've caught you they'll give me a bit of respect. Maybe Uncle will spare me, when he comes to punish us. Maybe—"

Somehow, suddenly, Fishcake's Stalker was standing behind Brittlestar. She gripped his chin and his red hair and twisted his head round so sharply that the noise of his neck snapping echoed across the hard like a gunshot. The last thing Brittlestar saw was his own surprised face reflected in her bronze mask. His finger tightened on the trigger of his spear-gun, which was pointing at the sky. A silver harpoon shot up into the sunlight, up through the steam from the idling engines, high into the clear air above the city.

Fishcake had just enough of his wits left to throw himself down beside Brittlestar's flapping body as bullets began to bang and whine among the parked limpets. He watched the harpoon rise higher and higher, slower and slower, until it seemed to hang for a moment suspended in the blue sky, a flake of silver among all the gliding gulls. His Stalker bared her claws. As the harpoon started to fall she began killing Brittlestar's gang one by one, finding them by their scent and the sound of the guns they shot at her. By the time the harpoon clattered on the deckplate at the far side of the hard, they were all dead.

The Stalker sheathed her claws and helped Fishcake to stand, asking him gently if he were damaged.

"Anna?" said Fishcake, surprised. "I thought you had turned into. . ."

"The other is still asleep, I think," his Stalker whispered, and patted at her robe, which was smouldering where someone had fired a flare-pistol at her.

"I didn't think you would be so. . ." said Fishcake awkwardly, looking at the blood that smeared her hands and sleeves. On the deckplate beside him Brittlestar had stopped flapping and lay still. Fishcake remembered how, in Grimsby, Brittlestar had always been rather kind to him. He said, "I thought it was only *her* that would do things like that."

His Stalker said, "I have had to kill people sometimes. I had forgotten, but I remember now. I used to be quite good at it. In my work for the League. And at Stayns that time, to save poor Tom and Hester. . ."

"You know Tom and Hester?" asked Fishcake, almost more shocked by those names than by the sudden deaths of Brittlestar and his crew.

But his Stalker had taken him by the wrist and was leading him briskly towards the limpet he had chosen. She did not bother to answer his question, and as she climbed the boarding ladder and started to force the heavy hatches open she was hissing to herself about Shan Guo and ODIN. Kind, murderous Anna had sunk once more beneath the surface of her mind, and she was the Stalker Fang again.

8
ON THE LINE

Wren had been dreaming about Theo, but what he had been saying or doing in her dream she did not know; the details, which had seemed so vivid and so clear just a moment before, all faded in an instant as she woke. Her father was shaking her gently and calling her name.

"Bother," she mumbled. "What is it?"

She was in her bunk aboard the *Jenny Haniver*, snuggled beneath a lot of furs and blankets, because although it was spring the Bird Roads were still cold. Outside her porthole the sky was dark. She sat up, rubbing the sleep out of her eyes. "What is it?" she asked, more clearly this time. "Is something wrong? You're not ill?"

"No, no," said Tom, "and I'm sorry to wake you early, but there's a sight ahead that you won't want to miss."

Wren's father believed firmly that there were certain sights in the world which were so beautiful, or awesome, or educational, that Wren would never forgive him if he let her sleep through them. He often recalled his own first glimpse of Batmunkh Gompa, and his first sight of the Tannhäuser volcano-chain, and several times during the journey east he had dragged Wren out of her bunk to see a beautiful sunrise or the approach of some fine city. Wren, who was a teenager and needed her sleep, was not always as grateful as he expected.

But on this particular morning, when she came grumpily on to the flight-deck and saw what was framed in the *Jenny*'s nose-windows, she forgave him at once.

They were flying low, and beneath them stretched the same featureless, rut-scarred plain that they had been passing over for days. To the south, a white-ish smear of mist hung over the Rustwater Marshes and the Sea of Khazak, but that was not what Tom had woken her for. Ahead, rising like mountains into a murk of their own smoke, stood more Traction Cities than Wren had yet seen in her life. Lighted windows and furnace-vents shone like jewels in the pre-dawn dark. Towns and cities which Wren would once have thought impressive were rolling to and fro, but they were dwarfed by the colossal, armoured ziggurats at the eastern edge of the cluster, ziggurats whose ten or fifteen tiers of homes and factories rose from base-plates a mile across, all armoured like medieval knights and prickly with guns and the mooring-gantries of aerial warships. The *Jenny Haniver* had arrived at the line which marked the easternmost boundary of Municipal Darwinism. She was flying into one of the great city-parks of the *Traktionstadtsgesellschaft*.

Fourteen years earlier, while Wren was busy learning to crawl and alarming her parents by eating stones, beetles and small ornaments, the Green Storm had swept down from their strongholds in the mountains of Shan Guo to spread war and destruction across the Great Hunting Ground. Their air-fleets and Stalker armies had surged westward, herding terrified Traction Cities ahead of them and destroying any that did not flee fast enough. Then Arminius Krause, the burgermeister of Traktionstadt Weimar, had sent envoys to eleven other

German-speaking cities and proposed that they join together and turn to face the Storm before every mobile town and city was driven off the western edge of the Hunting Ground into the sea.

And so the *Traktionstadtsgesellschaft* was born. The twelve great cities, swiftly joined by others, swore that they would eat no mobile town until the Green Storm was destroyed. They would survive instead by devouring Mossie ships and forts and static settlements until they had made the world safe again for Municipal Darwinism, which every civilized person knew was the most natural, sensible and fair way of life ever devised.

They turned, they fought, and they forced the startled Green Storm to a stalemate. Now, a broad ribbon of no-man's-land wriggled across the Hunting Ground from the southern fringes of the Rustwater Marshes to the edges of the Ice Wastes, marking the boundary between two worlds. To the east of it the Green Storm were struggling to plant new static settlements and reclaim for their farmers land which had been ploughed up and polluted by centuries of Municipal Darwinism. To the west, life went on almost as before, with cities hunting towns and towns hunting villages; the only difference was that most mayors sent a portion of their catch to feed the *Traktionstadts*.

Over the years there had been all manner of battles as each side tried to break the line. Stretches of churned mud and empty marsh changed hands again and again, at the cost of thousands of lives, but always, when the months-long thunder of thrust and counter-thrust had faded, the line remained much as it had been before, a river of dead ground winding across a continent.

Now that the truce seemed to be holding, some of the braver merchant cities and industrial platforms from the west had come to see the line for themselves, and trading clusters had formed around each concentration of *Traktionstadts*. The *Jenny Haniver* was flying into one of them. Tom took her low, beneath the grey lid of the cities' smoke, and Wren peered down at the upper-works of cities and merchant towns, and then down again to the earth, where smaller towns were scuttling along the narrow ridges of land between deep trenches made by larger cities' tracks. She saw tiny scavenger-villes down there, and speedy fighting-suburbs which Tom said were called harvesters. The sky was filled with other airships, balloon-taxis and lumbering sky-trains. Once a squadron of ungainly flying-machines roared rudely across the *Jenny*'s bows. "Air-hogs!" said Tom, and grumbled about old-fangled inventions and pilots who had no respect for the ways of the Bird Roads, but Wren was thrilled; the flapping, tumbling machines reminded her of the Flying Ferrets, those brave aviators whom she had seen in action over Cloud 9.

A fighting city called Murnau slipped by outside the windows, a colossal armoured wedge, wormholed with gun-slits and sally-ports. Its tiers were long triangles, narrowing to a sharp prow where a ram jutted out beneath the city's jaws. It was breathtakingly big and powerful-looking, but the sky was brightening quickly now, and Wren could see five or six similar cities in the distance, stretching off in a long line down the western edge of the Rustwater Marshes. Some looked even bigger than Murnau.

The *Jenny*'s destination was much more peaceful. Hanging in the sky a few miles from Murnau was a small doughnut of deckplate, crammed with lightweight buildings and fringed with mooring struts, supported by a bright cloud of gasbags like a helpful thunderhead. Wren had been aboard that doughnut often during her brief time on the Bird Roads; in cold northern skies and sticky southern ones. Finding it here above this clutter of armoured cities made her feel a little as if she were coming home.

Airhaven!

The long-faced clerk at the harbour-office looked thoughtful when Tom asked him about the *Archaeopteryx,* and shuffled off to rummage in his filing-drawers, returning after a few minutes with a musty ledger which he said held details of every ship registered in the flying free port. "Cruwys Morchard, mistress and commander," he said, and peered through his pince-nez at a cloudy photograph of the aviatrix, paper-clipped to the page that held the *Archaeopteryx*'s details. "Ah, yes, I remember! A handsome woman. Buys up Old-Tech."

"What sort of Old-Tech?" asked Tom.

"Magnetical curiosities mostly, to judge by her customs-records. Harmless old gadgets and gewgaws from the Electric Empire. Though she also shops for medical supplies, and a little livestock. Just a lass, she was, when she registered with us. Eighteen years ago!"

"The year after London was destroyed," said Tom. He unclipped the picture and turned it round. It had been taken long ago, when its subject was still a young woman, her curly hair a cloud of darkness. "It *is* Clytie Potts!" he murmured.

"Eh, sir?" The clerk was a little deaf. He cupped one hand to his ear while the other snatched back the photograph. "What's that?"

"I think her real name is Potts," said Tom.

The clerk shrugged. "Whatever it is, sir, the Sky Gods must like her. There's not many last eighteen years in the air-trade." And to prove his point he turned the ledger round and showed Tom and Wren the index-pages, where, amid a long list of airships, there were many names crossed through in red, with neat little notes beside them saying things like "missing", "crashed" or "Exploded at her Moorings".

The clerk thought that Ms Morchard had bought her ship in the Traction City of Helsinki, and when Tom slipped a golden sovereign under the cover of the ledger he suddenly recalled that she had purchased her at Unthank's airship-yard there. But where she had come from before that, where she had found the money for an airship, and what precisely her business was, he did not know; and, alas, old Mr Unthank and all his records had been destroyed ten years ago when one of his apprentices lit a cigar inside the envelope of an unexpectedly leaky Cosgrove Cloudberry. ("You can still see the scorchmarks along the edges of Helsinki air-harbour," the clerk said helpfully, as if he hoped it might earn him another sovereign, but it didn't.)

Outside his little office, the High Street was starting to come to life, and stallholders were rolling up their shutters and laying out trays of vegetables and fruit, flowers, cheeses and bolts of cloth. Watching them, Tom recalled following Anna Fang past these same stalls on a honey-coloured evening twenty years before. It had been his first visit to Airhaven. He remembered how Hester had slunk along beside him, hiding herself from the gaze of passers-by behind her upraised hand. . .

"Oh gods!" said Wren, stepping out of the harbour

office behind him and pointing to someone on a nearby quay. "Look who it is!"

For an instant, confused by his memories, Tom thought that it might be Hester come to find them. He felt strangely disappointed when he saw a shapely aviatrix in a pink leather flying suit.

Wren was jumping excitedly up and down and calling, "Ms Twombley! Ms Twombley!"

The aviatrix, who had been deep in conversation with some of her comrades, looked round in surprise, then strode gracefully across the quay to find out who was hailing her with such enthusiasm. "It's Orla Twombley," Wren told her father. "She used to work for Brighton." And as the aviatrix drew nearer her puzzled frown changed into a smile of recognition. She and Wren had not known each other well, but each was glad to find that the other had come safely out of the battle on Cloud 9.

"It's Wren, isn't it?" Ms Twombley asked, and took Wren's hands in hers. "The little slave-girl from the Pavilion? I had imagined you dead, or captured by the Storm. How good to see you safe and well! And this fine gentleman is your husband, I suppose?"

"Father," said Tom, going bright red. "I'm Wren's father."

"And wasn't I always thinking Wren was one of those Lost Girls!" cried Ms Twombley, astonished. "A poor motherless orphan from away out in the western sea somewhere. . ."

"Motherless, but not fatherless," said Wren. "It's a long story. But I am glad to see you so well, Ms Twombley. I thought you'd been shot down. . ."

"That was a bad night, to be sure," the aviatrix

admitted, and shook her head at the memory of the dog-fights that had raged around Cloud 9. "But it'd take a lot more than a few Stalker birds and poxy old Fox Spirits to bring down my *Combat Wombat*. I re-formed the Flying Ferrets. We work for Adlai Browne, Lord Mayor of Manchester. He's bringing his city up to the line, and he sent us ahead as his advance-guard."

Wren nodded. They had passed Manchester a week before; a huge, grimy city lumbering south-eastward, bristling with cranes which had been busy fitting shiny new plates of anti-rocket armour over its upper tiers.

"But what has brought you here?" asked Orla Twombley. She looked expectantly at Tom, but Tom said nothing. He had been wondering if those had been some of Ms Twombley's flying machines which had cut up the *Jenny Haniver* on her approach, and whether he should complain to her about them, but Ms Twombley was so beautiful that he couldn't quite bring himself to.

Wren jumped in quickly. "We've come looking for an old friend of Dad's. She calls herself Cruwys Morchard. You don't know of her, I suppose?"

"The archaeologist?" Orla Twombley nodded. "I saw her once at the Pavilion, in Brighton. She used to buy Old-Tech from Pennyroyal. In fact, I think they were supposed to have been an item at one time – but then, Pennyroyal's name has been linked with so many ladies. Even with me!"

"But I thought that you and Prof Pennyroyal were. . ." said Wren.

"Oh, only in his wife's imagination, and in the gossip pages of the *Brighton Palimpsest*," laughed Orla Twombley. "I just flirted with the old rogue a little, to make sure he'd renew the Ferrets' contract. Mind you, when I heard how brave he'd been that night I almost wished I *had* been his lover. Who could have thought that an old relic like Pennyroyal could outwit the Stalker Fang. . ."

Wren laughed. "Is that what people say he did?"

"Haven't you heard of it?" cried Orla Twombley, as if Wren had confessed to not knowing that the world was round, or that high-collared flying-suits were out of fashion. "It has been the talk of the season out here on the line! Isn't Prof Pennyroyal the great hero of the world? And has he not been dining out on the stories of his exploits aboard all the *Traktionstadts*?"

"He's here?" cried Tom.

"Aboard Murnau, at this very instant," the aviatrix confirmed. "I know, you must ask him about your friend Cruwys Morchard! He is sure to know all about her! If I know him he'll be having breakfast now at Moon's, down on Murnau's second tier."

"Oh, yes, Dad!" said Wren cheerfully. "Come on, let's find him, and ask!"

Tom put a hand to his chest, to the wound that Pennyroyal's bullet had made. He didn't want to go and have breakfast with the man who had shot him. And yet Pennyroyal had behaved decently enough aboard Kom Ombo, and now he thought about it, he half-recalled Pennyroyal telling him a story once about an aviatrix he knew who had ventured inside the wreck of London. Could her name have been Cruwys Morchard?

"I'll take you to see him myself," said Orla Twombley, and it was settled. She led them both away towards the centre of Airhaven, where balloon taxis were waiting to ferry people to the towns and cities below.

As their taxi sank towards Murnau, Wren prattled excitedly about the exploits of the Flying Ferrets and how their midge-like flying machines had hurled themselves at giant air-destroyers over Brighton. But Tom heard none of it. He was too busy thinking about the mystery of Clytie Potts. Where was her airship's home port? Why was she buying Old-Tech and medical supplies? Why livestock?

An answer had occurred to him a few nights before while he lay awake puzzling over his encounter with her at Peripatetiapolis. It occurred to him again now, as he pondered what the clerk had just told him. It was a wild, unlikely sort of answer, and he didn't quite dare to believe it, for he was afraid it might have more to do with his own nostalgic longing for London than with a cool assessment of the facts. He must wait and see what Pennyroyal knew, he decided. Perhaps Pennyroyal would remember something about the *Archaeopteryx* and her mistress that would prove Tom's theory, one way or the other.

He found that he was quite looking forward to meeting his murderer again.

9

BREAKFAST AT MOON'S

The taxi set down on a platform outside an entry-port in Murnau's armour, where there were a lot of guards and questions. The guards were polite enough, but reluctant to let dubious-looking characters like Tom and Wren up to Tier Two even when Orla Twombley promised that she would vouch for them, and showed the guards the ornamental sword she'd been presented with for shooting down three of the Green Storm's destroyers at the Battle of the Bay of Bengal. At last, exasperated, she said, "They are old, old friends of Professor Nimrod Pennyroyal!" and that was enough; the guards stopped being merely polite and became quite friendly; one of them put through a telephone call to his commander, and a minute later Tom, Wren and Ms Twombley were aboard an upbound elevator.

In these days of peace Murnau had taken to opening the shutters in its armour during the daylight hours, to let the sunlight in. Even so, Tier Two felt gloomy. Many and many a time on their way from the elevator station Tom and Wren passed empty places where whole streets had been collapsed by rockets and flying bombs. The buildings which still stood had Xs of tape across their window panes, giving them the look of drunks in comic-strips. On every square inch of wall there were posters and stencilled slogans, and you did not have to speak New German to understand that they were urging the young men of Murnau to volunteer for the *Abwehrtruppe*, Murnau's military. Most of the young men Wren could see had taken their advice and were dressed in smart, midnight-blue uniforms. The few who weren't, those who were missing an arm or a leg, or half their face, or who were being pushed along in bath-chairs, all wore medals to show that they had done their bit against the Storm. A lot of the young women were uniformed too, but not so magnificently as the men. Orla Twombley said, "Murnau women are not allowed to fight, poor dears. They play their part by working in the factories and the engine-district while their menfolk crew the guns."

They crossed a square called Walter Moers Platz, heading for the tall, narrow café named Moon's. A shutter had been opened in the city's armoured cowling a few streets away, letting in the bright spring sunshine, but it came too late for the trees and grasses in the little park at the centre of the square, which were all dead and brown and withered after years in the shade. Through the bare branches Wren caught glimpses of silent fountains and a rusting band-stand. She thought this the saddest city she had ever been to.

But when she followed Orla Twombley through the front door of Moon's, it was as if she had stepped out of Murnau and into another city altogether. The café's scuffed and mismatched furniture looked faintly arty, and the walls were covered with paintings and drawings and photographs of people having fun. It reminded Wren of Brighton, and the resemblance was deliberate. There was a generation of young people aboard Murnau who had lived all their lives with war and duty. They had heard about the sort of freedom people enjoyed on other cities, and were determined to taste it for themselves.

And so they came to Moon's; the artists and the authors and the poets and the young men on leave from the *Abwehrtruppe* who dreamed of being artists and authors and poets, and they did their very best to be Romantic and Bohemian.

They weren't very good at it, of course. There was something too stiff about the careless poses they struck in Moon's tatty old leather armchairs. Their casual, baggy clothes were too well-pressed, and their too-long hair was always neatly combed. The few real artists amongst them, like the painter Skoda Geist, they found rather scary. So when Nimrod Pennyroyal arrived on Murnau they had welcomed him eagerly. Here was a man who had made his fortune by having highly Romantic adventures and writing books about them, and who had once been mayor of Brighton, that most artistic of cities. Yet unlike Geist he never laughed at them, or mocked their poems and paintings; quite the contrary; he was always ready to praise their little efforts, and happy to let them buy him drinks and meals.

He was in the middle of an enormous breakfast when Tom and Wren walked in on him. Quite literally in the middle of it, for the couch he sat on, in an upstairs room, was surrounded on all sides by small tables laden with rolls and cooked meats, fruit, croissants, algae-waffles, fried eggs and mushrooms, toast, kedgeree, omelettes, jam and cheese. A silver coffee-pot sent curlicues of steam up into the splay of sunbeams from the taped-over windows, and all around, packed on to other couches or sitting rather daringly on the floor, artistic young Murnauers listened as he described the book he was at work on.

". . .I have just reached the bit where I faced that

dreadful Stalker Fang," he explained, through a mouthful of moss-loaf. "Rather a painful episode to put on paper, for I don't mind admitting that I was scared. I quaked! I quivered! I never *planned* to fight her, you understand – I do not mean to set myself up as some sort of Hero. No, I came on her by accident while I hurried through the gardens in search of a way to escape from the Storm. . ."

His audience nodded eagerly. Some of them had served in Murnau's skirt-forts and faced Stalkers themselves, and most recalled the dreadful battles of the year '14, when Green Storm airships had landed squads of the Resurrected on Murnau's upper tiers. They all wanted to hear how this valiant old gentleman had managed to overcome the most terrible Stalker of them all.

But Pennyroyal, for once, seemed lost for words. His mouth hung open, he set down his fork, and one by one his listeners turned to see the newcomers standing in the doorway.

"Two old friends to see you, Professor!" said Orla Twombley, finding herself a place to sit among the Murnauers.

"Tom!" said Pennyroyal, standing. "And Wren! My dear child!"

He came to greet them with his arms outstretched. Their sudden appearance had surprised him, but he was genuinely happy to see them both. He had always felt guilty about shooting Tom, but by saving Wren from the Lost Boys, helping her fly the *Arctic Roll* to Kom Ombo and then magnanimously allowing them to keep the little airship, he hoped that he had made up for that unfortunate incident at Anchorage. Now that Tom's horrible wife had vanished, Pennyroyal felt glad to count the Natsworthys among his friends.

"My dears!" he beamed, hugging them each in turn. "How happy I am to see you! I was just telling my friends here about our adventures on Cloud 9, which are to be the subject of my forthcoming book. A respectable Murnau publishing house, Werederobe and Spoor, has paid a whopping advance for a modest account of my part in the downfall of the Stalker Fang and the rise of General Naga, that peace-loving gentleman. You will both feature in the tale, of course! After all, Wren, was it not you, my loyal former slave-girl, who flew the *Arctic Roll* up to Cloud 9 to rescue me when all hope seemed gone?"

"Was it?" asked Wren. "That's not how I remember it. . ."

"She is modesty itself!" cried Pennyroyal, glancing over his shoulder at his young friends, and to Wren herself, rather more urgently, he muttered, "I had to alter the facts a little, just here and there, to add some colour, you know."

Wren looked at her father, and they both shrugged. She thought how tiring it must be to be Pennyroyal, and build a past for yourself out of so many interlocking lies. He must have to spend such a lot of time tinkering with his stories to make sure they fitted, and surely he must live in fear of the day when the whole shaky edifice collapsed?

But perhaps Pennyroyal felt that the rewards made it all worthwhile. He certainly looked as if he were prospering. He wore an outfit of his own invention which managed to make him look important and military without actually being a uniform: a short, sky-blue dolman tunic over a red waistcoat (both covered in frogging and pointless silver buttons), a lilac sash, purple breeches with gold embroidery and a six-inch crimson stripe, and bucket-topped boots with gold tassels. Compared to the Pennyroyal she had known in Brighton, Wren thought he looked quite tasteful and restrained.

He made room for Wren and Tom on his own couch, and invited them to help themselves to some of his breakfast while he introduced his friends. Wren was not used to meeting so many new people so quickly. She managed to grasp that the bespectacled man in civilian robes was Sampford Spiney, Murnau correspondent of a journal called *The Speculum*, who was writing a profile of Pennyroyal, and the quiet, bespectacled young woman clutching an enormous camera was his photographer, Miss Kropotkin. The rest of the introductions passed in a blur of ranks and names. The only person whom Wren was really interested in – a tall, lean young man who stood on his own by the stove – Pennyroyal seemed not to know, which was a pity. He wasn't as handsome as some of the other young officers, and his old blue greatcoat was shabby and travel-stained, but there was something magnetic about him that kept pulling her eyes back to his wry, watchful face.

Pennyroyal poured coffee for his guests, and there was some polite chat about the truce, the weather, and the handsome advance that Pennyroyal had been paid by his new publishers. Then he asked Tom, "How is the good old *Arctic Roll*? And what has caused you to bring her here?"

"She is the *Jenny Haniver* again now," said Tom, "and we have come looking for someone. A lady."

"Indeed?" Pennyroyal narrowed his eyes thoughtfully; he considered himself a bit of an expert on the fairer sex. "Anyone I might know?"

"I think so," said Tom. "Her name is Cruwys Morchard."

"Cruwys!" cried Pennyroyal. "Yes, by Poskitt, I know her well. Great gods, but it must be twenty years since I first ran into her." (The journalist Spiney scribbled in his notebook with a stub of pencil.) "She called on me at Cloud 9 a couple of times," Pennyroyal went on. "Still flying that *Archaeopteryx* of hers, and still as big a mystery as ever. . ."

"Why a mystery, sir?" asked one of the Murnauers.

"Why, because nobody knows where she comes from," said Pennyroyal. "Shall I tell you what I know of her? It is an extraordinary tale. . ."

"Oh, please do, Professor," cried Wren. "And tell us just the truth, with no alteration of the facts or added colour. . ."

"Oh, yes, please!" cried half of Pennyroyal's audience, and *"Bitte!"* agreed the rest, when their Anglish-speaking friends had translated for them.

"Very well," said Pennyroyal, but Wren's request had made him nervous. "Perhaps I should say, it is a *fairly* extraordinary tale. I believe I have heard stranger in my time. But Cruwys Morchard stays in my mind anyway, because of her extraordinary personal charms, and because of the way I met her."

"It was in Helsinki, some nineteen years ago," (said Pennyroyal). "The city was hunting for semi-stats out near the Altai Shan. I was down in the Gut, paying a call on a very charming young salvage supervisor named Nutella Eisberg, when Ms Morchard came aboard with a couple of companions – rough-looking coves, but touchingly devoted to her. Walked right in off the tundra, they did (the city's jaws being open at the time so that the maintenance crews could clean its teeth), and asked the Foreman of the Gut for sanctuary.

"It caused a bit of a stir, I can assure you! This was the year after London went off bang. There had already been a few atrocities by Green Storm fanatics, and the cities of the eastern Hunting Ground were getting edgy. I think the Helsinki folk would have kicked Ms Morchard and her friends straight back into the Out-Country, for fear they might be saboteurs or spies, but luckily I happened to be passing at the time, and I said I'd vouch for her. Her beauty touched me, d'you see? And her youth, of course, for at that time she was not much older than Wren is today."

(Everyone turned to stare at Wren, who blushed.)

"I took Ms Morchard to the city's upper tier with me," Pennyroyal continued, "and I even offered to let her come and stay in my own suite at the Uusimaa Hotel, if we could find suitable accommodation for her hairy friends. But she said, 'I have no need of charity, sir. I have a great deal of money, and I have come to this city to buy an airship. If you wish to help me, perhaps you might introduce me to an honest second-hand airship-dealer.' Well, I took her straight to old man Unthank. And do you know, she *did* have money! Wrapped up in a secret belt and concealed about that charming person were dozens of gold coins, and each of her companions was similarly burdened. I got a look at the stuff while she was bargaining with Unthank, and I recognized it at once; London gold, each piece stamped with the portrait of Quirke, the god of that unlucky city!

"You may imagine my astonishment! London was gone. Had I not seen with my own eyes the baleful flash of its explosion? 'How did you come by all these Quirkes, my dear?' I asked, and Ms Morchard, after a moment's confusion, confessed that she was an archaeologist, and that she had been hunting for salvage among the ruins of London!"

A ripple of excitement spread among Pennyroyal's listeners. People whispered eagerly to each other in New German (a handsome language; the words had corners). Tom leaned forward eagerly in his chair. A young lady in a frock decorated with hundreds of blue eyes said, "But Herr Professor, London's wreck is haunted!"

"Indeed," replied Pennyroyal. "In the months that followed London's destruction a dozen different scavenger suburbs went hastening east to devour its twisted and blackened remains. None of them ever returned."

"Because the air-fleets of the old Anti-Traction League caught them as they neared the debris field and bombed them to bits," said a clear, faintly mocking voice. The young man whom Wren had noticed earlier had come to the edge of the circle of Pennyroyal's friends and was standing there with his hands in his coat-pockets, listening intently. His eyes twinkled. His long mouth widened sideways in something that was almost a sneer.

"So we are told, sir," Pennyroyal agreed, glaring at him. "So we are told. But have we not all heard eerier rumours?"

The Murnauers nodded and muttered. It seemed they all had.

"Cruwys Morchard was a rational, scientific sort, like our friend here," Pennyroyal went on. "She paid no heed to talk of ghosts. But she had seen things inside London that had turned her hair grey! No sooner had her party landed among the ruins than a fork of mysterious lightning came crackling out of the debris and destroyed their airship! More lightning followed, leaping upward from the dead metal and striking all around the explorers, as if it were drawn to the warmth of the blazing ship – or perhaps to the warm bodies of Ms Morchard and her comrades! One of her party was burned to ashes. The others panicked and fled, but the ruins seemed to shift and twist about them, so that they could not find their way out of the debris fields. A dozen of them died during the week it took them to struggle back to the Out-Country. And it was not just the lightning that killed them. There were . . . *other things*. Things that made even the valiant Ms Morchard grow pale as she spoke of them. Things that drove men mad, so that they flung themselves from high places in the wreckage rather than face them."

"What sort of things?" asked the young lady with the eyes on her dress, all agog.

"Ghosts!" whispered Pennyroyal. "I know, Fräulein Hinblick, you will tell me there is no such thing; you will say that nobody returns from the Sunless Country. But Ms Morchard swore to me that she had met with phantoms in the ruined streets of London. And since Ms Morchard is the only person who has ever walked those streets and lived to tell the tale, I think we should take her word for it."

There was a silence in the room. It seemed to have grown rather cold. Fräulein Hinblick snuggled closer to her companions, and a young man with medal-ribbons and a wooden hand said softly, "It is a haunted place. When I flew with the *Abwehrtruppe* I saw it from a distance. Ghostly lights flash and glimmer there at night. Even the Green Storm fear it. Over the rest of the old eastern Hunting Ground they have put settlements and forests and farms and windmill-fields, but for a hundred miles around the wreck of London there is nothing."

Tom leaned forward in his seat. It was time for him to try out the theory that he had been working on over the past few days. He was shaking slightly. He said, "I think Ms Morchard may have been deceiving you a little. You see, I believe that she comes from London. I knew her when she was Clytie Potts, a member of the Guild of Historians. Somehow, she survived MEDUSA. Perhaps she made up her tale of ghosts and lightning to keep people from going to London? To scare off scavengers who might try to loot the wreck? Could it be that other Londoners survived the explosion and that she uses the *Archaeopteryx* to fly in and out of the ruins, ferrying supplies to them?"

The young Murnauers were far too polite to say that they didn't believe him, but Wren could see by their faces that they did not. Only the shabby young man watched him with interest.

"Medical supplies and livestock," Tom said hopefully. "That's what the clerk at Airhaven told us she carries. . ."

Pennyroyal shook his head. "A nice idea, Tom, but a bit unlikely, wouldn't you say? Even if anyone had survived that terrible disaster, why would they still be living in the ruins, all those hundreds of miles behind the Green Storm's lines?"

Wren felt embarrassed for her father. She wished he had tried out his crazy-sounding idea on her before he let everybody else hear it. Poor Dad! He really missed his old city, even after all these years; that was why he had let his imagination run away with him.

The breakfast-party was beginning to break up, the room filling with a low buzz of conversation as Tom spoke eagerly to Pennyroyal, and Fräulein Hinblick explained what had just been said to some of her friends who spoke no Anglish. A few of them looked doubtfully at Tom, and there was some laughter. Wren turned to search for Orla Twombley and found the shabby stranger standing close behind her.

"Your father's imagination is almost as vivid as Professor Pennyroyal's," he said.

"Daddy is a Londoner himself," Wren told him. "It's only natural that he should be interested in what has become of London."

The man seemed satisfied. He was better looking than Wren had thought at first, and younger, too; just a boy really; eighteen or nineteen, with clear, pale skin and a faint stubble showing on his chin and upper lip. But his ice-blue eyes seemed to belong in a much older face. They stared past Wren at her father as he said, "I should like to talk to him. But not here." He thought for a moment, then reached inside his coat and took out a square of thick, creamy card, which he gave to Wren. Curly writing was embossed on it; an address on the *Oberrang*, Murnau's upper tier. "My father is giving a party tomorrow afternoon. You should both come. There we may speak in private."

He studied her face for a moment. Wren looked down at the invitation, and when she looked up again the young man had turned away; she saw the skirts of his coat swirl as he reached the stairs and started down; his hair glinted gold in the lamplight. Then he was gone.

Wren turned to her father, but Tom was talking to the journalist Spiney, trying not to give too much of the truth away as Spiney quizzed him about how he knew Prof Pennyroyal. Wren went over to Orla Twombley instead. "Who was that man?" she asked. "The one who interrupted the Professor's story?"

"Him?" The aviatrix looked round quickly and, seeing that the young man had left, said, "His name is Wolf Kobold. Son of Kriegsmarshal von Kobold, the old soldier they made mayor of Murnau when this war began. Look, there they are together in that print above the fireplace. . . Wolf's a brave fighter. Handsome too, don't you think?"

Wren did, but she was too shy to admit it. She tried not to blush as the aviatrix steered her across the still-crowded room to show her the picture. There stood the Kriegsmarshal, a stern, stiff gentleman whose enormous white moustaches made him look as if a wandering albatross had chosen his upper lip as a perch. Beside him was the young man to whom Wren had just spoken, looking younger still – the picture must have been five or six years old, for it showed Wolf as a rather angelic schoolboy. Wren wondered what had happened to him in the years since to make him so grim.

"He'll be Kriegsmarshal himself when the old man finally retires or dies," Orla Twombley was saying. "Until then, he has been acting as mayor of one of Murnau's harvester-suburbs. He drops into Moon's sometimes, when he visits Murnau on family business, but he's a solitary type. I've never talked with him."

Wren showed her the invitation she'd been given, and Orla whistled softly. "Wren, my dear, you *are* going up in the world! I declare, you've barely been aboard this city an hour, and already you've been invited to the Kriegsmarshal's garden party. . ."

10

THE BLACK ANGEL

O oh, what's this? Here on the high seas of the desert, where the rippling horizons seem more liquid than land, something solid has appeared. It is just a speck at first; a dark triangle shimmering above the silver mirages that lie across the dunes, but it grows clearer and harder by the moment; a blade, a shark's fin, a black sail bellying in the desert wind. Listen; you can hear the sand singing under racing tyres. Look; you can see the sun's reflection like diamonds in a line of portholes.

Imagine a pond-skater, but magnify it until it is as big as a yacht. Fix a wheel to each of its long legs, and raise a mast above it. Then set it skimming over sand instead of water. It is a sand-ship, the vehicle of choice for desert scavengers and bounty-hunters, and as it passes, if we turn to look, we can see what has brought it into this mineral ocean. The region ahead of it is crowded with towns, their smokestacks and upper-works dancing behind the curtains of reflected heat which sway above the dunes.

This is a rare event; the nearest thing to a trading cluster that you will find in the dried-out, town-eat-town world of the desert deeps. A big, slow suburb which should be preying on fishing-hamlets along the far-off coast has blundered into the sand-sea by mistake, and been hunted to a standstill by a pack of speedy predators. The hunters have huge wheels, huge jaws, huge engines and huge appetites to match. They have cornered their prey in a dusty bowl of sand called

Bitumen Bay, ringed by mined-out hills. They are tearing it apart, and for a day or so, while they are too busy digesting their catch to eat each other, an uneasy peace prevails. Merchants go from one fierce town to another, and far-wandering airships appear out of nowhere to flog Old-Tech and knick-knacks. Even the swift, shy scavenger-towns come creeping close to try and sell the scraps they've found among the sands.

The black sails of the nameless ship crinkle and flutter like the petals of an opium poppy as its pilot brings it up into the wind, slowing, sweeping round in a long curve that will take it into the shoal of other sand-ships around the cluster.

The townlet of Cutler's Gulp had parked itself on the slopes of an enormous dune a half-mile from the feeding-frenzy and kept its engines idling, ready to take off in a moment should any of the predators show signs of fancying it for dessert. It was a long, low thing, its single deck overshadowed by fat sand-wheels. It consisted mainly of engines, and of the bloated ducts and flues and exhaust-pipes which served them. The inhabitants made their homes in what little space was left, stretching their awnings between the ducts and building small dwellings of mud and papier-mâché on the few bare patches of deck among the engine-housings. Sand-ships came and went from garages in its belly, and a jaunty black and white striped air-trader called the *Humbug* came buzzing across the dunes to touch down at the harbour; a blank space near the bows where a couple of the mud buildings had recently collapsed.

The master of the *Humbug* was a merchant named Napster Varley. *Varley & Son*, said the signs on his ship's engine pods, but little Napster Junior was only three months old, and not yet taking an active part in the running of the business. Varley had hoped that a wife and child might give him the respectability he needed to escape from these tinpot desert trading towns and set up in one of the big cities. But so far they had brought him nothing but noise, annoyance and expense, and if he had not needed his wife to help him pilot the *Humbug* he would have kicked them both overboard months ago.

As the sunk sank westward and the shadows started to lengthen Varley found himself ambling aft along the Gulp's ramshackle walkways with the boss of the place, Grandma Gravy.

They made an odd pair. Napster Varley was a slight, pasty young man, with flakes of sunburned skin peeling off his snub nose. He was a keen reader of business books, and in one of them (*How to Succeed at the Air Trade* by Dornier Lard) he had read that "*a successful businessman must always dress distinctively, that his customers shall remember him*". So despite the heat he wore a purple frock coat, a fur stovepipe hat and a pair of baggy yellow pantaloons with a crimson windowpane check.

Grandma Gravy, meanwhile, covered herself with so many layers of flapping, rust-coloured shawls and robes and skirts and jellabahs that she looked as if one of the nomad tents of the deep desert had decided to get up and walk about. But if you peered closely at the space between her massive shoulders and her wide-brimmed hat you could see, behind the close mesh of her fly-proof veil, a fat, yellowish face and a pair of tiny, calculating eyes which glittered slightly as she studied Mr Varley.

"Got somefin to sell," she told him. "Aye. Found it out in the deeps, few weeks by. Valooble."

"Really?" Varley dabbed at his neck with a handkerchief and waved the flies away. "Not Old-Tech, is it? The price of Old-Tech has dropped something shocking since this truce began. . ."

"More valooble'n Old-Tech," muttered Grandma Gravy. "Mossie airship gone down, dinnit? My boys saw the fires in the sky. My town was first at the wreck. Not much left, no. Jus' a few struts and engine parts and this item, this valooble item. . ."

She led him up a metal stairway and in through the door of one of the mud-brick towers which rose like termite-hills out of the tangle of ducts at the townlet's stern. Inside were more stairs, and Grandma panted and rattled as she climbed them. The hems of her robes were bedecked with magic charms; a human jawbone, a monkey's hand, little greasy-looking leather pouches filled with gods-knew-what. Grandma Gravy had a reputation for witchcraft, and used it to keep her people in line. Even Varley felt a little nervous as he followed her up the winding stairs, and he touched the medal of the God of Commerce which hung round his neck beneath his paisley cravat.

They came to an upper room; hot, and filled, like the rest of Grandma's tower, with a brownish haze and a faint smell of burnt fat. In the middle of the room someone lay chained by the feet to a ring in the metal floor. A boy, Varley thought, until she raised her head and looked up at him through tangles of filthy hair and he saw that she was a young woman. She was dressed in rags, and there were bruises on her throat, and sores on her bony ankles where the shackles had rubbed.

"Sorry, Grandma," said Varley quickly. "I'm not buying no slaves." (He had no moral objection to the slaving business, but the great Nabisco Shkin, in his book *Investing In People*, advised would-be slavers to buy only the healthiest stock. Varley could see at a glance that this scrawny little quail was already half dead.)

"She's far more valooble than just some slave," said Grandma Gravy in her rasping, breathless voice. She waddled across the room and grabbed the captive by her hair, twisting her face towards Varley. "What do you think she be?"

Varley fished a monocle out of his breast pocket and squinted through it at the captive's dull, almond-shaped eyes. Her skin, under all the dirt and sunburn and exposure-sores, had once been ivory-coloured. He shrugged, growing tired of the game. "I don't know, Grandma. Some kind of half-breed eastern trash. Shan Guonese? Aino? Inuit?"

"Alooshan!" crowed Grandma Gravy.

"Bless you, Grandma."

"From Aloosha." Grandma Gravy let the woman's head drop and came waddling back to where Varley waited. Her breath went *hur, hur, hur* behind the fly-proof veil. "Know 'oo she is then, young trader? She's that Mossie general's wife. She's the queen of the Green Storm!"

Varley said nothing, but his posture changed. He took his hands out of his pockets and licked his lips and his eyeglass flashed. He'd heard a story about Lady Naga's airship going down in the sand-sea. Was this her? It could be. He'd seen a picture of her once in the *Airman's Gazette*, and he tried hard to remember it, but she had been in her wedding finery, and anyway, all these easterners looked the same to Napster Varley.

"Found this on her," said Grandma Gravy, and produced from inside her tent of robes a signet ring. Gold, with an oak-leaf design. "And look at that cross round her neck: that's Zagwan workmanship."

Varley held a silk handkerchief to his nose and went close to the woman. "Are you Lady Naga?" he asked, very loudly and slowly.

She stared at him, and nodded faintly. "What has become of Theo?" she asked.

"She's talking 'bout some Zagwan kid what was travelling with her," Grandma Gravy explained. "We stuck him in the engine pits. Dead by now, I s'poze. Anyway, merchant, what I'm asking is, what's to be done with her? I can't go on keeping her in luxury like this. She's too weak to sell for a common slave, but she ought to be valooble to someone, aye? The Queen of the Mossies. . ."

"Oh, indeed," said Varley thoughtfully.

"I been thinkin' we might skin her, see," suggested Grandma Gravy. "Her hide might fetch a tidy sum, aye? We could turn her into a nice rug, or some scatter-cushions."

"Oh, Grandma Gravy, no!" cried Varley. "It's her *brain* that is the valuable part!"

"You mean a paperweight or somefin?"

Varley leaned as near to Grandma as he could bear, and tapped one finger on his temple. "What she knows. I could take her to Airhaven and offer her to the *Traktionstadtsgesellschaft*. They might pay well for her."

"Then you'll buy her whole? What'll you give?"

"Oh, well, of course, I will have transport costs to factor in, and other overheads, and this unfortunate truce has upset the market, but let me see. . ."

" 'Ow much?"

"Ten gold dollars," said the merchant.

"Twenty."

"Fifteen."

" 'Course," said Grandma Gravy thoughtfully, "I could always make little talismans out of her fingies and toes and sell 'em off individual. . ."

"Twenty it is," said Varley hastily, and started counting the coins out into her hand before she could up the price.

The black sand-ship found a berth in one of the garages on the flanks of Cutler's Gulp. Its robed and hooded pilot furled its sails, and then jumped down to make the ship fast. He seemed to be only a servant, or a crewman, for when his work was done he stood waiting patiently until a woman came down from the ship to join him. Then, together, they climbed the stairs and started along the iron walkways that bridged the townlet's furnace-pits, heading for the huddle of cantinas and coffee-shops near the stern. Beggars stretched out bowls to them, then saw their faces and thought better of it. Rough desert types with half-formed plans of robbery and violence changed their minds and backed into the shadows under ducts. Even the dogs ran away.

The woman was tall, and very thin, and she carried a long gun on her shoulder. She was dressed all in black; black boots, black breeches, black weskit and a long black duster coat that flew out behind her like black wings when the wind caught it. In a place where everyone went masked or veiled you might have expected her to wear a black veil too, but she chose to go bareheaded. Her grey hair had been tied back, as if she wanted everyone to see that she was hideous. A terrible scar ran down her face from forehead to jaw, making it look like a portrait that had been furiously crossed out. Her mouth was wrenched sideways in a permanent sneer, her nose was a smashed stump, and her single eye stared out of the wreckage as grey and chill as a winter sea.

Her name was Hester Shaw, and she killed people.

She had appeared in the desert six months earlier. Her companion, a Stalker named Mr Shrike, had carried her aboard El Houl, one of the towns which was eating the wreck of Cloud 9. She had been ill, and Shrike had demanded that the townspeople take care of her. They did not want to argue with a Stalker, so they called a doctor, who examined the woman and declared that there was nothing wrong with her beyond a few cuts and scrapes and a sort of settled melancholy that he had seen before in the survivors of calamities.

"Has she lost someone who was dear to her, Mr Shrike?" he asked.

"SHE HAS LOST EVERYTHING," the Stalker replied.

So the woman lived for a week or two in one of the sackcloth-curtained cubby-holes which passed for houses on the under-decks, and the Stalker cared for her, and fed her on bread and milk which he mashed up for her with his metal hands, and the people watched and whispered and tried to imagine what relationship there could be between this dazed, ugly woman and the Resurrected man.

Then, one day, the township's engine-master came to visit Shrike and said, "Stalker, I want you to kill me someone. The sheikh who rules this town is old and fat. He takes too much of the salvage for himself. Kill him for me, and I'll see you live in comfort on the topmost tiers, with fine food and a feather bed for your um, ah..."

He was still hunting for a word that might describe Hester when Shrike said, "I WILL NOT KILL."

"But you're a Stalker! Of course you kill!"

"I CANNOT. MY MIND HAS BEEN . . . TAMPERED WITH."

The engine-master scowled, and wondered about throwing the useless Stalker off his town, but he didn't see how it could be done. He shook his head, and was about to leave when the scarred woman said quietly, "I'll kill him for you."

"You?"

"I'm Hester Shaw. My father was Thaddeus Valentine, the famous secret agent and assassin," she said. "You want your sheikh dead? Give me a weapon and tell me where to find him."

"But you're only a woman!" objected the engine-master.

So Hester Shaw found herself a fork and a crowbar and climbed the stairs to El Houl's upper tier. She kicked open the doors of the sheikh's house. She killed the sheikh. She killed his guards. She killed his dogs. She moved through the smoky rooms like a plague and left nothing alive behind her. She was more like a Stalker than her Stalker, who would only watch and wait for her.

With the money the engine-master gave her she bought a sand-ship and a few guns, and she and her Stalker left El Houl for ever, much to the relief of its inhabitants. Since then, she had become one of the legends of the deep sands; the woman bounty-hunter and her companion, the Stalker who would not kill. Even Theo Ngoni had heard a garbled version of the story, as he toiled away in the engine pits of Cutler's Gulp, but the man who'd told him had spoken partly in Arabic, and had referred to the Stalker as a djinn and to Hester Shaw as the Black Angel. So it came as a complete surprise to him when he glanced up that afternoon to see them striding along the walkway which led above his station, and recognized them both.

For a moment Theo could not remember where he had seen either of them before. Cloud 9 seemed such a long time ago. Even the wreck of the *Nzimu* seemed long ago. He dimly remembered how he had dragged Lady Naga out through a rent in her cabin wall as the airship filled with fire, and how they had clung to a hawser on the steering vanes while the wreckage sank towards the desert, but it all seemed like something that had happened to somebody else; or something he had only read about.

He had been working hard ever since, on eighteen-hour shifts, whipped and beaten and abused, given little water and less food. He had begun to have bad dreams even when he was wide awake, and at first he thought it was just another dream when he saw Wren's mother walking above him in the dazzling sunlight. But he shook his head, and pinched the sweat from his eyes, and she was still there, and the terrible Stalker beside her.

"Mrs Natsworthy!" he shouted, and let go of the handles of the fuel-hopper which he had been pushing towards the furnaces. Grandma's overseers were on him almost at once, smashing him to the deck with their clubs of woven rope. But Wren's mother had heard him, he was sure, for he saw her horrible face turn and stare at him in the instant before he fell.

"LEAVE HIM," grated the voice of the Stalker, louder than the clatter of the townlet's engines, and no more human.

The overseers backed off. It had fallen very quiet in the engine pit. Theo could hear the men's quick breathing. He tried to stand, but he was too weak; he fell on his knees on the hot, sandy deck. "Mrs Natsworthy," he said again, meeting the eye of the woman on the walkway. He did not really think that she could help him, and he knew that as soon as she turned away the overseers would beat him to death. He just wanted her to know that he was here. Maybe she would be able to tell Wren one day that this was what had become of him. He said, "We met. Remember? On Cloud 9?"

"I KNOW YOU," said the Stalker Shrike.

"I don't," said Hester Shaw. Hearing her old name shouted out like that had unsettled her. She stared at the boy in the pit below her; a gaunt, black boy like a bundle of burnt sticks. His teeth were bared in something that she supposed was meant to be a smile, and blood was running down his face where the townsmen had struck him. "Who is he?" she asked Shrike.

"HE IS THE ONCE-BORN CALLED THEO, WHO WAS WITH YOUR CHILD ON CLOUD 9."

"Is he?" Hester had vague recollections of Wren having a boy in tow that last time they'd met. Perhaps they'd even been introduced. Hester wished he had not called out to her. She was trying to forget her past. She had only come to Cutler's Gulp for fresh water and supplies. She didn't want to get involved.

But as she started to turn away Shrike caught her arm. "YOU CANNOT LEAVE HIM HERE."

"Why not?"

"HE WILL DIE."

"Everybody dies," said Hester.

"YOU CANNOT LEAVE HIM HERE."

"Damn you, Shrike. What did that Green Storm witch do to you, to make you so soft?"

"YOU CANNOT LEAVE HIM HERE."

"Well, you ain't taking him!" shouted a voice from the pit. The foreman of the furnaces, Daz Gravy, had come out of his shady lair to see what all the fuss was. Stalkers didn't frighten Daz; he was Grandma Gravy's favourite grandson, and around his fat neck hung dozens of charms she'd given him to ward off bullets and the evil eye. All he cared about was keeping Grandma's engines running smooth. He grabbed Theo by his iron slave collar and heaved him back towards his abandoned hopper. "He's ours. We found him, square and fair. Dragged him out of a wrecked Mossie airship. Grandma says we can do what we like with hi—"

In a single motion Hester swept the gun off her shoulder, flipped up the safety catch and shot him dead. He fell with a wet thud and a clattering of good-luck charms. Hester shot his companions down so quickly that the shots and the echoes of the shots all ran together, like a drum-roll. She ran down the iron stairs and held out her hand to Theo, but he was shaking too badly to stand, and so the Stalker had to heave him up and carry him away from the engine pit like a child. Hester followed with her gun held ready. In the silence that had come after the gunshots she could hear the shuffling sounds and the mutterings as people stepped quickly out of her way.

For some reason, as she ran after Shrike to the sand-ship and Shrike unsheathed his claws and severed the mooring-ropes, she kept remembering Stayns; how she and Tom had run from slavers' men there, and Anna Fang had saved them. She fired a warning shot across the garage as she scrambled up her ship's side, and cursed herself for being maudlin. This wasn't Stayns, and Theo wasn't Tom, and anyway, she didn't want to think about it.

Napster Varley heard the shots and shouting as he readied his airship for the sky, and he swore under his breath, hoping that nothing would delay his departure from the Gulp. Grandma's boys had slung Lady Naga into his hold a few minutes before, and he was shivery with excitement at the thought of the price she would fetch out on the line. If he lingered too long Grandma Gravy might think better of selling her. So he didn't run outside to watch the sand-ship go racing off across the desert. He ordered his wife to put the baby down and go fire up the engines, and blacked her eye when she did not go quick enough. "Move it, you dozy mare!" he shouted, over the baby's wailing. "Let's leave these sand-hoppers to their squabbles. We've business to attend to!"

11

WOLF KOBOLD

om was uncertain about accepting Wolf Kobold's
invitation; he had been brought up to know his
place, and he knew that it wasn't on the
Oberrang, which towered above the rest of Murnau like
an ornate crown. It took Wren several hours to persuade
him.

"You really need to talk to this Wolf person," she told
him. "He seemed so interested in what you had to say
about Clytie Potts. I'm sure he knows something."

Tom shook his head. "I'm not sure I really believe any
of that myself. It was just an idea; I have no proof.
Pennyroyal didn't believe it, and he's the man who claims
that Ancient rubbish-tips were really ritual centres and
that the Ancients had machines called 'eye-pods' where
they could store thousands of songs on tiny little
gramophone records. If *he* thinks my London theory is
unlikely, maybe it really is just a daydream."

Wren tried another tack. "Don't you think it would be
good for my education, though? To mix a little in high
society? Orla said she has a friend who can lend you
formal robes. . ."

It was hard work, but she won him round in the end.
Next afternoon they went aboard Murnau and took an
elevator to the *Oberrang*, Tom looking awkward in his
borrowed robes, Wren wearing her usual aviator's gear,
because she felt it suited her and she knew that nothing
she could buy in the bazaars of Airhaven could compete
with the finery the rich ladies would be wearing.
Looking around at her fellow passengers as the elevator

grumbled upwards, she wondered if she had made the right decision; she drew some strange looks from the smart officers in their blue dress uniforms and the ladies in elaborate hats and gowns. She heard several people whisper, "Who is that extraordinary girl?"

It was a relief when the elevator stopped and she took Tom's arm and walked out of the terminus building with him, into bright sunlight. Like the rest of Murnau the *Oberrang* was covered by an armoured roof, but large sections had been folded open to let in the light and air. The party-goers walked towards the spiky bulk of the Town Hall along a boulevard called the Über-den-Linden, with a glass pavement through which you could look down on the trees in a park on the tier below. It must have been beautiful in the old days, before the war, but now the trees were all dead, and the bare, scratchy branches reaching up towards her gave Wren an eerie feeling.

A broad swathe of parkland ringed the Rathaus, Murnau's spiky, gothick Town Hall. There, upon a sparse, patched, mossy lawn, the Kriegsmarshal's garden party was getting under way. Brightly-coloured pavilions and marquees had been erected, and lines of coloured flags strung among the dead trees and the battle-damaged colonnades, along with Chinese lanterns which would be lit later, when it grew dark. Enormous numbers of people were wandering about, for the Kriegsmarshal of Murnau was entertaining the mayors and councillors of all the other cities in the cluster. A band played on a flag-decked podium, and people were dancing complicated, formal dances that looked more like applied mathematics than the old-fashioned northern jigs and reels than Wren had learned in Vineland. She wished she had listened to her father and stayed away from this do. She'd only once attended anything as grand as this; that had been on Cloud 9, and she had been there as a slave, handing round trays of drinks and nibbles. . .

She was just about ready to flee back to the elevators when Wolf detached himself from a small group of officers standing near the band and came to greet her. He had smartened himself a little, but even in formal uniform and a scarlet sash there was something faintly careless and shabby about him. The sword at his side was heavier and cheaper than the ornate ceremonial weapons the other men wore; it looked as if it had been *used*. His grin was full of sharp teeth. "My friends!" he called out, bowing low to Tom, taking Wren's hand and kissing it. "I am so glad you could come!"

Wren was not used to having her hand kissed. She blushed and bobbed a curtsey. Wolf's thumb brushed the raised weal on the back of her hand; the brand of the Shkin Corporation, whose property she had been in Brighton. She snatched her hand away quickly, ashamed, but Wolf just looked inquisitively at her, as if it did not trouble him at all that she had been a slave.

"You have led an interesting life, Fräulein Natsworthy," he said, taking her arm, leading her and Tom through the busy garden.

"Not really, Mr von Kobold. But I suppose I've packed quite a bit in the last six months or so. . ."

"Please," he said, "call me Wolf. Or at least 'Mr Kobold'. 'Von' is an old honorary title; my parents use it, but I have no time for such nonsense." He bent closer to Wren and said, "You need not feel ill-at-ease among these silly women in their silly frocks. Most of them have been living in safer cities than Murnau since the war began, and have only come back now that the guns are quiet. Look at them! They are like overgrown children. They know nothing of real life at all. . ."

Wren felt glad of his company, and pleased at the slightly envious way the Murnau women watched as she walked by with him, but it disturbed her a little that he had been able to guess so easily how she was feeling.

"You must forgive me for bringing you here," Wolf went on, addressing Tom. "I thought it would be a good opportunity to talk. I had not realized how lavishly my family entertain since this foolish truce began. Come, we will go inside. . ."

He steered them past the bandstand towards the looming, armoured walls of the Rathaus, but halfway there they were headed off by a formidable-looking lady in a gown of grey silk so stiff and pointy that she looked armoured, too. "Wolf, dear heart," she said sweetly, "everyone is asking me who your friends are. . ."

Wolf bowed neatly and indicated Wren and her father. "Mother, let me present Tom Natsworthy, an aviator, and his daughter, Wren. Tom, Wren; my mother, Anya von Kobold."

"Delighted," said his mother, though she seemed rather pained as she looked Tom and Wren up and down, as if it physically hurt her to meet anyone so common. "Wolf has developed such quaint, democratickal notions since my husband gave him command of Harrowbarrow: one simply doesn't know *who* he is going to bring home next. Aviators. How very *interesting. . ."*

"Ignore her," said Wolf, as his mother moved on to greet a clump of aldermen and their wives. "She knows nothing of life out here on the line. She deserts Murnau whenever the fighting starts, and flies off to a hotel on the upper tiers of Paris. All she knows or cares about are clothes and pastries."

He spoke loudly enough for his mother to hear, and a lot of the other guests looked round, shocked and disapproving. Tom, embarrassed, asked innocently, "Harrowbarrow? Is that the name of your suburb? I don't believe I've heard of it. . ."

Wolf stopped glaring at his mother's broad back and smiled. "It is very small, sir; barely a suburb at all; just a little specialized place which came into Murnau's possession during the war. But it is my own, you know, and I have hopes for it; high hopes."

As he ushered them into the Rathaus Wren wondered what sort of place it might be, this Harrowbarrow. The fighting suburbs she had seen on the journey east had looked horrible; low, vicious and armoured like woodlice. Yet Wolf spoke of his with affection. She supposed it was the same sort of pride you met among aviators, who would never hear a bad word about their own ship, even if she was just some leaky sky-tug. . .

Once inside, the sounds of the garden party quickly faded. Wolf took his guests into a large, silent room where slender metal pillars held up the roof, giving Wren the feeling that she had stepped into an iron forest. There were chairs, and they all sat down while Wolf rang the bell for a servant and ordered refreshments. Then he waited a moment, studying Tom and Wren as if he was not quite sure that he had done the right thing in bringing them here.

"London," he said at last. His face twisted into the same wry grin it had worn the previous day when he was listening to Pennyroyal's story. "I understand that you were once a Londoner yourself, Herr Natsworthy?"

Tom nodded, and told him about his training in the Guild of Historians and how he had happened to be out of the city when the MEDUSA device went off.

"Interesting," said Wolf, when he had finished. Then, rather cautiously, he said, "I have my own London story, you know. That is why I came to listen when I heard what old Pennyroyal was saying yesterday. Look. . ." He reached into his pocket and pulled out a small disc of metal, which he tossed to Tom. "If you are who you say you are, Herr Natsworthy, you will know what that is. . ."

Tom turned the disc over in his hands. It was the size of a large coin, and there was a coat-of-arms embossed on it. He had not seen such a thing for nearly twenty years, but he knew it at once, and gave a little gasp. Wren saw tears in his eyes when he looked up again at Kobold. "It is a rivet-head from one of London's tier-supports," he said. "From one of the lower tiers, I'd guess; it's only iron, and the ones on the upper levels were all brass. . ."

Wolf grinned. "My souvenir of London," he said.

"You've been there?" asked Tom.

"Briefly. About two years ago, before I was given my own suburb, I persuaded Father to let me join a *kommando* of the *Abwehrtruppe* on a raid deep into Mossie territory. We were attempting to destroy their central Stalker works. Unfortunately we never got there; we were attacked, and my own ship was forced down on the plains not far from Batmunkh Gompa. Alone, I sought shelter in the wreckage of London. I was scared, of course, for I had heard nothing but ghost stories about that dreadful old place. But the Mossies were hunting for me, and it seemed better to take my chances with the ghosts than let them catch me. So I wandered into that landscape of rust, looking for water and food and a place where I might shelter. . ."

He paused. Music from the party drifted through the corridors of the old building, faint and ghostly.

"It is a curious place, the debris field," he said. "I saw only the very south-easternmost fringe of it. The wreckage is terribly twisted and flung about. Hard to believe that it was once a great city, although here and there one sees something familiar; a door, a table, a pram. Those rivet-heads, for instance; they were scattered everywhere. I pocketed that one you are holding, thinking that if I ever made it home I would want some proof to show my friends that I had been inside the wreck of London.

"Towards nightfall, as I struck north into the interior where the ruins rise high and eerie, something happened. I'm not sure what. I noticed movements in the wreckage. Too deliberate to be animals. They seemed to follow me. After a while there were noises, too; unearthly groans and wailings. I drew my revolver and loosed a couple of shots into the shadows, and the noises stopped. In the silence, I became aware of another sound. It seemed like machinery, although it was far off, and never clear enough for me to be certain. I sat down among the debris to rest and . . . I blacked out. Later I seemed to remember someone coming up behind me – but perhaps that was only a dream, the memory is very unclear.

"The next thing I knew, I was ten miles away, lying in the open country west of the wreck, hidden from Mossie patrols beneath the foliage in an old track-mark. My wounds had been bandaged with field-dressings, my canteen had been filled with water, and my pack with bread and fruit."

"By whom?" asked Tom eagerly.

Wolf looked sharply at him. "You do not believe me?"

"I didn't say that. . ."

Wolf shrugged. "I have never told anyone of this before. All I know is; there is somebody inside the wreck of London. They are not Mossies, or they would have killed me when they had the chance. But they have their secrets, and they guard them well."

Wren looked at her father. She thought Wolf's story far spookier than Pennyroyal's. "Who could it be?" she asked.

Tom didn't answer her.

"I have often wondered," said Wolf. "I've asked around. Some of my lads aboard Harrowbarrow are ex-scavengers who've lived rough in some bad places, and seen some strange things there. *They've* never heard of scavs living inside London. But a couple of times I've heard mention of the *Geistluftschiff* – the phantom airship. It crosses no-man's-land in silence, when the wind's from the west, and flies off into Mossie territory. No markings. Not part of any known unit, ours or theirs."

"Ghosts again," said Wren.

"Or the *Archaeopteryx*," said Tom. His voice trembled slightly. He was trying not to make his feelings too obvious, but he was moved and excited by what Wolf had told him, and what he suspected it might mean. "The *Archaeopteryx*, flying home to London."

Wolf leaned forward. "I believe your theory, Herr

Natsworthy. I believe survivors of MEDUSA live on secretly inside the wreck."

"But why would anyone want to?" asked Wren. "There's nothing left there, is there?"

"There must be something," said Wolf. "Something that makes it worth staying there, and guarding. I have done a little research of my own into Cruwys Morchard since I heard you ask about her. Our intelligence corps keeps a file on most ships that pass through these skies, and their notes on the Aerial Merchant Vessel *Archaeopteryx* made interesting breakfast-time reading. It seems your Ms Morchard has been buying a lot of Old-Tech in the last few years."

"She is an Old-Tech trader," said Tom, reasonably.

"Is she? It doesn't look to me as if she ever *sells* many of the old machine-parts she buys. So what becomes of them? Perhaps she just flies home with them to London. And what was London famous for?"

"Engineering," admitted Tom, rather reluctantly. He was remembering the man he had seen with Clytie on the docking pan at Peripatetiapolis; a man with a gleaming, shaven head. "And Engineers," he said.

Wolf nodded, watching him. "What if some of those Engineers of yours have survived? What if they live in the debris fields? What if they are building something there? Something so wonderful that it is worth living twenty years inside a ruin to preserve the secret of it! Something that could change the world!"

Tom shook his head. "No; no. Clytie would never work for the Guild of Engineers. . ."

"The Clytie you knew might not. But she may have changed her mind, in twenty years." Wolf stood up and walked to the windows, which he flung open, letting in the sounds of the party on the lawn. "Come," he said, beckoning them out with him on to the balcony. Below, the bright gowns and uniforms of his parents' guests speckled the garden like petals; like butterflies. For a moment, as he gazed down at them all, the young man's face wore a look that could almost have been hatred.

"The truce will not last long," he said. "But while it does, we should make the most of it."

What does he mean "we"? wondered Wren. She wasn't sure how her father's dream had suddenly been swallowed up by Wolf Kobold's, and she still wasn't entirely sure that she liked this attractive young man.

"I have often thought of returning to London," Wolf went on. "The war has kept me too busy, though. But now I see my chance. I've been finding out about you, Tom Natsworthy. It seems you are a fine aviator. And that old League ship of yours could be just the vessel for a jaunt behind the enemy's lines. . ."

"You mean that I should go to London?" asked Tom. "But that's impossible! Isn't it? We'd never get past the Green Storm's patrols. . ."

"You couldn't get across here," agreed Wolf, looking past the garden party and the buildings at the edge of the *Oberrang* and out across the scumbled mires of no-man's-land towards the Storm's territory. "Naga's entire ninth army is dug in out there in the mud, waiting for us to make a move. Even if they didn't shoot you down, our own side would assume you were trading with the enemy and open fire on you. But there are places north-east of here, where the line is less well defended."

He turned to Tom with a boyish grin. "Harrowbarrow could get you across. I often take her hunting in no-man's-land. She'll get you right up to the borders of

Storm-country where an aviator of your skill could easily slip across the line and follow the old track-marks east. That's what Clytie Potts must have been doing all these years, after all."

"And will you be coming with us, Mr Kobold?" asked Wren.

Tom glanced at her. "You're not coming, Wren. It's far too dangerous. I don't even think I should go myself. . ."

Wolf laughed. "Of course you will go!" he said. "I can see it in your eyes. You want more than anything to know what is going on in London. And I will come with you, because this peace bores me and I long to see what lies in the debris fields. Don't worry; I will make all the arrangements, and I will pay you well for your trouble. Shall we say, five thousand in gold, transferred into an Airhaven bank account?"

"Five *thousand*?" cried Tom.

"I come from a very wealthy family," said Wolf. "I'd rather see the fortunes of the von Kobolds spent on an expedition like this than frittered away on garden parties. Of course, for that sort of sum I shall have to insist that Wren accompany us as co-pilot. She is a young woman of great courage, and we will need her help to fly all that way." (He smiled at Wren, who felt herself start to blush.)

"I'm still not sure," said Tom, but he was. How could he refuse? He had never had much money, and had never wanted much, but he had Wren's future to consider. The sum this boy was offering would make her a rich woman, and if Wren *were* to set up as an air-trader when he was gone, it would do her no harm to be known on the Bird Roads as the aviatrix who had been inside London.

The truth was, he longed to return to his city and find out what was left of it; to see for himself if anything (or any*one*) had survived. He longed to take Wren with him, too, so that she could see for herself the place where her father's adventures had all begun. And so it was easy for him to find ways to justify going, and taking her, and to belittle all the dangers they would face. After all (he told himself), he and Hester had flown the *Jenny Haniver* to far worse places, in their young days...

"It is decided, then," said Wolf. "Move your ship into the Murnau air-harbour. We shall meet in a day or two to discuss arrangements. But please don't mention to anyone where we are going; not to anyone at all. The Storm and the other cities have spies everywhere."

They shook hands before going back down together to the garden, to the laughter and the music and the lengthening shadows. Pennyroyal had arrived, surrounded by bright young women and waving cheerfully at Tom and Wren as they passed. Wolf excused himself and went to speak to his father. He looked awkward and slightly nervous standing beside the old Kriegsmarshal, and Wren found herself liking him more; she had had parent problems of her own. It was Wolf's experiences in the war that made him seem hard sometimes, she thought; underneath, he was probably shy and kind, just like Theo.

Wondering what it would be like to travel east with him, she squeezed her own father's hand. "If you go," she said, "I'm coming too. Like Wolf Kobold said. Don't think you can make me stay here. So there's no point even trying to argue about it. I can look after myself."

Tom laughed, for it was such a Hesterish thing to say.

He looked at Wren, and saw her mother's strength and stubbornness in her. "All right," he said. "We'll see."

Between Wolf Kobold and his father the conversation did not flow so easily. Somehow, somewhere in the years, they had lost the easy friendship that they had had when Wolf was little. They thought in different ways now, the Kriegsmarshal and his son. Still, the old man seemed to think that he should take advantage of Wolf's rare visit to try and talk seriously to him. He led him away between the dead trees, through dry brown beds of withered shrubs which, before the war, had been one of the glories of Murnau. They crossed a footbridge over a boating lake (the lake drained, of course, its dry floor scabbed with rust) and climbed some steps to a little pillared gazebo where a statue of a goddess in antique dress gazed out over the tier's brim.

"This was one of your favourite spots when you were a lad," said the Kriegsmarshal, stroking his moustaches, as he always did when he felt nervous. "You used to be fascinated by this little lady on her pedestal. . ."

"I don't remember," said Wolf.

"Oh yes. . ." The statue's face was streaked with damp, as if she had been weeping green tears. The Kriegsmarshal pulled out his pocket-handkerchief and started trying to clean her up. "You always wanted to know who she was, and I would tell you how she represented Murnau. Strong but gentle. Nobility. That's it." Working away at the mossy statue meant that he did not have to meet his son's gaze. He said, "You should come back, Wolf. Your mother misses you."

"My mother will go skulking off to Paris again as soon as this truce breaks down. Anyway, what do you care? Everyone knows your marriage has been a sham for years."

"Well, *I* miss you."

"I'm sure that is not true."

"When I suggested you take charge of that harvester-suburb I meant it to be for a month or two. I did not intend you to live there permanently! You belong here, Wolfram! Damn it, you should be preparing to take over from me. I'm just an old soldier. Now that peace is returning Murnau needs younger men to guide it. Men of vision."

"The peace will not last," said Wolf.

"How can you be so sure? I think Naga means well. I have fought against him, remember. He held out against Murnau for six weeks on the Bashkir Gradient. His people fought like tigers, but he made them spare all the prisoners on the towns they captured. He never used Tumblers unless he had to. And when he heard I'd been wounded by one of his snipers he sent me a get-well present; a vest of Old-Tech body-armour, with a note that said, 'Sorry we missed you.' He may be my enemy, but I like him more than most of my friends."

"Very touching," yawned Wolf, who had heard that story many times before. "But the Mossies must still be exterminated."

"Nonsense!" said his father crossly. "The *Traktionstadtsgesellschaft* was not founded to exterminate anyone, only to defend honest cities from the Storm. Let Naga and his Anti-Tractionists live up in their horrible mountains in peace, as long as they promise not to trouble us."

Wolf rounded on his father angrily, but did not say anything. Instead he walked to the edge of the gazebo and looked out between the dead trees, east across the rough, torn landscape that the war had made to the plains beyond, imagining London out there somewhere, waiting.

After a while, Kriegsmarshal von Kobold said, "Manchester is coming east. I had a communiqué from the mayor, Mr Browne. . ."

"Ah! Our paymaster."

"It is true that Manchester has helped to finance our struggle. . . He plans to hold a conference aboard his city as soon as it reaches the line. The mayors of all the *Traktionstadts* are to meet and decide how to proceed. I plan to make the case for a lasting peace with the Storm. I would like you to be there, Wolfram. There at my side, so that everyone can see you are my heir. . ."

"I shall be going home to Harrowbarrow tomorrow or the day after," said his son. "I have business to attend to."

"With your sky-tramp aviator friends?"

Wolf shrugged.

The Kriegsmarshal turned away, hesitated, then shook his head and marched briskly down the steps and across the bridge. He had fought countless battles against the Storm; met Stalkers in hand-to-hand combat on the steps of his own home in the red winter of '14, but his own son always defeated him.

Wolf stood alone and watched him go. After a while, he had the uncomfortable feeling that *he* was being watched, too. He turned, and there was the statue of the goddess gazing at him with her calm, blind eyes. Despite what he had told his father Wolf could remember how, as a little boy, he had liked to sit in the statue's lap and look up at her while his father told him stories of Murnau's glorious past. He drew his sabre and hacked through the slender neck with three furious blows, sparks flaring as the blade sliced stone. Then he kicked the severed head down the stairs into the empty lake, and strode quickly away through the gardens to start preparing for his journey.

12

THE SAND-SHIPS

It seemed to Theo to be raining. He could not feel the rain, for he was indoors, in bed. He could not see the rain, for it was dark. But he could hear it, the gentle hiss of steady-falling rain, and even the sound was refreshing after those parched days on Cutler's Gulp. It rushed and sighed and soothed and shushed, and wove together his disjointed dreams.

And sometimes, briefly, he came fully awake, and knew that the hissing rain-sound was just the noise of the sand singing beneath the wheels of the black sand-ship.

"Don't be afraid," someone told him.

"Wren?" he asked.

"Was she with you when you were taken by Grandma Gravy's boys? Were Wren and Tom with you?"

"No, no," said Theo, shaking his head. "They're far away. They're in the north, on the Bird Roads. Wren sent me a card at Christmas. . . I hoped I might find her when we reached the north. . ." Remembering the wreck of the *Nzimu*, he struggled to rise. "Lady Naga. . . What about Lady Naga?"

A hand touched his face, gentle and shy. A mouth brushed his forehead. "Don't be afraid, Theo. Sleep."

He slept, and woke again, and saw that the woman who sat beside him was Wren's mother. Above her head an argon globe in a squeaky gimbal swung to and fro, sloshing black washes of shadow up the cabin walls. When the shadows hid Hester's face Theo could imagine that it was Wren sitting there beside his bunk, but when she saw that he was watching her she said harshly, "Awake, are you? You'd better pull yourself together. There's no room for slackers on my sand-ship." It was as if she hoped that he would not remember the gentle things she had said to him earlier.

Theo tried to speak, but his mouth was drier than Bitumen Bay. Hester reached out roughly and raised his head and pushed a tin cup against his lips. "Don't drink too much," she said. "I can't spare it. I was only in Cutler's Gulp for food and water and thanks to you I had to leave before I found either. That lout I shot was Grandma Gravy's golden boy. She's not best pleased."

The sand went on singing against the hull of the speeding ship. Theo slept again. Hester stood up and climbed the ladder to the open cockpit, where Shrike stood at the tiller, his green eyes glowing. The ship was west of the sand-sea, running across plains of roasted shale. Away in the east a band of pale light showed on the horizon. The wind thrummed in the rigging. "He keeps going on about someone called Lady Naga," Hester said. "I think she must have been with him when the scavs found him. Ever heard of Lady Naga?"

Shrike said, "THERE ARE SHIPS BEHIND US."

"What? Damn!"

Hester had expected the old witch at Cutler's Gulp to send someone after her. Grandma's reputation for black magic meant that her men were likely to be more scared of Grandma than they were of Hester or her tame Stalker. She squinted at the horizon until she could see them too; the thin, sharp shapes of their sails, like the teeth of fish. She had expected one or two, feared three, but Grandma had sent six, ranging in size from a tiny cutter to a big, twin-hulled dune-runner. "I suppose we ought to be flattered," she said.

The sun rose out of the ragged hills astern, and the lookouts on the masts of the pursuing ships saw the black sail ahead. A flare rose from the dune-runner, signalling "chase to leeward". A few minutes later there was a puff of smoke aboard one of the smaller ships and Shrike and Hester saw a dune a few hundred yards astern explode in flames and flung sand.

"THEY WILL SOON BE IN RANGE," Shrike said impassively. "IF THEY HIT OUR TYRES WHILE WE ARE TRAVELLING AT THIS SPEED THE VEHICLE WILL BE DESTROYED."

"Damn," said Hester again. She went below to the gun-locker and took out something she had stolen from a bandit she'd killed way out in the Djebel Haqir. It was an automatic jezail, taller than her, with pretty silver chasing on its walnut stock. If the bandit had been sober he might still have been alive; it was a good gun, with a range of several miles. Hester loaded big brass shells into the chambers and filled her pockets with more. She checked that Theo was still sleeping. He was; curled up like a child, gentle and vulnerable. Hester made herself turn away. If she wasn't careful she would start to care about him, and she knew too well that when you cared about people you opened yourself up to all kinds of pain.

She climbed out into the light, which was hard and white. The scouring wind was full of sand, and the ships were closer. The one which had fired first was smallest and fastest; it was coming up quickly on the starboard quarter, and Hester could see the men on its hull taking aim at her with some kind of swivel-mounted cannon. It puffed out white smoke and she felt the shot whisk past her, exploding among a stack of biscuit-coloured rocks a hundred yards to larboard.

She wiped her nose on her sleeve and steadied her gun against the cockpit rail. "Be easier if you could do this," she told Shrike, pushing her sand-goggles up her forehead and squinting through the jezail's telescopic top-sight. "I can hardly see them. . ."

"I CANNOT," said Shrike. "I HAVE TOLD YOU MANY TIMES. SOMETHING DR ZERO DID TO ME; SOME BARRIER IN MY MIND. . ."

"I wish I had your Dr Zero here right now," grunted Hester, trying to focus on the little knot of men busy with their sponges and ramrods around the swivel-gun. "I'd put a barrier in *her* mind." She squeezed the jezail's trigger and cursed as the stock slammed against her shoulder. The empty cartridge-casing went tumbling astern. Where the bullet had gone, Hester could not say, but she had not hit her target. She was no sharpshooter. Her talent wasn't shooting, only killing.

Luckily, the men on the other ship were no better than her; shot after shot went past her as she worked her way steadily through a pocketful of ammunition. She was about to start on the second pocket when the other ship suddenly veered off course.

"Did I do that?" she asked.

The enemy ship was out of control. Maybe one of Hester's stray shots had severed a cable or pierced a tyre. It curved across the line of ships, and a three-wheeler close behind it swerved wildly and collided with a little armed yacht. Tangled together, both ships overturned and started to cartwheel impressively across the sand, shedding spars, wheels, sails and scraps of broken mast. The leading ship had overturned too, throwing up a billowing scarf of sand that hid the remaining three for a while, but they emerged again, vague at first, then sharp and clear and gaining fast. Bullets from a steam-powered machine gun mounted on the big dune-runner started thumping against the woodwork close to where Hester crouched. She said something filthy and lay down out of sight.

"THEY ARE TRYING TO CAPTURE THIS SHIP, NOT DESTROY IT," Shrike guessed. "NOW THAT THEY HAVE LOST THREE OTHERS, GRANDMA GRAVY WILL NOT WANT THEM TO RETURN WITHOUT A PRIZE."

"Well, that's comforting," said Hester, looking up at him from ankle-height as the bullets whanged off his armour. "What are you going to do when they board us?"

"IT WILL NOT COME TO THAT."

"What if it does?"

"THEN I SHALL DEFEND YOU IN ANY WAY I CAN," said the Stalker patiently. "I WILL SNATCH AWAY THEIR WEAPONS. I WILL RESTRAIN THEM. I WILL STAND BETWEEN THEIR BLADES AND YOUR BODY. BUT I WILL NOT KILL THEM."

"And if they kill me?"

"THEN I WILL KEEP THE PROMISE I MADE YOU ON THE BLACK ISLAND."

Hester squeezed off a couple more shots at the dune-runner. Overhead, the sails were starting to fill with holes, but the silicon silk was tough and did not split. "Why did she do this to you?" Hester shouted. "I mean, tricking you into smashing that Anna Fang thing, fine, but why couldn't you just go back to normal once the job was done?"

"I AM SURE THAT DR ZERO HAD HER REASONS FOR LEAVING ME WITH A CONSCIENCE."

"Well, I miss the old Shrike."

"AND I MISS THE OLD HESTER."

"What's that supposed to mean?"

But she never found out, because at that moment the dune-runner pulled alongside, and grappling hooks came hurtling across the narrowing gap between the two ships, and it was time to drop her jezail and pull out her pistols and fight.

The hammer-blows of bullets against the hull got into Theo's dreams, so perplexing and out-of-place in the quiet green spaces he was drifting through that he had to wake up to find out what they meant. He lay on the bunk for a moment, wondering where on earth he was and why it was jolting about so. The row of portholes on the wall above him were shuttered so that it was shady in the cabin, but just above his head someone had stretched a golden cord right across from one wall to the other. Theo wondered why anyone should do such a thing. Was it a washing line? If so, it was more beautiful than any washing line he'd seen before; so bright, so shimmery. He put his hand out to touch it, and his fingers slid straight through it. It was made from warm light.

Theo sat up. There were more of the cords stretched all across the cabin, like a cat's cradle. Every now and then there would be a thud against the hull and another would appear. They were shafts of sunlight, poking in through the bullet holes which were appearing in the cabin walls.

Dizzy with sleep, Theo rolled off the bunk and landed on the deck. The smooth wood bucked beneath him as the sand-ship sped over the rough desert floor. Theo started crawling towards the metal ladder at the rear of the cabin. He could hear shouting above him, and the slam and cough of handguns. As he reached the foot of the ladder a man came down it head-first, dead, his turban smouldering where the flash from Hester's pistol had set it on fire. Theo looked up the ladder, through the open hatch. A confusion of struggling shapes blocked out the sun.

He climbed the ladder. Out on the deck in the white, blinding light a scruffy battle was taking place, almost silent apart from the stamp and scuff of feet on the deck-boards. A ragged brown dune-runner was keeping pace with the sand-ship, attached to it by ropes and grappling hooks. Men had jumped across the gap, thinking it would be easy to overpower a one-eyed woman and a Stalker who would not kill, but three of them were already dead, tangled in the rigging or draped across the rail. A fourth was struggling with Shrike, who had taken his gun and was holding him away from Hester. A fifth circled Hester, who had thrown her empty pistols aside and was holding a knife, jabbing it at the man each time he lunged at her. He had a sword, much longer and heavier than Hester's knife, but he had not yet worked up the courage to get close enough to use it.

Theo stood unnoticed in the cabin hatchway. The fight and the desert swirled around him, the heat and light came down on his head like a fall of bright water. On the deck at his feet lay a boarding-axe, and the light seemed to pour from its blade. He picked it up and hacked at the rope which stretched from the nearest of the grappling hooks. The rope was old and greasy and parted easily after a few blows. The sand-ship lurched, starting to pull away from its attacker. Theo scrambled towards the next hook. "Theo!" he heard Hester shout. He looked up. A man stood in the dune-runner's rigging, grinning at Theo and aiming a blunderbuss. Hornets were buzzing past, and Theo felt one sting his arm. A knife appeared, sticking out of the man's neck, and he dropped the blunderbuss and fell out of the rigging into the storm of sand between the two ships.

Theo looked at Hester. She had flung her knife at the man with the blunderbuss, now she was defenceless. Without thinking he swung the flat of his hatchet at the swordsman who was attacking her. The man still hadn't noticed Theo and the blow caught him by surprise. He crashed sideways against the rail and over it, away into the swirling dust. Shrike dropped the man he had captured after him, and Theo saw them clamber to their feet in the sand-ship's wake and stagger painfully away, waving at the surviving ships, which were slowing and starting to turn, dismayed by their losses and abandoning the chase.

"Good work," said Hester.

Theo nodded, still dizzy, but proud that he had won her respect.

"You all right?" she asked.

He looked down at his arm, where the hornet had stung. It hadn't really been a hornet, of course, but the wound was a scratch, not deep. He knelt on the deck and watched Hester pick up the hatchet and cut the remaining ropes. As the dune-runner veered away pilotless she turned and said, "Stupid! I didn't rescue you so you could get yourself killed." But Theo sensed beneath her scorn a sort of rough kindness, and remembered the gentle way she had sat with him in the night, and knew that she was not so unlike Wren after all.

The dust was clearing. The black ship ran on, slowing now, because its sails were full of holes. It began to pass through the shadows of tall towers of rock around whose summits hopeful vultures wheeled. Some of the towers looked like crude, wind-worn statues, and perhaps they were, for all sorts of civilizations had made their mark on the old earth and some had left some very strange things behind. The towers filled the desert ahead, whittled by the wind into flutes through which the dry breeze moaned. In their crisscross shadows Theo began to feel safe again.

The sand-ship slowed, slowed, and came into a shady place where dwarf acacia trees grew. Shrike flung out the anchor and furled the sails. He jumped overboard and scaled one of the smaller towers, climbing the fissured rock quickly and easily like a steel lizard. He stood for a while on the summit and then clambered down, calling out that the pursuers had turned tail, and that nothing else was moving in the desert. The sand-ship creaked under his weight as he came back aboard. Theo, who had always hated Stalkers, recoiled from him.

Shrike sensed the boy's unease. "I WILL NOT HARM YOU," he said. "EVEN IF I WANTED TO, I COULD NOT."

"Why?" asked Theo, remembering how Shrike had spared the man he caught during the battle. "That's what Stalkers are for, isn't it? Harming people?"

Shrike's steel teeth gleamed as he tried to smile. "NOT IN DR ZERO'S OPINION."

131

"Dr Zero? *She* built you?"

"I WAS BUILT BY THE NOMAD EMPIRES. I AM OLDER THAN THE STORM. OLDER THAN MUNICIPAL DARWINISM. THE LAST OF THE LAZARUS BRIGADE. BUT I WAS REBUILT BY OENONE ZERO, AND SHE MUST HAVE ALTERED ME. NOW, IF I THINK OF KILLING ONCE-BORN, MY HEAD FILLS WITH PICTURES OF ALL THE ONCE-BORN I HURT AND KILLED BEFORE, AND I CANNOT DO IT."

"Dr Zero's *here*!" said Theo eagerly, remembering his promise to protect Oenone. "She's aboard Cutler's Gulp! She's called Lady Naga now. They said she was being sold to that trader Varney. . . We have to go back! We have to help her!"

Hester, coming out of the cabin with food and the makings of a fire, looked coldly at him. "We don't *have* to do anything, boy. We're not going back. And if you mean Napster Varley, I saw his *Humbug* lift off from the Gulp as we were pulling away. Anything he bought there he'll have taken with him."

Shrike hissed like a thoughtful kettle. "WE COULD GO AFTER HIM."

"Not you as well!" cried Hester angrily. "For all the gods' sakes, Shrike, she's the vet who neutered you! What do you care if she's been 'slaved?"

Noises came from inside Shrike's armoured skull. Theo wondered if they were the sounds of thoughts whizzing through the Stalker's brain. "IF I CAN FIND HER, SHE WILL TELL ME WHY SHE HAS DONE THIS TO ME. WE COULD GO NORTH, SELL THE SAND-SHIP AND BUY AN AIRSHIP. NAPSTER VARLEY'S VESSEL IS SLOW. ITS WIDMERPOOL-12 AËRO-ENGINES ARE INEFFICIENT. WE COULD CATCH IT UP DESPITE HIS HEAD START."

Hester turned away from him and kicked the gunwales of her sand-ship. "I like the desert," she said angrily. "It's good. It's simple. It's clean. I can make a living here."

"YOU ARE NO MORE ALIVE THAN ME," said Shrike.

"No?" Hester glared at him. She was good at glaring; she could glare better with that one eye than most people could with two. "Well, isn't that what you wanted? Didn't you always want to make a Stalker of me, so we could wander about dead together?" She appealed to Theo. "Shrike wants to make me like him. That's the only reason he's stayed with me since Cloud 9 came down. He's not got the stomach any more to kill me himself, so he's been waiting for one of these sand-rats to do it for him. Then he'll take my carcass to his old friends in the Storm and get me Resurrected."

"Oh!" said Theo, horrified. Resurrection was the worst fate he could imagine, yet Hester spoke of it as if it was nothing.

"I won't care," she said. "I'll be dead. He can do what he wants with what's left."

"NO," said Shrike. If he could whisper he would have whispered it, but all Shrike's words came out the same, loud and sharp and scraping. He wished Oenone Zero had done something about his voice instead of tinkering with his brain. He said, "WHEN YOUR DEATH COMES, I WILL HAVE YOU RESURRECTED, AS WE AGREED LONG AGO. BUT I CAN WAIT. I WANT TO SEE YOU LIVE AGAIN AND BE HAPPY. YOU WILL BE NEITHER WHILE YOU STAY IN THIS DESERT."

Hester sat down and hid her face in one hand. She was only in her middle thirties but she looked ten years older, and very tired. Theo felt sorry for her. He wanted to put his arms around her, but he didn't think she'd like that. He glanced at Shrike, but the Stalker seemed to have said all that he was going to.

133

"Mrs Natsworthy," said Theo, "it's not just Dr Zero who's in danger. It's lots of people. The truce depends on her. Who knows what General Naga might do if he doesn't get her back? He loves her."

"He's a fool, then," muttered Hester. "People shouldn't love each other. It only leads to trouble." She looked at Theo. "I don't care about your truce. I don't care about General Naga or this wife of his."

She jumped down on the sand and started walking away from the ship, gathering dry acacia branches to make a fire. Although she kept her back to Shrike and Theo she knew that they were both watching her. She felt shivery, and cold despite the heat, as if she had a fever coming on, but she knew it wasn't fever.

At first, when she found herself alone with Shrike, she had been terrified. She had remembered his ghoulish plans for her, and imagined that he was going to kill her at once. But when she learned that he couldn't or wouldn't kill, she had decided that Shrike was the person she belonged with. Had it not been Shrike who rescued her, all those years ago, after her own father tried to murder her? Shrike had looked after her when she was a child, long before she met Tom; now her life with Tom was over, and she was with Shrike again. There was a rightness about it.

Anyway, she was glad of someone to talk to. During these months in the desert she had told him things that she had never told anyone before. She told him about her first meeting with Tom, and how she had fallen in love with him; about the *Jenny Haniver*, and Wren. And she told him how she had betrayed Anchorage, and murdered Piotr Masgard, about how she had driven her own daughter away.

Shrike did not judge her the way a human being would have done; he just listened patiently. Hester felt that when she had told him everything, then she would be able to forget her previous life; she would become as blank as the sand and the red rock hills, and her memories would not be able to hurt her any more.

And now this boy had dropped into her life like a shower upon the desert, making all sorts of things stir under the parched surface. Hope, for instance. Little dreams. She tried not to let them grow, but couldn't stop them. Theo was still in touch with Wren and Tom, and one day he might tell them of his meeting with Hester in the sand-sea. She liked the idea that he might have something good to say about her. She imagined her husband and daughter, in some far-off harbour, hearing that she had done something good again, just once, to balance all the bad things.

She turned and started lugging her bundle of branches towards the ship. "All right, old Stalker," she said when she drew near. "All right. All right then. Let's sell this old tub and find ourselves an airship."

13

TIME TO DEPART

AMV Jenny Haniver
Murnau Air Harbour
21st May

Dear Theo,
I thought I should write to you, because I am
starting on a journey, and it may be dangerous,
and I shouldn't want to die and disappear and
leave you thinking that I just hadn't got in touch
because I couldn't be bothered. A wealthy
Murnau gentleman, Wolf Kobold, has hired us to
do a little exploring, and we have been in Murnau
Harbour for the past week, loading provisions and
making plans. Mr Kobold has left now, gone
north to a suburb he runs called Harrowbarrow
(he's important enough that he can just
commandeer Abwehrtruppe airships to give
him lifts, which makes you wonder why he
needs us, but I think he likes to do things for
himself really, and not make use of all the
privileges his position brings). Tomorrow we
shall fly out to join him on Harrowbarrow, and
our journey will begin. So I am going to leave
this letter at the Air Exchange and hope that
they will pass it on to the captain of a west-
bound ship who will pass it on to someone
else, and before the year's out it might, with
luck, find its way to Zagwa, and to you.
This is all rather complicated to explain, but I

*shall try. It seems that some survivors may be
living still among the ruins of London. This is
news to me, because I didn't even know that
London had any ruins – I thought it had been
completely burned up. But apparently there are
quite a lot of bits left, scattered about in the Out-
Country west of the Green Storm fortress at
Batmunkh Gompa. Wolf Kobold went there
once, and wants to go back and find out more,
and Dad is keen to take him, not just because
of all the money he is paying us, but for old
times' sake. And I want to go, too. It sounds
exciting; just the sort of adventure I used to
imagine when I was stuck in Anchorage. I've
seen old pictures of London, and heard Dad's
stories of it, but imagine actually being there,
and walking in the ruins of those streets Dad
walked along when he was little! I'm a
Londoner's daughter, which makes me a
Londoner too, in a way; at least, it's part of me,
and I want to see it nearly as badly as Dad.*

*Sorry: no time to write more. Dad is over at the
air-chandler's, settling our account, and I
promised him I would prep the Jeunet Carots for
take-off before he gets back. Hopefully by the time
this reaches you I will be safe in friendly skies
again. If not, look for me in London.*

Wren hesitated, then wrote carefully at the bottom of the
page:

> *With love,
> From Wren*

She blotted the letter and started to read through it, then realized that if she did she would lose her nerve and crumple it up, the way she did almost all her letters to Theo. She folded it quickly, and slipped it into an envelope.

A few days earlier, while she was studying the price-list in the window of a photographer's shop at the Murnau Air Exchange, Prof Pennyroyal's journalist friend Sampford Spiney had appeared and offered to photograph her for free. She had sat in the sunshine near the harbour mouth while his colleague Miss Kropotkin took half a dozen portraits, and Spiney chatted pleasantly and listened with interest to Wren's account of her adventures in Brighton. She had done her best not to expose any of Pennyroyal's fibs, though several times Spiney had picked her up on something that contradicted one of the Professor's accounts. "He does tend to exaggerate a little," she admitted at last, and the reporter seemed quite satisfied.

The finished photographs had arrived at the *Jenny*'s berth that morning. Wren thought they made her look grown-up and serious, and they didn't show her spots too badly, so she slipped one into the envelope along with her letter before she sealed it. She liked the idea that Theo would have it to remember her by if they never met again.

Letter in hand, she set off through the busy harbour, making for the Air Exchange. She had not gone far when she met her father, coming back from the chandlery where he had been settling the *Jenny*'s account. She guessed the bill had been fairly enormous, for not only had the little ship been repainted and refuelled and overhauled but Dad had bought a new compass and altimeter and filled her holds and lockers with tinned food and bottled water, and laid in stocks of rope and envelope-fabric, spare valves and hoses and engine-parts, enormous rolls of camouflage netting, and everything he could think of which might be needed on a voyage into hostile territory. Still, it was affordable enough when you remembered what Wolf Kobold was paying them, and Dad didn't look too shocked.

Wren waved to him, then remembered the letter and tried to hide it behind her.

"What's that?" he asked.

"Just a letter," said Wren. "I was going to ask one of the balloon-taxi men to—"

Tom took the letter and looked at the address. "Wren!" he cried. "Great Quirke! You can't send this! If the Murnau authorities find out you're writing to somebody in Zagwa they'll think you're a spy, and we'll both end up in a prison on the *Neiderrang*!"

"But Murnau's not at war with Zagwa! The Zagwans are neutral!"

"They're still Anti-Tractionists." Tom put one arm around her shoulders and started to lead her back to the *Jenny*. "I'm sorry, Wren."

Just then, from a neighbouring pan, they heard a loud, familiar voice. "Of course, I used to fly my own ships. Got quite expert at it, riding the Boreal hurricanoes and so forth. But I can't be bothered on these little inter-city hops. I remember a time in Nuevo Maya when. . ."

Pennyroyal was strolling towards a smart and expensive-looking dirigible taxi, whose crew were waiting beside the gangplank for him to board. His companion, a handsome high-Murnau lady in a dress which had probably cost more than the *Jenny Haniver*, was listening with great attention to his anecdote, and looked annoyed when he broke off to call out, "Tom! Wren! How are you, my dears? Have you met my dear friend Mrs Kleingrothaus? We are just on our way up to Airhaven. We have been invited to dine with Dornier Lard, the airship magnate, aboard his sky-yacht there."

"Airhaven!" cried Wren. "Then you could take this letter for me, couldn't you? Just leave it at the harbour-office and ask them to put it aboard a ship bound for Africa. . ."

Pennyroyal glanced at the envelope as she pressed it into his hands, along with a silver coin to pay for postage. "Zagwa?" he hissed. "Good lord. . ."

"I know the Murnauers would not approve, but you aren't afraid of them, are you?" urged Wren.

"Of course not!" said Pennyroyal at once, with a glance at his companion to make sure she understood how brave and helpful he was being. He tucked Wren's letter into the innermost pocket of his coat and winked slyly at her. "Never fear, Wren! I shall make sure young Ngoni gets your *billet-doux* if I have to take it to him in person!" He looked at Tom. "I noticed at the Air Exchange that you are scheduled to leave Murnau tonight."

Tom nodded. He knew that Pennyroyal wanted to know where the *Jenny Haniver* was bound, but he wasn't planning to tell him.

"I heard a rumour that you were working for young Kobold?"

"We talked," said Tom, casually.

Pennyroyal nodded, beaming. "Excellent, excellent," he said. "Well, we mustn't keep Mr Lard waiting, must we, dear?" He made his bow and wished Tom and Wren *bon voyage*, but as his lady-friend strolled gracefully towards the waiting ship he turned and called, "Don't miss the June edition of *The Speculum*, Tom! Available in all good newsagents, and the lead article is to be Spiney's piece on me!"

Tom waved, wondering where he would be come June. *The Speculum* was published in several languages and sold aboard all sorts of different cities, but he didn't think he would be able to buy a copy among the ruins of London.

14

GENERAL NAGA

Twenty miles away, at the westernmost edge of the Green Storm's territory, General Jiang Xiang Naga stood on a fire-step in a forward trench and studied the lights of Murnau through the brass eyepieces of a periscope. An aide twiddled the knobs on the periscope tripod and the instrument turned slowly, showing Naga the neighbouring lights of smaller cities and countless suburbs, another *Traktionstadt* further down the line.

"New cities are arriving almost daily from the west," said one of the officers standing in the trench. "Intelligence says that even Manchester, one of the last great urbivores, is moving towards the Murnau cluster. Excellency, they are preparing an attack."

"Nonsense, Colonel Yu," snorted Naga, turning from the periscope. "They are trade towns, taking advantage of the truce to come and do business with those fighting cities."

"Yes, to sell them fresh weapons and supplies!" insisted Yu. "This truce is providing the barbarians with a breathing-space; a chance to rearm. . ."

"It is giving us the same chance," said his neighbour, General Xao, a short woman with a creased yellow face like an old purse. She smiled. She had lost three sons to the Green Storm's war, and it was a long time since anyone had seen her smile. "More than a month now, and nobody killed anywhere on the line," she said. "Even if the townies break truce tomorrow, it will have been worth it. Listen."

Naga listened. He could hear the low voices of soldiers in the neighbouring trenches, the whisper of the breeze in his wolf-skin cloak, and faintly, far off, the song of a bird. Was it a nightingale? He wished he knew. He would have liked to tell his wife, when she came home from Africa, "We heard a nightingale singing, right out there on the front line!" But he had been too busy all his life with war to study such things as birds. If the peace held, he thought suddenly, he would learn all about them; birds, and trees, and flowers. He would walk with Oenone in green meadows, and they would point out the birds and blossoms to one another, and he would be able to tell her what each was called. . .

"There!" he said, and his mechanical armour broke the stillness with a hiss and a clank as it swung him down off the fire-step. He clapped Colonel Yu on the shoulder with a steel hand like a Stalker's gauntlet. "There! That's what we have been fighting for, Yu Wei Shan. We didn't go to war because we want to smash cities, but because we want to be able to hear the birds sing again. And if fifteen years of war won't do it, maybe we will have to try talking to the barbarians instead." He waved his arm, indicating the wastelands that lay beyond the wire; the immense shell-craters and concrete city-traps, the wrecked suburbs foundering in weeds, the million bones. "We were supposed to be making the world green again," he said, "and all we have been doing is turning it into mud."

It was something his wife had told him once. It had sounded better when Oenone said it. Later, in the airship, on his way to the sector headquarters at Forward Command, he found himself longing for her. If she were here he would find it easier to keep to this difficult road she'd set him on. Half his people thought that he was mad for trying to make peace with the cities, and he sometimes wondered if they weren't right. But what choice did he have?

The Green Storm was in a bad way. Naga had had no idea how bad until he seized power. Under the Stalker Fang the Storm had always made sure that soldiers like him were never short of food or equipment. But in their own lands everything was falling apart; the people who used to run things in the old League days had all been arrested when the Storm took over, and the young fanatics who had taken their places didn't know how to do their jobs. In the liberated zones which Naga and his comrades had fought so hard to clear of mobile cities, no one seemed to know what crops to plant, or how to arrange the plumbing and transport systems in the ramshackle new static settlements. No one knew where the money was to come from to pay for anything. Stopping the war would help; the old administrators whom Naga was releasing from the prison-colonies of Taklamakan might know what to do, but the task was huge. Too huge, Naga sometimes felt, for an ignorant soldier like him. . .

Still, he knew that if he could talk to Oenone she would soon soothe all his doubts away. The white sky slid past his window. He dozed, and he could almost smell her, and feel the warmth of her small body. Where was she? he wondered. He wished that he had not let her volunteer for that mission to Zagwa. But she had wanted to go, and he could think of no one more likely to bring the Zagwans over to his side than little Zero, with her unwarlike ways and that quaint old god of hers.

Forward Command was a disabled Traction City, squatting on a low hill north of the Rustwater behind defensive walls built from its own cast-off tracks. It had been part of the Storm's front line during the battles of the previous year. Now that the *Traktionstadts* had been driven back beyond the marshes, it was turning into a full-scale settlement; clusters of civilian houses were sprouting on the slopes below the city, and in the fields around them some kind of root crop seemed to be failing miserably. Wind turbines dotted the steppe, flailing their long arms like idiot giants.

A gaggle of officers waited on the docking pan, fussing around a dark-skinned servant-girl whom Naga vaguely recognized. He could tell from twenty yards away that they had bad news.

"Excellency, word has come from Africa. . ."

"This is your wife's servant, Excellency, the mute girl, Rohini. . ."

"She arrived on foot at the Tibesti static, out of the desert, all alone."

"Your wife, Excellency – her ship was jumped by townie warships a day out from Zagwa. The Zagwans must have betrayed her, Excellency. Lady Naga is dead."

Later, in one of the citadel's council-rooms, she told him everything; how three townie airships had ambushed the *Nzimu*, how her crew had fought to defend his wife, and how they had been overwhelmed. She wrote it all laboriously out on papers which an aide read aloud.

When she was a little girl, Cynthia Twite had dreamed of being an actress. Her parents had both been actors; arty, Anti-Tractionist types from the Traction City of Edinburgh who had fled their home for what they imagined would be an idyllic life in a static in Shan Guo. They had always encouraged their daughter to dress up and perform, fondly believing that she might be a star one day. And how right they had been!

Good, tolerant people that they were, they had been taken aback by the sudden rise of the Green Storm. "Not *all* city people are barbarians," they kept telling Cynthia, rather plaintively, as ferocious Green Storm slogans crackled out of the loudspeakers which the new regime had erected all around their settlement. But Cynthia thought it all very exciting; she enjoyed the flags and uniforms, and the war-like songs she got to sing at school, and she loved the Stalker Fang, so strong and shiny. She soon grew tired of hearing her mum and dad moaning, and reported them to the Storm as Tractionist elements.

After they were taken away she went to live in a government-run orphanage at Tienjing. From there she was recruited into the intelligence wing, and then into the Stalker Fang's private spy network. That was when Cynthia discovered that she had inherited her parents' love of theatre. Putting on disguises, adopting other names and voices and mannerisms, these were the things she most enjoyed, and she knew that she did them very well. Her only regret was that she could never claim the applause which she deserved. But it was tribute enough to watch the tears trickle down Naga's face while he listened to all the dreadful things the townies had done to his wife.

Naga had probably never wept in public before. His aides and officers looked quite appalled. Even General Dzhu, who had hatched the plan to kill Lady Naga and helped Cynthia to infiltrate her household, looked uneasy when he heard his old friend sniffling and saw the tears drip off his chin. In the end, he cut short Cynthia's performance. He had arranged Lady Naga's death because he wanted to shock Naga out of his silly notions of peace with the cities, not to destroy him.

"Enough!" he said, holding up his hand to stop the man who was reading out Cynthia's words. "Naga, you should not listen to any more of this. Two things are clear. We cannot trust the Zagwans. And the truce with the Tractionist barbarians must end. My division is ready to attack tomorrow, if you command it."

"And mine," said several other officers, all at once.

"Destroy All Cities!" shouted another, seizing on a Green Storm slogan from simpler times before the truce began.

"No," said Naga angrily.

There was a mutter of surprise from everyone in the chamber. Even Cynthia had to remember she was playing a deaf mute and stop herself from crying out.

"No!" the poor fool said again, thumping the table-top with his mechanical hand. "Oenone would not have wanted to see the world go tumbling back into war on her account."

"But Naga," insisted General Dzhu, "she must be avenged."

"My wife did not believe in vengeance," said Naga, trembling. "She believed in forgiveness. If she were here she would say that the actions of a few townies in the sand-sea do not mean that *none* of them can be trusted.

We must continue to work for peace, for her sake." He looked straight at Cynthia, who modestly averted her gaze. "What of this girl? What reward can we offer her? She has been brave, and loyal."

Annoying, having to wait while someone wrote down his question on a piece of paper before she could scribble her answer. She allowed herself a little smile as she wrote it, and it pleased her to think that everyone else in the room thought she was smiling because she was such a good, loyal girl.

I ask only that I be allowed to serve General Naga just as I served his beloved wife.

15

THE INVISIBLE SUBURB

Dawn found the *Jenny Haniver* above the scarred brown moors of no-man's-land. The cheerful cluster of cities that surrounded Murnau had sunk below the south-western horizon sometime in the small hours, and the only city in sight now was a far-off, armoured hulk called Panzerstadt Winterthur, grumbling north on sentry duty. The *Traktionstadtsgesellschaft* and the Storm each kept watch on this region out of habit, for they had been outflanked before, but neither seriously imagined the other launching an attack across this marshy, pockmarked landscape, which only grew uglier and less inviting as the light increased. There was nothing down there beneath the mist except the immense track-marks of towns.

Some of the older marks were a hundred yards across, steep-walled canyons running straight into the east, their bottoms filled with loose shale and chains of boggy ponds. Looking down at them, Tom thought he recognized the tracks of London, which he and Hester had followed long ago. Soon he would follow them again. This time, Quirke willing, they would lead him home.

"Well, I can't see a suburb anywhere," said Wren, wrapping her wet hair in a towel as she came through from the galley, where she had been washing in the sink. The lemony scent of her shampoo filled the flight-deck as she went to each window in turn, looking down at the slabs and slopes of mud all shining in the grey dawn. "Nothing!"

"We must be patient," said Tom, but he could not help feeling uneasy. It did not seem like Wolf Kobold to be late... He circled again. The *Jenny* felt light and playful, as if pleased to be back in the sky. Her holds were empty, on Wolf's instructions; presumably he envisaged himself flying home from the wreck of London with a shipload of loot. But where was he?

The radio gave a sudden crackle and began to squeal. It had been tuned in advance to a frequency which Wolf had provided, so it seemed safe to assume that the shrill, ear-splitting noise coming out of the speakers was the call sign of Harrowbarrow's homing beacon.

Tom scrambled over to turn down the volume, while Wren ran back to the windows. The land below them was as featureless as ever. "I can't see any suburbs," said Wren. "It must still be over the horizon."

"Can't be," said Tom, wincing as the signal increased again. "It sounds as if we're right on top of it."

It was Wren who spotted the movements in a broad track-mark about a mile to the east. The pools of water there were emptying away, and the trees and bushes that had grown around them were starting to move, turning and twisting and falling one against another. The floor of the track-mark heaved upwards into a high dome of earth, which split and slithered and fell away to reveal a bank of immense, spiralling drill-bits and then a scarred, armoured carapace. A grey fist of exhaust smoke punched into the sky.

"Great Quirke!" murmured Tom.

In the Wunderkammer at Anchorage-in-Vineland there had been the shell of something called a horseshoe crab. Later, when she was trying to explain what Harrowbarrow looked like, Wren would often compare it to that crab. The suburb was small – barely a hundred feet across, and about three times that in length. It was entirely covered by its armoured shell. The front end was a broad, blunt shield, into which the drill-bits were being retracted now that it was on the surface. (The shield also covered Harrowbarrow's ugly mouth-parts, and could be raised when it wanted to tear chunks off the small towns it hunted, or gobble up a Green Storm fort.) Behind the shield, Harrowbarrow tapered to a narrow stern, protected by overlapping plates of armour. Several of the plates were sliding aside, and Wren glimpsed heavy tracks and wheels beneath them, and a metal landing apron which slid out slowly on hydraulic rams, flickering with landing lights.

"Is that where we're meant to put down?" asked Wren.

Tom said that he supposed it must be. "Kobold said his place was specialized," he said wonderingly, "but I had no idea. . ."

He didn't like the look of this place, but he told himself that it was just the first step on the way to London, and guided the *Jenny* carefully down on to the landing platform.

Wolf Kobold was waiting, ready to answer all their questions. It was nearly a week since Wren had seen him, and she had forgotten just how striking he was. The grey dawn and the landing lights and the wind flapping his coat-tails about made him look more handsome and piratical than ever. But Wren had always had a soft spot for pirates and at least Wolf's smile was friendly and welcoming.

Not so his town. All she could see beneath the folded-back armour were blocks of drab grey flats, punched with tiny windows. The people looked grey and drab too as they hurried forward to take the travellers' bags; stocky; scowling scavengers in capes and overalls, with goggles or beetlish dust-masks shielding their eyes from the gathering daylight.

"No, Harrowbarrow does not exactly burrow," Wolf was saying, in answer to something Tom had asked him. "We cannot bore through bedrock or anything like that – it would be far too slow a way to get about! But there are great many nice deep track-marks crisscrossing our world, and their bottoms are mostly filled with loose shale and silt and tumble-down; more than enough of it to hide this little place."

They watched while his men secured the *Jenny Haniver* to the mooring apron, and then followed him through an alley between the metal buildings and forward along Harrowbarrow's central street. Stairways rose from it to the second storeys of the buildings, poky tenements squashed in under the armoured roof. Others led down through the deckplate to engine-rooms whose heat came up through the pavement and the soles of the travellers' boots. An alcove between the snaking air-ducts held an eight-armed image of the Thatcher, all-devouring goddess of unfettered Municipal Darwinism.

"Is this your first visit to a harvester?" Wolf asked, watching his guests' faces as they walked along beside him. "We make no pretence at gentility here, as the larger cities do. It's a good, sound place, though. It was a scavenger once, till it got captured by a hunting city up in the Frost Barrens. They thought it might be useful for the war-effort, so they delivered it to Murnau whole, and my father gave it to me to knock into shape. I've recruited people from other harvester-suburbs to help me. Rough types, but loyal."

The whole place smelled like a stove; smoke and hot metal. Wren thought that if she had to live underground she would take every chance to go outside and breathe fresh air, but the Harrobarrovians did not seem inclined even to venture out on to the landing apron; they stayed in the shadowed parts of their suburb, and those whose business took them into the daylight hid their eyes behind sunglasses and goggles and wrapped themselves up against the cold in pea-jackets and grey felt mufflers.

"Not many women aboard," said Wolf, with a sideways look at Wren. (She couldn't tell if he were apologizing to her for the lack of female company or hinting at how pleasant it was to have a visit from a pretty aviatrix. Both, maybe.) "No families live here. It's a hard life aboard Harrowbarrow. You mustn't mind my lads if they stare."

And stare they did, their mouths hanging open in their stubbly faces, as their young mayor led his visitors up a rackety moving staircase into the Town Hall, a crescent-shaped building which stood on stilts, overlooking the dismantling yards inside the suburb's jaws. It was ugly, and rather small, but Wolf had furnished it well. There were hangings and tapestries to hide the metal walls, and well-chosen works of art, and when his servants closed the shutters to hide the views of machinery outside, it had a homely feel.

Wolf took them to a long, narrow dining room, the ceiling painted blue with little white clouds as a reminder of the sky outside. "You have not breakfasted, I trust?" he asked, not waiting for an answer as he ushered them to seats around the dining table, making sure that Tom took the place of honour at the head. Another man entered; elderly, short and sallow, with pocked skin and complicated spectacles. Wolf greeted him warmly and held out a chair for him, too. "This is Udo Hausdorfer, my chief navigator," he explained. "When I am away, it is he who keeps things running smoothly. One of the best men I know."

Hausdorfer nodded, blinking at each of the guests in turn. If he was one of the best men Wolf knew, Wren would not have liked to meet the rest, for Hausdorfer looked like a villain to her. But she could see that Wolf liked him; more than liked him – if she had not known better she would have taken them for father and son. She could not help thinking how much more at ease Wolf was with this shifty-looking old scavenger than he had seemed with his real father.

Serving women with eyes like bruises moved silently about carrying plates and dishes and pots of coffee. Kobold smiled at his guests and raised his cup.

"My friends! How pleasant to have new faces at my table! I am happy to say that we have real, fresh coffee, taken from a scavenger town we ate last Tuesday. The fruits of the hunt!"

"You are still hunting?" asked Tom. "I thought the *Traktionstadtsgesellschaft* had sworn not to eat other towns until the war was won. . ."

Wolf laughed. "A silly, sentimental notion."

"I thought it rather noble," said Tom.

Wolf looked thoughtfully at him as he slurped his coffee. Then, setting down his cup with a clatter, he said,

"It may be noble, Herr Natsworthy, but it is not Municipal Darwinism."

"What do you mean?" asked Tom.

"I mean that I have lived aboard Murnau, and I have seen at first hand the way our great Traction Cities have tied themselves up in petty rules and taboos." He speared a kipper with his fork and used it to point at Tom. "The big cities are finished! Even if they win this war, do you think the *Traktionstadts* will ever hunt again as real cities should? Of course not! They will cry, 'Oh, we must not hunt Bremen; Bremen gave us covering fire when we bogged down on the Pripet Salient,' or, 'It would be wrong to chase little Wagenhafn, after all that Wagenhafn did for us in the war.' That is why they cannot defeat the Mossies, you see. They insist on helping each other, and as soon as you start helping others, or relying on others to help you, you give away your own freedom. They have forgotten the simple, beautiful act which should lie at the heart of our civilization: a great city chasing and eating a lesser one. *That* is Municipal Darwinism. A perfect expression of the true nature of the world; that the fittest survive."

"And yet you're part of their alliance," argued Tom. "You fight in their war."

"For the moment, because it suits us. The Storm must be smashed. But I never let my people forget that we are free. We hunt alone, and we eat whatever we can cram into our jaws."

Tom looked unhappy. Wren hoped he was not about to say something that would offend Wolf. "You make Harrowbarrow sound no better than a pirate suburb," he mumbled at last.

Wolf was not offended. He laughed. "Thank you, Herr Natsworthy! I have always suspected that piracy is the purest form of Municipal Darwinism!"

"But you're only temporary mayor of this place, aren't you?" asked Wren. "I mean, you're heir to Murnau. . ."

Wolf shrugged, and ate his kipper. "I shall never take over my father's job. Not if he begged me. Why rule a lumbering mountain full of merchants and old women when I could be out here, hunting, free? Places like this are the future now. When the Mossies and the big cities finish tearing each other to pieces in this endless war, Harrowbarrow and others like it will inherit the earth."

"Gosh, well, I hadn't thought of it like that," Wren stammered. She was sure he was wrong, but he was so certain of himself that she could not think of a counter-argument.

Wolf laughed again. "I'm so sorry. I should not talk politics at breakfast time! And I have not even filled you in on the details of our journey. We shall set off soon, heading due east across no-man's-land. If all goes well we should reach the Storm's outer defensive line sometime after midnight. I have found just the place for the *Jenny Haniver* to cross unnoticed. Until we reach it, you must make yourselves at home. You are my guests."

He bowed, and his eyes were fixed on Wren. Tom wondered if there was still time to pull out of this expedition; or at least to find some excuse to take Wren back to Murnau, away from this attractive, dangerous young man. But he so wanted her to see London. . .

And anyway, it was too late. Through the thin walls came the scrape and boom of the suburb's armour sliding shut, and the dull bellow of its engines starting up again. Harrowbarrow crawled on its way along the bottom of its chosen track-mark, gathering speed, shoving its bank of drills into the earth, working itself deeper until it was just an unlikely, moving mound, like a rat under a rug, grinding eastward towards the rising sun.

16
FISHCAKE ON THE ROOF
OF THE WORLD

Remember little Fishcake and his Stalker? Not many people do. The death of Brittlestar and the theft of the *Spider Baby* had been a surprise to Brighton, but the other Lost Boys had instantly started to squabble among themselves for possession of Brittlestar's slaves and houses, and by the time the bullets and the battle-frisbees stopped flying nobody remembered the odd events which had sparked off all the trouble.

A few days later a raft-town cruising in the crater-maze east of the Middle Sea reported losing fuel from its storage-tanks, and the captain of a submersible diving for blast-glass on the crater floors claimed to have seen a strange craft swim by above him, silhouetted against the sunlit surface. But the captain was a drunkard, and the few people who believed his story just shook their heads and muttered that the Lost Boys must be up to their old tricks again.

From crater to flooded crater the *Spider Baby* crept north and east. It crossed a spur of the Great Hunting Ground, swimming along flooded track-marks and scuttling nervously over the ridges between them, while the ground shook beneath the weight of prowling cities. It crept through the Rustwater Marshes, and found its way at last into the Sea of Khazak. The sea had been a battlefield not long before, and there were sunken suburbs and drowned airships lying all over its silty floor. Fishcake burgled their rusting fuel-tanks, and surfaced in a cleft on the rocky shore of the Black Island to recharge the limpet's batteries. Then he submerged again and pressed on eastward.

The *Spider Baby* had passed beyond the edge of Lost Boy charts weeks earlier, but Fishcake's Stalker seemed to have a map of this country in her mind. Beyond the sea a broad river curved down out of the eastern hills. Fishcake did as she told him, following the river east, past Green Storm airbases and under bridges rumbling with convoys of half-tracks and armoured trains. Pontoons had been stretched across the river in case townie raiders tried to sneak inland in boats, but the *Spider Baby* slid under them, passing like a ghost through the lands of the Storm.

"Why don't you make yourself known?" asked Fishcake, looking through the periscope at settled statics, farmland, the green lightning-bolt banners flapping confidently from forts and temples. "These are your people, aren't they? When they see that you're alive. . ."

"They betrayed me," his Stalker hissed. "The once-born have failed me. They follow Naga now. I shall make the world green again without them."

"But you'll have me, won't you?" said Fishcake nervously. "I can help you, can't I?"

His Stalker did not answer him. But later, while he was resting, he woke to find her sitting at his side. She was Anna again, and she touched his hair with her cold hand and whispered, "You are a good boy, Fishcake. I am so glad of you. I should have had a son of my own. I should have liked to watch a child grow, and play. I never see you play, Fishcake. Would you like to play a game?"

Fishcake felt himself turn hot with shame. "I don't know any games," he murmured. "They didn't – at the Burglarium – I mean, I don't know how to."

"Poor Fishcake," the Stalker whispered. "And poor Anna."

Fishcake huddled himself on her lap, wrapping his arms around her battered metal body and laying his head against her hard chest, listening to the tick and shush of the weird machines inside her. "Mummy," he said quietly, just to find out what shape the word made in his mouth. He did not remember calling anybody that before. "Mummy." He was crying, and the Stalker comforted him, stroking his head with her clumsy hands and whispering an old Chinese lullaby that Anna Fang had heard in her own childhood, on the Bird Roads, long ago.

And Fishcake slept, and did not wake until she turned into the Stalker Fang again and stood up, dumping him on to the floor.

Mile by mile, up rivers, through marshes, clumping on its eight steel feet through empty valleys, the *Spider Baby* edged its way eastward. One night, when Fishcake went out on to the hull to breathe fresh air, the moonlit mountains of Shan Guo stretched along the horizon ahead of him like a white smile.

The river shallowed, choked with rocks and boulders which spring floods had washed from the overhanging hillsides. The *Spider Baby* moved only by night, stalking up white rushing rapids in the starlight, hiding at dawn in the dense forests of pine and rhododendron which cloaked the river banks. The Stalker Fang grew impatient during these delays; she bared her claws and listened enviously to the convoys of Green Storm airships which passed overhead from time to time. But when she was Anna she liked the forests. She held Fishcake's hand and led him down the quiet, resin-scented aisles between the trees, or turned girlish and silly and threw pine cones at him. "We're playing!" she whispered excitedly, as he chased after her laughing, throwing pine cones of his own. "Fishcake, this is what playing feels like!"

Fishcake lived for the times when she was Anna. He hated the Stalker Fang, and Anna did too. "She scares me," she told him once. "The other one. So cold and fierce. When she comes, I can't even hear myself think. . ."

But the Stalker Fang was scared of Anna, too. Each time she regained control her first question was always, "How long was I malfunctioning? What did the Error do? What did it say?" That was her name for the Anna part of her; *the Error*.

"This unit is damaged," she declared. "I need repair."

"I don't know how," whined Fishcake. "I don't know anything about Stalker brains." If he had, he would have shut down the Fang part of her and made her be Anna all the time. Then they could take the *Spider Baby* away into the empty mountains somewhere and live there and be happy together, the Lost Boy who wanted a mother and the dead woman who wanted a child. But he knew it was hopeless. If the Fang part of her found out that Fishcake had tried to help the Error, she would kill him.

So he went east and north with her, following her whispery directions, while the river grew steeper and narrower, until one night the *Spider Baby* surfaced in the plunge-pool beneath a tall white waterfall and Fishcake realized that it could carry them no further. At first he felt relieved. But the Stalker Fang was not disheartened for a moment. "We shall leave the limpet here and walk," she whispered.

"Walk to where?" asked Fishcake.

"To talk to ODIN."

"How far is it?"

"It is two hundred and ninety-four miles away."

"I can't walk that far!" protested Fishcake.

"Then stay here," his Stalker said. She left the limpet and started to feel her way up the steep, spray-wet ladder of rocks beside the cataract. Fishcake quickly filled a burgling-bag with provisions, ready to go after her. When he scrambled out on to the hull he found her waiting for him. She was still the Stalker Fang. She had decided that he might be useful to her after all.

"There is a hermitage on Zhan Shan," she whispered. "We shall break the journey there."

Zhan Shan was a volcano so huge and high that Fishcake had been piloting the *Spider Baby* across its lower slopes for days without even noticing. The whole world seemed to form the roots of Zhan Shan, and its head was lost above the clouds. The narrow tracks which wound up and up across the lava fields were lined with shrines. Raggedy silk prayer-flags clapped and fluttered and tore away in wisps of silk and cotton, carrying prayers to the realms of the sky gods.

"This is a holy mountain," said Fishcake's Stalker, turning into Anna again and picking him up, because the path was steep and the air thin and he was close to exhaustion. He wondered why she had come back now. Had it been the sound of those flags flapping which had woken her?

"No one knows how it came to be," she whispered. "Perhaps it was the gods who put it here, perhaps the Ancients. Something ripped the land open, and the hot blood of the earth welled out and made Zhan Shan and all the young mountains north of here. Ash and smoke blocked out the sun. The winter lasted for decades. But look how beautiful this land is now!"

"You can't see it."

"I remember it. I loved these mountains, when I was alive. It is good to be home."

After a day and a night, Fishcake saw a light ahead, twinkling at him through the twilight and the silent-falling snow. They passed a field where a few hairy cattle stood with blankets of snow on their backs. Beyond it lay a tiny house with a steep roof and eaves that curled up at the corners like burning paper. It was built from the black volcanic stone of the mountainside, but there were shutters and a pillared porch made of carved wood painted red and gold and blue, which gave it a cheerful look. A dog trotted out to greet the travellers, and slunk off whimpering when it sniffed the Stalker.

"What is this place?" Anna whispered.

"Don't you know?" asked Fishcake. "You brought us here."

"I have never been here before. I just followed the road the other me set us on."

Fishcake looked critically at the little house. "She said there was a hermitage. She said we'd break our journey there. Is this it?"

His Stalker did not know.

The door had two gold eyes to ward off evil. Fishcake thumped with his small fist on the planks between them. He heard a movement behind the door, then silence. He knocked again. Above, on the sheer buttresses of the mountain, the evening mist made ghosts.

The door opened. A person in a red robe of some thick, crude-woven fabric. A woman, Fishcake decided. She had a brown face, hollow and large-eyed, and her hair had been shaved down to a shadow on her bony skull. "We need food, please, Missis, and water," Fishcake began, but the woman was not even looking at him. She stared over his head at the Stalker. Her mouth moved, but no words came out, only little whimpering sounds. She put her left hand to her face, and then her right, and Fishcake saw that the right hand was not really a hand at all, just a shiny metal hook.

"Anna?" the woman said. She took a step backwards into the darkness of her little house. "No! You are not her!" she said. "I tried and tried, but you are not. . ."

"Sathya!" whispered the Stalker, and lurched past Fishcake to wrap her steel arms around the frightened woman. Fishcake shouted out, because he thought for a moment that she had turned back into the Stalker Fang again and was murdering the stranger. When he saw that she was just embracing her he felt relieved, and then jealous.

"Sathya!" his Stalker whispered, tracing the lines of the woman's face with her metal fingertips. "I haven't seen you since – oh, that night at Batmunkh Gompa, the snow, and the fire, and Valentine. . . Oh Sathya, how old you've grown! And your poor hand! What happened to your hand?"

Sathya looked at her, and looked at Fishcake, and fainted with a little sigh, collapsing on the flagstone floor.

"She was my friend, my student," the Stalker whispered, crouching over her. Her blind bronze face looked round at Fishcake. "What is she doing here? What has become of her?"

Fishcake shook his head uneasily. How was he supposed to know anything about this hermit-lady? His Stalker was the one who knew her. He said, "We ought to nick some food and get going before she wakes up."

"No! We must help her! I want to talk to her!"

"But what if the other half of you comes again? *She* won't want to talk, will she? *She'll* just kill. . ."

"Then you must watch for her," his Stalker whispered. "You must warn Sathya when you think the other one is about to come. But perhaps she will not come at all." She stroked Sathya's face. "Such memories, Fishcake – all sorts of new memories! They make me stronger, I can feel it. Now help me; where is her bed?"

That was easy; the hermitage had only one room, and the bed was in the far corner; a big bed, heaped with furs and blankets, with a fire of cattle-dung burning in a space beneath it. Anna laid Sathya down and gently drew a coverlet over her. Sathya stirred.

"Anna, is it really you?" she asked.

"I think so," the Stalker whispered.

Sathya started to sob. "Anna, it is all my fault! I should have let you rest peaceful, but I couldn't bear it! I made a deal with Popjoy."

"Who is Popjoy?"

"An Engineer. He Resurrected you. He promised me that you'd be yourself again, but you didn't remember me, you didn't remember anything, you said you weren't Anna. . ."

"Sssssh," the Stalker whispered, holding Sathya's hand, pressing it against her cold bronze lips. You brought me back, Sathya. Your love brought me back."

"Oh, oh," moaned Sathya, and hid her face in the blankets, while Fishcake watched and waited for Anna to turn into the Stalker Fang. But she did not change, and slowly he started to hope that this meeting with her old friend had given her the strength to keep the Stalker Fang at bay for good.

He slept on the floor that night, pillowed on rugs, warmed by the dung burning in the pot-bellied stove. The voices of Sathya and the Stalker washed over him and around him, speaking of places he had never been to and people he had never met, dropping now and then into languages he didn't know.

He woke hours later, to morning sunlight and the steady sound of a pump. Rubbing the sleep from his eyes, he went outside into the bright morning mist. His Stalker was sitting on the porch, her back to the sun-warmed wall, her blind mask turned inquisitively towards the sounds that Sathya was making as she worked the handle of the pump at the far corner of the house. It looked hard work for someone with only one hand, so Fishcake went to help. When they had filled Sathya's big leather bucket they took a handle each and started carrying it to the house. "You're wondering what this is for, I suppose?" said Sathya. "Well, it's a bath, for you."

Fishcake yelped, protested, and almost dropped the bucket. He didn't think he'd ever had a bath before, and he didn't see why he should break the habit of a lifetime now. But Sathya and his Stalker would not listen to any excuses; working together they stripped off his grimy clothes and dumped him into Sathya's zinc bath, and soaped and scrubbed him, and washed his lousy hair.

That was the happiest day of Fishcake's childhood, and he would remember it always. The sun rose high and burned away the mist, and all around Sathya's lonely house the snowfields shone clean and dazzling, each summit exhaling a breath of wind-blown snow into the diamond sky. Sathya washed Fishcake's clothes, and gave him some of her own to wear while they were drying; worn canvas trousers and a woollen shirt. He chopped wood for her, tugging big logs out of a pile that had been brought up to the hermitage as a gift by the people living in the deep valleys below, and splitting them with an axe. His Stalker helped him carry the split logs into the lean-to behind the house, and then Sathya led him down to the dry-stone enclosure where the cattle were. They frightened Fishcake at first, because they were so big and so alive, but Sathya showed him how gentle they were. He thought they were funny; the way their hairy black ears twitched like mittened hands to bat flies away, and their pink tongues curled around the mouthfuls of hay he held out to them. He watched while Sathya milked the cow, and then carried the pail back to the house for her, careful not to spill a drop of the foamy, steaming milk.

Meanwhile, Anna had unsheathed one of her claws and was using it to carve an off-cut of wood she had found in the lean-to. When she had finished she pressed the thing she had made into Fishcake's hands. It was a little wooden horse, trotting with its head up and its tail flying out behind it like a flag.

"What is it for?" asked Fishcake, turning it over, surprised.

"For you," whispered his Stalker. "It's a toy. For playing with. My father used to carve toys for me when I was a little girl."

Fishcake looked at the horse in his hands. If he had been a normal child he would have had lots of toys; he would have spent whole afternoons lying on the carpet inventing worlds of his own with toy animals and cities. If he had been a normal child he might already think himself too old to play with little wooden horses. But he was a Lost Boy, and he had never owned a toy before. And he started to cry, because the horse was so beautiful, and he loved it so much.

Later, he and Sathya walked down to the river; a white rush of a river that spilled under a rickety rope-and-bamboo bridge and went shouting and splashing away towards the wooded valleys. They threw stones into the rapids, while Sathya's dog barked and bounded up and down the bank. Fishcake found the pole from an old prayer-flag washed down in last spring's thaw from some shrine high on Zhan Shan, and threw that in too, and they watched the river carry it away. The sun was going down. The valleys filled with shadow and the mountains glowed amber and rose.

"You should stay here, Fishcake," said Sathya, over the roar of the water.

"I can't," Fishcake replied, not wanting to even think about it. "The Stalker. . ."

"She can stay too." She looked away from him, far away, beyond the mountains, into her own troubled past. "After I lost my hand and the Stalker took charge at Rogues' Roost and the Green Storm seized power, I went a little bit mad, I think. I kept trying to tell people that she wasn't really Anna, but they wouldn't listen. The Storm wanted to execute me, but there were a few officers – Naga was one of them – who took pity on me, and they arranged for me to come and live here instead. The Stalker Fang must have signed the order, I suppose; that must be how she knew to find me here. I expect the others have all but forgotten me by now. I'm not allowed to leave, but the people in the valley settlements look after me; they bring me wood and honey and tea, and in return I go up on to Zhan Shan and tend the high shrines, and pray for them to the Sky Gods and the Mountain Gods."

"Don't you get lonely?" Fishcake asked.

"Of course I do. It's a better life than I deserve, after the things I did when I was young. But if you wanted to stay for a while, there would be room for you. Just until you are ready to move on, or old enough to move down into the villages and make a life for yourself there. . . Fishcake, you're only a child."

They walked together back to the house. The Stalker stood outside like a statue, her face tilted towards the mountains. Hearing them coming she turned and whispered, "I must go now."

"No!" said Sathya.

"No!" cried Fishcake, feeling his perfect day slipping

away from him. He wondered if his Stalker had changed again, but she was still Anna.

"I have been thinking," she said patiently. "The Engineer who Resurrected me is still alive, isn't he?"

"Dr Popjoy is a great man now," said Sathya bitterly. "The Storm gave him a villa of his own; the house on the promontory at Batmunkh Gompa."

"I will go there," said Anna. "I will ask him to look inside my head and destroy the other part of me. The Stalker Fang must not be allowed to survive. Who knows what she is planning?"

"She wants to talk to somebody called Odin," Fishcake offered. "That's why she came here."

"And who is Odin?" asked his Stalker. "I do not trust her. I will make Popjoy quiet her for ever. If he cannot, he must destroy us both."

"Oh, Anna!" cried Sathya, trying to hug her, but the Stalker drew away.

"I cannot stay here," she whispered. "If I change again, I might kill you. I must leave now, before my other self returns."

Sathya started to cry and plead with Anna to change her mind, but Fishcake knew that there was no point arguing. He'd come a long way with his Stalker, and he knew that the Anna part of her was just as stubborn as the other. He felt in his pocket, and his hand closed around the little horse she'd carved for him. "I'm coming too," he said.

"No, Fishcake," said both women at once, the dead and the living, in perfect unison.

"You need me," he insisted. "Even the *other* you needs me. How far is it to this Batmunkh Gompa? Miles of walking, I expect. You can't do it all alone, blind. . ." He was crying, because he did not want to leave the hermitage behind, but he did not want his Stalker to leave *him* behind either. He held tight to the toy horse and tried hard to look brave. "I'm coming too."

17

STORM COUNTRY

Evening in no-man's-land. Harrowbarrow had been moving slowly east all day, waiting motionless beneath the shale whenever an air-patrol flew by above, surfacing sometimes when the sky was clear to let a haze of exhaust smoke billow out like fog from vents at its stern.

Travelling underground in a burrowing mole-suburb was one of those things that sounded terribly exciting but quickly grew dull when you actually did it, thought Wren. She walked briskly through Harrowbarrow's smoggy, roasting streets, and the citizens stared at her as she passed, and turned so that they could carry on staring when she had gone by. She was afraid that her haircut and her clothes, which had made her feel so fashionable and grown-up in Murnau, just made her outlandish to these burrowing folk.

She would have felt happier staying safe in the Town Hall, but Wolf Kobold had invited her down to join him on the bridge. He had invited Dad, too, but Dad was not feeling well, and Wren didn't want Wolf thinking they did not appreciate his invitation, so here she was, passing the glass-brick windows of the Delver's Arms and taking a left on to Perpendicular Street, a ladder-way that dropped into the suburb's depths.

The bridge was a moveable building, spanning Harrowbarrow's dismantling yards, with big greasy wheels at either end set in rails on the yard walls so that it could trundle forward to the jaws to oversee a catch or aft to watch the workers in the salvage stacks. Chains dangled from it, swaying and clanking with the suburb's lurching motions, and two men lounged on guard duty at the foot of the ladder that led up into it. One of them stepped out to bar Wren's way as she reached for the bottom rung, but his mate said, "Easy, she's His Worship's girl."

"I'm not anybody's girl," retorted Wren, but the men didn't hear her. The scraping and grinding of shale against the suburb's hull was deafening, and something about these hard, leather-faced scavengers made Wren's voice come out very small and girly. She felt their eyes upon her as she pulled herself up the ladder, and heard one of them shout something to the other that made both of them laugh.

"Wren!" Wolf cried happily, when she emerged through the hatchway in the bridge floor and stood breathless and bewildered, looking about her at all the racks of levers, the banks of dials and switches, the rows of gauges, the speaking-tubes sticking down like stalactites out of the low metal ceiling. He sprang from his swivel-chair and came to greet her, side-stepping nimbly as Hausdorfer and the other navigators hurried past him with rolled-up maps or orders for the engine-rooms.

"I'm glad you could come down! How's Herr Natsworthy?"

"All right," Wren replied. "He's having an after-dinner nap, I hope. . ." (Dad had not felt well since they came aboard the burrowing suburb, and he was looking pale and weak. She had left him with strict instructions to get some sleep, but, knowing him, he was probably in Wolf's library, studying charts of the land ahead.)

Wolf took her arm. "You worry about him."

"I think Harrowbarrow is too hot and stuffy for him," said Wren. She didn't want to explain about Dad's heart-trouble. Dad put so much effort into trying to convince everyone, including himself, that he was all right, it would have felt like a betrayal to tell Wolf how ill he really was. "He'll be fine," she promised, smiling as brightly as she could.

"Good," said Wolf, as if they had settled something. He guided Wren to a place near his chair where a big brass thing covered in knobs and levers poked down through the ceiling. There were two eyepieces at the bottom of it. Wolf pulled it down until they were at the right level for Wren to look through. "I thought you'd like a look at the view."

Wren had almost forgotten that there were such things as views. The hours passed so slowly aboard Harrowbarrow that it already seemed like days since she had seen the sky, or the earth. Yet when she looked into the eyepieces of the periscope she saw them both; the sky deep blue and almost cloudless, a crescent moon hanging bright above the weed-grown walls of the track-mark which the suburb was running through.

"Where are we?" she asked.

"Close to the Storm's country," Wolf replied.

"Then why are there no fortresses? No settlements?"

Wolf chuckled. "The Storm haven't enough troops left to garrison all the new territories they captured. Out here they just have armoured watchtowers every few miles. Air patrols too, sometimes."

"Then it'll be easy to get the *Jenny* across?"

"Easy enough. I have prepared a little diversion that will keep the Storm's lookouts busy."

Wren frowned. He hadn't mentioned anything about a diversion when they planned this trip, in Murnau. But before she could ask him what he meant Hausdorfer approached them, and Wolf turned to speak in German with him. After a few words he grinned, and slapped the older man on the shoulder, and Hausdorfer started bellowing orders down the speaking tubes in a language Wren didn't even recognize – Slavic? Roma? The suburb shuddered and canted, changing course.

"When we're moving slow like this I send scouting parties out ahead of us on foot. Some of them have just come in to report. We're almost at the Storm's front line." Wolf slapped her on the shoulder and grinned; he was having fun. "You should fetch your father. We'll be going through within the hour."

Where the deep, twenty-year-old track-marks of London cut through the Green Storm's border they had been filled with banks of earth, topped by stone-filled wicker gabions, iron huts and rocket batteries. Ten years earlier a pack of harvester-suburbs had tried to break through there, and their ruins had been added to the fortifications; upended sections of chassis and track, pierced with gun-slits and painted with the angry slogans of the Storm: *Stop The Cities! The World Made Green Again! We Shall Wash The Good Earth Clean In The Blood Of Tractionist Barbarians!*

In the rocket-battery at Track-mark 16 a sentry

thought she heard the growl of land-engines and went out on to the parapet to look, but all she could see was the mist. That morning's patrols had reported all the barbarians sitting safe and snug and stationary on their own lines, almost like real people. The engines probably belonged to a Green Storm half-track taking soldiers out to some advance listening-post in no-man's-land. Poor devils. Sentry duty stank, and Track-mark 16 was a worthless sewer. The soldier went back inside where there were hot noodles and a stove to sit beside, and letters from her family in Zhanskar.

Tom was dreaming of London when Wren came to wake him. In his dream, he had already reached the wreck site, and to his delight the old city was not nearly as badly damaged as he had feared. In fact, all that had changed was that Tier Two was open to the sky, and the sun shone brightly down into the streets of Bloomsbury, where Clytie Potts was waiting for him on the steps of the Museum. "Why did you wait so long to come home?" she asked, taking his hand.

"I didn't know," he said.

"Well, you're here now," she told him, leading him in through the familiar portico. The dinosaur skeletons in the main hall all turned their bony heads to look at him, and mooed their greetings. "Now you can get on with the rest of your life," said Clytie. He looked past her and saw his own reflection in a sheet of ancient tinfoil that hung in one of the cabinets, and he was not old and ill-looking but well again, and young.

"Dad?" asked Clytie, turning into Wren, and he woke

reluctantly to the stuffy dark of Harrowbarrow, groping for his green pills.

"Are you all right?" Wren asked him. "We're nearly at the line. Wolf says to make ready. . ."

The thought that they would soon be leaving made Tom feel a little better; so did the pleasant memory of his dream. He dressed and followed Wren aft to the hangar near the suburb's stern where the *Jenny Haniver* sat waiting to resume her journey. Wolf met them there. "Get your stuff aboard," he ordered. "Be ready to move out as soon as I come back."

"Where are you going?" asked Tom, surprised that they were not to take off at once.

"To the bridge. We are not across the line yet, Herr Natsworthy. I am arranging for a little distraction so that the Mossies don't spot us crossing."

He left, hurrying forward along one of Harrowbarrow's tubular streets. Tom and Wren stowed their bags in the *Jenny*'s gondola, then waited outside, standing close together in the noisy turmoil of the hangar. The note of the idling engines changed suddenly, rising from a murmur to a scream, and Wren grabbed at Tom for support as the suburb surged forward.

"What's happening?"

Tom was not sure, but even in the windowless hangar there was an immense feeling of speed. With all its auxiliary engines churning, Harrowbarrow raced along the track-mark, throwing up a thick bow-wave of soil and vegetation as it rose to the surface. The startled Green Storm soldiers had time to fire off a few salvoes of rockets, which burst harmlessly against the suburb's armour. Then the barriers, the fortresses and the rocket-projectors were slammed aside as Harrowbarrow tore through the front line into Storm territory. Sally-ports popped open in her flanks, and squads of fierce scavengers swarmed out with guns and knives and maces to attack the survivors scrambling from their dugouts. With a steep skirl of engines Harrowbarrow swung itself sideways, smashing the walls of the track-mark down, toppling a watchtower.

A moment later Wolf ran into the hangar, shouting, "Go! Go!" and yelling orders in Roma and German to the men waiting by the hangar door-controls. Heaving on brass handles, they started to haul the doors open. As smells of damp earth and cordite swilled into the hangar, Tom and Wren caught their first glimpse of what was happening outside. In the red glow of countless fires a battle was raging across the steep, mashed sides of the track-mark. Harrowbarrow was still turning, so the scene slid past quickly, but there was time to see the flattened barrack-blocks, the spiky tangles of barbed wire showing spidery against the flames, and the figures struggling and slithering and scrambling in the mud; the flash of gunfire; the glint of blades, the sliding, tumbling dead.

"Get aboard!" shouted Wolf, shoving Wren up the *Jenny*'s gangplank. "We must be well on our way before reinforcements arrive."

"All this, just so we can cross the line?" cried Tom. "You never said. . ."

"I said I would get you across," Wolf shrugged. "I did not say how. I thought you realized there would be a little unpleasantness involved."

"But the truce. . ." said Wren.

"The truce will hold; we've given them no reason to think we're part of the *Traktionstadtsgesellschaft*. . ."

"All those poor people. . ."

Hurrying her on to the flight-deck, Wolf grinned kindly at her, as if her soft-heartedness amused him. "They're not people, Wren; only Mossies. They chose to live like animals on the bare earth. Now they will die like animals. . ."

Harrowbarrow had turned right around now; its bows pointed back the way it had come; its stern, and the open doors of the hangar, pointed east into Storm country. Tom was working frantically at the *Jenny*'s controls. Wren felt the engines coming to life, but she could not hear them above the louder roar of Harrowbarrow's own engines and the battle going on outside. A few bullets sparked against the frame of the hangar doors, but most of the Green Storm defences had been silenced. Wolf slapped Tom hard between the shoulder blades and shouted, "Go! Fly! Now!" Tom glanced at Wren and then, grabbing the control-levers, he cut the power to the *Jenny*'s mooring-clamps and took her quickly up and forward, out of the hangar, eastward along the foggy floor of the track-mark.

Wren left the flight-deck and ran aft to the stern cabin. Through the long window there she had her last sight of Harrowbarrow, a leviathan wreathed in fog and battle-smoke, rearing up to gobble and crush another Green Storm fortress before it sank down into the track-mark and drove westward. The *Jenny* was flying fast, the branches of trees in the floor of the track-mark scratching and snatching at the gondola's keel. Soon even the glow of the fires faded into the fog astern, and there was no sound but the familiar purr of the Jeunet Carot engines.

"I doubt any Mossies noticed us leave," said Wolf. How long had he been standing behind her? Wren turned. He was watching her kindly, eager to allay her fears. "If they did, my boys will have killed them by now. Hausdorfer will smash a few more of their defences and then head back into the badlands before reinforcements come. The Storm will think it was only a greedy scavenger town, hungry for scrap metal and Mossie blood. They won't come looking for us."

"You didn't tell us," said Wren coldly. "You said it would be easy to cross the line! You didn't say we'd have to fight a battle."

"That *was* easy," said Wolf. "You can't even imagine what a real battle's like, Fräulein Aviatrix."

Wren pushed past him, and went back to the flight-deck. Tom was staring out through the big forward windows: nothing out there but mist. Sometimes a buttress of earth and rocks where the wall of the track-mark they were flying in had partially collapsed. Each time that happened Tom would make a quick, calm adjustment to the steering-levers, guiding the *Jenny* expertly around it. Wren envied him for having something to concentrate on. All she could think of were those struggling figures she'd glimpsed through the hangar doors. She felt guilty for having been part of the attack, and more and more afraid. Despite what Wolf said, she was sure the Storm must know that the *Jenny Haniver* had pierced their line; at any moment rockets or Stalker-birds would come howling out of the mist, and they would be the last thing she would see.

"I'm sorry," said her father softly, sounding as shocked

and miserable as her. "When he said he knew a place where we could cross, I just thought. . ."

Wren said, "How could he do that? All those people?"

"There's a war on, Wren," Tom reminded her. "Wolf's a soldier."

"It's not just that," she said. "I think he enjoys it."

"Some people are like that," agreed Tom. He had recognized the light in Wolf's eyes as the battle raged; Hester had had the same look, that night at the Pepperpot when she murdered Shkin's guards. He said, "Wolf has some strange ideas, but then he's led a strange life. He's very young, and he's never known anything but war. Underneath, I think, he's a decent young man."

"Must be pretty deep underneath," said Wren.

Tom smiled. "I knew a man called Chrysler Peavey once. A pirate mayor, boss of a suburb nearly as fierce as Harrowbarrow, but he wanted more than anything to be a gentleman. Wolf's the other way round; a gentleman who wants to be a pirate. But there's another side to him. He's treated us well, hasn't he? Now we've got him away from his suburb we might see that side of him again."

Wren nodded cautiously, as if wishing she could believe him. Tom wished he believed himself. He had been wrong to accept Wolf's offer, he was certain of that now. What would become of Wren if anything happened to him on this flight and she was left with only Wolf Kobold to look after her?

But as the *Jenny* flew on, mile after lonely mile, and no rockets or birds appeared, he began to feel more hopeful, and started to remember the sense of peace which had come to him with his dream of the museum.

He did not like what Kobold had done, but at least they were on their way. From somewhere ahead, beyond these midnight plains, he could feel the tug of London's gravity, drawing the *Jenny Haniver* and her passengers towards it like a dark star.

18
THAT COLOSSAL WRECK

After a few hours the fog thinned, and Wren was able to see properly for the first time the landscape that she was flying over – or rather flying *in*, for Tom was still keeping the airship as low as he dared, hiding her behind the steep fans of dried mud which towered between London's old track-marks. As far as Wren could see the land around her was not much different from the plains the cities rolled across back on their side of the line. The Green Storm had cleared these eastern steppes of Traction Cities, but they had not yet built settlements of their own. Sometimes, through clefts in the walls of the track-mark, the distant lights of forts or farmsteads showed, far off across the churned, weed-tangled land; but if they were keeping watch at all, they were not watching for a single small airship.

London's wake ran ruler-straight towards the east. Each of the city's tracks had ploughed a trench two hundred feet wide and often almost as deep. Tom steered the *Jenny* along the northernmost one until the ribbon of sky above him started to turn pale. Then he set her down to wait out the hours of daylight.

Later, sitting watch on the silent flight-deck while he slept, Wren looked up into the sky and saw dozens of Green Storm airships pass over, very high and heading west. Then the rhythmic wing-beats of a flock of Stalker-birds caught her eye, also flying west. She pointed them out to Wolf Kobold, but he said, "Nothing to worry about. Routine troop movements."

As angry as she had been at him the night before,

Wren felt glad that he was there with them; glad of his soldierly certainty; his confidence. And already, as Harrowbarrow fell behind, he seemed to be softening, just as Tom had promised. His voice and his expression had grown gentler, and when Wren asked him to do something he obeyed meekly, as if conceding that, aboard the *Jenny Haniver*, she was the expert.

He was right about the birds, though. None came low or close enough to see the *Jenny*'s russet envelope amid the red earth of the track-mark.

That night they flew on, and the next day passed in the same way, except that there was a deep, clear pool of water close to where Tom set the airship down, and Wren swam in it. The water was numbingly cold, its surface filled with bright reflections which shattered ahead of her. She turned on her back and floated, feeling her swimming-dress balloon around her, listening to the silence. Her old life, Vineland and Brighton, seemed impossibly far away.

Stones scampered down the steep wall of the track-mark and plopped into the water, spreading rings of overlapping ripples towards her. Wolf was clambering between the trees which jutted from the track wall. He saw Wren and waved. "Just taking a look!" he called.

Wren swam ashore and changed quickly into her clothes, making sure that the *Jenny Haniver* was between her and Wolf. When she emerged, wet-haired and shivery, she could not see him, but when she scrambled up to the top of the track-mark she found him lying on a flat, grassy ledge, peering through a pocket telescope across the Storm's country.

"What can you see?" she asked.

"Nothing to worry about."

He handed Wren the telescope and she put it to her eye. Southward, a plain of brown grass rolled away towards distant, blue hills. A cluster of the Storm's silly wind-turbines flickered in the sunlight above a small static. Further east, something else was moving; a long, low town, Wren thought at first, then realized that it couldn't be.

"Supply train, heading west with provisions for their armies," said Wolf. "They've laid railways all the way from the mountains of Shan Guo to the Rustwater. That's how I got home from London last time; hiding in a freight-car. Most of the trains aren't manned."

"What, not even a driver?" asked Wren, focusing on the black, electric locomotive at the front of the train, a blunt, windowless thing, charging along like a bull.

"The engine *is* the driver. A Popjoy Mark Twelve Stalker, controlled by a Resurrected human brain. Some poor dissident or captured soldier whom the Storm have turned into a train-engine. They aren't worth getting sentimental about, Wren. They're savages, and it is either them or us."

Wren knew he was referring to last night's battle; apologizing, or explaining. She tried to think of a riposte but nothing came.

"Look, it's slowing. . ." said Wolf, taking back the telescope. "Must be a bridge or weak bit of rail there. That would be a useful place to climb aboard, if we ever need to."

"What do you mean?"

Wolf grinned at her. "If anything goes wrong with your airship, we'll be walking home. A lift aboard one of those trains will cut weeks off the journey."

Wren nodded. She knew he was hoping to unsettle

her, and refused to let him. "Look," she said, pointing. "The trees grow close to the rails there. You could hide there while you waited for a train."

Wolf laughed, pleased by her show of bravery. "I like you, Wren! There are no girls in Murnau who would make a journey like this, and stay so cool about it. You are – how would you say it – cold-blooded."

"Must take after my mum," said Wren.

🥟 ⛩ 🥟 ⛩ 🥟

"Not far now," Tom announced, as he started the engines that night. Wren had gone aft to catch up on her sleep in the stern-cabin, but Wolf was pacing the flight-deck, pausing from time to time to stare out over the control-panels into the blackness ahead, waiting impatiently for a glimpse of London. "We're close," he said softly, as if to himself. "We're very close now. . ."

Sails of dried mud thrown up by London's tracks blotted out the night sky. Twice the sounds of the engines woke birds, which came flapping past the gondola windows and startled Tom. The second time he cried out, and brought Wolf springing to his side.

"It's all right," Tom said sheepishly. "Nothing. Just birds. I was in a fight with the Storm's flying Stalkers, years ago. I've been nervous of birds ever since. . ."

"You're a brave man, Herr Natsworthy," said Wolf, relaxing, going back to his pacing.

"Brave?" Tom laughed. "Look at me. I'm shaking like a leaf!"

"Even brave men feel fear. And the things you've done. . . Wren has told me some of the wonderful adventures you had when you were young."

186

"They didn't feel wonderful at the time," said Tom. "I was just scared stiff, mostly. It was only luck that brought me through alive. Every time I tried to do anything, it all went wrong. . ."

They flew on. After a few hours Wren relieved Tom at the controls. He switched on the coffee machine and shook Wolf, who was dozing on the window seat. "Coffee?"

The young man frowned. "What time is it? Are we at the debris fields?"

"Not yet."

"Dad?" said Wren, from the pilot's seat. "Dad, look!"

Forgetting the coffee, Tom went to stand beside his daughter, leaning over the banks of control levers to peer out through the nose-windows. The sky was pale, the first hint of dawn starting to show behind the distant mountains. Closer than the mountains, black against the sky, stood a squat, windowless tower, blocking the track-mark ahead. For a panicky instant Tom wondered if the Green Storm had built a fortress here to guard the wreck of London.

"It's a wheel," whispered Wolf, staring over Wren's shoulder, fascinated.

As Wren eased the steering-levers back and the *Jenny* rose and the rounded thing slid by beneath her Tom saw that the other man was right; it was buckled, corroding, shaggy with weeds, but unmistakeably one of London's wheels. Beyond it the Out-Country mud was strewn with immense, dark shapes; more wheels, lengths of twisted axle, strange melted masses of metal flung out from the exploding city. Cast-off tracks were strewn across it all, like ruined roadways leading towards the mountain of scrap that was just coming into view through the mist ahead.

Tom held his breath. He remembered the last time he had seen London, blazing and wracked by explosions, on the morning after MEDUSA. Hester had been with him then; they had been cast adrift together in the *Jenny*, and she had comforted him, and made him turn away from the sight of his dying city. By the time he looked again the wind had blown them far from London.

"Do you want to land?" asked Wren.

Tom rubbed a hand quickly across his eyes and looked at Wolf. Wolf said, "Not yet. This is just the western edge of the debris fields. Nothing here but wheels and tracks and a few burnt-out suburbs that came looking for salvage and got bombed by the Anti-Traction League. . ."

"Or blasted by the ghost-lights," joked Wren, and then wished she hadn't, because the silly ghost-stories she had heard in Moon's did not seem silly at all now. The silent wreckage of London was slipping past on either side of the gondola: empty-windowed husks of broken buildings looming out of the night like a fleet of ghost-ships.

"We'll head eastward for a bit," Tom decided.

The landscape beneath the *Jenny Haniver* was altering quickly. Soon she reached the main debris field, where the earth was completely hidden by deep, dense heaps of tangled scrap. She passed over a burnt-out suburb, wheels and engine-array dissolving into the greater ruin of the city it had come to feast on. Trees stirred softly in the clefts between steep-tilted jags of deckplate. Ahead the wreckage heaped upward into spiny hills. Tom sighted a flat place, half-hidden by the overhanging plates of a sloughed-off track, circled back to check it and set the *Jenny* down quietly and carefully in the shadows there.

"Gosh!" whispered Wren, in the silence that closed in once Tom had killed the engines.

Wolf Kobold opened the hatch, letting in cold, moist air and a smell of wet earth. "Nobody about," he said. "No welcoming committee. . ."

Tom could feel his heart pounding. He struggled to calm himself. Furtively swallowing one of his green pills, he found an excuse to stay on the flight-deck while Kobold and Wren busied themselves outside, tethering the *Jenny* securely with landing-anchors and draping her engine pods and steering fins with the camouflage netting he had brought from Murnau. She was too big to hide, but with luck passing airships or Stalker-birds would miss her, tucked into that rusty cave of track-plates with the netting softening her outlines.

They gathered the things they needed: their canvas packs; lanterns; the old gun that Tom had never used, taken down from the locker above his pilot's chair. Outside, the sky above the debris fields was turning grey; stars fading as the dawn approached. They drank tea, and Wolf took a nip of something stronger from his hip-flask.

"Perhaps you should stay here with the ship, Wren," Tom suggested. "At least until we've had a look around. . ."

"We should stick together," said Wolf firmly, and no one disagreed; they were on the ground again now, back in his realm, and they let him go ahead, a torch in one hand and his pistol in the other, as they stepped out one by one into the shadows of the lost city.

It seemed silent at first. An eerie, awful, graveyard silence, broken only by the footfalls of the newcomers. *The white gardens of the Moon must be this quiet*, thought Tom. But gradually, as they picked their way along the narrow, aimless tracks he became aware of small sounds. Drips of water pattered down from overhangs; a scrap of curtain flapped in an empty window; flakes of rust shifted and stirred, piled in deep drifts among the hollows of the wreckage.

"No one about," muttered Wolf.

"How does it feel to be home, Dad?" asked Wren.

"Strange." Tom stooped to run his fingers over a buckled metal sign which lay among the rust-scraps underfoot, tracing the familiar name of a London street; *Finchley Road, Tier Four.* "Strange and sad. . ."

"Quiet," warned Wolf, standing a little ahead of the others, watchful, his gun in his hand.

"If there's anyone here they must have heard the *Jenny*'s engines when we set down," Tom reminded him. "They know we've arrived. I wish they'd show themselves. . ."

A bird cried, away in the ruins somewhere. They pressed on eastward, pulling on their goggles to shield their eyes against the peach-coloured glare of the rising sun. The debris fields had looked big from the windows of the *Jenny Haniver*, but from ground-level they were simply vast. London was another country; a mountainous island whose central peaks stood several hundred feet high. Parts of the wreck were still recognizably the remains of a city; there were whole streets of empty-eyed buildings, and a row of upside-down shops with the fading, blistered signs still in place above their doors. But in other sections everything was so twisted, so jumbled-up, so distorted that it was hard to say what it had been before MEDUSA. And twice, among the enormous heaps of rust, Tom made out subsidiary wrecks; the carcasses of suburbs. He remembered hearing in Murnau about suburbs that had gone to tear salvage from the wreck soon after it fell, and had never come back because the Anti-Traction League had bombed them. But these suburbs, deep in the ruins, one with its jaws still clamped around some tasty mass of scrap, did not show the scars of any bomb or rocket blasts. It looked to Tom as if the reason they had never gone home was because they had *melted*.

At the top of a low rise he stopped and shouted, "Hello!"

"Ssshh!" hissed Wolf, whirling round.

"Yes, Dad!" said Wren. "Someone will hear you!"

"That's what we want, isn't it?" asked Tom. "Didn't we come here to find people, if there are people here at all? And Wolf, you said yourself that they weren't hostile. . ." He cupped his hands to his mouth and shouted again, "Hello!" Echoes ran off and hid themselves among the wreckage. As they faded there was a shrill, trilling whistle, but it was only another bird.

The path led through a shadowy canyon between the rust-crags and then out into sunlight again. Tier-support pillars, broken gantries and shards of deckplate lay jumbled together, blackened and fused by unimaginable heat. The travellers scrambled over a tangle of rusting six-inch hawser, like gnats creeping through a bowl of congealed spaghetti. Beyond it a wrenched rind of deckplate arched over the pathway. As they passed beneath it Wren sensed movement above her and looked up, but it was only a bird – a nice, ordinary, non-Stalkerfied bird –

gliding higher and higher on the thermals which were rising from the sun-warmed wreck. They moved on, passing through the cool shade of the arch and out into sunlight again.

And behind them a sudden babble of shouts and howls broke out, spinning them around, making Wolf curse and Wren grab for her father's hand.

The steep screes of rust-flakes beside the path had come alive with raggedy, careering figures, and more were letting themselves down on ropes from hiding places in that twisted arch. Wolf aimed his gun at one of them, but Tom shouted, "No, don't!" and snatched at his arm so that the shot went wide. Before Wolf could fire again he was surrounded by grimy young people with home-made weapons, all shouting, "Hands up!" and "Don't move!" and "Throw down your guns!" Some of them had feathers in their hair, and had drawn stripes of rusty mud across their faces like war paint. One, a girl in a grubby white rubber coat, jumped down close to Wren and pointed a crude crossbow at her.

Wren had had all sorts of things pointed at her since she left Anchorage; everything from clunky old Lost Boy gas pistols to shiny new machine guns. It never got boring. She knew of nothing quite so uncomfortable as finding that your life was suddenly in the hands of someone you had never met, who did not seem to like you very much and who could snuff you out in an instant by simply squeezing a trigger. She raised her hands and smiled weakly at the crossbow-girl, hoping she wasn't prone to twitchy fingers.

Tom was trying to explain to his captors that he was a Londoner and a Third Class Apprentice in the Guild of Historians, but they didn't seem interested. Someone had snatched Wolf's pistol and was pointing it at him. Wolf looked so angry and ashamed at being captured that Wren felt sorry for him, and wished she could think of something she could say to comfort him. It had not been his fault, and she was glad that her father had stopped him shooting anybody.

The man who seemed to be the leader of the ambush came stumping over to peer suspiciously at Wren. He was older than the others, short and square-ish, with cropped grey hair and a tattoo just above the bridge of his nose in the shape of a little green compass. Wren sensed that he was afraid of her, which was a bit rich when you considered that he had a dozen heavily armed juvenile delinquents on his side. He was clutching a gun of his own; a strange thing, covered in wires and tubes, with a flat zinc disc where the muzzle ought to be.

"Well, young woman?" he demanded tetchily. "What is your game? What are you doing in London?"

Wren tilted her chin at him and tried to look haughty. "We've come to see Clytie Potts," she said.

"What?" The man looked surprised. "You know Clytie?"

"This one keeps saying he's a Londoner, Mr Garamond," shouted one of the boys who had captured Tom.

"Rubbish!" The man looked at Wren again, chewing his lower lip as he considered what to do.

"Very well, everyone," he said at last. "Bind the prisoners' hands. We shall take them to the Lord Mayor."

19

THE HOLLOWAY ROAD

With their hands tied in front of them, surrounded by the fierce-looking young Londoners, the travellers resumed their journey. Their captors did not lead them east, into the heart of the debris field, as they had expected, but turned north instead. The girl guarding Wren pointed with her crossbow towards the central heights and said, "Lots of 'ot zones in there. Round 'ere too, only not so bad. If you'd kept going you'd have ended up slap bang in Electric Lane. Nasty."

Wren had no idea what she was talking about, and before she could ask, Mr Garamond shouted angrily, "Be *quiet*, Angie Peabody! Stop fraternizing with the scavengers!"

"I ain't fraternizing with nobody!" cried the girl indignantly.

"We aren't scavengers," said Tom politely. "We are simply—"

"Be *quiet*!" insisted Garamond, like a teacher struggling to keep an unruly class in order. He held up his hand for silence. Around his neck on a length of cord hung a curious little machine with many aerials, and he was frowning at a gauge on its top. "Sprite!" he shouted suddenly. "Everybody down!"

His young followers obeyed him instantly, flinging themselves down in the mud and pulling Tom, Wren and Wolf down with them. There was a faint buzzing sound that grew quickly louder and higher-pitched until it passed beyond the reach of human hearing; then a gigantic arc of lightning crackled across a gap between two spires of melted deckplate.

"What was that?" gasped Wren, trying to rub the after-image off her eyes as crossbow-girl helped her to her feet.

"Lingering energy from MEDUSA," said Tom's guard, cheerfully. "We call 'em 'sprites'. That one was pretty pathetic compared with the monsters we used to get. In the old days the whole of London was hot. . ."

"*Please* be quiet, Will Hallsworth," shouted Mr Garamond, waving the party onwards. Hallsworth glanced at Wren and grimaced like a cheeky schoolboy, making her smile. She decided that she had been captured by far worse people than these young Londoners in her time.

The path they were following veered away from the deeper ruins, and they passed through no more hot zones. Twice they crossed places which were almost free of wreckage, stretches of open ground where crops were ripening. Among the rubble heaps scrap-metal windmills rose like rusty sunflowers.

They descended into a broad, v-shaped valley, whose walls were dead buildings and whose muddy floor lay deep in shadow. Looking up, Wren saw that the sky was hidden by the branches of overhanging trees and by a complicated mesh of knotted ropes and hawsers, through which dead branches and scraps of fabric had been threaded, forming a sort of roof. A few shafts of sunlight shone in, falling like spotlights on the airship which lay tethered on the valley floor.

"The *Archaeopteryx*!" cried Tom, recognizing the handsome little ship he had last seen pulling away from Airhaven.

"So this is where they hide her. . ." Wolf sounded grudgingly impressed. He was starting to forget the indignity of his capture, and was looking about with as much interest and curiosity as the others.

They passed the silent airship, then a line of battered tanks labelled *Fuel* and *Lifting Gas*, and finally a small guard-post with tattered deckchairs, and views of old London tacked to the tin walls. The valley ended at a sheer cliff of metal, and Garamond ordered his party into a tunnel which seemed to lead under it.

The roundness of the tunnel, and its ribbed walls and roof puzzled Tom, until the Londoners lit lanterns and he realized that it was one of the old air-ducts which lay looped like lifeless snakes throughout the wreck. Rails had been laid along the bottom of the duct, and a couple of wooden trolleys stood ready at the buffers. Above them, on the curving wall, an old enamel sign gleamed in the lantern-light. It was the name-plate from a London elevator station; a broad red ring in the middle of a white square, crossed by a vertical blue bar. In white letters on the blue were the words HOLLOWAY ROAD.

"This is how we get 'eavy cargoes out of the *Archy* and into London," whispered Wren's guard, Angie. "The Mossies' spy-birds can't see us if we keep inside this old duct. We call it 'taking the tube'."

"The Hollow-Way Road," said Wren, reading the sign again. "Oh, very funny. . ."

"Well, yer gotter 'ave a laugh, ain't yer?"

They followed the Holloway Road for what felt like a mile or more, sometimes by lantern-light, sometimes through patches of sunshine that spilled in through rents in the skin of the old duct. The way twisted and turned, and the floor sloped steeply sometimes where the duct dipped down into a hollow of the earth or lay draped across another section of wreckage. Underfoot, the dust between the rails was stamped with the prints of passing boots.

At the end of the duct they passed more makeshift cargo-trolleys, another set of buffers, and emerged into daylight again to find a pathway of metal duckboards leading between two steep hills of scrap. Beyond the hills stretched an open space which had been cleared of wreckage. Kitchen gardens had been laid out in raised beds full of peaty soil, and people broke off from picking cabbages and digging potatoes to stand staring as the prisoners were led by.

Tom stared back. There were not just people inside London; there were *lots* of people. He looked at their faces, but there was no one he recognized. It didn't matter; they were Londoners, that was what was important. Many of them bore the marks of old injuries; he saw missing limbs and fingers, a man with a burnt face, a blinded woman being guided along by her children, who were telling her excitedly about Tom, Wren and Wolf. Scars everywhere. *Hester would have felt at home here*, he thought, and he wished that the wind had blown the *Jenny Haniver* the other way on that morning after MEDUSA, and carried him and Hester into London instead of away from it. How different things might have been if they had lived in the debris fields. . .

At the far side of the garden area a massive section of deckplate lay propped upon the ruins, forming a low-ceilinged cave. Garamond led his party in through the long, letterbox-shaped opening. The iron roof was so low that everyone had to stoop, but in the shadows dozens of small huts and houses had been erected, built from scraps of metal and wood. Crowds were waiting there, alerted by the children who were running excitedly ahead of the procession. "Where's Miss Potts?" shouted Garamond over all the noise, and a bald-headed gentleman in a grubby white rubber coat (*An Engineer!* thought Tom, uneasily) replied, "She's at the Town Hall, Garamond."

The procession went marching on, deeper and deeper into the metal-roofed cavern until the deckplate overhead was so low they had to bend almost double to save themselves from cracking their heads on the old bolts and fittings that poked down from it. "This is why it's called Crouch End," said Wren's friendly guard. "It ain't a very convenient place to live, but in the old days, with sprites and Mossies and Quirke-knows-what else to hide away from, a roof over our 'eads was very welcome. . ."

"Angie Peabody," barked Mr Garamond, "I thought I told you to shut your cakehole!"

Wedged in under the lowest corner of the deckplate was a building fashioned out of an old Gut Supervisor's office and bits of many other things, all nailed and bolted together in a workmanlike way and painted a cheerful shade of red. LONDON EMERGENCY COMMITTEE someone had written above the door, in careful capitals. Garamond left his charges outside while he went in and had a muffled conversation with someone. Then he came out again and pushed the door wide open. "Step along now, prisoners," he said. "And show a bit of respect. You are entering the presence of the Lord Mayor of London!"

The floor inside the building had been dug out so that

there was no need to stoop. Tom went first, with Will Hallsworth at his side, warning him to watch out for the steps. He tripped down them anyway, and landed in a big, slope-ceilinged room where a map of the debris fields covered one wall, marked all over with tickets and flags and mysterious red pins. Around a battered old tin table in the centre of the room a dozen people were gathered, looking as if they had been in the middle of a meeting when they were interrupted by the arrival of Mr Garamond and his prisoners. One of them was Clytie Potts. She stood up when she recognized Tom. "Oh, Quirke!" she said.

Beside her, another of the committee was already rising to greet the new arrivals, and his shabby red robe and chain of office marked him clearly as the Lord Mayor. Tom felt relieved. For a moment he had feared that he was about to come face-to-face with Magnus Crome, the sinister Engineer who had ruled London in his childhood. But this ancient, portly gentleman with tufts of white hair sprouting like steam around his ears was not Crome. And after the relief came astonishment, for Tom found that he knew that round, red face, and meeting it here was even more of a shock than his first encounter with Clytie Potts.

"Chudleigh Pomeroy!" he cried.

"I – Great Quirke and Clio!" the old man said, his white eyebrows leaping in surprise. "By the Sacred Black Flannel of Sooty Pete! If it isn't young Apprentice Thing! Young Whatchamacallit! Young, um. . ."

"Natsworthy," said Tom. He had always been a little afraid of the Deputy Head Historian, but meeting him here, realizing that he had survived down all these years and against all these odds, made him weep with happiness. He wiped the tears away and said in a wobbly voice, "Tom Natsworthy, Mr Pomeroy; Apprentice Third Class. I've come home."

20

CHILDREN OF MEDUSA

Chudleigh Pomeroy called for refreshments to be brought from the settlement's communal kitchen, and fussed at his colleagues to clear away their piles of paper and make room at the table for the visitors. Tom, who was starting to recover from his shock, turned to look at the other committee-members. Two of them were Engineers – a small, brown-skinned man and a rather severe-looking old lady, as bald as two pebbles, and wearing tattered white rubber coats. The rest were just ordinary Londoners; people of all shapes and sizes and several different colours, including a wiry, leathery little man who waved at Angie, prompting her to wave back and say, "'Ullo, Dad!" He looked to Tom as if he'd been a Gut labourer before MEDUSA went off; certainly not the type of person you would have found in London's council-chamber in the old days.

At last three seats were cleared for the newcomers. Chudleigh Pomeroy beamed at them as they sat down. "Pleased to meet you, Miss Natsworthy," he said, reaching across the table to shake Wren's hand when Tom introduced her. "And Herr Kobold. We've heard a lot about the bravery of your city and its allies. Miss Potts here keeps us up to date with the war news. Welcome to London."

"Thank you, sir," said Wolf, bowing neatly, his hand moving to where his sword-hilt would have been if Mr Garamond had not taken his sword away from him. "This is not my first visit. The last time I was here I found myself ejected before I could actually meet any of your people. . ." He smiled slyly at the puzzled faces around him and quickly explained the story of his first visit to the debris fields.

"Great Quirke!" muttered Garamond. "I remember him now. . ."

"You're not the first lost soldier to seek shelter here," said Pomeroy. "The lost and wounded of both sides blunder into the fringes of the wreck sometimes. We couldn't risk any of them going off and blurting out our secrets to the outside world, but we didn't want to murder them or anything, so we came up with the notion of simply scaring them away. A few mysterious moans are usually enough to set the bravest of 'em running, but now and then we come across one who's more inquisitive. When we do, we knock 'em out with chloroform before they can see anything and dump them outside the wreckage. Most of them get the message. You're the first to return."

"So why didn't you knock *us* out and carry *us* into the Out-Country?" asked Wren.

"Good question," grumbled one of the committee-men, glaring at Garamond.

"It wasn't practical!" said Garamond huffily. "They came in by airship, not on foot. They seemed like scavengers, not castaways. And Mr Natsworthy here doesn't look any too healthy. If my lads had chloroformed him he might never have woken up. . ."

Tom started to protest that there was nothing wrong with him; that he would have positively welcomed a good, bracing dose of chloroform. Luckily, before an argument could develop, the food arrived; bread and butter, apple crumble and home-baked biscuits, elderflower wine in old tin water-bottles.

"I see you have learned to live off the bare earth," said Wolf Kobold softly. "Just like the Mossies."

Clytie Potts smiled brightly at him; she was taken with this handsome young newcomer, and missed the faint edge of disgust in his voice. "Oh, we grow all sorts of things in the patches of soil between the rust-heaps. It's very fertile. Some of the survivors were workers in the agricultural districts before MEDUSA and they have taught us all about growing food. And our scavenging-teams find all sorts of things among the ruins: tinned goods; sugar; tea. There are less than two hundred people in London now, so we've enough for everyone."

"We hunt, too," said Angie eagerly. "Rabbits and birds and things make their 'omes in the debris fields. . ." She stopped as Mr Garamond turned to glare at her; the other youngsters had been made to wait outside, and Wren suspected that Angie wasn't supposed to be in the committee-room at all.

"And Clytie brought in a few goats and sheep aboard that ship of hers," added the quiet, elderly lady Engineer.

"But I don't understand," Tom was saying. "I mean, how did you survive at all? How do you come to be here? I thought. . ."

"You thought we were all dead," said Pomeroy kindly, "which, by the way, is what I thought about you; that villain Valentine told me you'd fallen down a waste-chute in the Gut. I've felt guilty ever since about having sent you down there that night. Wine?"

He filled a motley collection of tin beakers and enamel mugs, and another of the committee handed one to each of the newcomers while Pomeroy sat beaming at them, gathering his thoughts. Then, while they ate and drank, he told them of the last hours of London; of how the tension between the Guild of Historians and Crome's power-hungry Engineers had ended with open warfare in the halls of the Museum, and of how Katherine Valentine and Apprentice Engineer Pod had set off up the secret stairway called the Cat's Creep to try and stop MEDUSA being used.

"Soon after that," he said, "the Engineers attacked in force, and things grew rather confused. We fought like tigers, of course, but they had Stalkers and things, and they drove us back into the Natural History section. There weren't many of us left by that time; Arkengarth and Pewtertide and Dr Karuna had all been killed, and Clytie here was hurt pretty badly. I decided to make a last stand behind that old model of the Blue Whale – it had been taken down from the ceiling for some reason, and was lying on the floor, where it made a passable barricade. And as we crouched behind it, waiting for those Resurrected fellows to come and finish us, suddenly, *Boom*! The building started to come apart at the seams. . ."

"Mr Pomeroy threw me in through the whale's mouth," said Clytie Potts, looking sadly down at her hands as she spoke, as if the memories still upset her.

"Yes," agreed Pomeroy, "and then, with extraordinary presence of mind, I jumped in after her. Just in time! I think the whole of Tier Two must have given way at that point. Light blazed in at me through every rent and bullet-hole in the whale's hide, and I felt it start to roll, to slide, to tumble through the air! After that I don't remember much. Surfing down the sides of disintegrating cities inside fibreglass whales isn't really my cup of tea, I'm afraid, and I passed out fairly promptly. . ."

"The whale eventually came to rest between two fallen tier-supports over on the southern edge of the main debris field," explained Clytie, taking up the story. "Some workers from the salvage-yards found it there, and helped us out. That was when I saw what had happened to the city. It was... Oh, I can't begin to describe it. There was fire everywhere, and dirty smoke boiling into the sky, and explosions going off all the time, so that there was always wreckage rattling down, and ash falling softly everywhere, like black snow. And sometimes, out of the middle of the ruins, a huge claw of white light would come crackling, groping its way across the ground as if it was feeling for us. . ."

"Yes, those were dicey times," said Pomeroy, nodding solemnly. "The League was about, too, hungry for revenge. We watched some of our fellow survivors venture out of the wreckage to give themselves up to a League patrol and they were all shot on the spot. So Clytie and me and our salvage-yard friends decided to stay put. After a while we started to make contact with other little groups of survivors, and we banded together and wondered what to do. We thought about sneaking back west along the track-marks, but where would that get us? Just into the slave-holds of some scavenger-town probably, where we'd be no better off than with the League. So in the end we decided to stay here. London might have come a cropper, but it was still London, eh? Still home. . ."

His colleagues all nodded and muttered agreement, and Pomeroy gave the wall of the committee-room an affectionate pat, which made it wobble alarmingly.

"We moved into Crouch End because it seemed safe from sprites," explained Clytie, "and we were hidden here from the air-patrols that the League kept sending over in those early days. There's a big section of the Gut lying fairly undamaged about a half-mile east of here, and we salvaged a lot of useful stuff from it; even a trunk-full of money. So later, when the League patrols thinned out a bit, some of us were able to sneak out and buy the *Archaeopteryx* and start picking up a few other things we needed. . ."

"It must have been dangerous," said Tom, thinking of his own experience of crossing the Green Storm's lines.

"Impossible, sometimes," admitted Clytie. "But we usually manage a few trips a year. . ."

"Collecting Old-Tech, I gather," said Wolf Kobold.

Clytie looked uncertain. Several of the councillors shifted uncomfortably in their salvaged chairs.

"And what about these Engineers?" Wolf Kobold went on, nodding at the bald-headed man and woman. "You seem very friendly with them, considering it was all their fault that London exploded in the first place."

The lady Engineer said softly, "Not all of our Guild supported Magnus Crome and his insane plans. Those of us who opposed him were banished to lowly jobs in the prisons and factories of the Deep Gut. I suppose that's what saved us. All Crome's supporters were with him on Top Tier when MEDUSA failed."

"We've been very glad of our Engineers over the years," said Angie's father, the wiry former labourer. "They've knocked up all sorts of handy contraptions for us – bicycle-powered electric hotplates, solar collectors, windmills, lifting gear. Electrical guns that can knock out the Green Storm's mechanized spy-birds. Dr Abrol here –" he pointed to the other Engineer, who grinned modestly – "has built a receiver which allows us to listen in on the Storm's radio-traffic, so we'll have fair warning if they ever do come looking for us. And Dr Childermass, our Deputy Mayor, used to be head of the Mag-Lev Research Division. It's she—"

"Now, Len," said the lady Engineer in a warning voice.

"The Green Storm must know that you're here," said Wolf. "All these windmills and fields and so forth. They must have seen you."

"I suppose so," said Clytie Potts.

"Yet they choose to leave you in peace. Perhaps they think you are Anti-Tractionists, like them?"

"Well, they'd be wrong then," said Angie's father, sensing the challenge in Kobold's question and bristling. "They don't know our plans, no more than you do. . ."

"Len," said Dr Childermass, and Chudleigh Pomeroy cut in hurriedly to say, "Anyway, now that young Natsworthy and his chums are here, we'd best make them comfortable; decide where they're to stay and so forth."

"Oh, we don't want to trouble you," Kobold told him. "We'll just stop a few days, have a nose about, and then head back to the *Jenny Haniver*. . ."

"But you can't leave so soon!" protested Pomeroy. "You've only just got here!"

"What he means is, you can't leave at all," said Mr Garamond, who had been listening impatiently to all this from his perch near the door. "These are important times for London. We can't risk having you tell somebody we're here."

"Come, Garamond," said Pomeroy, "Mr Natsworthy is a Londoner like us!"

"That's as maybe, but his daughter isn't, and as for this other gentleman... As head of the Security Sub-Committee it's my duty to point out that we don't know them, and we can't trust them."

"Hear, hear," said Angie's father, nodding vigorously. "It'd be a right shame if we hung on here for all these years only for some nosey parker to go and squeal about us to a scavenger just when we're about ready to—"

"*Len!*" snapped Dr Childermass.

"But I'm afraid Garamond's right," said Pomeroy apologetically. "I think it would be best if our young people keep a twenty-four hour guard on the Holloway Road and the airship-park. Tom, Wren, Herr Kobold; I hope you will consider yourselves our guests, but I'm afraid that there is absolutely no question of you leaving. Another biscuit, anyone?"

21

PAGING DOCTOR POPJOY

ixty miles beyond dead London, where the young mountains of Shan Guo rose steeply from the plains, stood the fortress-city of Batmunkh Gompa. It guarded a pass through which, for centuries, Traction Cities had kept trying to break into the fertile Anti-Tractionist kingdoms of the east. But now that the Green Storm had pushed their frontier westward, it had become a sleepy, faded shadow of itself, like a harbour from which the sea had retreated. A small garrison still manned the Shield-Wall, but the city served mainly as a base where armies and supply-convoys paused on their way west to the new battlefields of the line.

In the valley behind it, along the pleasant shores of the lake called Batmunkh Nor, lay stilted fishing-lodges and the pretty, steep-roofed villas and weekend homes of senior Green Storm officials. One, prettier than the rest, stood among pine trees on a finger of land pointing out into the lake. The lights in its teardrop windows made long reflections in the water, and the roofs curled at each corner like the toes of a sultan's slippers in a fairy-tale. Anyone bold enough to peek between the bars of its high, spiked gates would notice some curious statuary in the gardens and a name-plate beside the paved drive which read:

Dun Resurrectin'

It was the home of another survivor of MEDUSA; Dr Popjoy, late of the Guild of Engineers, and more recently head of the Resurrection Corps. The villa was his reward from the Storm for all the armies he had built them.

"That is the house," said Fishcake's Stalker, when he described what he could see as they came down the mountain road that night. "When Sathya was stationed at Batmunkh Gompa we went for boat-trips on the lake and looked at that house from the water. It belonged to an artist then; a master calligrapher. Sathya used to say that when she was old and rich she would live there herself."

Fishcake stopped at the last steep turn of the road above the lake-shore. He was cold and tired, footsore after the long trek from the hermitage, and very afraid that they would be challenged as they neared the outskirts of the city. He had insisted on walking most of the way, although his Stalker had offered to carry him, because he did not want her to think that he was weak. An ache had begun in the back of his knees after a few miles, and had now spread to every part of him, making it hard to walk at all. He knew that he should be happy that the journey was over, but he just felt afraid.

When his Stalker turned to find out why his footsteps had stopped he said, "Don't go down there."

"But Popjoy can mend me," she whispered. "Then I will be Anna all the time."

"You don't need him!" Fishcake said. It seemed to him that she was mended already. She had been Anna ever since the day they climbed up on to Zhan Shan. He was dimly starting to understand that the Anna part of her was made stronger by memories; the fluttering flags written with prayers to her old gods had woken her again, and the familiar mountains and the talks with Sathya had made her stronger than ever; perhaps the Stalker Fang part had been crushed for good. Why risk trusting this Popjoy person?

But he was too tired and shivery to explain all that to his Stalker. She came and picked him up and said, "Don't be afraid, Fishcake. Dr Popjoy will mend me, and then we shall go back to Sathya. Now be my eyes again, and tell me, is there anyone about?"

There was no one, and no one challenged them as she carried him to Popjoy's gate. It was late. Batmunkh Gompa was a glittering curtain of lights drawn across the sky beyond the lake. Snow was falling, flakes patting Fishcake's face like chilly little fingers; like the cold fingers of the ghosts of children.

The Stalker set Fishcake down and smashed the gates' strong locks and Fishcake pushed them open, looking nervously at the lighted windows of the house which showed through the trees at the far end of a long drive. His Stalker took his hand as they stepped together through the gateway, the gates swinging shut behind them. "We shall ask Dr Popjoy to give you some food, before he works on me," she promised.

"What if he won't?" asked Fishcake. "Work on you, I mean?"

"I will make him," whispered the Stalker. "Don't worry, Fishcake."

Fishcake looked again towards the house, and put a hand in his pocket to clasp the little horse she'd made him. He still didn't want his Stalker to put herself at the mercy of this sinister-sounding Engineer. He almost pulled her back through the gates, but already it was too late. In the garden ahead, where shadows lapped beneath the trees, things were moving. Spiky shapes which had looked like statues suddenly turned their heads; green eyes lit like flames.

"Stalkers!" whispered Fishcake's Stalker, hearing the clank and hiss as they came to life. She sounded scared.

"But *you're* a Stalker," Fishcake said.

"Oh, so I am. Thank you, Fishcake. I forget, sometimes. . ." She pushed him gently behind her, out of harm's way, and unsheathed her claws.

The house had three guardians; big, polished battle-Stalkers customized by Dr Popjoy, finned and spiked like heraldic dinosaurs. Light silvered their spade-shaped, featureless faces as they loped across the snowy lawns. Fishcake's Stalker limped towards them. They were stronger, but she was cleverer. She dodged their clumsy, flailing blows. Her blades flashed as she drove them through the couplings of each Stalker's neck in turn. Sparks spewed and fluids squirted. The beheaded bodies lurched aimlessly about, colliding with each other and falling over, thrashing and clattering on the flagged path like armoured break-dancers as Fishcake's Stalker turned towards him. She reached out to him with one hand, and then snatched it away, touching her own face. Her eyes flared; her head jerked.

"No!" she whispered.

"Anna!" wailed Fishcake. He squidged himself back against the cold bars of the gate as she struggled with herself. She shook herself and came towards him. She grabbed his chin, twisting his face upward. She was not Anna any more. What had made her change? Had the fight with the other Stalkers tripped some circuit in her head? Or had Fishcake done it himself, by reminding her of what she was? He shook with sobs, wishing there was some way he could bring Anna back.

"What is this place?" she hissed, listening to the wind in the trees, the lap of waves along the lake-shore. "How long was the Error in control?"

"D-doctor Popjoy," was all that Fishcake could say, through his tears. "He lives here. . ."

"Popjoy?"

"Anna thought, she thought. . ."

"She thought that he could make her even stronger," the Stalker whispered, and gave a hissing laugh.

"What about Sathya?" he said. "What about my horse? Remember. . ."

"Be silent." She let Fishcake go and went over to the ruined Stalkers, who were falling still at last. Bending down, she felt across the ground until she found a wrenched-off head. She unplugged one of the cables from her own skull and inserted it into a socket on the head. The dead Stalker's eyes began to glow again. She lifted the head and held it up in front of her like a lantern. As she swung it towards Fishcake he understood that she was looking out at him through its eyes. He wondered if she was disappointed, after all their time together, to see how small and frail he was.

"Come," was all she said. "We will see Popjoy, as the Error intended. I will make him expunge her permanently."

Fishcake wanted to run, but he went with her instead, as he always did. He didn't know what "expunge" meant, but he could guess. He wanted to hold his Stalker's hand, in the hope that his touch might somehow bring Anna back, but she was not in a hand-holding mood; she flapped him away and went limping fiercely along in front of him, still holding up the baleful head.

As they neared the house a dozen big Stalker-birds launched themselves from the trees outside and began to circle the intruders, closer and closer, slivers of light falling from their beaks and claws. Fishcake tried to hide himself in the folds of his Stalker's filthy robe, but she just raised her arms and whispered to the birds in some battle-code, and they settled meek and watchful on the lawns, waiting for her next instruction.

The front door was ironwood, bound and studded with actual iron, but it splintered easily under a few kicks from the Stalker Fang's good leg. Behind it lay a pillared atrium where a Resurrected butler lumbered out of an alcove to bar the way. "WHAT IS YOUR BUSINESS?" it droned.

"I have come to meet my maker," replied the Stalker Fang in her usual, cool whisper. She smashed the butler to pieces and left its wreckage scattered on the tiles. Fishcake scurried after her across the atrium, through another shredded door and down three stairs into a sunken den walled with soft draperies and lit by the toffee-coloured glow from three tall uplighters. A small, bald-headed old man was rising from his couch to ask what the commotion was about. He went very still when he recognized his visitor. A glass fell from his hand, splashing wine across the carpet.

"Keep away! My birds will fetch help! They'll fly to Batmunkh Gompa and. . ."

"Your birds are under my control now, Dr Popjoy," whispered the Stalker. "Stupid creatures, but they have their uses." She moved towards him, swinging the head in her outstretched hand so that the light from its eyes swept the room. Fishcake glimpsed things running away – Stalkerized insects and animals, a dog with the head of a dead girl. On a plate balanced on the arm of Popjoy's couch sat a neat wedge of fruitcake, which Fishcake snatched and crammed into his mouth. Eating messily, he pushed open a door in the far wall and looked through into some sort of workshop; cadavers on slabs and shelves heaped high with curious machinery.

"It wasn't me!" Popjoy was whimpering, assuming that the Stalker Fang had come for revenge. "I didn't know Shrike would attack you! It was all that girl's doing; that Zero girl! She's dead now; did you hear? The Townies got her, down in Africa. Naga's quite cut up about it, they say; sticks to his quarters and won't issue orders. Everyone will be relieved to hear that you're back! You'll be on your way to Tienjing, I suppose? To reclaim power? I can help you. . ."

"Tienjing no longer matters," whispered the Stalker, holding the head out to stare at him. "The Green Storm no longer matters. The world will not be made green again by air-fleets and guns and the squabbling of the once-born."

"Of course not, of course not." Popjoy edged away until he was pressed against a wall and could edge no further. His face shone sweatily in the green light. "So what can I do for you, Excellency? What small service can this feeble once-born offer. . .?"

The Stalker did not answer at once. She moved the severed head, following the flight of a Resurrected bee around a lamp on a side-table. Then, in a voice softer even than her usual graveyard whisper she said, "I remember things."

"Ah. . ."

"I remember being Anna Fang."

"Oh? Interesting." Fishcake, who was watching from behind the sofa, could see that Popjoy really *was* interested, despite his fear.

"The memories overwhelm me sometimes," the Stalker confessed. "It has been worse since I reached Shan Guo. Sometimes it is as if I *become* her. . ."

"Then the stuff I installed has started to work at last!" cried Popjoy triumphantly. "The damage you suffered must have dislodged something, or perhaps in repairing itself your brain has made some connection that I could not achieve with my crude instruments. . ."

"How is it possible?" demanded the Stalker. "Are they real memories?"

"Hard to say," mused Popjoy. "How do you define a real memory? But it's nothing to be frightened of. I think I can correct it. . . May I take a look? Inside?" He tapped his own bald head, and grinned, his fear replaced by a nervous excitement. "If you could wait till morning, when my laboratory assistants arrive to help me with my little retirement projects. . ."

"No." The Stalker Fang was already moving towards Popjoy's workshop. "No one must know that I am here. You will do it now. The boy can help you."

The workshop stank of death and chemicals. Racks on the walls held shiny displays of scalpels and bone-saws. Fishcake, who still didn't trust the old Engineer, helped himself to a long, thin-bladed knife and hid it inside his coat.

The Stalker Fang shoved a cluttered bench aside and

knelt down on the floor, in the spill of light from a hanging argon-globe. Kneeling, her bowed head reached halfway up Popjoy's chest. The Engineer circled her, licking his lips and fidgeting. "You, boy," he snapped, holding out his hand to Fishcake without ever looking at him. "Pass me that tray. . ."

The tray was metal, covered with delicate, finely-made instruments. It rattled and clattered in Fishcake's shaking hands as he passed it over. The instruments made a mockery of the crude tools he had used to repair his Stalker. He saw the Engineer wince at the sight of the cheap iron bolts with which he had fixed her death mask in place.

"Who made these repairs? A real bodge-job. . ."

"The child has done well," said the Stalker, and Fishcake felt proud.

Popjoy had surgeon's fingers; slender and clever. Within half a minute he had the mask off, baring the dead woman's face beneath. Another half minute and the top of her skull-piece came free and was laid on a table. "Lamp, boy," he said, and strapped the small torch which Fishcake passed him around his head. He peered down into the tangle of machinery and preserved brain-tissue inside the Stalker's skull.

"Sometimes she is just Anna, for days and days," said Fishcake, hoping that Popjoy would take the hint, destroy the Stalker part of her and save his Anna. "It was the Anna bit that wanted to come here, so you could help her. I think Anna Fang is trapped inside her somewhere, and sometimes when she remembers who she is the Stalkerish side shuts down. . ."

"The ghost in the machine. . ." Popjoy looked at him and winked. "I'm afraid not, lad. Nobody returns from the Sunless Country, you know." He selected a long, thin probe from the tray and inserted it into a crevice of the Stalker's brain. The Stalker's head lifted with a jerk; her dry lips moved; she whispered, "Stilton. . . I'm so sorry. I didn't want to hurt you, but it was the only way. . ."

"Anna?" said Fishcake eagerly.

Her eyeless, desiccated face turned towards him. "Fishcake?"

"It's her!" Fishcake told Popjoy, "Keep her! Hold on to her! Don't let the other one come back!"

Popjoy was busy with his probes and instruments. He didn't even bother to look at Fishcake. "You have it all wrong, boy," he said. "These memories aren't a person. They're just residue which the Stalker-brain has scoured out of the dead brain-cells of the host. Eighteen years too late, mind, but better than never. . ."

Something sparked, down inside the Stalker's head; the flash lit up the inside of her mouth, which had fallen open. She jerked again, and said, "No tricks, Popjoy."

"What, you think I'd sabotage my finest work?" cried Popjoy, hurt. "I am just making a few minor adjustments."

"You have found the Error? The memories? Remove them!"

"Great Quirke, certainly not!"

"Remove them!"

"But Excellency, they are what distinguish you from the mindless Stalkers, the battle models. . . They are what make you the finest Stalker of the age; the pinnacle of Resurrection technology. . ."

Either Popjoy's words or the pleading tone that had

crept into his voice caught the Stalker's attention. She nodded cautiously, prepared at least to hear him out.

"Those memories have always been there, submerged beneath the surface," the Engineer explained. "They give you levels of experience and emotion which no other Stalker of mine can draw on. Recently, thanks to the damage Mr Shrike inflicted, they have become intense, overwhelming your conscious mind. But we should soon be able to strike a healthy balance."

"What are they?" insisted the Stalker. "Where have they come from? Why do I remember being Anna?"

"I'm really not sure," admitted Popjoy, groping for a tiny pair of pliers and setting to work. "The fact is, the brain I fitted you with isn't quite like anything else I've ever seen. Certainly not one of those clunky modern models we London Engineers built, and not like old Mr Shrike's, either. It's much older, and much stranger.

"You see, when your friend Sathya first took me to Rogue's Roost all those years ago and ordered me to bring Anna Fang back to life, I panicked a bit. I knew it was impossible. So to buy myself some time I set up an expedition and took a Green Storm airship out into the Ice Wastes, hunting for an Old-Tech site that I'd heard rumours of ever since I was an Apprentice in dear old London. The Engineers had looked for it, but never found it. I had better luck. Right up to the top of the world we went; so far north we started going south again. And there, half buried in the snows of a tiny, frozen island, we found a complex built by some forgotten culture which must have flourished in the days before the Nomad Empires. Inside the central pyramid sat a dozen dead men and women on stone thrones.

Some had been crushed by roof-falls or encased in ice, but there were a few who, when we entered their chamber, began to whisper to us in languages we couldn't identify. They were Stalkers, of a sort, although they had no armour or weapons, and they'd clearly not been built to fight."

"Then why?" asked Fishcake's Stalker.

"I think they were built to remember," said Popjoy. He rummaged in a drawer for a set of Stalker's eyes and started wiring them into his patient's empty sockets. "I think that when a great leader of that culture died, their scientist-priests would take the body to the pyramid at the top of the world and stick a machine in their head and there they'd sit, *remembering*. They'd remember all the things they'd done in life, and pass on those memories to their successors, and tell the stories of the times they lived in so they'd never be forgotten. Except they *were* forgotten, of course; their culture vanished from the earth, and the Nomad Empires who came after them picked up a crude version of the same technology and used it to build undead warriors like old Mr Shrike.

"That pyramid was the only relic of the first Stalker-builders, and I'm afraid my Green Storm minders dynamited it for fear some other scavenger would stumble on the secret. But in one of the smaller buildings, among a lot of religious paraphernalia and irrelevant old texts, I unearthed an almost complete Stalker brain. I took it back to Rogues' Roost for study and repairs, connected it to a brain of my own design which controls your motor functions and such-like, and installed the whole caboodle in the carcass of old Anna Fang."

The Stalker tilted her head on one side. "So *am* I Anna Fang?" she asked.

"No, Excellency," said Popjoy. "You are a machine which can access some of the memories of Anna Fang. And they give you strength." He replaced her mask and skull-piece, fastening them into place with neat new bolts. "You want to make the world green again; you yearn for it. That's not because you have been set to obey Green Storm instructions, like some brainless battle-Stalker, but because you can subconsciously remember how much Anna Fang wanted it; you can remember what the townies did to her, and to her family, and how it felt when those things happened. Her memories, those feelings, are what drive you."

"I remember dying," said the Stalker, not in the hesitant voice of Anna but in her own harsh hiss. "I remember that night at Batmunkh Gompa. The sword in my heart, so cold and sudden, and then that sweet boy kneeling over me, saying my name, and I couldn't answer him. . . I remember it all."

She unplugged her cable from the severed Stalker head and slung it aside. When she reinserted the cable into her own skull her new eyes filled slowly with green light. "Now it is time for us to go."

She stood, and turned, and Popjoy's smile faded. "Excellency, you can't leave now! I need to make further tests and observations! With your help I might be able to make more like you! I've spent so many years trying to repeat my success with you, and all I've been able to turn out are tin soldiers and silly curiosities. . ."

"You have an airship?"

"Yes. A yacht, in the hangar behind the house. Why?"

"I am not Anna Fang," said the Stalker thoughtfully. "But I am here to do what she would have wanted. I shall take your ship, and fly to Erdene Tezh. There I shall speak with ODIN."

"No!" said Popjoy. "No!"

"You have heard of ODIN, I see."

"My old Guild. . . But even they. . . It was impossible, the codes are lost. . ."

"The codes are found," the Stalker said. "They were recorded in the Tin Book of Anchorage. I saw them on Cloud 9. I have carried them safe in my head ever since."

"It's madness! I mean, ODIN. . . Don't you understand the power of it?"

"Of course. It is the power to make the world green again. Where the Storm has failed, ODIN will succeed."

Popjoy clenched his plump hands into fists, as if he was about to attack her. "But Excellency, what if it goes wrong? We barely understand these Ancient devices. Remember MEDUSA! ODIN would be incomparably more dangerous than MEDUSA. . ."

The Stalker's claws slid from her finger-ends. "Your opinion is irrelevant, Doctor. You are no longer needed."

"But, but you *do* need me! Your memory problems. . . With the right trigger, they could flare up again. . . No!"

The Stalker Fang caught him as he tried to dodge past her to the door. "Thank you for your assistance, Doctor," she whispered.

Fishcake shut his eyes tight and covered his ears, but he could not quite block out the crunch and spatter of Popjoy's dying. When he looked again his Stalker was helping herself to things from the shelves; fragments of circuitry, wires and ducts, the brains of lesser Stalkers.

The walls of the workshop had been redecorated with eye-catching slashes of red.

"Find food and water for yourself, boy," she whispered. "I shall need your help when we reach Erdene Tezh."

22

WREN NATSWORTHY INVESTIGATES

London (!!!)
28th May

I've always thought that only smug, self-satisfied people keep diaries, but so much has happened in the past few days that I know I'll forget half of it if I don't write it down, so I have cadged this notebook off of Clytie Potts and made a promise to myself to write a journal of my time in London. Maybe if we ever get back to the Hunting Ground I can turn it into a book, like one of Prof Pennyroyal's. (Only true!)

It seems hard to believe that it is only two days since we arrived in the debris fields. So much has happened, and I have met so many new people, and found out so much, that it feels as if I have been here a year at least.

I'll try to start at the beginning. After our meeting with the Lord Mayor, Mr Garamond and some of his young warriors took Dad back to where we left the Jenny Haniver and made him move her round into the same secret hangar where the Archaeopteryx is kept. They say she will be safer there, and won't be seen by the Green Storm spy-birds which cruise over from time to time. But I think it's also so they can keep an eye on her; they keep saying we're not prisoners, but they obviously don't want us sneaking off. They seem terrified that we'll tell some other city that they're here, which seems a bit pathetic – I mean, what do they have that another city would want to cross hundreds of miles of Storm Country to eat?

Later, after an evening meal in the communal canteen, we were all three of us brought to this house, which is to be our home while we're in London. I say house, but it's really just a sort of hut; a lot of sheets of old metal bolted and welded together at the base of one of the old brake-blocks which supports Crouch End's roof. There are wire grilles over the window-holes, but I don't know if they've been put there to keep us from escaping or just because there's no glass in London. Inside there are three rooms, linked by a lot of winding passages, the floors dug down into the ground so that we can stand upright inside. It's a little damp, but homely enough, and close enough to the edge of Crouch End that the sun shines in for a half-hour or so in the evenings, which is nice. Dad has the biggest room, Wolf is next to him, and I have chosen for myself a little semi-circular chamber at the back; one wall is made from an old tin advertising sign (Stick-Phast Paste – Accept No Imitations), and I have a window that lets in a little sunlight, and the light of the moon some nights.

I thought that Wolf would try to escape or something, but he seems quite content at the moment, very interested in this little world the

Londoners have made for themselves. He's a strange person. It's hard to tell what he is thinking.

Dad is just glad to be home, of course. I was half hoping he'd find True Love with Clytie Potts, but it turns out she's married (to an Engineer called Lurpak Flint, who flies her airship for her, so she's not just Clytie Potts and Cruwys Morchard but Clytie Flint as well – I've never known a woman with quite so many names).

29th May

I think I like London. It's funny, I've come so far, and I've ended up in a place that's very like Anchorage-in-Vineland. It's secret, and hidden, and so small that everyone knows everyone else, which is both good and bad. Sometimes I think I can't wait to get back on the Bird Roads, but at other times I wish I was a Londoner myself. And it's beautiful. You wouldn't think there would be beauty in a great smashed-up heap of rubbish, but there is. In all the clefts and stretches of open earth, trees and ferns grow, and in every soil-filled nook among the debris too. Birds sing here; insects buzz about. Angie says that in another month the scrapheaps above Crouch End will be pink with foxgloves.

Angie is my best friend here. (Her name is short for Ford Anglia – her dad, Len Peabody, named all his children after Old-Tech ground-cars.) She's sensible and funny, which is a good combination, and she reminds me of a badger or a mole or *something; small and stocky and slightly furry, always busy with something. She's been all over the debris fields, because she goes on patrol with Garamond's militia, keeping an eye out for intruders and the Green Storm. All the young Londoners are always going off on patrol, or hunting, or scouring about for salvage in the farthest corners of the wreck. I suppose the Emergency Committee think it's a way of using up all that teenage energy. I'd like to go with them, and use up some of mine, but Garamond says I can't, because he still doesn't trust me. What a fuss-pot that man is! He says that me and Wolf (Wolf and I?) have to spend our days helping the old folk dig over the vegetable plots, or listening to Dad talk History with Mr Pomeroy.*

2nd June

For all their kindness I am starting to feel sure the Londoners are hiding something from us. Wolf has said this from the first, but I thought he was wrong. Now I'm starting to believe him. It's just little things; like the way people look at us, and the way Dr Childermass kept shushing Len Peabody that first morning – what was she afraid he'd tell us? Sometimes, when Dad and Wolf and I go into the communal canteen in the middle of Crouch End where everybody eats, people who are deep in conversation about something suddenly stop and start talking about the weather instead. And when Dad asked Clytie Potts why she had been collecting Kliest Coils and other bits of Electric Empire technology she went all red and changed the subject.

Last night, I heard voices outside again while I was trying to get to sleep, so I went to my window and pulled the curtain aside (it's just a bit of old sack really) and what do you think I saw? Engineers! Lavinia Childermass and half a dozen others! They were leaving Crouch End and walking off up a track that leads eastward over a steep ridge of debris. Where were they going? It looked a lot more purposeful than just a moonlit stroll. Do they do this every night? Maybe that's we why I hardly ever see any of the Engineers around in the daytime – they must be catching up on their sleep!

Well, I always dreamed of being a daring schoolgirl detective, like Milly Crisp in those books I used to read when I was little. So this afternoon I wandered off on my own up that track that I saw the Engineers taking last night. From the top of the ridge you can see it winding on across the debris fields for about half a mile, towards a really big, wedge-shaped chunk of wreckage that looks as if it must have been a section of London's Gut.

Nobody about, but something flashed in one of the holes or window-openings in the side of that big old chunk. Then, all of a sudden, I heard footsteps behind me and there was Mr Garamond with a couple of his favourite young warriors, Angie's brother Saab and a girl called Cat Luperini. "What are you doing here?" he shouted, all purple with rage, nearly as cross and ugly as Mum. I tried to explain that I'd just felt like stretching my legs, but he wouldn't have any of it. "You're on the edge of a hot zone!" he shouted, and Cat got hold of me and started steering me back towards Crouch End. Saab leaned over and said, "You mustn't go wandering off like this, Wren. That's a dangerous part of the fields. We don't want you to get crisped by a sprite."

He was quite kind about it, actually. I like Saab. But if that part of the wreckage is so dangerous, why is there such a well-trodden track leading through the middle of it?

Later, I talked about some of this with Wolf. He doesn't believe in the sprites at all. When I reminded him about the one that almost fried us on our first day here he just laughed and said it had been "remarkably well-timed". He thinks the sprites are a sort of trick the Engineers have dreamed up to keep people out of the wreck. He's got a point, hasn't he? I mean, if they can make those electric anti-Stalker guns, why not sprites too?

Well, I'm not going to let stupid old Garamond put me off. He leaves a couple of his people on guard outside our hut at night, for fear we'll try and run off to sell this little static to a predator, but the guards don't really believe we will, and they usually just chat and then fall asleep. Tonight, as soon as all is quiet, I am going to creep out and see what's really going on in that *big old wedge of rust they have out there.*

(If this is the last entry in this journal, you'll know that Wolf is wrong about the sprites, and I've been roasted crispier than Milly Crisp herself. . .)

Wren put away her pencil, slipped her notebook into the inside pocket of her flying-jacket and lay waiting. She listened to Tom's soft, steady breathing coming through the gaps in the tin wall from the room next door, and wondered what he was dreaming about. Did he have any suspicions about the Londoners? He had not said anything. He just seemed happy to be home.

In the room to her right she could hear Wolf moving about. Little metal noises; clicks and scrapings. What was he up to? Outside, Mr Garamond's guards spoke softly to one another.

Wren did not remember going to sleep, but she must have done, because she woke suddenly to find that the luminous hands of her wristwatch stood at half past three.

"Oh Clio!" she groaned, rolling off her bedding and scrambling to her feet.

She went to the door and looked out into the narrow passage. For some reason she felt uneasy. Wolf's door was half-open, moonlight spilling through. She crept to it, and peered into his tiny room. His bed-roll was empty. Wren ran to the window, and stifled a cry as the steel-mesh shutter came free in her hands. Wolf had unfastened it somehow, and hung it back in position after he climbed out so that the guards would not notice anything wrong.

"Oh, Gods!" Wren whispered, thinking of the *Jenny*

Haniver. She had not forgotten the ruthless streak in Wolf's nature. What if he were already creeping away through the debris fields to steal the *Jenny*? How long had he been gone? Was it the sound of his going that had woken her?

She scrambled out under the loosened grille and peeked around the corner of the hut. The guards were sitting on the doorstep, bored and sleepy; one was already snoring, and the other's head was nodding. Wren tiptoed away, then ran between the silent shacks and huts and out of Crouch End. The ruins of London were a maze of stark moonlight and inky shadows. Eastward, a figure showed for a moment on the spiky skyline.

Wolf! Wren started after him, relieved that at least he was not heading for the *Jenny*. So what *was* he doing? Snooping about, she guessed, just as she had been planning to snoop. It annoyed her to think that he had beaten her to it. She had wanted to learn London's secrets herself, and impress him with her discoveries over breakfast. . .

She started to go after him, up the track that she had taken earlier. She told herself there was no reason to be afraid; the Londoners were softies, and even if they caught her they would do nothing worse than return her to her prison and screw the window-grilles down tighter. But she could not help feeling tense, and when a shape suddenly stepped out of the shadows beside the path to grab her she cried out loudly and shrilly.

An arm went round her middle, and a strong hand covered her mouth. She twisted her head around and saw Wolf Kobold's face above her in the moonlight. "Shhhh," he said softly. His hand left her mouth, but lingered for a moment on her face. "Wren. . . What are you doing out here?"

"Looking for you, of course," she said, her voice wobbling slightly. "Where are you going?"

Wolf grinned, and released her. He pointed along the moonlit road to the enormous segment of wreckage which lay ahead. In some of the openings lights were moving about, bobbing like marsh-lanterns.

"Listen!" he said.

Across the wastes of moonlit metal came a low rumbling noise, rising and falling, then cutting out altogether. White light flashed and flickered out of the openings in the hulk.

"Sprite?" asked Wren.

Wolf shook his head. "Machinery of some sort. The same sound I heard two years ago."

"Engineers come up here at night," she whispered, hoping to impress him with her discoveries.

Wolf just nodded. "I've seen them too. And I've seen people bringing crates up here; crates filled with salvage from the debris fields. And Engineers poring over plans. Why? What are they building in there, Wren?"

Wren felt a little annoyed that he had found out more than her. Milly Crisp never had this sort of competition. She tried to look as if his findings came as no surprise to her.

"Let's find out, shall we?"

Side by side they hurried on, and soon reached the Gut-segment. It really was immense; a sea-cliff pitted with countless caves where ducts and corridors had once linked it to the rest of London. Wolf clambered in through one of them, and reached back to haul Wren up behind him. "It looks like some kind of factory from

London's Deep Gut," he whispered. "It seems to have survived almost intact. . ."

They moved deeper. The floors were tilted at a slight angle, making walking tricky. Metallic noises echoed along the drippy corridors. They reached a bolted door, retraced their steps, climbed a flight of sloping, metal stairs. They passed a wall stencilled with the symbol of a red wheel and the words *London Guild of Engineers: Experimental Hangar 14*. The higher corridors were lit by shafts of stuttering white and orange light that grew brighter as Wren and Wolf crept on into the heart of the building. The steady, reassuring glow of argon-lamps shone through hanging curtains of transparent plastic.

Wren felt more excited than afraid now. She let her hand brush against Wolf's, and he gripped it and squeezed it reassuringly as he pushed the curtains aside.

Together, hand in hand, they looked down into an immense open space at the centre of the hangar.

"Great Gods!" Wren whispered.

"So that's it!" said Wolf.

"Put your hands up, Mr Kobold," said another voice, quite close behind them. "You too, Miss Natsworthy. Both of you, put your hands up and turn around very slowly."

23

THE CHILDERMASS EXPERIMENT

"Hester?" mumbled Tom, waking slowly. He had been dreaming of the old London Museum again, but this time it had been Hester who was leading him through the dusty galleries. In his dream, he had been happy to see her.

Now someone was crouching beside his bed, shaking him. He remembered that it could not be Hester, and sat up. A lantern dazzled him. He turned his head away, and saw a couple of Garamond's boys in the doorway. The person who had woken him was Clytie Potts.

"There's a problem, Tom. It's Kobold and your daughter. Oh, they're quite all right, but – I think you'd better come. . ."

Out across the ruins. Moonlight and scrap-metal. Clytie walked with Tom, the two of them surrounded by silent Londoners, some carrying guns.

"What has Wren been doing?" he asked as they hurried him along.

"Spying," said Clytie. "She and Kobold were found . . . where they should not be."

"Wren's just a girl!" Tom protested. "She may be inquisitive and foolish, but she's not a spy! What was she spying *on,* anyway? What is this place you found her in?"

"Easier to show you than explain," said Clytie.

Tom pulled his coat more tightly around him. It wasn't just the cold that made him shiver. He had a feeling that he was close to learning the secret of his city. Had Wren discovered it already for herself? Was that was this was all about? He felt proud of her bravery, but worried, too, in case she was in danger.

In an open doorway at the foot of a wall of wreckage Dr Childermass and five of her fellow Engineers stood waiting; six bald heads like a clutch of eggs. "Mr Natsworthy," said the Engineer, with a faint, weary smile. "You may as well see the project. No doubt your daughter and her friend will tell you about it anyway. As long as we can dissuade our more excitable colleagues from shooting them, that is."

Up a stairway, through a plastic curtain, and out on to a narrow metal viewing platform where Garamond and a gaggle of his people stood around Wren and Wolf Kobold. They had both been made to kneel, and their hands were tied. Dr Childermass said, "Oh, don't be such a twerp, Mr Garamond!"

"They were in a restricted area! Spying!" Garamond complained.

"Only because you let them come here," retorted the Engineer. "Really, Garamond, your people are appallingly slack. Now let them go."

Garamond and his young followers reluctantly freed their prisoners and let them stand. Tom ran to hug Wren, intending to tell her how foolish she'd been, but just as he reached her he noticed what lay below, filling the hangar, and surprise drove all the words out of his head.

It was a town. Not a large town, nor a very elegant one (most of the buildings on its upper deck were missing and there were no wheels or tracks) but a town none the less. It had no jaws, but in most other ways it seemed to Tom to match the basic blueprint of a London suburb; those small places like Tunbridge Wheels and Crawley which London had built to carry her excess population during the golden age of Municipal Darwinism.

"Pretty, isn't it?" asked Clytie, gazing down with a look of awe and affection at the unfinished town.

Dr Childermass said, "The fruit of many, many years of hard work, now nearing completion."

A big saw was at work somewhere beneath the town, which was resting on a cradle of rusty stanchions. A spray of sparks scattered across the hangar floor like boisterous glow-worms.

"You *built* this?" asked Tom, letting go of Wren and moving over to stand at the edge of the platform, gripping the pitted metal of the handrail to convince himself that it was not all a dream.

"Not quite," said the Engineer. "The chassis and most of the upperworks were here already. My division began working on this project long before MEDUSA. Luckily this experimental hangar was deep enough in the Gut to survive without too much damage."

"But why didn't I know about it?" Tom wondered. "I mean, if London was building a whole new suburb, surely it would have been news?"

Dr Childermass shrugged. "It was a secret. My Guild was very keen on secrecy. Anyway, this little place was only intended as a prototype. Experimental Suburb M/L1 is its official designation. We designed it as an answer to London's problems, but Magnus Crome was never keen on it. He thought that MEDUSA was a better solution, and gradually he withdrew more and more funding from my Mag-Lev Research Division and diverted it to MEDUSA. Now, those of us who survived MEDUSA's failure have been able to pick up the work. It is not just the Engineers' project any more, Tom. Everyone in London has worked together on it."

"And please don't think of it as a suburb," said Clytie. "It may be small, but to everyone in London it is a city; our new city. Soon we shall climb aboard it and leave these debris fields behind for ever."

Tom gazed down at the tiny forms of Londoners clambering over the new city, laying cables, welding girders, marking out the shapes of streets and buildings on the bare deckplates.

"But it's got no wheels," Wren pointed out.

"I can see you don't know what Mag-Lev stands for, my dear," said Dr Childermass.

"It's a code-name, isn't it?" asked Tom, who didn't know either.

"Oh no," Dr Childermass said. "Mag-Lev is just a shorter way of saying Magnetic Levitation."

"It floats!" said Wolf, gazing down at the new city entranced. "Like a gigantic hovercraft. . ."

Dr Childermass gave him a graceful nod, pleased that at least one of her listeners was keeping up. "Rather quieter than a hovercraft, Herr Kobold, and not nearly so hungry for fuel. More like a very large, low-flying airship. You see those silvery discs along the flanks and underbelly?"

Tom, Wren and Wolf nodded in unison. There was no missing the discs; dirty metal mirrors fifty feet across, swivel-mounted like an airship's engine pods.

"Those are what I call Magnetic Repellors. Once they

are powered, the whole city will be able to swim in the currents of the earth's magnetic field. It will hang a few feet above the ground – or above the water, indeed; it makes no difference. The small prototypes we made worked splendidly. All we need do now is to complete the electro-magnetic engine which powers the repellors—"

"The Kliest Coils!" cried Wren, like a plucky schoolgirl detective making a brilliant deduction.

"Yes," admitted Dr Childermass. "We were having trouble generating enough power, until Mr Pomeroy told me about Dr Kliest's work on the Electric Empire machines. I guessed at once that something like that was what we needed. Clytie has managed to acquire several dozen, along with the materials we need to fabricate new ones."

Wren glanced at Wolf, and saw him gripping the handrail and staring at the little city with the wide, shining eyes of someone who has been granted a vision of the future.

"So you see why we're nervous about spies," said Clytie Potts. "It's taken us nearly twenty years to put New London together. We'd hate a scavenger to get wind of it now that we're so nearly finished."

"New London!" said Tom softly. "Of course. . ." You could not go on calling a place "Experimental Suburb M/L1" for ever; not if you meant to live aboard it, and carry the culture and memories of your city away on it to new lands. *New London.*

"I'll help!" he said. "I mean, if you can use me. I can't stay here, eating your food, getting in your way, doing nothing while you all do so much. I'm a Londoner. I want to see London move again as much as any of you.

I'm no Engineer, but I kept the *Jenny Haniver* ticking over all right, and at Anchorage I helped Mr Scabious build the hydro-electric system. I'll stay, and help. . . That is, if Wren doesn't mind. . ."

"Of course I don't," said Wren, and Tom could see that she was just as impressed as him by New London. "And I expect Mr Kobold will want to help too," she said, turning to draw their companion into the conversation.

But Wolf Kobold was gone. While everyone was listening to Dr Childermass and looking down at New London, he had slipped silently away.

Garamond turned white and started shouting things about securing the perimeter and organizing searches. Dr Childermass stared hard at him. "See?" she said. "Slack."

❧ ❧ ❧ ❧

News of Wolf's escape went ahead of Tom and Wren. By the time they reached Crouch End they found search parties being organized, armed with crowbars, crossbows and even lightning guns. "We'll catch 'im!" Angie Peabody vowed, buckling on a quiverful of crossbow-bolts. "He ain't going to sell New London out to no dirty pirate suburb."

"Oh, be careful," Wren warned. "He's dangerous. . ."

"There are dozens of us and only one of your friend, Miss Natsworthy," snapped Mr Garamond. "And we know these debris fields a lot better than him. It's Kobold who's in danger, not us. Come along everyone! Move out!"

"We'll come with you," said Tom.

"I think not, Mr Natsworthy. As far as I'm concerned,

you and your daughter are Kobold's accomplices. You're staying here."

"Nonsense, Garamond," snapped Chudleigh Pomeroy, emerging from his hut in dressing-gown and nightcap. "Tom and Wren have as much to lose as any of us. Kobold is probably planning to make off aboard that airship of theirs."

Wren hugged her father. "You stay here, Daddy," she said, and, snatching a lantern, ran off with Angie and her brother Saab. Tom watched them go; the bobbing lamps disappearing into the hillocks of scrap, Mr Garamond yelling orders which were meant to be military but made him sound like a panicky teacher in charge of a school outing. "At the double! Work in pairs! Watch where you're pointing that Lightning Gun, Spandex Thrale!"

Fanning out across the rubble, the searchers moved away from Crouch End, combing every path and cranny of the rust-hills for traces of Wolf. "He can't have got far," Wren heard people whispering. *But he could*, she thought; *he's a soldier; he's already made his way back to Harrowbarrow once before; hundreds of miles through Green Storm territory. Hiding from us in a maze the size of London won't be hard.*

At least he had not made it to the airship-hangar yet. The *Jenny* and the *Archaeopteryx* sat where they had been left, untouched. Garamond loudly detailed Saab and a few others to reinforce the guard on them, and the search parties moved on.

"It's useless," said Wren miserably, as she and Angie tramped away from the hangar, along that narrow path she had come in by on the first day. "He could be anywhere. He's skilled at hiding. His whole *suburb* hides."

"Oof!" said Angie.

It seemed a funny sort of reply. Wren turned to look at her friend, and found herself, for the second time that night, unexpectedly face to face with Wolf Kobold.

"You've found me, Wren!" he said brightly. "Now it's your turn to hide. . ."

He stooped over Angie, who had crumpled at his feet, knocked down by a blow from behind with some heavy object – there was no shortage of blunt instruments in the debris fields. Wren opened her mouth to scream for help, but before she could force a sound out Wolf straightened up again, pointing Angie's crossbow at her.

Wren wasn't sure if she was supposed to raise her hands or not. She flapped her arms uncertainly, wondering if Angie were alive or dead. "You'll never get away!" she said. "There are guards in the airship hangar, with lightning guns. . ."

"I don't need an airship, Wren," said Wolf, laughing. "I thought once that the Engineers' secret might be something I could carry away aboard your *Jenny Haniver*, but now I've seen how wrong I was. I shall have to bring Harrowbarrow east. . ." Keeping the crossbow pointed at her he started pulling off Angie's belt, with its quiver of bolts and canteen of water. "Look, I have all I need for a trek across the Out-Country. I'll ride on one of the Storm's convenient Stalker-trains. Hausdorfer will have Harrowbarrow waiting for me just across the line." He grinned at Wren, and held out one hand. "Why not come with me?"

"What?"

"You're wasted in the life you lead, Wren. Trailing about after your dad. How long is he going to keep you trapped here, skivvying for these mudlarks? Come home to Harrowbarrow with me."

"And watch it eat New London?" asked Wren. "I don't think so."

"Then think harder. This new technology the lady Engineer has developed is wasted on the Londoners. Well-meaning fools! They haven't even put jaws on their new city. I'm going to take it for myself, and use it to make Harrowbarrow the most powerful predator on earth. A *flying* predator, armed with electric weapons! Think of it!"

Wren was. She didn't like it.

Wolf laughed again, and blew her a kiss as he turned away. "There'll always be a place for you in my Town Hall, Wren," he said.

Wren bent over Angie. The girl groaned as Wren touched her face, which she hoped was a good sign. "Help!" she screamed, as loudly as she could. "Help! Help! He's here! Over here!"

They came running: Saab, Garamond, Cat Luperini. Someone with more medical know-how than Wren bent over Angie and said, "She'll be fine, she'll be fine." But of Wolf there was no sign, and although the others kept hunting him until the sky above the wreck turned grey with morning he was not sighted again; he had faded away, as if he had been just another of London's ghosts.

PART TWO

24
MANCHESTER

The clang and tremor of docking clamps engaging shook Oenone from her dreams. She struggled to stay asleep, but the dull, hungry ache in her belly kept nagging at her, and she came awake groggily. She had been dreaming of home; the islands of Aleutia; grey stone and grey sky and grey winter sea, she and her brother Eno haring downhill in the sharp cold. The images faded quickly in the stuffy heat of the *Humbug*'s hold.

It was morning. The new-risen sun was poking in through rents in the *Humbug*'s envelope. Oenone lay curled on the floor of a wire-mesh pen, surrounded by crates and boxes full of dodgy gadgets and unsold trade-goods which Napster Varley must once have hoped would make his fortune. There was no mattress in the pen, and Oenone was so stiff from sleeping on the hard deck that she could barely move. She lay there for a while, wondering what it was about her prison which seemed different this morning. Then she realized. The rattling engines which had been drilling their noise into her ears all the way from Cutler's Gulp had stopped.

She could hear voices down below her in the gondola. Varley was shouting at his wife, as usual. As usual, the baby was crying. Oenone had never known a baby that cried as much as Napster Junior.

She drank water from the tin jug Varley had left her, peed in her cracked enamel chamber pot, and said her morning prayers. By the time she had finished all was quiet below. She waited fearfully to see what would happen next.

To her relief it was not Varley who came up through the hatch, but Varley's wife. Mrs Varley was not exactly friendly towards the prisoner in the hold, but she was friendlier than her husband. She was a freckled, doughy girl with unruly red hair and frightened eyes, one of which was currently swollen shut and surrounded by yellowish bruises. Varley had bought her somewhere, and she had not made as good a wife as he had hoped. He beat her, and Oenone had often heard her screams and sobs echoing through the airship. She had come to feel a sort of comradeship with this exhausted young woman, as if they were both prisoners together.

"Napster says to give you breakfast," Mrs Varley said now, in her quivery little voice, and pushed a bowl of bread through the bars, along with half an apple.

Oenone started to shovel the food into her mouth with both hands. She felt ashamed, but she couldn't help it; a few weeks of captivity had turned her into a savage; an animal. "Where are we?" she managed to ask between mouthfuls.

"Airhaven," said Mrs Varley. She looked about fearfully, as if she was afraid her husband might be lurking among the stacks of crates, ready to leap out and black her other eye for talking to the cargo. She leaned close to the mesh of the cage. "It's a town that flies!"

"I've heard of it. . ."

"And it's above something called the Murnau cluster," Mrs Varley went on, her excitement getting the better of her fear. "There's more cities down there than I've ever seen in my life. A big fighting one, all hidden in armour, and trade towns too, and Manchester! Napster says Manchester's one of the biggest cities in the world! He read about it in one of his books. He reads a lot of books, does Napster. He's trying to improve himself. Anyway, it's lucky we got here today because there's a big meeting of mayors and bigwigs there and Napster's gone down there to. . . To see if one of them will buy you off him, Miss."

Oenone thought she was used to being helpless and afraid by now, but when she heard that, she was almost sick with fright. She had spent most of her life hearing about the cruelty of the men who ruled the Traction Cities. She forced her hands out through the mesh and snatched at Mrs Varley's skirts as the girl turned away. "Please," she said desperately. "Please, can't you let me out of here? Just let me ashore. I don't want to die on a city. . ."

"Sorry," said the girl (and she really was). "I can't. Napster'd kill me if I let you go. You know the temper he's got on him. He'd throw my baby overboard. He's often said he would."

The baby, as if it had overheard, woke up in its crib down in the gondola and began to bawl. Mrs Varley tugged her skirts out of Oenone's grasp and hurried away. "Sorry, Miss," she said, as she started down the ladder. "I have to go now. . ."

Manchester, which had been rumbling eastward all spring, detouring now and then to eat some smaller town, had finally reached the Murnau cluster the previous afternoon. Bigger and brasher than the fighting city, it squatted like a smug mountain a few miles behind the front line. Its jaws hung half-open; officially so that its maintenance crews could clean its banks of rotating teeth, but it gave the impression that it had half a mind to gobble up a few of the small trading-towns which thronged around Murnau's skirts.

One by one, the towns gathered in their citizens and started to crawl away, for they all knew that Manchester's arrival meant trouble, even if didn't eat them. Adlai Browne was a well-known opponent of the truce, and most of the cities of the *Traktionstadtsgesellschaft* were in debt to him. He had poured a lot of money into their war with the Storm, and now he wanted to see something in return. His couriers, flying ahead of the city, had summoned their leaders to a council of war in Manchester Town Hall.

By nine o'clock that morning airships and cloud-yachts were converging on Manchester's top tier from every city and suburb on the line. Watched from a safe distance by polite crowds of onlookers, the mayors and Kriegsmarshals made their way into the Town Hall, where they took their places on the padded seats of the council chamber and waited for the Lord Mayor of Manchester to mount the steps to the speaker's pulpit. High above them, in the dome of the ceiling, painted clouds parted to let beams of painted sunlight through, and a burly young woman who was supposed to be the Spirit of Municipal Darwinism flourished a sword, putting to flight the dragons of Poverty and Anti-Tractionism. Even *her* eyes seemed fixed upon the podium beneath her, as if she too were eager to hear what Adlai Browne would say.

Browne leaned with both hands on the carved pulpit-rail, and surveyed his audience. He was a squat, florid man, whose immense wealth had made him permanently dissatisfied with everything around him. He looked like an angry toad.

"Gentlemen," he said loudly. ("And ladies," he added, remembering that there were several mayoresses among his audience, as well as Orla Twombley, leader of his own mercenary air force.) "Before we begin this historic conference of ours, I just want to say how very proud I am to be able to bring my city here, and to tell you how much your long years of sacrifice and struggle are appreciated back west, by the ordinary folk of more peaceful cities."

There was polite applause. Kriegsmarshal von Kobold leaned over to his neighbour and muttered, "It is our money they appreciate. We've paid a fortune down the years for all the guns and munitions they have sent us. No wonder Browne is scared at the thought of peace. . ."

"Now, I'm a plain-speaking fellow," Browne went on, "so I won't mince my words. I haven't just come here to pat you on the back. I'm here to stiffen you up a bit; to give you a bit of a boot up the proverbial. To remind you, in fact. . ." (He paused, letting the young man who was translating his words into New German catch up with him.) "To remind you," he went on, "that Victory is at hand! I know how much you have all welcomed this truce, this chance to open your cities to the sky again and enjoy a few months' peace. But we who dwell a little further from the battle-lines, and fight the Green Storm in our own ways, are maybe able to see a few things that you can't. And what we see right now is an opportunity to scour the earth clean for ever of the menace of Anti-Tractionism. And it is an opportunity which we must seize!"

There was another spattering of applause. Mayor Browne looked as if he had expected more, but acknowledged it anyway, turning to check who his supporters were – von Neumann of Winterthur, Dekker-Stahl from the Dortmund Conurbation, and a few dozen battle-hardened mayors from harvester-suburbs. He signalled for quiet before the applause had a chance to peter out of its own accord. "Some of you think I speak too boldly," he admitted. "But Manchester has agents in the lands of the Green Storm, and for weeks now all of them have been telling us the same thing. General Naga is a spent force. That little Aleutian dolly-bird he fell for is dead, and the old fool has lost the will to live, or fight, or do anything but sit alone in his palace and rail at the gods for taking her off him. And without Naga, the Storm is leaderless. Gentlemen, this – oh, and ladies – this is the moment to attack!"

More applause, stronger this time. Several voices called out "Well said, Browne!" and "We'll all be in Tienjing by Moon Festival!"

Kriegsmarshal von Kobold had heard enough. He stood up and shouted in his best parade-ground roar, "It would not be honourable, Herr Browne! It would not be honourable, to take advantage of Naga's grief like that! We know the real cost of war, out here on the line. Not just money, but *lives*! Not just lives, but *souls*! Our own children are turning into savages, in love with war. We must do all we can to make sure this peace lasts!"

A few people cheered him, but many more shouted for him to be quiet, to sit down and stop spouting defeatist Mossie clap-trap. Von Kobold had not realized that so many of his comrades would be ready to listen to Browne's warmongering. Had these few months of peace been enough to make them forget what war was like? Did they really think there would be any winners if they let the fighting start again? They were as bad as Wolf! He glared about him, feeling indignant and hot and foolish. Even his own staff officers looked embarrassed by his outburst. He started to shove his way along the row of seats towards the nearest exit.

"Gentleman," Adlai Browne was saying, "what I'm hoping we can thrash out today is not so much a battle plan, more a menu. The lands of the Green Storm lie before us, defended by a weary, ill-equipped army. Whole static cities like Batmunkh Gompa and Tienjing, countless forests and mineral deposits which the barbarian scum have refused to exploit, all lie waiting to be eaten. The only real question for us is how shall we divide the spoils? Which city shall eat what?"

Feeling sick, the old Kriegsmarshal pushed his way out of the council-chamber. The sounds of cheering and booing and furious arguments followed him all the way down the corridors of the Civic Hall and into the park outside, but at least out there the air was fresh and the breeze was cool. He hurried down the steps and ducked under the security barriers which Browne's people had erected to keep sightseers at bay. The crowds had gone now, except for a few picnickers on the lawns. Paper hats and placards lay strewn among the fallen blossom on the metal paths. A discarded newspaper blew past, Nimrod Pennyroyal's photograph on the front page. *Ridiculous!* thought von Kobold. The whole world tilting back into chaos and all the papers were interested in was the latest gossip about that absurd writer fellow. . .

He strode across the grass to an observation balcony. Standing against the railings he breathed in deeply, gazing eastward towards the armoured ramparts of his own city, and then east again, to no-man's-land. It was three weeks since Wolf had left Murnau. What was he doing now? Where was that nasty suburb of his? What would become of it if the war began again?

"Von Kobold?" asked someone close behind him. "Kriegsmarshal von Kobold?"

He turned, and saw an impertinent, overdressed stranger with ginger whiskers. The young man looked slightly demented. Kobold almost regretted that he had left his staff officers behind in the council hall. But he was not going to let himself be scared by a ferrety little scrub like this, so he drew himself to attention and said, "I am von Kobold."

"Varley." The stranger held out a hand, and he could think of no good excuse not to shake it. "Napster Varley," said the man, beaming at him. A gold tooth blinked like a heliograph. "I popped down here, hoping to speak to your little conference, but they wouldn't let me in. So I was hanging about, waiting for it all to finish so I could buttonhole one of you on your way back to your airships, and I noticed you wandering about. Stroke of luck, isn't it?"

"Is it?"

"Oh, it is indeed, Herr Kobold!" (*Hair* Kobold; his pronunciation made the Kriegsmarshal wince.) "You see, sir, I'm in the air-trade. A dealer in curiosities. And curious is the word for the little item I've got aboard my ship, sir, just waiting for the right buyer. So when I saw you, sir, walking through the park here, all alone, like, I said to myself, 'Napster,' I said, 'the Gods of Trade have sent him here so you can go and tell him what a bargain is waiting for him, up at Airhaven.'"

"Airhaven?" said von Kobold, and glanced to leeward, where the flying town was drifting above a haze of city-smoke a few miles away. Nobody was going to lure him to a place like that! A free port, probably a nest of Mossie spies and assassins. He stepped away from Varley and started walking back towards the Civic Hall, calling over his shoulder, "Whatever you're selling, Mr Varley, I am not interested."

"Oh, yes, you are, sir!" said the merchant, hurrying to catch him up. "Least, you will be when you find out what it is. Could be important, sir. For the war effort, like. I'm only trying to do my bit, sir."

Von Kobold stopped, wondering what on earth the man was talking about. Shady scavengers were always emerging from the Out-Country with bits of Old-Tech which they claimed would end the war. Most of them were charlatans, but you could never be sure. . . "If you think it might be important," he said, "you should take it to the authorities. Either here in Manchester, or in Murnau. They'll know what to do with it."

"Ah, but I don't suppose they'll reward me for my troubles, will they, sir? And I've taken considerable trouble to acquire this item, so I shall want a considerable reward."

"But if you are a good Municipal Darwinist and you think this thing can help us. . ."

"I'm what you might call a Municipal Darwinist second, sir," said Varley, "and a businessman first." He shrugged, and muttered, somewhat perplexingly, "Scatter cushions! Grandma had the right idea! I never thought it'd be so hard to find a buyer. . ."

Von Kobold turned away again, but before he could walk on, the merchant's hand closed on his sleeve. "Look, sir!" he said. He was holding out some sort of photograph. Von Kobold, who was too proud to wear his reading-glasses in public, could not make it out. He pushed Varley away, but the merchant stuffed the photograph into the breast pocket of his tunic and said ingratiatingly, "I expect you'll want to come and arrange a price, sir. You'll find my ship on Strut 13, Airhaven Main Ring. Varley's the name, sir. And the reserve price is ten thousand shinies. . ."

"Well, of all the infernal. . ." von Kobold started to say, but he was interrupted by the voice of his aide, Captain Eschenbach. The young man was hurrying down the steps of the civic hall, and Varley, seeing him, ducked between some nearby bushes and went scurrying away.

"Was that fellow bothering you, Kriegsmarshal?" asked Eschenbach, drawing level with von Kobold.

"No. A crackpot; nothing."

"You should come inside, sir," the young man said. "They are discussing battle plans. Deciding which city attacks which sector of the enemy's territory. Browne has bagged the static fortress called Forward Command for Manchester; Dortmund is to take everything on the east shore of the Sea of Khazak. There'll be nothing left for us, sir, if you're not quick. We don't want to lose out. . ."

"Lose out?" Von Kobold narrowed his eyes, scanning the park for Varley. There was no sign of him, unless he was aboard that balloon taxi lifting off from a platform at the tier's edge. "Is this what it has all been for?" he asked. "Just so men like Adlai Browne can turn the Storm's lands into one enormous all-you-can-eat buffet? Why can't we let them live in peace?"

Eschenbach frowned, trying hard to understand but not quite managing it. "But they're Mossies, sir."

Von Kobold started to walk towards the council hall. "Poor Naga," he said. He climbed the stairs, and went inside to fight his city's corner, forgetting all about the photograph which Napster Varley had pushed into his pocket.

THEO IN AIRHAVEN

By late afternoon the sky around Airhaven was humming with traffic. Everyone knew that Adlai Browne had brought Manchester east for the sole purpose of getting the war started again, and the air-traders were eager to do as much business as possible before they took off for safer markets, further west. To and fro between the cities and the flying town went the freighters and the overladen balloons, while high above them, ever-watchful, the Flying Ferrets wheeled like flocks of starlings. But Orla Twombley's airmen were on the lookout for Green Storm attack-ships, and they paid no attention to a greasy little Achebe 100 which came puttering out of the west that evening to slip into a cheap berth on Airhaven's docking ring.

She was called the *Shadow Aspect*, and she had been captured from the old League long ago, and converted into a merchantman. She was not much, but she was the best that Hester had been able to afford after she sold her sand-ship. All the way from Africa Hester had grumbled about her leaky cells and racketing engines, and cursed the used-airship dealer who had sold her such a death-trap. But Theo, who had been doing most of the flying, had grown used to the *Shadow*'s little ways; he secretly thought she was a fine old ship, and in the quiet of the night-watches he had whispered kindly to her, urging her on her way, "Go on; just a little longer; you can make it. . ."

And now she *had* made it; the long voyage was over, and the sight of all those cities arranged on the earth below him like monstrous chess-pieces filled Theo with anger and fear. Cities were his enemies. They had been the enemies of his people for a thousand years. What was he thinking of, coming into the heart of this vast cluster of them? He had no hope of rescuing Lady Naga from whatever prison the townies had penned her in. She would not have expected him to try; she would not want anyone to die for her sake. . .

The *Shadow*'s docking-clamps clanged against the strut. Theo cut her engines, and the sounds of Airhaven spilled into the gondola; shouts of merchants and stevedores, rattling chains, a hurdy-gurdy playing somewhere, a trader manoeuvring at the next strut. A boy with a bucket and a long-handled squeegee came running to clean the *Shadow*'s windows, but Hester waved him away, and a glimpse of her angry, hideous face was enough to send him scuttling off.

Hester was in a foul mood. She had hoped to overtake the *Humbug* in mid-air, where she thought she could board it and rescue Lady Naga with ease. But although the *Shadow Aspect* had no cargo, and four engines to the *Humbug*'s two, it had taken Hester too long to discover where Napster Varley was going, and he had beaten them to Airhaven. Boarding the *Humbug* would be difficult here, where there were harbour officials and security men and passers-by who would interfere. She looked round at Shrike, standing statue-still in the shadows at the rear of the flight-deck. "Better hide yourself, old machine," she said.

"YOU MAY NEED ME."

"Not here. There are a lot of townies aboard, and if they see you stalking about they'll think we're Green Storm. Anyway, somebody might remember your last visit, when you tore the place half to pieces looking for me and Tom. Wait in the hold; if I need you, I'll call you."

Shrike nodded, and climbed the companion-ladder into the envelope. Hester pulled up her veil, slipped on dark glasses, and opened the exit-hatch. "Coming?" she asked Theo.

The tavern called The Gasbag and Gondola had survived through all Airhaven's changes, and still occupied the same sprawling assemblage of lightweight huts that Hester remembered from her first visit to the free port. But in the intervening years the air-trade had split, like the world below, into townies and Mossies, and the Gasbag and Gondola had become a townie haunt; *No Dogs, No Mossies*, read a scrawled message in white paint above the door. The traders clustering around its small, dirty tables came from Manchester and Dortmund and Peripatetiapolis, from Nuevo Mayan steam-ziggurats and Antarctic drilling cities. Framed posters and cartoons on the walls mocked the Green Storm, and the dartboard was printed with the bronze face of the Stalker Fang.

Hester stopped at the shrine to the sky gods, just inside the door, and sighed irritably as Theo cannoned into her. She rummaged in her coat pockets and found a few pennies which she dropped into the airship-shaped charity box of the Airman's Benevolent Fund. A fat waitress bustled over, eyeing them rogueishly as if she thought that Theo was Hester's boyfriend, and that Hester had done rather well for herself. Hester felt suddenly proud, as if it were true.

"We're looking for Varley," she told the woman. "Trader. Lately in from Africa. Heard of him?"

"You're in luck. He's by the window there. Watch out though; he came back from Manchester in a nasty mood."

Outside the circular window which the waitress pointed at, the evening clouds were glowing as the sun began to set, but the young man who sat at the table beside it was not enjoying the view. He was reading a book, and reaching out from time to time to pick half-heartedly at a bowl of chargrilled locusts.

"Napster Varley?"

"Who's asking?" Varley's eyes narrowed suspiciously, looking Hester up and down. He closed his book. It was called *The Dornier Lard Way to Successful Haggling* and a dozen pages had been marked with mean, grubby stubs of paper. When he saw Hester looking at the title he hastily turned it face down. "I don't know you," he said. "What ship you from?"

"*Shadow Aspect*," said Hester.

"Never heard of her." He studied Theo, and asked him, "What city do you come from? What's your business?"

"We're from—" Hester started to say.

Varley cut in. "I asked the boy."

Theo, who was not a good actor, wished Wren was there instead of him. He still remembered the way she had run rings around old Pennyroyal and Nabisco Shkin with her stories back in Brighton. Doing his best to emulate her, he lied, "We're from Zanzibar."

"We heard you had something that we might want to buy," said Hester.

Varley looked interested, but still suspicious. "Sit

down," he said, pushing a chair out with his foot. "Have a locust. So what have you heard about my business, and where did you hear it?"

"Grandma Gravy," said Hester.

"You trade with Grandma?"

"We're old friends. She told me you had a very important prisoner aboard."

"Shhh!" hissed Varley. He leaned across the table and said in a smelly whisper, "Don't talk about my merchandise that way, lady. I don't know who's listening. The Airhaven authorities don't like the slave trade. If they thought I was trying to shift a live cargo on their patch there'd be hell to pay."

Theo felt so angry and disgusted that he could happily have hit the man. He still bore the scars and bruises of his time in Cutler's Gulp, and the shame of his captivity on Cloud 9 had never completely faded: he knew all too well what that harmless-sounding phrase "live cargo" meant.

Hester seemed unmoved. "Found a buyer yet?"

"I opened negotiations with the Kriegsmarshal of Murnau a few hours ago," said Varley, looking shifty. "Nothing's been finalized."

"I'm interested in buying," said Hester.

Varley snorted, shook his head, and returned to his locusts, eating greedily now, as if talking business had brought back his appetite. "You couldn't afford what I'm asking," he said, through a crunchy mouthful.

"Maybe I could."

Varley looked up sharply, and spat out a wing-case. "You ain't from Zanzibar," he said. "Your fancy-boy might be pretty, but he's a lousy liar. Who are you?"

Hester said nothing, and kicked Theo's ankle under the table, warning him to stay quiet too.

Varley grinned. "Gods almighty!" He lowered his voice to a whisper again. "You're the Storm, ain't you? I been wondering if any of you lot would turn up. Don't worry; I'm broad-minded. Gold is gold to Napster Varley, whether it comes from the coffers of a *Traktionstadt* or the treasure-houses of Shan Guo. So what's she worth to you, your empress? You'll have to hurry, mind. Everyone's saying the fighting'll break out again in a day or so. You'll want to get her safe in Mossie-land before that happens, won't you?"

"What are you asking?" said Hester.

"Ten thousand in gold. Nothing less."

"Ten thousand?" Theo had a hollowed-out feeling in the pit of his stomach. For a moment he had let himself imagine that it might just be possible to buy Lady Naga back, but. . . Ten thousand in gold! Varley might as well ask them for the moon!

"I'll think it over," said Hester calmly, pushing back her chair. "Come on, Theo."

Varley waved a locust at her. "You do that, honeybunch. My ship's the *Humbug*, over on Strut 13. Just bring me the money, and hand it over nice and polite."

"We'll want to see the merchandise first," said Hester.

"Not till I've seen the money. And I've got three big lads on watch, so don't think about trying anything funny."

Out on the High Street, electric lamps were being lit. Large moths zoomed about in the twilight, pursued by enterprising boys with nets who planned to roast them and sell them as tasty snacks. Some lingering maternal instinct made Hester flinch each time one of the urchins darted close to the unfenced edges of the quays. She told herself not to be so soft; these kids were born in the sky; too canny to fall; even if they did, the Airhaven authorities had stretched safety nets between the mooring struts to catch anyone who stumbled overboard.

She leaned against the handrail on the outer curve of the street and pretended to be watching the last smears of sunset fading in the west. She was actually studying Strut 13, where the black-and-white striped bulk of the *Humbug* lay at anchor. There were indeed three men loitering on the quay outside her single hatch. They were, as Varley had promised, quite big.

"He's out of his depth," Hester said.

"Who?" asked Theo. "Varley?"

"Of course Varley! He's got the biggest prize of his career and he doesn't have the faintest idea what to do with it. He's terrified that someone'll get wind of his prisoner and try to take her; hence all the hired muscle. But he daren't approach the *Traktionstadts* directly for fear they'll just swipe Lady Naga off him and give him nothing but a medal for his troubles, and when he tried doing it privately, they gave him the brush-off; that's why he came back from Manchester 'in a nasty mood'. That's why he's hunting for new ideas in books. Us turning up is like an answer to his prayers. He's an amateur, Theo."

"But he still wants ten thousand in gold," said Theo.

"He'll settle for less. Half, even."

"That would still be an enormous lot of money, and we don't have anything at all! We're here to rescue Lady Naga, not buy her! We can handle Varley and his three men easily. You rescued me, didn't you? And I heard what you did at Shkin's place last year. . ."

Hester glanced away, remembering the men she had

killed to free Tom from the slaver's tower in Brighton, and the shocked, betrayed way that Tom had looked at her afterwards. That had been their last evening together. "It's not just a question of getting Lady Naga out," she said. "We have to get her away; right away, past all these fancy cities and safe across the Green Storm's lines. If we cause a fuss getting her off Varley's ship we won't get half a mile before those flying machines catch us and. . ."

She reached out and snatched a passing moth, dropping the crumpled body into the net of one of the urchin-boys, who said, "Ta, missus!"

"Are you saying we should give up?" asked Theo, as the boy moved on.

Hester was silent, staring across the High Street.

"Mrs Natsworthy?"

"No," she said, quite softly. She did not look at him. Her attention was fixed on a man who had just emerged from the doorway of a large, shabby building called the Empyrean Hotel. She reached back, found Theo's arm and squeezed it encouragingly. "No," she said again. "We don't have to give up. We just have to find someone who can give us an enormous lot of money."

26
RUINED!

The conference aboard Manchester had dragged on and on, as the leaders of the *Traktionstadts-gesellschaft* hammered out the details of their new offensive. And "offensive" was the word, thought Kriegsmarshal von Kobold as he clambered out of the gondola of his air-yacht and walked stiffly home to the Rathaus. His wife had already set off for Paris aboard the liner *Veronica Lake*, scared away by the rumours of war. He did not miss her. He had seen so little of her these past years that he did not feel he even knew her any more. Glad that he would not have to spend another evening with her in their over-decorated, over-scented official suite, he climbed the stairs to the small room on the top floor which he made his home when she and Wolf were away. The white walls, bare but for a portrait of his son, focused his attention on the windows, the bats flitting black outside against the afterglow, the sky streaked with the wind-combed con-trails of flying machines.

Such a peaceful evening, thought the Kriegsmarshal, pulling papers from the pockets of his tunic and throwing them down on his bed. Yet in the morning he would have to sign the orders that would take his city back to war. Young men would be recalled to their units; snout-guns and airships made ready. . . Already, the women and children were on their way to peaceful cities further west. And tonight the armour would be closed. It might be months before he would be able to look out again at the evening sky from his own bedroom window.

He hung up his tunic, and used the telephone above his dressing-table to talk to his housekeeper, telling her that he would dine in his own room that night, and asking her to send up bread, cold meat, a glass of beer. As he returned to the door to check that he had not locked it he noticed a face staring at him from the pile of papers on the bed.

He picked up the photograph, wondering what on earth it was doing there, among the tedious, typewritten transcripts of Browne's speech. A woman's face. It took him a moment to realize that this was what Varley had stuffed into his pocket in the park. In all the misery of the afternoon's planning sessions he had almost forgotten that seedy air-trader. Now he grew furious. To think that a slaver was operating within a few miles of Murnau, which had never had anything to do with slavery, and had always made it a point of honour to free the slaves of every town it ate! And to think that Varley could imagine that he, von Kobold, would be interested in buying the poor, miserable-looking waif in this picture!

Photo in hand, he strode back to the telephone, winding the handle furiously and shouting at the startled operator to put him through at once to his chief of security. While he waited for the man to answer he fumbled his spectacles on, and looked more closely at the photograph. The girl was an easterner; dirty, bruised, huge-eyed with fear. She seemed faintly familiar, though Kobold could not think why. That small, vulnerable mouth, those crooked teeth. . .

He remembered, suddenly, where he had seen her before. Intelligence had sent him pictures of General Naga's wedding. The bride in her red finery. Thick, black brows and tilted cheekbones. That mouth.

"Herr Kriegsmarshal?" crackled the telephone. "What is it?"

Kobold hesitated, still staring at the photograph. "Nothing, Schiller," he said softly. "It doesn't matter."

He returned the telephone gently to its cradle, then took a pistol from the dressing-table drawer, buckled on his heavy fighting sword and put on the precious *Kevlar* body-armour which his enemy had sent him all those years ago. He did not usually bother with armour, but it seemed appropriate that Naga's gift should protect him when he went to rescue Naga's wife.

He pulled a greatcoat on over the top and ran down the stairs, past the housemaid who was coming up with his dinner. "Sorry, my dear," he told her. "Change of plan." But he took the beer, drinking it as he hurried down to his private docking pan. The ground crew were moving his yacht *Die Leiden Des Jungen Werthers* into her hangar for the night. "It's all right, men," he called, tossing the empty beer-stein aside as he marched towards them across the pan. "I am taking her out again."

"Tonight, sir?"

"Not much fuel in her tanks, sir."

"I don't need much," said the Kriegsmarshal. "I'm only going up to Airhaven."

"Nobody of that name here," said the clerk at the Empyrean Hotel. A dusty argon globe buzzed and flickered, light fluttering over threadbare carpets and tobacco-coloured walls. Stairs went up into shadow.

"Nice place," muttered Theo.

Hester leaned across the receptionist's desk. Behind her veil her blunt profile looked as hard as a fist. Theo was afraid that she was going to do something terrible to the insolent young man in the pillbox hat, but she just said, "You're sure? *Nimrod* Pennyroyal. He's a writer."

"Oh, I know who he is, lady," said the clerk, with the same witless grin. "Everyone's heard of Pennyroyal. But we ain't got no one of that name staying here."

"I just saw him leave," said Hester. "A fat man. Old. Bald."

"That was just Mr Unterberg," said the clerk. "A commercial gentleman from Murnau, staying in room 128. He said he was popping round to the harbour office to. . . Look, here he is now!"

Hester and Theo both turned as the lobby door opened, letting in the noise of rowdy parties from the High Street bars, a few lost moths, and the man they were looking for. He had shaved off his beard, put on blue-tinted spectacles and swapped his usual fine clothes for the dowdy pin-striped robes of a commercial traveller, but Hester and Theo recognized him at once.

"Oh, great Poskitt!" he gasped as they went to meet him. "Oh, Clio! Oh, ruddy Nora!"

"We'd like a little chat," Hester explained.

She expected him to scream for help, to call for the police and Airhaven militia. After all, last time they met, Hester had tried to murder him, and only her soft-hearted daughter had stopped her. But Pennyroyal seemed more frightened of the clerk on the front desk than of her. He peeked nervously past her at the youth (who was watching wide-eyed, with his mouth hanging open) and hissed, "We can't talk here!"

"Your room then," said Hester.

Pennyroyal obeyed meekly enough, fetching his pass-key from the astonished clerk and motioning for Theo and Hester to follow him up the stairs. Hester couldn't help feeling she had missed something. She had never met anyone as pleased with himself as Nimrod Pennyroyal. Why would he pretend to be someone else?

Room 128 was on the top floor; sloping ceilings, a tap dripping into a grimy metal handbasin, empty wine bottles on every level surface. Pennyroyal sank into a wicker chair beside the window. Hester let Theo in, and kicked the door shut behind him.

"If you've come looking for Tom and Wren," the old man whimpered, "they took off days ago. Gone north, on some job for a fellow named Wolf Kobold."

"Tom and Wren were here?" asked Theo.

Hester seemed disconcerted by this sudden news of her family. She stared at Pennyroyal for a moment, started to say something, stopped, and then recovered herself and snapped, "That's not why we came. We need money, Pennyroyal."

Pennyroyal let out a humourless bark, like a seal with bronchitis. "Money? You've come to me for money? Ha! Never been much of a reader, have you, Hester? Haven't you heard?"

"Heard what?"

"Why do you think I'm hiding in this dump?" He crouched down and pulled a tattered newspaper from beneath the heap of empty bottles and discarded socks under the bed. Shoving it at Hester and Theo he said bitterly, "See? I'm ruined! Ruined! And it's all thanks to that daughter of yours!"

The paper was called *The Speculum*. A picture of

Pennyroyal filled most of the front page. Beneath his smug, smiling face, heavy, black type screamed,

LIAR!
THE REAL NIMROD B. PENNYROYAL UNMASKED!
By our Murnau correspondent SAMPFORD SPINEY
(See pages 1–24)

Theo took the paper and leafed quickly through the first few pages. "'Many experts have long believed that "Professor" Pennyroyal's archaeological work is suspect...'" he read. "'No proof has ever surfaced to support "Professor" Pennyroyal's stories of his adventures in America and Nuevo Maya...'" Then he turned to the end of the article, and gave a cry of surprise, for there was Wren. The photograph was small, and she had done something to her hair since he last saw her (or had she been standing on a slope when it was taken?) but it was her. He scanned the paragraphs beneath the picture, and glanced nervously at Hester before he read them aloud.

"'Mr Thomas Natsworthy, a respectable air-trader, is none other than the husband of Hester Shaw, whose death Pennyroyal describes so touchingly in the closing chapters of his bestseller, *Predator's Gold*. Fans of that book may be surprised to learn that Ms Shaw was alive and well last Moon Festival, when she and her husband separated, and that the couple have a charming daughter, Miss Wren Natsworthy (15), who says of Pennyroyal, "He does tend to exaggerate a little."

"'It is the opinion of this writer, and of an increasing number of the Professor's readers, that Pennyroyal exaggerates more than a little; that he is in fact nothing more than a fraud; a charlatan; a confidence-trickster; a lounge-lizard and a master of deceit whose presence upon Murnau's upper tiers offends against every tradition of that noble city.'"

Hester chuckled appreciatively behind her veil.

"You see?" said Pennyroyal. "The little minx! Talking to Spiney like that behind my back! Or did he trick her? Twist her words about? I wouldn't put it past him. He will use any ammunition to hurl at me. I would set my lawyers on him, but alas, all proofs of my adventures burned with Cloud 9. Now Werederobe and Spoor are claiming that I have deceived them and want me to repay the advance on my latest memoir. And I can't! I've spent it! Already warrants have been issued for my arrest in Murnau and Manchester! Where am I to go? What am I to do? I fled here hoping my friend Dornier Lard would take me away aboard his sky-yacht, but he refused to know me! And I dare not try to buy passage on any common trade ship, lest the aviators recognize me and alert my creditors. Unless. . ." He gawped at Hester, trying to hide his fear of her and look plaintive and appealing. "Do you have a ship, Mrs Natsworthy? Perhaps, for old times' sake. . . Theo, dear boy, you remember how we got off Cloud 9 together; you and me taking turns to pilot the dear old *Arctic Roll*. . ."

"Money," said Hester firmly.

"Oh, of course I can pay my way!" Pennyroyal began to fumble his clothes open, exposing his bulging, white-furred belly and a canvas money-belt with many pouches. He took off the belt and started emptying coins on to the floor. "Just a little portable wealth I carry with me in case of emergencies," he explained. "Only pocket money, really, but you are welcome to it if you can take me away from here, and keep quiet about it. . ."

"Pocket money?" Hester stirred the heaps of coin with the toe of her boot. "There must be four hundred shineys here, Pennyroyal."

"Five hundred!" said the old man eagerly, pulling a roll of coins out of the lining of his coat and throwing it down with the rest.

"It's a wonder you could walk."

"Well, it's all yours, if you can help me."

Hester nodded, thanking him. "Take it, Theo," she said.

"But it's not enough. . ."

"It's enough to get me aboard the *Humbug*. Once I'm past those heavies on the quay I'll improvise."

Theo still didn't see how she planned to satisfy Varley's greed with five hundred in assorted gold bits, but he crouched down anyway and started shovelling the coins into his pockets. Pennyroyal watched with a strange expression, both pained and hopeful. "Which quay is your ship on?" he asked. "What is she called? Is she fast? I was wondering about Nuevo Maya; I don't believe *The Speculum* is very widely read in Nuevo Maya. . ."

"You're not coming with us," said Hester.

"But you said. . ."

"I didn't say anything, Pennyroyal. You've been doing all the talking yourself, as usual. I wouldn't trust you aboard my ship, and even if I did, you wouldn't want passage to where I'm going."

Pennyroyal started to whimper. "But my money! My money!"

"We can't do this!" cried Theo, turning to Hester. Pennyroyal had kept him as a slave once, and he knew he should be glad that the gods had finally punished him for all his lies. But he didn't feel glad; he felt as if he were robbing a helpless, frightened old man. "We can't just take his money!"

"Think of it as a charity donation," said Hester, pulling the door open.

"I shall inform the authorities!" wailed Pennyroyal.

"What, and give your hiding place away? I don't think so."

"It's for a good cause, Professor," promised Theo, lingering behind as Hester strode out of the room. He touched the old man's trembling hand and said gently, "We'll pay it back. Lady Naga's a prisoner in a ship here. We're going to get her to Shan Guo. When we do, General Naga will be so grateful. . . He'll pay back ten times what we took from you."

"Lady Naga?" whined Pennyroyal. "What are you talking about? She's dead!"

"Theo!" shouted Hester, halfway down the stairs.

With a last worried glance at Pennyroyal, Theo turned and followed her out of the room, out of the Empyrean Hotel, out into the chilly, starry night.

The clerk on the front desk watched them go, then wound the handle of the hotel's telephone and asked the operator to connect him to his brother, who worked in Airhaven's radio-telegraph office. "Lego?" he whispered. "It's me, Duplo. Can you send a message down to Murnau, double quick?"

Alone in Room 128, Pennyroyal took a few deep, shivery breaths to calm himself. Curiosity was starting to get the better of his self-pity. What had young Theo meant? Could Naga's wife really still be alive? Was she really in Airhaven? And if she was, what would the *Traktionstadts* not give to get her for themselves? Why, the man who captured her would be a hero, no matter what alleged irregularities lay in his past. . .

Pennyroyal poured himself a brandy to steady his nerves, and lifted the stained curtain aside to look out at the big, sleepy shapes of the moored airships down on the docking ring. *Humbug*; that was the name Hester had let slip. He'd not heard of her, but it would be easy enough to find out what strut she lay at. And there were sure to be some burly townies in the High Steet taverns who could help him out if things turned nasty.

In his mind's eye, the beastly stories that *The Speculum* had printed about him finally began to fade, and a new, more favourable headline appeared; something along the lines of *Pennyroyal Captures Leading Mossie. . .*

27

STRUT 13

ow cloud, blowing in from the west on the night wind, spread like a white carpet fifty feet beneath Airhaven, hiding the earth below and all but the uppermost tiers of the largest cities there. An air-yacht in the midnight-blue livery of Murnau came gliding through the cloud-tops, curving towards a berth on the far side of the docking-ring; probably some toff from the *Oberrang* come up to risk his inheritance in the casinos. As she leaned over the handrail of an observation deck on the High Street the smell of mist reminded Hester of a night at Rogues' Roost, long ago.

Beneath her was Strut 13. The *Humbug* lay alongside, the three guards lounging at the foot of her gangplank. A light showed in her gondola, another in a window low down in her envelope.

Hester turned to Theo. "Go back to our ship. Get her ready to pull out. If all goes well, I'll be coming aboard with Lady Naga in a few minutes."

"You can't go down there alone!" Theo protested. "What if something goes wrong?"

"Then you'll leave without me. Go east and tell your General Naga what really happened to his wife." Hester was eager to get Theo safely out of the way so that she could start doing what she did best. She leaned over and kissed his cheek, feeling the warmth of his skin through her veil. Everything was so intense in these moments before action, as if her brain wanted to drink in everything; every sound, every smell.

Theo nodded, and started to say something, then

thought better of it. He walked away fast along the High Street, dodging the crowds of aviators who meandered between the bars and cafés. Hester watched till he was out of sight, thinking how badly she would have fallen in love with him if she'd been twenty years younger. Then, cursing herself for a sentimental goose, she ran down the stairway to Strut 13.

The men on guard were as bored and dozy as she'd been hoping. They were the sort of shabby, down-at-heel aviators who hung around the High Street bars looking for work. Varley must have hired them to guard his precious cargo, but they would rather have been off drinking than standing out here in the cold. She considered just killing them, and keeping hold of Pennyroyal's gold for herself, but she couldn't take them all down without a fight, and she didn't want to risk that yet. She called out, "Where's Varley?"

The men came to life, trying to look hard and competent. "Who's asking?" said one, pointing a spring-loaded spear-gun at her.

Hester shook the bag she was holding and let them hear the chinkle of Pennyroyal's gold. *Is chinkle a word?* she wondered. She always grew very calm at times like this, and small questions like that became intriguing. *Tom would know. . .* But she mustn't think about Tom.

One of the guards was backing up the *Humbug's* gangway, calling through an open hatch to someone inside. After a moment he jerked the spear-gun at Hester, and the others stood aside to let her go aboard.

In the *Shadow Aspect*'s gondola Theo was warming up the engines, testing the rudder controls, and hoping that no one aboard Airhaven would notice, for he had not asked anyone's permission to depart. Behind him, Shrike paced to and fro, his heavy footfalls shaking the deck. "SHE SHOULD NOT HAVE GONE ALONE," the Stalker said.

"I told you. . ."

"YOU ARE NOT TO BLAME, THEO NGONI. BUT SHE SHOULD NOT HAVE GONE ALONE." He let out a grating, mechanical noise which Theo supposed was the Stalker equivalent of a sigh. "I SHOULD BE HELPING HER TO FREE DR ZERO. IN OTHER TIMES I WOULD HAVE DONE IT EASILY. TAKEN OUT THE AIRHAVEN POWER PLANT, SOWN CONFUSION, AND GONE ABOARD THE *HUMBUG* WHILE THE ONCE-BORN WERE LOOKING ELSEWHERE. . . BUT I COULD NOT DO THAT WITHOUT KILLING."

"You wouldn't get far afterwards, either," Theo pointed out.

Shrike didn't seem to hear him. He stood at a porthole, staring out at the night and the silent, tethered ships. "I AM GOING TO HELP HER."

"But you can't! If you're seen. . ."

"I WILL BE CAREFUL."

Before Theo could stop him, Shrike opened the hatch and jumped down on to the docking strut. No one was about. He crossed the strut in two long strides and dropped over the edge, his armour rippling with reflections from the harbour lights as if he were made of quicksilver. The underside of the strut was in shadow, hatched with girders. Shrike crept along them until he was beneath the docking quays, and waited while a puttering dirigible balloon-taxi passed beneath him on its way to the central ring. Then he began to pull himself along Airhaven's underbelly towards Strut 13.

The dirigible taxi pulled in against one of the docking-platforms in the centre of Airhaven, and its wicker gondola creaked as Sampford Spiney scrambled out, followed by Miss Kropotkin and her enormous camera. The journalist had been at a dinner on the *Oberrang* when he received the message from Airhaven, and he had not had time to change out of his formal robes. He swayed slightly as he made his way across the mooring platform to where the clerk from the Empyrean was waiting.

"Well? Are you the one who claims to have seen Pennyroyal?"

"He's been staying in my hotel, sir."

"Is he there now?"

"No, sir. He ran out not long after I sent word to you. . ."

"Ran where?"

"I don't know, sir. Some people came to talk to him. Then he went running off. I can show you his room, sir. . ."

"His room? His room? Great Thunderer! I can't interview a room! Find me Pennyroyal himself, or you'll not see a cent out of *The Speculum*."

The clerk hurried towards the stairs which led up to the High Street, and Spiney went with him, snapping at his photographer to follow. "And make a note, Miss Kropotkin," he added as they climbed, "I'm pretty sure that was the Kriegsmarshal's sky-yacht we passed as we came in. What's the old man doing in Airhaven? Gambling? Seeing a woman? Could be a story in that. . ."

The *Humbug*'s gondola reeked of wet nappies. The living quarters at the stern were full of them, draped on lines strung above the heating ducts. Poorly-made bookshelves covered the walls, sagging under the weight of Varley's self-help books. In one corner a slimy-nosed baby snuffled and started to cry. "Hush, hush, hush," his mother said, looking up nervously as one of Varley's heavies pushed Hester in.

Varley was waiting for her, looking more feverish and ferrety than ever, a half-eaten supper on the table in front of him. He'd taken off his jacket. His trousers were held up by snakeskin braces. "On your own this time?" he asked Hester. "Got my ten thousand?"

"Five," said Hester. "That's all we can get hold of."

"Then I'll be selling your Lady Naga to another buyer."

"Oh, yes, I noticed the enormous queue all up the gangplank when I came aboard," said Hester. "That was sarcasm," she added as Varley sprang up to peer through a porthole. "Face it, you haven't got any other buyers. You'll have to do business with me, before someone bigger and tougher hears who you've got stashed in your hold and comes to take her off your hands for free."

Varley glared at her and said nothing. She opened her bag on the kitchen table, and shook out a pile of small, plump money-bags. They jingled loudly, as well they might; two were full of Pennyroyal's savings and the other eight were stuffed with nuts and washers which she and Theo had bought at the all-night chandlery on the High Street. "Ten bags," she said, opening one and tipping out a stream of gold. "Two hundred and fifty shineys in each. Captain Ngoni will be bringing you the rest when I can assure him your cargo is alive and well."

Varley eyed the money hungrily, but he wasn't happy. "That black kid of yours is a captain? The Green Storm must be running short of men as well as money. . ."

Hester chose another money-bag and emptied a second shining drift of coin across the table-top. ("Look! Pretty!" said Mrs Varley, bouncing the baby on her knee.)

"Take it or leave it," said Hester.

Varley still hesitated. "I want to see your face," he said sullenly.

"Believe me, you really don't."

The merchant sniffed, kicked a toy aside, and told his henchman, "Watch her, and don't go thieving any of my money." Then he pushed past Hester and vanished up a companion-ladder into the *Humbug*'s envelope. The other man reluctantly prised his eyes away from the heap of gold on the table and watched Hester instead. The baby gurgled. The woman sang it a song that Hester remembered faintly from long ago, but she quickly stopped when Hester looked at her.

"You from Oak Island?" Hester asked.

The woman shook her head. "Red Deer."

You could see Red Deer Island from the hills above Hester's childhood home on Oak Island, when the weather was fine. No wonder she recognized the song. She hoped she wouldn't have to kill this woman and her baby.

"Napster bought me in the wife-auction there. . ." the woman started to explain, and then stopped suddenly again, because she had heard her husband's footsteps on the ladder, coming back down. She shifted closer to the table to give him room as he dropped into the cabin, dragging his frightened cargo behind him.

Pennyroyal peered into half a dozen of the High Street's crowded drinking-holes before he found what he was looking for. In fact, they found him; a gang of rowdy young militia officers up from Manchester on a twenty-four-hour pass, clutching girls and bottles, making their unsteady way from a casino above Strut 1, where they had been betting their pay on Ancient games of chance like Pick-a-Sticks and Buckeroo. Pennyroyal scurried alongside, calling out, "Excuse me, gentlemen," and "I say," but they paid him no attention until he shouted, "I am Nimrod Pennyroyal!"

The Mancunians turned to stare at him.

"Shove off!" said one.

"Scrag him!" suggested another.

"Chuck him off the docking ring!" roared a third.

"Hoorah!"

"No," said a fifth man, slightly more sober than the rest. "He *is* Nimrod Pennyroyal. I recognize him from the papers."

"Chuck him off the docking ring anyway!"

"Hoorah!"

"He's that fake explorer bloke, ain't he?" said one of the girls, peering at Pennyroyal as if he was some mildly interesting animal in a zoo.

"I am not a fake!" Pennyroyal shouted. "I have come to ask your help! There is a high-ranking member of the Green Storm secreted aboard an airship down on the docking ring, and I need the help of some loyal Tractionists to take her into custody!"

"Huh huh huh huh," went one of the Mancunians, laughing at some private joke. The rest struggled to follow what Pennyroyal was saying. One or two reached for their swords. "A Mossie? Here?"

"Lady Naga herself! I've been operating undercover to discover her whereabouts. All that stuff you read in the papers was just a ruse, designed to make the enemy think I was in disgrace. I've actually been working for the *Murnauer Geheimdeinst* all along, you know."

The Mancunians looked blank. None of them had heard the German name for Murnau's intelligence service before. Pennyroyal cursed their ignorance (but only quietly) and pulled out the old envelope on which he had jotted down the *Humbug*'s details from the arrivals board in the Floating Exchange. He squinted at his own crabbed writing for a moment, then flourished the envelope like a battle-flag. "Come gentlemen!" he cried. "Follow me to Strut 13, and to glory!"

A bruised face; a mat of greasy hair, a thin body shaking and shaking inside a sackcloth dress. Hester was astonished at the flood of pity she felt as she watched Lady Naga come creeping down the *Humbug*'s companion ladder. *She's not much older than Wren*, she thought, and for a moment she wanted to rush forward and hug the poor, frightened creature and comfort her and tell her that she was safe now.

But she wasn't safe, not yet, and anyway she would not have wanted to be hugged; she seemed as scared of

Hester as she was of Varley. When Varley shoved her forwards and said, "This nice lady's come to buy you," she hung back and let out a whine like a scared animal. Hester, in her black coat and her black veil, looked like the Goddess of Death.

"You're Lady Naga?" she asked.

"Oenone," said the young woman, blinking fearfully at her. Her glasses were held together by sticking plaster and one of the lenses was cracked.

"Course she's Lady bleedin' Naga," crowed Varley. "Look at her signet ring, and that Zagwan pendant thing. They're extra, by the way. Now go and get me the rest of my money."

Hester nodded and glanced past him, judging the distance between herself and the man with the spear-gun at the bulkhead door. She turned, back to the wall, one hand moving slowly to the knife inside her coat, and saw out of the corner of her eye the baby reach towards the pile of money-bags on Varley's table.

What happened next happened very slowly, but not slowly enough that she had time to stop it. The child's fat hand grabbed the bag; the bag fell; the bag burst. Across the deck at Varley's feet there went scattering a storm of nuts and washers. Varley, realizing he'd been tricked, let out a yell. Hester snatched her knife and threw it underarm at the man on the door, hitting him in the throat. His spear-gun went off as he fell, but the spear went high, passing over Hester's head; she heard it thud into the bulkhead above her. Mrs Varley was screaming. The baby howled. Something struck Hester a sudden, stunning blow on the top of her head. A flash of purple light went off inside her skull. She cursed and tried to turn, confused, imagining someone had got behind her.

Things were falling all round her, punching her shoulders, thumping on the deck. She went down on her knees among them and saw that they were books. The dead man's spear-gun had detached one of Varley's home-made bookshelves from the wall, and it had struck her as it fell. It was a stupid sort of injury, but that didn't make it any less serious. The spilled books seemed to whirl around her. *Dodgy Dealing for Beginners. Investing in People. Make Your Fortune on the Bird Roads – and Survive to Spend It!* She felt sure she was going to be sick.

Varley had an arm round Oenone's throat. "Come on, lads!" he shouted. "Get her! Get her!" Hester remembered the men outside. Squinting with the pain in her head, she tried to stand up. Footsteps shook the gondola as the heavies from the mooring strut came aboard. Hester reached into her pocket and tugged out her pistol, shooting them one at a time as they came barging through the cabin door. The gas-pistol made soft coughing sounds which she hoped would not be heard out on the High Street. The men fell on top of the body of their friend, and one of them kept struggling, so she shot him again. She could feel blood running down her face. She swung the gun towards Varley, but fainted before she could pull the trigger.

The next thing she knew, the merchant was wrenching the gun out of her hand. He had a stupid, mad grin, and his nostrils kept flaring. He pulled down Hester's veil and his grin grew even wider, as if her ugliness was some sort of victory for him. He spat in her face. "Well," he said. He put down the gun (a dangerous thing to use on board your own airship) and pulled a knife out of his belt. "Nobody's going to miss you."

He looked surprised when his wife picked up the gun and shot him. It seemed to take him a moment to understand that he'd been killed. His grin faded slowly, and he sank down on his knees beside Hester and bowed his head and stayed there, kneeling, dead.

"Oh, God," murmured Oenone.

Mrs Varley lowered the gun. She was shaking. The baby howled and howled. Oenone scrambled across the cabin and helped Hester to her feet.

"You'd better go now," said Mrs Varley. She pulled a nappy down from one of the lines and started scooping the gold into it.

Hester touched the searing, throbbing place where the shelf had hit her, and her hand came away wet and red. She felt drunk. She held on to Oenone for support and said, "We came to rescue you. Me and Shrike."

"Mr Shrike? He's here?"

"Theo too. There's a ship waiting." With Oenone's help she started limping towards the exit hatch, which seemed suddenly to be miles away. "Gods, it hurts," she grumbled. Somehow they reached the top of the gangplank. Out on the docking strut, a man was waiting. He was all alone. He had probably heard that last shot. The wind flapped his long, blue greatcoat open, and moonlight shone on the hilt of the heavy sabre in his belt.

Hester groaned, nauseous and weary. She had no strength left to fight him with.

"Lady Naga?" said the stranger. "I'm just in time, I see."

Oenone cringed against Hester as the stranger walked towards her, putting one booted foot on the gangplank. In the dim light from the *Humbug*'s hatchway his face looked stern, but not unkind. He held out a hand. "I am

Kriegsmarshal von Kobold. You must come with me to Murnau. Quickly, please."

Hester gripped the gangplank rail and glared at him. "You'll have to get past me first."

Von Kobold looked respectfully at her. Her scarred face did not shock him, nor did the blood that matted her hair and dripped from her chin. He gave her a little bow. "Forgive me, young woman, but that does not seem too great a challenge. I take it you are an agent of the Storm, come to free your empress? Even if you were not wounded, you could never get her away from here. A dozen cities stand between you and your own territory, and not all of their leaders are as understanding as I. Come with me to Murnau, and I shall find a way to send you and your mistress home to General Naga."

A blurt of noise from the docking ring made him look round. Someone was shouting; running figures showed against the lighted windows of an all-night Ker-Plunk parlour. "We have to trust him," whispered Oenone, and helped Hester down the gangplank. But by the time they reached von Kobold it was too late; the deckplates were thrumming with the stamp of booted feet. Along the strut towards them came six red-coated men with drawn swords, and behind them, urging them on, the podgy, hopping shape of Nimrod Pennyroyal.

"There they are!" Pennyroyal shouted. "They're escaping! Stop them!"

"Who are you?" barked Kriegsmarshal von Kobold, in such a military voice that the men stopped short. Up on the High Street passers-by began to gather at an observation platform to see what was happening down on Strut 13.

"We, sir, are officers of the Manchester Civic Guard,"

said the tallest and most sober of the newcomers. "We have been informed that a dangerous Mossie is concealed aboard this airship. . ."

"Blimey!" said one of his comrades, pointing. "It's her! Naga's wife, just like the old man said!"

"What, in that get-up?" asked another.

"It's her. I seen her picture in the *Evening News*. Blimey!"

"You're under arrest!" said the leader, striding towards Oenone.

"Stand back, sir," snapped von Kobold, and drew his sabre. "The lady is my prisoner, and I will not deliver her into the hands of your warmongering mayor."

"Now, steady on!" called Pennyroyal, who didn't want a squabble between Murnau and Manchester to ruin his chance of some favourable headlines. But before he could say more the light of a flashbulb blinded him. A small man in formal robes walked out on to the increasingly crowded strut. There was a girl behind him, fumbling a new flashbulb into place on the top of her camera.

"Mr Pennyroyal!" the newcomer called out pleasantly. "Sampford Spiney of *The Speculum*. Been looking for you everywhere. Do you have any message for your many disappointed fans?" His voice was affable and faintly snide; it faded into silence as he saw the Mancunians with their drawn swords, von Kobold with his sabre, Oenone supporting Hester, who had crumpled to her knees at the foot of the *Humbug*'s gangplank. "I say!" he murmured excitedly. "What's all this?"

But the leader of the Mancunians was tired of talking. He raised his sword and tried to barge past von Kobold, but the Kriegsmarshal barred his way. Sparks flew as their swords met, directly contravening Airhaven's strict fire-prevention laws. Up on the High Street people screamed. The Manchester swordsman screamed too, stumbling away with blood running down his arm. Von Kobold turned to face the others. "Defend yourselves!" he shouted, and most of them started to edge back, frightened of this fierce old soldier who seemed ready to take on five of them at once. Only one held his ground. He was a young man, red-cheeked and running to fat. In addition to his uniform sword he had a revolver. He pointed it straight at von Kobold, and fired twice.

Theo, waiting aboard the *Shadow Aspect*, heard the shots. He ran to the hatch. He tried to tell himself that those bangs had not been gunfire, but he knew that they had, and he knew that they had come from the direction of Strut 13.

An alarm bell began to jangle. Theo jumped down on to the mooring strut and started to run towards the docking ring. A squad of men in the sky-blue uniforms of Airhaven were storming down a stairway from the High Street, crossbows held ready. From a docking pan near the Town Hall a red fire-fighting dirigible was lifting off, ready to train her hoses on any blaze that broke out.

Theo stood helpless, halfway between the *Shadow Aspect* and the docking ring. What could he do? How could he help?

A horrified scream reached him, blowing on the wind. Another. More shots. He turned, and went hammering back to the *Shadow*.

As Kriegsmarshal von Kobold fell the man who'd shot him sprang forward, reaching for Lady Naga. Hester heaved herself up to face him and suddenly, although she had done no more than glare at him, he dropped his gun and shouted, "Yaagh!" Looking down, Hester saw the sharp blades that had been driven up through the deck from beneath. There were five of them, and two had gone through the Mancunian's boot, and through the foot inside it. He screamed again, wrenching himself free, and the blades slid back through the deck, leaving ragged holes. "Get this, Miss Kropotkin!" Spiney was ordering his photographer.

The deckplate heaved. An armoured fist punched up through the quay from beneath; clawed fingers widened the hole, and Shrike scrambled out. He flared with light as another flashbulb fired, silvering his armour, his fingertips and his gruesome metal grin.

"Stalker!" screamed the Mancunian gunman, trying to hop away. Shrike picked him up and flung him off the edge of the strut; he flailed at the empty air for a moment and then fell with a terrible shriek, and landed bouncing in the safety net. Shrike hurled one of his friends after him; the rest turned to run, and collided with the first squad of Airhaven militia arriving from the High Street.

Hester fainted again and fell down on the hard quay, waking a few seconds later when the Airhaven fire-boat swung overhead, dowsing everyone with freezing water. There seemed a general belief that whole squads of Stalkers had been landed on Strut 13. Dozens of alarm bells were ringing, making horrid discords. At the end of the strut the Mancunians were fighting with the Airhaven men, who had somehow got the idea that they were Green Storm raiders in disguise. "No, no, no!" Pennyroyal was yelling. Below the strut the Mancunians Shrike had thrown off it were scrambling up the mesh of the safety net to the neighbouring quay, where aviators from a Florentine highliner leaned out to haul them to safety.

Below that, dark against the cloud-layer, the plump shape of an airship moved, rising upwards.

"The *Jenny Haniver*," said Hester, looking down at it through the holes in the deckplate. Then she realized that it couldn't be; it wasn't Tom coming to her rescue this time, but Theo, in the *Shadow Aspect*.

Shrike had seen it too; or heard the mutter of its engines. He picked Oenone up under one arm, as if she were a parcel. He turned and reached for Hester, but Hester was dragging herself away from him towards von Kobold.

In the scrum at the far end of the strut one of the Mancunians was yelling, "It was Pennyroyal! Pennyroyal lured us here! Into the claws of the Storm's Stalkers!"

"That's not true!" Pennyroyal shouted, skipping backwards as an Airhaven soldier made a grab at him. "I'm the victim here! What about my money?"

The *Shadow Aspect* came up like a surfacing whale at the end of Strut 13. Hester saw Theo inside the gondola as she turned von Kobold over. The fat Mancunian's gun had made two charred holes in the front of von Kobold's coat. But he was only winded. Beneath his coat she saw the dull sheen of Old-Tech body-armour. He raised a hand to cup her face. "They breed you brave in the Green Storm's lands," he whispered.

"I'm not. . ." said Hester, but there wasn't time to explain.

"Tell Naga that not all of us want this war," she heard von Kobold say. Then she passed out, and Shrike swept her up and loped towards the *Shadow* with the bolts from Airhaven crossbows rattling against his armoured back.

Pennyroyal scurried away from the scrum of men at the end of the strut and ran into Spiney. The journalist had been directing Miss Kropotkin while she took the pictures which would appear on the front of the next day's papers beneath the headline *Manchester Men Battle Bravely Against Naga's Raiders!* He flung himself at Pennyroyal with a vulpine grin. "What's your part in all this then, Nimrod? How long have you been working for the Green Storm?"

Pennyroyal shoved him aside. An airship was manoeuvring away from the strut with a deafening howl of engines, and he had a sudden, terrible fear that it was the *Humbug,* taking off with his gold still aboard. "What about my money?" he shouted at it.

"How much have they paid you, Pennyroyal?" called Spiney stepping into his path again and flapping at Miss Kropotkin to bring her camera.

Pennyroyal gave a feeble roar of rage and pushed Spiney hard with both hands. Spiney fought back, flailing at Pennyroyal's face, grabbing him by the collar. So much was happening on Strut 13 that no one saw the two writers stumble across the quay and plunge off the edge. Their screams harmonized for a brief moment as they fell.

On the *Shadow*'s flight-deck Theo pushed all the engines to full power, preparing to shove the airship out into the open sky beyond Airhaven's shadow, but as he reached for the steering levers a steel hand clamped his wrist.

"THERE ARE TWO ANTI-AIRCRAFT HARPOON BATTERIES ON AIRHAVEN HIGH STREET," the Stalker Shrike announced. "AS SOON AS WE CLEAR THEIR AIRSPACE THEY WILL FIRE ON US."

"But we can't stay here!" shouted Theo, waving at the windows. The glass was already starred by hits from a dozen crossbow bolts, although no one had dared to fire anything more dangerous yet, for fear of igniting a blaze which might engulf the whole of Airhaven.

"GO DOWN," said Shrike. "DROP INTO THE CLOUDS. THEY WILL HIDE US."

Theo nodded, angry that he'd not thought of that for himself. A moment later the *Shadow* swung its engine pods upright and forced itself down into the white billows beneath Airhaven.

🙶 🙶 🙶 🙶 🙶

"Aaaaaaaaah!" wailed Pennyroyal and Spiney, and then, "Oh!" as the safety net beneath Strut 13 caught them and held them safe. They bounced together, as if they had dropped into a giant's hammock.

"Great Poskitt!" whimpered Pennyroyal, thrusting the journalist away from him and trying to stand upright. He had forgotten the net's existence until its thick, yielding mesh broke his fall. "I thought we were done for!" he gasped.

"You're done for all right, Nimrod!" Sampford Spiney cackled. He had been just as scared as Pennyroyal, but he wasn't about to show it. "Consorting with the Storm;

taking part in a brawl; accessory to the attempted murder of a Kriegsmarshal – here, was that bint on the strut really Naga's wife? That's what your Manchester friends are saying. . ." Excited at the thought of all the startling reports that he would soon be filing, the journalist began to bounce happily up and down.

"*Do* stop doing that, old man," pleaded Pennyroyal. "You're making me feel all queasy. . ."

"Not half as queasy as you'll be when you see the next edition of *The Speculum*." Spiney chuckled, bouncing harder. Odd noises started to come from the net; faint creaks; small twanging sounds.

"Spiney, I really think you should stop! This net looks old, and it's already taken the weight of a brace of fat Mancunians tonight. . ."

With a sound like plucked harpstrings the bolts which attached one edge of the net to the underside of Strut 14 started to come free. Spiney stopped bouncing, and let out a strangled yelp.

"Help!" shouted Pennyroyal, as loudly as he could, but although Strut 13 was crammed with people the only one who heard him was Spiney's photographer, Miss Kropotkin. Her face appeared over the edge of the strut. She stretched down towards the stranded men with one hand, but she could not reach them. Pennyroyal started trying to claw his way up the steep net towards her, but only succeeded in pulling some of the bolts on that side free as well. "Oh, Poskitt!"

"Miss Kropotkin!" Spiney shrieked. "Fetch help! Fetch help at once, or I'll make sure you end up photographing pet shows and garden parties for the rest of your worthless—"

And with a presence of mind that ensured she would

never have to photograph another pet show as long as she lived, Miss Kropotkin raised her camera as the net gave way, and took the picture which would appear on page one of the next edition of *The Speculum* beneath the headline *Writers Perish In Airhaven Death Plunge Horror*.

28

STORM BIRDS

As the *Shadow Aspect* sank into the clouds Shrike strode aft. In the curtained-off cabin at the stern of the gondola Oenone was crouching over Hester, using her fingers to try and stop the blood which was pouring from the gash on Hester's scalp. She looked up at Shrike. "Is there a medicine chest? Just a first-aid kit even?"

Shrike stared at Hester's grey, shocked face. *Let her die*, he wanted to tell Oenone, *then use your skill to Resurrect her. In place of that scarred and ruined face give her a steel mask, more perfect than the Stalker Fang's. In place of her breakable body build her a body as strong as this one.* She would forget her life, but Shrike felt certain that her spirit would survive. Over the millennia that they would have together he would help her to recover it. His immortal child.

"Medical chest!" shouted Oenone. "Quickly, Mr Shrike!"

Shrike turned and found the *Shadow*'s first-aid kit in the locker above the bunk. As he handed it to Oenone a blow shook the airship. He went forward on to the flight-deck again. Theo was clinging to the controls, staring out of wet windows.

"WE ARE UNDER ATTACK," Shrike said.

"What?" the boy looked round at him, wide eyes white in his dark face.

"WE WERE HIT. A PROJECTILE. . ."

Theo turned to the window again. "I can't see another ship. I can't see anything. This cloud. . ."

And then the *Shadow Aspect* dropped out of the belly of the clouds, and they both saw the flanks of cities rising all around them, the sky between filled with the running-lights of dozens of airships. It was raining, and the drops flecked the windows and blurred everything into a kaleidoscope of glowing specks, but Shrike could tell by their trajectories that the other ships were not searching for the *Shadow Aspect*. They were not military ships at all, but freighters and liners, heading west.

"MURNAU IS EVACUATING ITS WOMEN AND CHILDREN," he said.

"Preparing for war. . ." whispered Theo, and then, remembering his plight, "What about us?"

"WORD OF OUR DEPARTURE MAY NOT HAVE REACHED THE OTHER CITIES YET."

"Well, it can't be long," said Theo. It seemed pointless to turn the *Shadow* eastward, for he did not believe they could escape from the Murnau cluster now, but he turned her anyway, peering out through the rain as she flew through a steep-sided canyon whose walls were the towering sides of Manchester and Traktionbad Braunschweig. He took the Shadow low so that the cities' tall wheels slid past on either side of the gondola. Other ships poured through the canyon high above, most of them flying west. Ahead, across a few miles of mud crawling with small, fierce-looking suburbs, stood Murnau. The great fighting city had shut its armour. Theo started to steer the *Shadow Aspect* around its northern flank, still at track-level. The rudder controls were sluggish. "I think the steering vanes are damaged," he said, tugging irritably at the levers.

Remembering the blow that he had felt as the ship

dropped away from Airhaven, Shrike went aft again. Hester was conscious, groaning as Oenone cleaned her wound. "Tom! Oh, Tom!" Shrike caught the sharp whiff of medical alcohol. He climbed the companion-ladder, stooping as he stepped out on to the axial catwalk that led along the centre of the envelope. At the sternward end was a small hatch, built for once-born and almost too small for him to squeeze his Stalker's bulk through. Outside, the *Shadow*'s rain-wet tail-fins shone silvery in the light from the passing windows of Murnau's skirt-forts. Holding tight to the ratlines, Shrike made his way out on to the lateral fin. At the rear of the fin something had wedged among the control-cables. Beneath the howl of the engines and the drumming of rain on the steep curve of the envelope above him, Shrike picked up another sound, a rhythmic clatter. Was this some new weapon? He let go of the ratlines with one hand, and unsheathed his claws.

The shape in the control-cables shifted suddenly, reacting to the flick of wet light from the blades. A white, frightened face gaped up at Shrike. "Great Poskitt!" it wailed.

Shrike realized what had happened. This once-born must have fallen from Airhaven as the *Shadow Aspect* departed. He sheathed his claws and reached out to drag him to safety, but the once-born misunderstood; terrified, he let go his tight grip on the cables and began to fall again, shrieking as he tumbled into the sky. Shrike lunged forward and grabbed him by the collar of his coat, swinging him round and safely up on to the fin again. The *Shadow Aspect* tilted, engines caterwauling, as Shrike heaved the man over the aileron flaps and started to drag him along the fin towards the open hatch.

The airship's sudden, uncertain movement drew the attention of lookouts in Murnau's skirt-forts. As Shrike and his dripping, barely conscious burden regained the flight-deck the forts' gun-slits started to prickle with light. It looked quite pretty, until the first bullets began tearing into the gondola. Windows shattered; pressure-gauges wavered as holes were torn in the gas-cells. The engines howled, still driving the ship eastward, past towering jaws, out across rainswept, shell-torn mud. The gunfire stopped. Theo checked the periscope. Astern, three points of light were pulling clear of the immense bulk of the armoured city; three bat-black shapes growing against the grey underbelly of the clouds.

High above, Orla Twombley wiped rain from her goggles and pushed her flying machine *Combat Wombat* into a dive that would bring it up on the *Shadow*'s tail. Behind her, the ornithopter *Zip Gun Boogie* and a rocket-propelled triplane called *No More Curried Eggs For Me* followed suit, wings slicing the wet air like blades.

Theo shouted out in fear and frustration. He knew that his sluggish, wounded *Shadow* could not outrun the Flying Ferrets. He saw Shrike turn towards him, and thought the Stalker was about to warn him of the pursuing machines. "I *know*!" he yelled.

But Shrike said, "THERE ARE STALKER-BIRDS AHEAD."

"What?" Theo tried to peer out through the rain-spattered forward window, but he could see only darkness and his own terrified reflection. Then a rocket from the pursuing machines tore past the gondola and exploded ahead, and he realized that the darkness was largely made of wings. Across the empty skies of no-man's-land, from the direction of the Green Storm's lines, an immense flock of Resurrected birds was flapping towards him.

"Christ!" cried Theo, and slammed the steering levers over, trying vainly to turn the ship about, for he would rather face rockets than the claws and beaks of the Storm's raptors. But the *Shadow*'s rudder-controls had been hit; she responded slowly, and long before she could come about the sky outside the gondola windows was filled with beating wings and the green pinpoints of the dead birds' eyes.

Astern, wind-lashed and drenched in the open cockpit of the *Combat Wombat*, Orla Twombley saw the cloud of wings. Cursing inventively, she swung her machine about and signalled to her companions to do the same. She had lost enough people to the Stalker-birds at Cloud 9; nothing would make her engage them in such numbers. She checked her men were with her, then soared back towards the fastnesses of Manchester, while skeins of birds, like the fingers of some gloomy god, closed around the *Shadow Aspect*.

On the flight-deck, Theo waited for beaks and claws to start tearing through the thin walls. Over the rumble of the *Shadow*'s engines he could hear whooshing wingbeats, the flutter of feathers as the birds turned, matching the little airship's course and speed.

"They're not here to attack us," said Oenone softly, coming to stand behind Theo, her hand touching his shoulder. "I think they're an escort. . ."

Theo leaned forward, looking up past the bulge of the envelope. The wounded airship was flying inside a dark nebula of wings, where the eyes of hundreds of birds glowed like green stars. The birds were immense; resurrected kites and condors, eagles and vultures. As the gas vented from the *Shadow*'s shredded cells hundreds of birds gripped her air-frame with their claws and bore her up, their wingbeats carrying her eastward across the track-scars and shell-craters of no-man's-land.

In through one of the shattered starboard windows came a smaller bird. It had been a raven when it was alive. It perched on the handle of a control lever and turned its head, its green eye whirring as it focused on Theo. It opened its beak, and the faint, crackly voice of a distant Green Storm commander came out of the tiny radio-transmitter inside its ribs. He was speaking in a battle-code which Theo did not recognize, but Oenone did. She replied in the same harsh language, and the raven spread its wings and flew past her through the window and away.

Oenone looked at Theo. "One of the Storm's forward observation posts saw us come under attack. They assumed we must be their agents. I have told them the truth; that I am Lady Naga, coming home. The bird gave me the coordinates of the landing field where they want us to set down."

Theo listened to the numbers she quoted, but he

barely needed to alter course; the birds were already shepherding the *Shadow Aspect* in the right direction. He flopped down in his seat and looked at Shrike. He was too wrung out with shock to feel more than mildly surprised when he saw that the wet, whimpering man the Stalker clutched was Nimrod Pennyroyal.

"What's *he* doing here?" he asked.

"It was an accident!" said Pennyroyal fearfully, as if he thought he was about to be accused of boarding the *Shadow Aspect* by stealth. "I fell. Spiney and I – we fell out of Airhaven and landed on your tailfin. Well, I did. Spiney carried on down, poor devil. Still, it serves him right." The thought of his enemy's death seemed to restore his spirits slightly, but only for a moment; his eyes wandered past Theo to the storm of birds outside. "Ngoni, am I a prisoner?"

"I think we're all prisoners, Professor."

"But you're Green Storm; they won't harm you! I was Mayor of Brighton. You'll tell them, won't you, I was always an Anti-Tractionist at heart? I only accepted high office so that I could subvert the system from within. And I treated captured Mossies well, didn't I? You can vouch for me; you had it easy on Cloud 9, didn't you – three good meals a day and you never had to carry anything heavier than a sunshade."

Oenone said, "I will tell them to treat you well."

"You will? Thank you!"

"But I don't know if they'll listen to me. It all depends on whether the units who control these birds are loyal, or whether they want me dead."

"Oh, Poskitt!"

Oenone squeezed Theo's shoulder, and said, "I must go and check on your friend."

"How is she?" asked Theo, ashamed to find that he had completely forgotten about Hester.

Oenone looked solemnly at him.

"She'll be all right?"

"I hope so. She has a serious head injury. I'll do all I can. Who is Tom? She keeps asking for him."

"Her husband. Tom Natsworthy. Wren's father."

Oenone nodded owlishly and went aft again. Shrike dumped Pennyroyal on the deck and followed her. Left alone with the old man, Theo wondered if he should tie him up or lock him in the toilet or something. But Pennyroyal looked too trembly and sodden to try anything, and the host of Storm-birds just outside the window were surely enough to keep him in his place. Theo lay back in his seat, tasting the blood that had trickled into the corner of his mouth from a small cut on his forehead. He thought of Zagwa and his family, and wondered if he would ever see them again. Whatever happened when he landed, he must try and get word to them.

"Letter for you," said Pennyroyal, rather sheepishly.

Theo looked round. Pennyroyal was holding out a filthy, crumpled envelope. "She left it with me to send on to you, but I must confess, I forgot. Found it in my greatcoat pocket earlier, when I was looking for a scrap of paper to jot down the *Humbug*'s berth on. Thought you might as well have it. Better late than never, eh?"

Theo turned the envelope over and recognized Wren's careful handwriting. He ripped it open, and pulled out the letter, hissing with frustration as the wet paper tore. Her photograph smiled at him; the same picture that had been in the newspaper; that long, clever face, not as beautiful as he remembered her, but real, and lovely. He spread the letter on the control desk and tried to read it. The rain had fogged and buckled it until only a few phrases were legible. *We are starting on a journey . . . loading provisions . . . didn't even know London had any ruins but. . . .* A few lines on was a word that might have been *survivors*. Then, at the foot of the page: *look for me in London.*

"London?" he said. He tried not to cry, but he couldn't stop himself. "She has gone to London?"

"What?" asked Pennyroyal, startled. "No, no; you've misread it; they set off on some job for Wolf Kobold, the Kriegsmarshal's son. London? Nobody goes to London; it's a ruin; haunted. . ."

There was only one more line that Theo could read. *With love,* it said, *from Wren.*

The sleeping quarters smelled thickly of blood and antiseptic oils. Hester lay with her head thrown back, her face whiter than the pillow it rested on. Looking down at her, Shrike hoped that she would die without waking. When she was a Stalker like him he would not have to suffer so much worry. Once-born were so fragile; so disposable. Loving one was agony.

Oenone knelt to check her patient's pulse, then looked up at Shrike. In all the chaos of the fight on Strut 13 and the flight from Airhaven there had not been time for her to say, "Mr Shrike! What are you doing here?" or "Mr Shrike, how nice to see you again!" and it was too late now. Instead, she said, "She is Hester Shaw, isn't she?"

"YOU KNOW OF HER?"

"Of course. I studied your past before I reawakened you."

Shrike sensed the airship descending. He went to a side window and looked out. Through the darkness of the birds' wings he could see long strings of lights flickering on the land ahead; lanterns and torches on the Green Storm's front line. City traps and concrete sound-mirrors poked out of the mud like tombstones. Knowing that there might not be time for conversation once they landed, he spoke to Oenone's reflection in the glass. "WHY HAVE YOU MADE ME LIKE THIS?"

"Like what?" she asked guiltily. "Do you not have all your memories back? I erased nothing; when you had destroyed the Stalker Fang I meant you to become yourself again. . ."

"I CANNOT FIGHT," said Shrike. He turned to face her, feeling his claws twitch inside his steel hands. A spark of his old Stalker fury ignited inside him somewhere, like an ember glowing in a cold hearth. He wanted to kill her for what she had done to him, but what she had done to him meant that he could not kill her. "YOU MADE ME WEAK," he said. "THE GHOSTS OF ALL THE ONCE-BORN I KILLED BEFORE HANG IN MY HEAD LIKE WET SHEETS. I HATE THE THINGS I HAVE DONE. WHY DID YOU MAKE ME FEEL LIKE THIS?"

Oenone moved closer. Her hand touched his armour. "I did not do it. I would not know how. These feelings come from inside you."

"WHEN THE ONCE-BORN NATSWORTHY KILLED ME, ON THE BLACK ISLAND, I REMEMBERED THINGS. THEY FADED AS SOON AS YOU REPAIRED ME, BUT I THINK THEY WERE MEMORIES OF THE TIME BEFORE I WAS A STALKER; WHEN I WAS ALIVE, LIKE YOU. . . IS THAT WHERE THIS WEAKNESS COMES FROM?"

"I suppose it's possible. . . Dr Popjoy had a theory

about the origins of Stalkers. . ." She smiled. Shrike saw her white, crooked teeth; the first thing he remembered noticing about her when she dug him out of his grave. "I think it's more likely that you have developed feelings and a conscience of your own. You are intelligent and self-aware, and you have had long enough to do it in, after all! I think you began the process long before I met you. I know how you saved Hester as a child, and how long you sought for her after she left home. That was one of the things that made me realize you were no ordinary Stalker. You have loved Hester since you first found her, haven't you?"

Shrike looked away. He was still a Stalker, and it was hard for him to talk about things like love. He said, "WILL THOSE MEMORIES OF MY ONCE-BORN LIFE EVER RETURN?"

"Perhaps. Perhaps, next time you die. But that won't be for a long, long time. I built you to last, Mr Shrike."

The ground was close now. Shrike looked down at Hester, thinking that he did not care how long he lived for as long as she was with him. He said, "I WANT TO KEEP HER SAFE AND STRONG, FOR EVER. WILL YOU HELP ME?"

Oenone did not understand what he meant. "Of course I will," she promised. She stood on tiptoe and kissed his face. Dabs of his preservative slime came off on her lips and the tip of her nose. "Congratulations, Mr Shrike. You've grown a soul."

29

FUN, FUN, FUN ON THE *OBERRANG*

In the argon-lit rain Harrowbarrow heaved itself out of the mud off Murnau's starboard side like a gigantic submarine surfacing in a very dirty sea. A boarding bridge was run out, and Wolf Kobold strode across and vanished into the larger city, where an express elevator carried him quickly up to the *Oberrang*. A bug was waiting for him there, along with an officer who began shouting at him as soon as he stepped off the elevator, "Sir, sir, come quickly! Your father is hurt!"

"Yes, I got your radio message," said Kobold wearily, settling himself into the bug's rear seat. How stupid, to be dragged all the way up here just so that he could pretend to be concerned about an old man he cared nothing for. Already he was longing to be aboard Harrowbarrow again, free of these mawkish conventions. He listened half-heartedly to the driver prattling about Airhaven and Green Storm spies as the little vehicle went swerving along Über-den-Linden to the Rathaus. Outside, young officers were saying farewell to their sweethearts and workers were heaving shut the last open sections of the city's armour, but Wolf barely noticed them. He stared at his own gaunt face reflected in the bug's hood and thought of the long trek he had just made across the Storm's territory, the sentry he'd strangled as he crept back through their lines into no-man's-land, where good old Hausdorfer had had the 'Barrow waiting. He thought proudly of London, and of the fantastical machines which would soon be his.

At the Rathaus, the servants led him to the main

drawing room. His father sat in an armchair, his chest bandaged, being fussed over by frock-coated medical men. Adlai Browne stood close by, having come across from Manchester with flowers and grapes and a disclaimer he wanted the Kriegsmarshal to sign, absolving the Manchester Militia of any liability for his injuries. Beside him stood the commander of his mercenary air force. Wolf had found Ms Twombley attractive once, but now she struck him as rather brassy; all that pink leather and mascara. He thought wistfully of Wren Natsworthy, her innocent beauty and bright, malleable young mind.

"Wolfram!" cried his father, waving the doctors aside and struggling up to hug him. "They told me you were away somewhere. . ."

"Just a little business trip," said Kobold, disgusted by the liver spots on the old man's arms, the white curls of hair that showed above the bandage on his chest. "I got home to Harrowbarrow the day before yesterday."

His father studied him. "You look thin, my boy."

Thin, unshaven, fever-eyed, Wolf waved his words away. "It's yourself you should be worrying about. They told me you're hurt."

"Just a few bruises, some broken bones."

"I got home just in time, it seems."

"What do you mean?"

"Great Thatcher! The Mossies tried to kill you, father! It was an act of war! We must retaliate immediately!"

"Just what I've been telling him!" boomed Adlai Browne, with the air of a man who had been waiting impatiently to resume an interrupted conversation. "We mustn't let them get away with it!"

"Nonsense, Browne," snapped von Kobold, wincing

with the pain as he slumped back down in his chair. "It was one of *your* drunken louts who shot me!"

"Youthful exuberance," protested Browne. "If you'd not been so keen to keep the prisoner for yourself. . ." He appealed to Wolf. "Have you heard the news? Naga's missus herself was loose on Airhaven, with a gang of Stalkers to protect her. Hatching some plot with that renegade Pennyroyal, apparently."

"I see." Usually Wolf would have scoffed at such talk; the panicky, exaggerated stuff that flew about whenever fat city men got a whiff of real war. But tonight a little panic suited him. The sooner war broke out, the sooner Harrowbarrow could begin its journey to London. "They got away alive, I take it?"

Browne turned to the aviatrix at his side. "You tell him, lass."

Orla Twombley bowed and said, "The airship was met over no-man's-land by more Stalker-birds than I've ever seen in one place. There must have been someone or something of value aboard. There was nothing I could do to stop it escaping."

It seemed to Wolf that there was plenty she could have done, had she not valued her life more than her duty. But he simply nodded and said, "This sounds bad. Who knows what plots the Mossies have set in motion, or what they've learned about our plans? There's only one thing for it."

"You mean – attack?" asked Adlai Browne hopefully.

"It's the best form of defence. The Mossies struck first. We must retaliate. Attack at once, all along the line."

Von Kobold rubbed his eyes. "Surely there must be another way. . ."

"If you don't feel up to commanding this place. . ." said Browne, all mock-solicitude.

"I shall do my part," the old man promised wearily. "You'll not call me a coward, Browne. If the other cities advance, Murnau will come too, and I'll command her. Unless my son would care to take his place on the bridge?"

He looked at Wolf, who shook his head firmly. "Sorry, Father. I must get back to Harrowbarrow. When the attack begins I'll gnaw a nice big hole for you in the Mossies' defences."

He shook his father's hand, bowed to Browne and Ms Twombley and went out of the room, leaving silence behind him, and a feeling of sadness, like a lingering smell.

"Well," said Adlai Browne, clapping his hands together. "I must inform the other mayors and Kriegsmarshals. Ms Twombley, you'll need to get your machines aloft. The obliteration of the Green Storm starts at dawn!"

30

SHE IS RISEN

"**F**ulfil The Vision Of The Wind-Flower" Air Field was an oblong of flat ground bulldozed out of the mud a few miles behind the Storm's front line. It was ringed with landing lights and bunkers and big, whale-backed barns of airship hangars. Anti-aircraft cannon squatted watchfully in emplacements made from earth-packed wicker barrels. Searchlights stretched out their colourless fingers to brush the *Shadow Aspect*'s envelope as the cloud of birds steered her towards her docking pan.

Soldiers came running as she touched down, and crowded into the gondola when Theo opened the hatch. White uniforms; crab-shell helmets; guns. Oenone emerged from behind the curtain at the back of the flight deck, and they recoiled from her and raised their weapons, alarmed by her filthy, bloodstained clothes and the Stalker who stood behind her. She held out her hand, letting the light glint on her signet-ring. "Before you shoot me," she said politely, "I would like you to take care of my companions. Mr Ngoni and Professor Pennyroyal are not enemies of the Storm."

The sub-officer at the head of the boarding-party bowed low, placing his right fist against the palm of his left hand in the old League salute. "You are safe now, Lady Naga."

Oenone returned the bow, nervous, still not quite trusting him. "There is a woman in the cabin who needs care. Is there a field hospital here?"

The soldier pointed towards a hummock of camouflaged bunkers on the horizon. "Shall I call stretcher bearers?"

"I WILL CARRY HER," said Shrike. He pulled the curtain aside and lifted Hester easily and carefully in his arms. Theo and the others made to follow him as he carried her to the open hatch, but the sub-officer, feeling things sliding out of his control, moved quickly to stop them, barring their way with a raised hand.

"She will be well looked after, Ladyship," he promised Oenone. "But you and these other foreigners must come with me. I have orders to bring you before the sector commander."

The part of the line where the *Shadow Aspect* had landed was commanded by the motherly General Xao. Sleepy-eyed but smiling she welcomed Oenone and her followers to the dugout where she had her headquarters. It was a pleasant place, as dugouts went; not too damp, the floor flagged with slates, the wooden walls whitewashed and hung with pictures. In the general's private quarters photographs of her dead family stood among the statues of her household gods on an elaborate shrine. A pot-bellied stove gave out a dry heat that made Pennyroyal's soggy clothes steam so much the general suggested he take them off, and made one of her plumper staff officers lend him a spare uniform and an elegant grey cloak. Oenone had also changed into Green Storm uniform, and had washed her face and hair; she still did not look like an empress, but at least she looked less like a street-urchin.

The general's servants brought rice wine; steamed rolls; tea. Theo pulled off his flying-jacket and tried to stop himself from falling asleep on the folding chair which another servant set out for him. After the things they had been through that night, it all seemed impossibly luxurious. Although he had grown to hate the Green Storm, he had never doubted the strength or courage of their army, and it was a relief to think of all those brave soldiers and powerful guns standing between him and the cityfolk. He was not even worried about Hester, now that she was safe in the field hospital.

The general said, "My people are preparing a ship to carry you home to Tienjing, my lady. Her captain is a friend of mine; a supporter of General Naga; her crew can all be trusted. A Stalker-bird has gone east already to take the good news to your husband. I hope that it will restore his spirits."

"He is ill?" asked Oenone, alarmed.

General Xao looked glum. "There have been no clear orders from Tienjing for weeks. We have warned your honoured husband about the build-up on the other side of the line, and the harvester-suburb that raided Track-mark 16 last month. We have told him that we cannot hold these positions if the cities attack; he does not seem to care. It is as if, when he heard word of your death, he gave up all hope."

Oenone looked for a moment as if she would cry. She said hoarsely, "Can't we contact him more quickly? I could talk to him by long-range radio. . ."

Xao shook her head. "I dare not risk it, Lady Naga. The barbarians could intercept your message, and try again to kill you."

"It was not the barbarians who tried to kill me the first time," said Oenone. "It was barbarians who saved me, with Theo's help."

"Indeed," nodded the general, smiling at Theo, and then at Pennyroyal. "We have heard of Professor Pennyroyal's bravery."

"*Professor Pennyroyal's* bravery?" Theo almost choked on the roll he was munching. He wondered if the general was slightly drunk. First her defeatist talk about not being able to hold the line and now this! "*What* have you heard?" he asked.

"We have listening-posts deep in no-man's-land which eavesdrop on the townies' radio transmissions," explained the general. She reached for some papers on her desk. "This is a news-bulletin which went out on Murnau's public screens a few hours ago." She skimmed the transcript's first two paragraphs, then cleared her throat and read, "'The raiders were helped by an agent within Airhaven; the notorious author, charlatan and former Mayor of Brighton, Nimrod B. Pennyroyal. As the Green Storm spy-ship left, several eyewitnesses saw the traitor Pennyroyal running after it, shouting, "What about my money?"

"A traitor? Me?" Pennyroyal looked outraged.

"Only to the Tractionist barbarians," said General Xao. "To our people you will be a hero."

"But – gosh! Will I?"

"To think that the mayor of a barbaric raft-town could come to see the error of his ways so clearly that he would risk his own life to free a Green Storm prisoner," the general went on. "Your statue will stand in the Hall of Matchless Immortals in Tienjing. Naga will reward you richly. He. . ."

A junior officer entered, bowing nervously and murmuring something in Shan Guonese. The general frowned, standing up. "Forgive me; I am needed outside."

"What is happening?" asked Oenone.

"Our sound-mirrors are detecting engine noise from the cities. . . We have been expecting an attack, but not so soon. Great Gods, I've still not had the reinforcements I asked for last month!" A bell began to ring on the bank of field-telephones in the next room; then another and another. General Xao snapped an order at her underling and said to Oenone, "Excellency, you must take ship at once. I will not risk. . ."

An enormous roll of thunder drowned out the remainder of her words. The floor shook, and dust sifted down between the planks of the low roof. Pennyroyal started to call on his peculiar gods again. Theo looked at the table where he had set down his teacup, and the cup was dancing, dancing to the boom, boom, boom of the thunder. A soldier came scrambling into the bunker, and although he was shouting his report in Shan Guonese Theo and his companions knew what it meant, even before General Xao turned to them and said, "It is beginning! All their cities are on the move! Dozens of cities! Hundreds of suburbs!"

They stood up, indignant at being plunged into another adventure before they'd had a chance to recover from the last. "What about Hester and Mr Shrike?"

"I will have your friends meet you at the airfield," shouted General Xao. "Now go quickly, and gods preserve us all. . ."

They followed a sub-officer out of the headquarters and through trenches where hundreds of soldiers were hurrying to their positions. The thunder from the west was shockingly loud. The sky above the front-line trenches pulsed with light. Pennyroyal looked terrified. Theo, wincing at the noise of the blasts, kept reminding himself that most of it was probably the Green Storm's artillery firing at the cities; any attack would soon be beaten off.

Only Oenone had been in the front line before. She recognized the complex shudderings of the earth in the same way a city-person would understand what each movement in their deckplates meant. She knew that somewhere, not far away, fighting suburbs were advancing at high speed behind a rolling barrage of snout-gun shells. She prayed as she ran, wondering if even God would be able to hear her above all the din.

They zigzagged through a communications trench and there ahead of them was the airfield. A corvette was waiting on a central pan while pods of Fox Spirits went snarling into the primrose sky from hangars dug into the hillsides behind her. She was called the *Fury*, and her engines were already in take-off position, the propellers a blaze of silver. As they crossed the muddy docking pan a half-track marked with the caduceus symbol of the medical corps came speeding up, slewing to a halt near the foot of the *Fury*'s gangplank. Shrike swung down out of its belly, and reached back to help the bearers bring Hester's stretcher out.

The sub-officer started urging Oenone towards the

ship, and Pennyroyal, needing no encouragement, trotted alongside. Theo was about to follow them when he remembered Wren's letter, which was still in the pocket of his flying-jacket, on the chair by the stove in Xao's headquarters.

"I have to go back!" he shouted.

Only Shrike heard him, as he carried Hester up the gangplank. He looked round to see Theo plunge back into the maze of trenches. "THEO NGONI!" he shouted. Sometimes he could barely believe the folly of the once-born.

"Stalker! Get her aboard!" called an aviator from the *Fury*'s open hatchway.

"WE MUST WAIT," Shrike insisted. "THE ONCE-BORN THEO NGONI IS NOT WITH US. . ."

A snout-gun shell burst near the western perimeter of the field, crumpling a rising Fox Spirit and spraying mud and gravel against the *Fury*'s envelope. Shrike looked towards the trenches, but could see nothing but smoke. Explosions were going off steadily, and he made out another noise beneath and between the slamming of the guns – the deep note of city engines and the high, squealing counterpoint of rolling tracks.

"Come aboard, Stalker, or we take off without you!" yelled the frightened aviator, holding his helmet in place as blast-waves chased each other across the docking pans.

Shrike bellowed, "THEO NGONI!" once more into the storm of sound, then turned reluctantly, carrying Hester up the gangplank and through the hatch. Oenone ran to meet him in the corridor. "Where is Theo? I thought he was with us?"

The *Fury* jolted and leaped quickly into the air.

Shrike carried Hester to the medical bay and laid her on a bunk. "LOOK AFTER THIS ONCE-BORN," he told the orderlies, and strode across the cabin to a window. Flying machines were swerving through the air outside, bullets from their machine-guns pummelling the *Fury*'s armour. Below, shell-bursts speckled the ground. All up and down the Green Storm's line the heavy guns were firing, while steam-trebuchets flung up their long arms and lobbed their bombs into the screens of drifting smoke which curtained no-man's-land.

"Naga, it has begun!"

General Naga sits slumped in his favourite chair, beside the window of the quarters that he used to share with Oenone. The spiral stairways of the Jade Pagoda rumble like organ pipes as a gale blasts around the old fortress, blowing snow upwards past Naga's windows.

His old friend General Dzhu waits in the doorway, shifting awkwardly from one foot to the other, unhappy at delivering such bad news. "We have reports of heavy fighting in a dozen sectors. The Rustwater marsh-forts are under attack, and we've lost contact with Xao's command post. . ."

"Ah," says Naga, without looking up.

On the low table beside him stand a teacup and a pot of green tea. The girl Rohini brings it to him every morning at this hour, and plays to him on the shudraga, but today Dzhu sent her packing, insisting he must speak to Naga privately. A pity. She is a good girl, and sometimes Naga thinks that her kindness is all that keeps him alive. The music she plays reminds him of his boyhood; hunting duck in the flooded atomic craters of south China, joining the League's air fleet that summer before London came crawling east. At the training college on Seven Tiger Mountain there was a girl called Sathya whom he had fancied, but she'd been in love with the Wind-Flower.

"Whatever happened to Sathya?" he wonders. "Do you think she's still at that hermitage we found for her on Zhan Shan?"

"Naga, we're at war!" his friend shouts. "What are your orders? Do I tell our commanders to stand, or withdraw?"

"Whatever you think necessary, Dzhu."

Dzhu sighs; turns to go; turns back. "There is another thing; it seems minor, but Batmunkh Gompa are reporting a lot of activity inside the wreck of London. . ."

Naga flaps his words away. "London? A few poor barbarians, Dzhu; we've known about them for years. They're harmless."

"Are we sure of that? What if they are a fifth column, waiting to assist the enemy as he advances? I have ordered increased surveillance. . ."

Naga tries to shrug, but his mechanical armour isn't made for shrugging. "I'm ill, old friend. I ache all over. I can't sleep, but I'm never properly awake. My head buzzes like a nest of bees. You should take over command."

"The people want you, Naga! You smashed the barbarians last spring, and they know you can do it again! They won't trust me!"

"I miss Zero," murmurs Naga. "I miss her so much."

Dzhu stares at him. "I'll tell Xao to make a stand, if I can reach her."

As he leaves the chambers, he sees Cynthia Twite waiting outside, watching him from the shadows. He forces her down a narrow stairway and out on to a balcony. Snowflakes flail at them, and the wind blows their hair about. "What's happening to him?" hisses Dzhu. "I thought once we got rid of the Zero girl he'd come to his senses and lead us to victory, but he just sits there! Is it just grief? Is he dying? Tell me!"

Cynthia smiles. "Green tea," she says. "A pot every morning, like his poor wife used to make him."

"You're *poisoning* him?"

"Just a little. Not enough to kill him. Just enough to keep him helpless."

"But we need him!"

"No we don't, you fool."

Dzhu is astonished. In the mountain kingdoms women respect men and young people respect their elders, but this girl talks to him as if he's a child!

"Haven't you heard the rumours, Dzhu? A Stalker killing Lost Boys aboard Brighton. An abandoned limpet found under a waterfall in Snow Fan Province. The murder of Dr Popjoy. It all adds up. It's all connected. Are you too blind to see what it means?"

Dzhu just stares at her. The snow's so thick that her face keeps breaking up like a bad goggle-screen picture.

"She is risen!" Cynthia hisses triumphantly. "Soon she will reveal herself to us, and save us from the barbarians. Until she does, we must make sure that Naga is weak. When he has let the barbarians smash his divisions and devour our western settlements the people will be ready to abandon him and welcome back their true leader!"

"You're insane!" says General Dzhu, turning to go and warn his friend of her.

One of the long pins which hold Cynthia's hairstyle in place is tipped with venom. She's been saving it for just such an emergency. The sharpened tip makes only the tiniest scratch on Dzhu's neck, but he's dead before he can even cry out. Grunting with effort and cursing his fat belly, Cynthia heaves the body off the balcony and watches it plummet through the snowflakes to the sharp mountainside hundreds of feet below. She's always had her doubts about Dzhu, and she has forged his suicide note already. It will be the work of a moment to plant it in his desk.

She thinks of her mistress, the Stalker Fang, out there in the mountains somewhere, waiting. If only she would show herself! Cynthia understands why the Stalker would want to punish the weaklings who flocked to Naga's banner, but surely she knows that she can still rely upon her faithful private agents. For a moment, as she slips back inside and strolls towards General Dzhu's quarters, she feels almost angry at her old mistress. It quickly passes. Whatever the Stalker Fang is planning will be dreadful and wonderful, and it is not Cynthia's place to judge her.

Theo had always had a good sense of direction. He found his way quickly through the maze of trenches and was almost in sight of the dugout when an explosion went off just beyond the wire, kicking fans of earth and smoke high into the dawn sky. He crouched as the mud came spattering down. A sea of smoke filled the trench.

Scared, fleeing soldiers blundered through it, throwing down their weapons as they ran, pulling off packs and bandoliers. Their mouths were open as if they were shouting, but Theo couldn't hear them; he had been deafened by the blast of the shell.

Dazed, he scrambled up on to a fire-step to see what they were running from. Beyond the bramble hedge of wire outside the trench, mountainous shapes were moving. Now and again, as the gusting wind hooked swags of smoke aside, he could see Murnau, only a few miles off, munching its way through the shell-battered city traps, while a dozen harvester-suburbs probed for mines or pitfalls. A nearby fortress was firing rockets towards it, but as Theo watched the ground began to tremble sluggishly and up from the mud at the fort's base an enormous, blunt, steel nose came shoving, lifting to expose giant drills and complicated mouth-parts, knocking the fort to pieces and gobbling them down. WELCOME TO HARROWBARROW said a crude white slogan painted on the armoured flank. Theo had plenty of time to read it as the weird suburb went grinding past him, crushing bunkers and wrecked gun-emplacements beneath its tracks. Signal lamps blinked on Murnau's upper tier, as if trying to call it to heel, but the suburb ignored them; it settled itself deep into the muddy earth again and went grinding on into Green Storm territory.

Theo jumped down from the step and stumbled on, confused by the smoke and the steep walls of earth that had been thrown across the trench by the explosions. Fresh blasts went off, spattering him with mud and muddy water, but it all happened in hissing, undersea silence, like a dream. He barely understood what was going on. How could the cities have broken through so easily? Where were the indomitable air-destroyers and thousand-Tumbler quick-response units that he had been told of in the Green Storm's propaganda films?

An airship drifted overhead, burning so fiercely that he could not tell which side it had belonged to. By its light he saw the dugout entrance, and ran gratefully through it. The command post had already been evacuated, but Theo's coat still hung on the back of the folding chair where he had left it. He pulled it on, feeling Wren's letter crinkle in the pocket, her photograph pressing against his heart.

He didn't hear the scream of the snout-gun shell descending. The first he knew of it was when the hot hands of the explosion lifted him off his feet. Then everything turned into light.

31

THE HOUSE AT ERDENE TEZH

The Stalker Fang pauses at the edge of the docking pan where Popjoy's air-yacht is tethered and turns her bronze face towards the west.

"What?" asks Fishcake. "What is it?" He looks westward, too, but he can see nothing; just the mountains. How sick he is of mountains! They stand guard like frost-giants all around this high, green valley, and their reflections shimmer in the windswept lake below the docking pan.

"Gunfire," the Stalker whispers.

"You mean the war is on again?" Fishcake strains his grubby once-born ears to try and hear what she can hear.

"I must work quickly. Come."

She starts limping towards the causeway, and Fishcake follows her, carrying on his shoulder one of the cases of equipment which she made him bring from Dun Resurrectin'. Overhead, the dead birds which followed her from Popjoy's place soar past, keeping watch for movements in the sky or on the steep pass at the valley's western end.

The causeway is two hundred paces long. At its far end is a rocky island where a house stands, dark and cold as a tomb. It was a monastery once, sacred to the gods and demons of the mountains, whose faces still leer out of niches in the outer walls. Later it was Anna Fang's home, a place of light and laughter where she relaxed between missions for the Anti-Traction League. She had planned to retire here, and raise horses in the steep green pastures, before Valentine's sword unravelled all her plans.

In the first years of the Green Storm regime there had been talk of turning Erdene Tezh into a museum, where schoolchildren could come to see relics of the Wind-Flower and tread the same floors which she had trodden. But the Stalker she had become forbade it. She had the house locked, and let it fall into ruin.

The gate whinges as the Stalker heaves it open. Fishcake crunches after her through the gateway where patches of snow lie blue in the shadows. Safe in the loop of the thick stone wall is a garden; dead trees and dead brown grass, a fountain lacy with icicles. Fishcake trots after his Stalker up the frosty path to the house. She does not smash the door down as he has been expecting, but extends one of her finger-glaives, inserts it into the keyhole, and moves it carefully about in there until the lock clicks. As she opens the door she looks back at Fishcake.

"Home again!" she whispers.

He follows her into the shadows. He can't be sure any more if she is Anna or the Stalker Fang. He thinks she may be *both*, as if Popjoy's tinkering blended the two personalities somehow. She has not been unkind to Fishcake, and she still shares her memories with him, but she does not play with him any more; she no longer takes his hand, or tousles his hair, or comes to hold him at night when he wakes from a bad dream. All he has left of that Anna is the carved toy horse, which he clutches tightly when he goes to sleep.

Whoever she is, the Stalker seems happy to be home. "Ah," she sighs, passing through a reception room where the ceiling has collapsed and bird droppings lie thick on a fine tiled floor. "Oh!" she says, crossing the atrium and peering into a long chamber whose shattered windows stare out across the mere to the white heights of the Erdene Shan. "She had such parties here! Such happy times. . ."

The wind hoots through holes in the walls. Beyond the party-room lies a bedroom, a canopied bed sinking like a torpedoed ship into a sea of its own mouldering covers. At the far side of the bedroom is another locked door. And beyond the door. . .

The room exhales stale air when she unlocks it. Fishcake, creeping in behind her, guesses that this part of the house has been sealed. It smells a bit like Grimsby. The walls and floor are covered in metal, with rubber mats to walk on. Cobwebs and plastic swathe a curious mountain of machinery; wires and tubes, screens and boxes, valves and dials and coloured flexes, keyboards torn from typewriting machines.

"Engineers were not the only ones who knew how to build things, back in the good old days," the Stalker whispers. "Anna was clever with machines, just like you, Fishcake. She even built her own airship out of odds and ends. She was attempting to make a long-range radio transmitter here. It never worked very well, and others since have had much more success. But it's a start. With what we brought from Popjoy's workshop, and the radio set from his yacht, I am certain we can boost the signal."

"Who are you signalling to?" asks Fishcake.

The Stalker lets out her hissy laugh. She takes him by the arm and drags him into the ruined bedroom, points through a hole in the roof, straight up, at the deep blue in the top of the sky.

"Up there. That's where the receiver is. We are going to send a message into heaven."

PART THREE

32

LONDON JOURNAL

19th June

*Seventeen days have passed since Wolf Kobold
ran away. Everybody seems to be forgetting him.
Even me, most of the time. Even Angie, now her
headache has faded and the lump is going down.
Most people think that there's no way Wolf could
cross all those miles of Green Storm territory and
get back to Harrowbarrow again. Even if he could,
he would never be able to bring Harrowbarrow
back east to eat New London, at least, not unless
war breaks out again. But work on New London
is going ahead even faster, just in case.*

*When I first found out what they are building I
thought they were all a bit mad, to be honest. But
when you see how hard everyone works here, and
how much they all believe in this crazy new city
the Engineers have dreamed up, you realize what
it must have been like in Anchorage when Freya
Rasmussen decided to take it across the ice to
America. That was a mad idea too, and I'm sure
there were a lot of people who thought it would
never work – my mum was so sure of it that she
betrayed the whole place to Arkangel when she
couldn't persuade Dad to leave. But she was
wrong, because it did work, didn't it? And I don't
want to be like Mum so I've decided to believe
that New London is going to work too.*

Anyway, Dad's been very keen to do his bit. At first he seemed intent on trying to help the Engineers, but the Childermass machines are so different from any technology he's seen before that I think he just got in the way. So he started helping the men lug bits of salvage up to the hangar, but I had a quiet word with Dr Childermass and explained about his heart trouble, and she had a q. word with Chudleigh Pomeroy, who took Dad aside and said what New London really needs is a Museum, so that even if it roams to the far side of the world the people who live aboard it will never forget the old London, and what became of it. "And since none of us have the time, Tom," he said, "perhaps you wouldn't mind putting together a collection?" So Dad has been appointed Head Historian and spends his days scouring the rust-heaps for artefacts that will say something to future generations about his London – everything from old drain-covers and tier-support ties to a little statue of the goddess Clio from somebody's household shrine.

Meanwhile, I've been out patrolling with the other young Londoners. Mr Garamond was v. opposed to it at first, but Mr Pomeroy told him not to be such a b——y fool, and Angie and her friends are all very friendly, and most impressed when I told them I'd been in an actual battle and seen Stalkers and Tumblers and stuff. (I didn't tell them how completely terrified I was, as it might be bad for morale.) Anyway, I've been right across the main debris field several times. It's very spooky, esp. at night, but Angie and Cat and the rest are good company, and I've been given a crossbow to use if we're attacked – I'm not sure I could actually shoot anyone, but it makes me feel a bit braver.

What I'd really like is one of the lightning guns the Engineers built to deal with Stalkers, but there aren't very many of those, and only Mr G's most trusted fighters get to use them; Saab and Cat and people. The Green Storm's Stalker-birds have been getting very nosy these past few weeks, and the danger bell at Crouch End is forever ringing, telling everyone to get under cover because some flea-bitten old dead buzzard is circling overhead, having a good look at us. Mostly we've just taken to ignoring them, but when one gets too close to the Womb the boys on duty in the crow's nests there shoot it down with their lightning guns; there are half a dozen hanging outside Crouch End now, all singed and charcoal-y.

There is one other way of getting rid of them; it's much more dangerous, and Angie and her friends treat it as a sort of sport. Last week, when we were out patrolling, a Stalker-bird came flying over us. We're supposed to hide when that happens, but Angie said, "Let's have a spot of Mollyhawking!" and jumped right out into the open, so I followed her. We went along one of the paths that winds between the wreckage heaps, and the bird came after us. I was worried it was going to attack, but Angie said they never do;

*they're just spies, and she meant to serve it right
for snooping.*

*We went on, walking quite fast, and soon I
began to realize that we were heading towards the
middle of the debris field, the bit they call Electric
Lane. Till then I'd tended to agree with Wolf
about the sprites – that they were just a fairy tale.
But up there in the middle of London, where
everything looks kind of scorched and melted, I
suddenly wasn't so sure. I asked Angie if it was
safe, and she said "safe-ish", which wasn't very
reassuring, but I didn't want her to think I was a
coward, so I kept going.*

*After a bit we came over a rise and there in
front of us was a sort of valley stretching right
across the middle of the debris field. It looked
quite peaceful, with ponds and trees on its floor,
but the wreckage on either side was all charred
and twisty-looking. Angie says that it's the place
where the core of MEDUSA fell, having melted its
way right down through the seven tiers of
London, and that's why MEDUSA's residue is
strongest there. I don't know if it's true. Anyway,
I only got a quick glimpse before Angie shoved
me into a hollow of the wreckage all overhung
with ivy. "Hide!" she said. The stupid old Stalker-
bird didn't see us, and went soaring out over
the valley. It hadn't gone fifty feet before a great
snaggly fork of electricity came crackling out of
the wreckage and roasted it; there was nothing
left but a puff of smoke and some singed feathers
that blew away on the wind!*

I got a bit shuddery afterwards, thinking what

would have happened to the Jenny if we'd flown into Electric Lane that first day.

PS Saab Peabody asked me out. I said I'd have to think about it and he said he supposed I had a boyfriend on the Bird Roads somewhere and I said I supposed I did. Silly, or what?

And now, because it's late, and tomorrow is a big day – the first test of the new city – I am going to go to bed.

33

THE TEST

The morning of the test dawned dull and cloudy, threatening rain. The wind came from the west in indignant squalls, scattering a confetti-storm of petals from the blossom-trees that had taken root among the debris of London.

Not wanting to impose himself on Wren, who was going up to the Womb with her new friends, Tom made the trek from Crouch End alone. He scanned the mounds of wreckage beside the track as he walked, for he had fallen into a habit of looking everywhere for fragments which might fit into the New London museum, and give the children who would one day be born upon the new city some notion of what Old London had been like. When you knew where to look, the rusting ruin-heaps were full of relics; street signs and door-handles, hinges and tea-urns. He spotted a pewter spoon with the crest of the Historians' Guild on its handle, and slipped it into his pocket. He had eaten with spoons like that every day of his childhood; it was like a shard of memory made solid, and he liked to think of those future Londoners looking at it and imagining his life.

Of course, they would never know the details; how he'd felt and what his dreams had been; his adventures on the Bird Roads, in the Ice Wastes and America. You couldn't expect a pewter spoon to convey that sort of detail.

Lately, watching Wren writing in her journal of an evening, Tom had wondered if he shouldn't try and write down some of the things that had happened to him, before it was too late. But he was no Thaddeus Valentine. He wasn't even a Nimrod Pennyroyal. Writing did not come easily to him. Anyway, it would have meant writing about Hester, and he didn't think he could do that. He'd not even spoken his wife's name since he came to London. If his new friends ever wondered who Wren's mother was, they kept it to themselves; perhaps they assumed that she was dead, and that Tom would find it painful to speak of her – which was not so far from the truth. How could he write about Hester for future generations when he did not understand himself why she had done the things she had, or what had made him love her?

Drawing close to the Womb, he caught up with a crowd of his fellow Londoners, all heading in the same direction. Clytie Potts was among them, and she greeted him warmly, glad of his company; her husband was aboard New London with the Engineers. "Dr Childermass is afraid her magnetic levitation system might work *too* well," she explained. "She wants an aviator on hand to steer New London down again if it goes too high."

"Really?"

"It's a joke, Tom."

"Oh. . ." Tom laughed with her, although he didn't find it funny. "I'm sorry. So much has changed since we were young. . . So many new inventions. . . I don't really know *what* New London is capable of." He thought of the Mag-Lev prototypes that Dr Childermass had shown him; platforms the size of dinner tables which manoeuvred around the Womb as if by magic, hanging several feet above the ground. If the new city survived, the Engineers were planning to apply the same technology to actual tables next; floating chairs and beds as well, and hovering Mag-Lev toys, which they would trade as curios to other small cities. Tom had even heard talk of Mag-Lev vehicles, which made him feel oddly sad, because if they worked they would surely bring an end to the age of airships, and his dear old *Jenny Haniver* would be obsolete.

The thought made his heart ache – or maybe that was the result of the climb from Crouch End. He swallowed one of his green pills, and went with Clytie through the entrance to the Womb.

Inside the shadowy hangar New London waited, squatting heavily on its oily stanchions and looking less likely to take to the air than any object Tom had ever seen. Small figures were running about on its hull, gesticulating at each other. The Engineers seemed to be having trouble with one of their magnetic repellors. Tom scanned the crowd of onlookers for Wren and saw her standing near the front with Angie and Saab and a few other young people whose names he could never remember. He felt proud of her, and glad that she was settling in here, and making friends. Seeing her from a distance, he was reminded of Katherine Valentine; she had something of Katherine's grace and liveliness; the same quick, dazzling smile. It had never struck him before, but then he had not given much thought to Katherine before he returned to London. Now that he had noticed it, the strange likeness was inescapable.

Wren seemed to sense him staring at her; she turned

and saw him, standing on tiptoe to wave at him over the sea of heads. Tom waved back, and hoped it was not bad luck to compare her to poor, ill-fated Katherine.

A handbell started to ring. "This is it," said Clytie. Engineers bustled through the crowd, warning people to stay back near the hangar walls. Everyone fell quiet, looking up expectantly. In the silence they heard Dr Childermass, who was aboard the new city, call out, "Ready everybody? Now!"

There was a humming sound that rose quickly until it was too high to hear. Nothing else happened. One of the stanchions near the new city's stern gave a long groan, as if it shared everyone's disappointment. Then the other stanchions began to creak and squeak as well, and Tom realized that it was because they were relaxing; New London, whose dead-weight they had supported all these years, was no longer pressing down on them. Scraps of rust came whispering down like November leaves. A forgotten paintbrush fell from a gantry and clattered on the Womb floor. The magnetic repellors swivelled slightly as Engineers in the city's control-rooms realigned them, but they still looked like big, misty mirrors; no crackling lightning; no mystical glow, just a faint flicker in the air around them, like a heat-haze.

Slowly, slowly, like some ungainly insect taking flight, New London rose from its scrap-metal cradle and turned a little, first to one side, then the other. It edged forward, and again Tom sensed that faint hum. "It works!" people started to whisper, glancing at each other's faces, making sure that they were not imagining this.

This was how it must have felt when the first airship flew, thought Tom, or when the divine Quirke first switched on London's land-engines. Lavinia

Childermass's machines were going to change the world in ways he could not imagine. Perhaps by the time Wren's grandchildren were born *all* cities would hover. Perhaps there would be no need for cities at all. . .

There was a sharp crack. Smoke squirted from some of the vents in New London's keel. The heat-haze ripple around the repellors vanished and the hovering city dropped gracelessly back on to its stanchions with a bellow of straining metal. The spectators groaned in disappointment, pressing themselves against the walls of the Womb as the stanchions swayed and workers ran forward to steady them.

"It don't work!" complained a woman standing close to Tom.

"It's a dud!" said another.

Lavinia Childermass appeared among the unfinished buildings at the edge of New London's upper hull. The Womb's acoustics and her own nervousness made her speech almost impossible to hear, but as Tom pushed his way to the exit he caught a few fragments of what she was saying: "A small problem with the Kliest Coils – mustn't give up – much work still to do – fine tuning – adjustments – wait a few more weeks. . ."

But do we have a few more weeks? Tom wondered. For as he stepped outside he heard the drone of Green Storm airships heading west, and another sound, which he thought at first was thunder, and then realized was the rumble of immense guns, somewhere beyond the western horizon.

34

DISPLACED PERSONS

"I see you're feeling better."

"This is *better*?"

"Well, conscious. That's an improvement."

Hester rubbed her eye and tried to bring the ceiling into focus. She felt as thin as water; as if her whole body was just a damp stain drying slowly on this hard, horsehair bed. A ghost leaned over her and solidified into someone she ought to know. She began to remember Airhaven; the girl she'd sprung from Varley's freighter; Lady Naga. She remembered the blow on her head, the fight on Strut 13.

"You've been very ill." Oenone talked like a doctor, and had changed her sackcloth dress for some kind of white military tunic, but she still looked like a schoolboy. Hester stared at her taped-together spectacles and crooked teeth. "You'll be all right now; the wound is healing well."

Hester remembered airships; the *Shadow Aspect* and then that big Green Storm job. Taking off into thunder. People yelling at each other; *her* yelling; Shrike holding her. Shrike must be disappointed that she'd survived. She raised her head from the pillow to look for him, but he was not there. She was alone with Oenone in a square, ivory-coloured room. Metal shutters had been folded open to let afternoon light in through a big window. On a chair in the corner her clothes were piled up, neatly folded, her pack and boots beside them on the floor. A couple of her larger guns were propped against the wall, solid and somehow reassuring in this unfamiliar space.

"What is this place?"

"We're at Forward Command," Oenone said. "It's an old Traction City which the Storm took years ago."

"Not in Shan Guo, then?"

"Not yet. The *Fury* was badly damaged when we left the line. The cities broke through faster than anyone expected, and their flying machines were everywhere. We limped this far, and we've been stuck here ever since. General Xao is here, too. She's trying to organize a second line of defence, and she's promised to send us on our way as soon as the *Fury* can be repaired. But at the moment her mechanics are too busy keeping fighting ships airworthy to work on the *Fury*. There's heavy fighting going on north and south of here. This place is just an island in an ocean of hungry cities. . ."

Hester half listened, trying to order her vague memories of her illness and the journey east. She knew now how Theo had felt after she rescued him from Cutler's Gulp. She wished she'd shown him more sympathy.

"What about the others?" she said.

"Mr Shrike is here, quite undamaged. He sat with you all the time you were ill, but today General Xao has persuaded him to go out to the front-line trenches to help build the defences. Manchester and a dozen other cities are closing in on us from the west, so she needs all the help she can get. I've sent word to him that you were stirring; he's bound to be here soon. He'll be delighted that you've pulled through."

"I doubt it," said Hester. "What about Theo?"

Oenone hesitated. "Professor Pennyroyal is here too. He's been flirting shamelessly with General Xao. . ."

"Theo? *What about Theo?*"

Oenone looked down, hiding behind her annoying black fringe.

"Gods and Goddesses!" Hester heaved herself sideways, off the bed. She tried to stand, but her head swirled. Something tugged at her arm and she looked down and saw a transparent plastic tube emerging from the flesh beneath her elbow, attached to a upturned bottle on a stand beside her bed. She cried out in horror and disgust.

"It's all right," Oenone promised, stopping her as she reached to tug the tube out. "It's an Ancient technique; a way of getting fluids into you. You've been unconscious for days; we had to. . ."

Shaking, Hester sat on the bed's edge, staring out of the window. Her sickroom seemed to be on the topmost tier of the disabled city; outside, rooftops and chimneys dropped steeply to a grey-green plain where clumps of soldiers were moving about; half-tracks dragging big guns into position. "She came for him, didn't she? Lady Death. . ."

Behind her, Oenone said, "He went back into the trenches, for some reason. . ." She came around the bed. Her hand brushed Hester's bony shoulder. "By the time we knew he had gone, it was too late. He must have run straight into the cities' bombardment. . ."

Hester reached out and grabbed the cord around Oenone's neck on which her cheap Zagwan crucifix dangled. She pulled it tight, dragging the younger woman's shocked face down to hers. "You should have gone after him! You should have saved him! He saved you!"

But it was herself she blamed. She should never have let Theo begin his harebrained rescue-mission. Now he was dead. She let go of Oenone and covered her own face, frightened by the tears that were spilling out of her, the horrible moaning noise she couldn't stop. She had promised herself she would never care about anyone again, and she should have stuck to it, but no, her stupid heart had opened up for Theo, and now he was dead, and she was paying the price for having loved him. She shouted at Oenone, "You should have prayed to that old God of yours! To keep him safe! To bring him back!"

Down on the plain below the city General Xao's troops were digging frantic foxholes and city-traps. The blades of their spades and picks glinted rhythmically like a shoal of bright fish turning. Up through the sickroom floor came the sounds of marching feet and bellowed orders from the lower tiers, where tired sub-officers were trying to forge new fighting units out of the drabbles of survivors who kept stumbling in from defeats in the west and north. Oenone and Hester sat side by side on the bed. After a while Oenone said, "If God could do things like that, the world wouldn't look the way it does. He can't reach down and change things. He can't stop any of us doing what we choose to do."

"What use is he then?"

Oenone shrugged. "He sees. He understands. He knows how you're feeling. He knows how Theo felt. He knows how it feels to die. And when we die, we go to him."

"To the Sunless Country, you mean? Like ghosts?"

Oenone shook her head patiently. "Like children. Do you remember what it was like to be a tiny child? When everything was possible and everything was given to you, and you knew that you were safe and loved, and the days went on for ever? When we die, it will be like that again. That's how it is for Theo now, in Heaven."

"How do you know? Did one of those corpses you resurrected tell you this?"

"I just know."

They sat side by side, and Oenone put her arm around Hester, and Hester let her. Something about this earnest, humourless young woman touched her, despite her best efforts. It was her goodness, and her silly, indomitable hope. She reminded Hester of Tom. They sat on the bed waiting for Mr Shrike, thinking about Theo in Heaven. Outside the window the day faded to a steel-grey dusk. The lights of advancing cities twinkled all along the western horizon.

Theo was not in Heaven. He was trudging on foot across an immense, wind-whipped steppe somewhere north-east of Forward Command. He had been walking for so long that his boots were starting to disintegrate and he had tied them together with strips of cloth, which kept coming undone, trailing in the mud.

He was not alone. Around him, the remnants of the Green Storm's forward divisions were spilling eastward, spurred on by tales of hungry harvester-suburbs and mercenary aviators raiding deep into Storm territory behind them.

When he clawed his way out of the ruins of General Xao's dugout on the first day of the war, Theo's first thought had been to get home somehow to Zagwa. But cities had been pushing through all along the line. Running from them, he had fallen in with this mass of defeated, fleeing soldiers and been swept along in the only direction that seemed safe; east. He had found a place on a half-track, but after a few days townie airships bombed the bridges on the road ahead and he had been forced to get off and hobble along with the stragglers, the walking wounded, the ones deafened or driven mad by what they had seen on the line.

Theo felt half-mad himself sometimes. Often in the night he woke shaking, dreaming of his time under the cities' guns.

Mostly, though, he just felt miserable. The landscape didn't help. It had been Storm territory for more than a decade, but the Storm had never known quite what to do with it. One faction had tried to nurture the natural growth of weeds and scrub that filled the old track-marks, and then another had attempted to bulldoze the track-marks flat and plant wheat. The result was an undulating, thinly-wooded country which turned quickly into a quagmire under the boots of the routed army. From time to time they passed wind-farms or small static settlements, but the buildings were all empty, the settlers fled, the fields and houses stripped by soldiers at the front of the column.

Theo wondered about Hester and Oenone and Professor Pennyroyal, and whether they had managed to escape. At first he hoped that they might come looking for him, but as the scale of the Storm's defeat became clear, he stopped hoping. How would they know where to look? If even half the rumours he heard were true whole armies had been smashed, and the eastern Hunting Ground must be filled with straggling columns of refugees like the one he'd joined, all trying to reach safety before the hungry cities caught them.

He reached the crest of a long slope and saw, away to the north, a jagged smear upon the plain. Some of his companions (he couldn't call them friends; they'd been too stunned and weary even to ask each other's names) had stopped to look at it, pointing and talking.

"What is it?" asked Theo.

"London," said a Shan Guonese sub-officer. "A powerful barbarian city which the gods destroyed when it tried to breach the walls of Batmunkh Gompa."

"The gods were with us then," said another. "Now they have turned their backs on us. They are punishing Naga and his whore for overthrowing our Stalker Fang."

A signals officer, his eyes swathed in bandages, said, "I am glad I cannot see London. It is a bad-luck place. Even looking at it brings misfortune."

"You think our luck can get any worse?" sneered the sub-officer.

A shout of "Airship!" went up from further down the column, and everyone fell flat, some crawling under bushes, some trying to scrape holes for themselves in the wet earth. But the ship that came rumbling overhead was just a Zhang-Chen Hawkmoth with the green lightning-bolt of the Storm on its tailfins. It settled on the plain a few miles ahead.

The troops around Theo went quiet. This was the first Storm ship they had seen for many days, and they were wondering what it meant. But Theo was more interested in London. He stared through the mist at its spiny, unwelcoming skyline, trying and failing to imagine it as a moving city. Was Wren really in there somewhere? He dug in his pocket and took out the photograph, studying her face as he had studied it many times on this march east, remembering their long-ago kiss. *Love,* she had written at the bottom of her letter, but did she mean it, or was it was just one of those *loves* you end letters with, carelessly, not trying to suggest longing or desire?

Still, it gave Theo hope to think that Wren might be so close. London's ghosts didn't scare him; well, not much. He'd survived the Rustwater and the Line and Cutler's Gulp, and he could not imagine any ghosts more terrifying than that. Like his Shan Guonese comrade, he didn't believe his luck could get any worse.

An officer in a motorized mud-sledge came roaring along the line, stopping at each cluster of soldiers to bellow through a loud-hailer. "Fresh orders! We are moving south-west! General Xao is making a stand at Forward Command."

Theo heard the soldiers around him muttering doubtfully. They did not believe the enclave at Forward Command could hold out for long. They wanted to push on to the safety of the mountains. Maybe in Batmunkh Gompa, which had stood for so long against the cities, there might be hope. . .

"Move!" the officer was shouting, as his sledge went slapping and growling on along the column. "Take heart! We are to join with General Xao and smash the barbarians! Food and supplies are waiting on the road to Forward Command!"

Even he didn't sound as if he believed it, but everyone knew the penalty for disobeying an order from the Storm. Wearily, the soldiers grabbed packs and guns, some grumbling, some cursing, others excited and vowing this time to stop the barbarians for ever.

Not Theo. He was glad to hear that General Xao was still alive, but this was not his war; beneath his stolen greatcoat he was not even in the Storm's uniform. He stowed Wren's picture safely in his pocket and slid away from the others, creeping unnoticed down into a flooded track-mark as they started to move off.

It was almost nightfall by the time he judged it safe to show himself again. He waded across the floor of the track-mark, and scrambled up the far wall on to flat ground. Nothing was left of the army he had travelled east with except for a few abandoned packs, a dead horse, some litter blowing about in the wind. The guns in the west were booming again as he started to pick his way across the plain towards the distant outline of the destroyed city.

Look for me in London.

35

UPLINK

The house at Erdene Tezh hums with the power of the old machines. Driven by a hydro-electric generator in the basement, lights gleam, needles quiver, and components stripped from antique Stalker-brains tick and chitter to themselves. The room is webbed with cables. In the middle of this nest of machinery the Stalker Fang stands, tapping at ivory keyboards. Bright little fireflies dance for her behind the glass of an old goggle-screen. She whispers to herself; strings of numbers, letters, cryptic code-words culled from her memories of the Tin Book; the forgotten language of ODIN.

None of it means anything to Fishcake. When his Stalker does not want him to fix or carry something he wanders the dead rooms, or goes out into the garden and looks at the fish frozen in the ice on the pond, or simply sleeps, clutching his beloved wooden horse. He is sleeping a lot now, as his mind and body withdraw from the hunger and the cold. He has not had much to eat, for although he brought a bag of food with him from Batmunkh Gompa it is running low. His stomach aches with hunger. He has mentioned the problem to his Stalker, but she ignores him. Now that her transmitter is finished she is no longer interested in Fishcake.

Sometimes he dreams of escaping from this place. He casts hopeful glances at the keys to Popjoy's air-yacht which, for reasons of her own, she has hung around her neck on a cord. He does not dare to snatch them, though; he knows he wouldn't get more than three paces before she cut him down.

Tonight, because the rest of the old building is so cold, Fishcake has made his way to her room again, hoping to curl up in the faint warmth of her machines. She is still at work, still typing her chains of numbers. The clatter of her steel fingers on the keys sounds like Lady Death playing dice with dead men's bones down in the Sunless Country. Hydraulics grizzle up above the ceiling somewhere, sending down a snow of crumbled plaster. Outside, where the real snow whirls around the roof and the Stalker-birds keep watch for snooping airships, a saucer-shaped aerial turns and tips to focus on a point high in the north-western sky.

Far, far above, something large and old and cold rides the long dark; frosted with space-dust, pocked by micro-meteors. Solar panels give off a tired gleam, like dusty windows. Inside the armoured hull a receiver listens patiently to the same wash of static that it has been hearing for millennia. But now something is changing; inside the static, like flotsam washing ashore in the surf, comes a familiar message. The ancient computer brain detects it, and responds. Many of its systems have been damaged over the long years, but it has others; fail-safes and back-ups. Power cells hum; glowing ribbons of light begin to weave through the coils of the weapon-chamber; ice crystals tumble away in a bright, widening cloud as heavy shields slide open.

ODIN gazes down into the blue pool of the earth, and waits to be told what it must do.

36

INTRUDERS

22nd June (I think. . .)

I'm writing this in a very dismal spot on the western edge of the ruins of London, listening to the guns in the west. How far does the sound of gunfire travel? No one here is sure. But it's pretty clear that the war is on again, and the Green Storm are losing. Already a few refugees have wandered through the edges of the debris fields – they've moved on of their own accord, or with a bit of prompting from Londoners hiding in the debris and making spooky noises, but what if more come?

And what if suburbs and cities come behind them? And what if Wolf Kobold is already on his way here aboard Harrowbarrow?

I'll say this for the Londoners; they don't give up easily. It's been decided that New London simply has to be ready to leave by the end of this week, and although Lavinia Childermass and her Engineers look doubtful, they know there's no alternative.

While the Engineers get busy in the Womb everyone else is starting to crate up the things that will be needed aboard the new city, and extra patrols have been sent out to keep watch on the western edges of the field for signs of approaching trouble. That's what leads to me being out here in the wet, instead of tucked up snug in my bed at

Crouch End. We've made a camp among the rust-heaps, and we'll sleep under the stars tonight (or at least under a sort of rusty overhang, which we are glad of since it will keep the drizzle off). Cat Luperini, who's in charge of our little band, says we should take turns to do guard duty. She's having first go, and I'm due to take over at

Wren dropped her pencil and closed the book. Through the steady patter of the rain she had clearly heard the sound of a bird calling; the signal which the patrols used to communicate with one another across the wreckage. She went to tell Cat about it, but the other girl had already heard. "It's Hodge's lot," she said. "They need us. . ."

The other members of the patrol – Angie Peabody and a small, shy boy named Timex Grout – were waking up, wriggling out from under their blankets and reaching for lanterns and crossbows. Wren's heart beat quickly; it seemed to be wedged somewhere in the region of her tonsils. *This could be it*, she thought. What if Ron Hodge's patrol on the south-western edge had seen the lights of Harrowbarrow? What if advance parties from Harrowbarrow were already sneaking through the debris fields, ready to kill anyone they met? She fumbled a bolt out of the quiver on her belt and fitted it into her crossbow.

The bird-call came again. Cat called back, and the patrol set off quickly through the drizzle. The moon shone half-heartedly behind the clouds. Wren was glad of its light, but she was still terrified that she would lose the others and be left wandering in this insane rust-scape all alone. Stories which she had had scoffed at in Crouch

End seemed very real out here in the night-shadows. She started remembering all the scary scraps of London folklore she had picked up from her father, the dark supernatural shapes that haunted the nightmares of the old city; the ghosts of Boudicca and Spring-Heeled Jack; the awful, salvage-stealing Wombles.

She almost screamed when a silhouette rose up in the path ahead, but it was just Ron Hodge, the rest of his patrol behind him.

"What's going on?" asked Cat.

"Intruder," said Ron shakily. "We got a glimpse of him, then lost him. He's round here somewhere."

"Just the one?"

"Don't know."

Cat took charge, ordering everybody to fan out and search. They called to each other as they crept through the spires and angles of the wreck, and they used words now as well as bird-sounds; sometimes just the sound of voices emerging from the dead scrap-piles was enough to make intruders turn tail and run.

There was no sign of anyone.

"What's that?" yelped Timex. Wren ran to him, scrambling through drifts of rust-flakes as crunchy as breakfast cereal. "There!" he hissed, as she reached him, and she saw it too, just for an instant, a movement between two nearby blocks of wreckage. She tried to call out for Cat and the others, but her mouth was too dry. She fumbled for the safety-catch of her crossbow, telling herself that if the stranger was one of Wolf's men from Harrowbarrow she would have to kill him before he killed her.

"Who's there?" shouted a voice. A familiar accent; Theo's accent. It made Wren feel shivery with relief. This wasn't an attacker; just some lost African airman, another deserter from the retreating Green Storm armies which the lookouts had sighted passing by. Cat had said that half a dozen had stumbled into the fringes of the debris field over the past few days, and it had been easy enough to frighten them away. Wren wondered what would be the best way to convince this one that the wreck was full of restless spirits. Should she leap out waving her arms and going "Woooooo"?

Just then, a lot of things happened at once. The stranger, who was closer than he had sounded, appeared suddenly around the corner of an old engine-block. Cat and Angie, coming over the crest of the wreckage behind him, unveiled their lanterns, the dazzling ghost-lights which had driven off so many previous interlopers. The stranger, alarmed, ran straight towards Wren and Timex, and Timex barged backwards, crashing into Wren, whose crossbow went off accidentally with a startling twang and a kick that nearly broke her arm. The stranger fell in the splay of light from the lanterns, and Wren, catching sight of his face, saw that he did not just sound like Theo, he *was* Theo.

"Ow!" he said weakly.

There was a sound of slithering rust-flakes as the other Londoners came running. Wren stood shaking her head, rubbing her wrenched arm, waiting to wake up. This was a dream, and a pretty poor one. Theo could not be here. Theo was in Zagwa. That was not Theo, lying there dying on the metal in front of her.

But when she edged closer, and Cat held up her lantern, there was no mistaking his good, handsome, dark brown face.

"Theo?" she said. "I didn't mean to. . . Oh Quirke!"

She started to claw at his soggy coat, looking for the crossbow-bolt.

Ron Hodge arrived, keen to assert himself now that the intruder had turned out harmless. "Leave him, Wren," he ordered.

"Oh, go away!" yelled Wren. "He's a friend! And I think I've shot him. . ."

But there was no hole in Theo's coat; no blood, no jutting bolt. Her shot had gone wide. "I just slipped," Theo said weakly, looking at Wren as if he did not believe it could really be her. He half sat up and stared warily at the young Londoners crowding round him. Wren couldn't take her eyes off him. How thin and pained and tired he looked, and how glad she was to see him!

Theo tried out a smile. "I got your letter," he said.

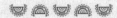

They made their way back to their camp, where Angie lit a small fire and heated up some soup for Theo, who was shivering with cold and exhaustion. Wren sat by him as he drank it. It felt strange to be with him again. She had been imagining him safe in sunny Zagwa. How did he come to be caught up in the Green Storm's defeats? She had asked, but he just said, "It's complicated," and she hadn't liked to press him.

She wondered if he still remembered kissing her at Kom Ombo Air-harbour, and supposed that he must; he had come all the way to London to find her, after all.

"We shouldn't be mollycoddling him," said Ron Hodge grumpily, pacing about at the edge of the firelight. "He's Green Storm."

"He's not!" cried Wren.

"He's in a Green Storm uniform."

"Only the coat," said Theo, lifting it open to show his flyer's clothes beneath. "I stole it from a dead man on the way east. I'm not Green Storm. I don't know what I am."

"He's a Zagwan," said one of Ron's group. "Zagwans are Anti-Tractionists. We can't let an Anti-Tractionist into London. Wren and her dad have already brought one spy among us; now she's asking us to take in a Mossie. . ."

"So what do you think we should do with him?" asked Cat Luperini. "Kill him?"

The boys looked sheepish.

"When daylight comes me and Wren will take him over to Crouch End," Cat decided.

Wren slept fitfully, curled up beside Theo. The wreckage made an uncomfortable bed, but even without the rivets and rust-flakes digging into her she could not have slept; she had to keep studying his sleeping face to make quite sure she had not dreamed him. And then she suddenly woke to daylight, and it was time to leave.

They walked eastwards, Wren and Theo together, Cat following with her crossbow. As they went, Theo told Wren his story, and she learned how he had met her mother, and how they had travelled together all the way to the Green Storm's lines.

"And after that?" asked Wren.

"I don't know. I think she's safe. Probably in Shan Guo by now."

Wren was not sure what to feel. She'd grown used to thinking that Mum was dead. It was unsettling to find out that she was still alive, and to hear the way Theo spoke of her, as if he *admired* her. And that she should be travelling around with that horrible Stalker, Mr Shrike – Wren didn't like to think about it, and she was almost relieved when Cat suddenly shouted "Down!" and she was able to concentrate on dragging Theo off the path and into cover.

A Stalker-bird coasted low over the ruins, so close that Wren heard the sound of its wing-feathers combing the air. Its too-big head swung mechanically from side to side.

Cat scrambled over to join Wren and Theo. "I saw it circling up high when we left the camp," she said. "I've been keeping my eye on it while you two nattered. I hoped it would go on its way, but it's watching us. Must have seen that fire we lit last night."

Wren peeked out from under the slab of deckplate which hid them. The bird had gone higher, circling. As Wren watched it flapped its raggedy wings and swooped off across the debris fields in the direction of Crouch End.

"They're definitely getting nosier," said Cat.

"Spy-birds," said Wren to Theo, thinking he looked scared. "They come over and take pictures of us for General Naga's album."

Theo shook his head. "That wasn't a spy-bird, Wren. That was a Lammergeyer. We had a flock of them aboard my carrier when I was with the Storm. They're used for armed reconnaissance." The girls looked blankly at him, as girls so often did when he slipped into the Storm's military jargon. "They're attack birds, Wren! I think your friends are in danger. . ."

The Green Storm's birds were certainly taking a great interest in the debris fields that morning. As Tom worked away wrapping and packing the treasures he had found among the ruins ready for their transfer aboard New London, he kept hearing the clang clang clang of the danger bell, warning any Londoner who was out in the open to beware. By lunchtime the still-smouldering carcasses of three more spy-birds were hanging outside the canteen, displayed as trophies by the keen lookouts who had shot them down with lightning guns when they showed too much interest in the Womb.

Tom felt pleased by the way the rekilling of the birds lifted his fellow Londoners' spirits, but he could not help wondering whether shooting them had been wise. Might it not just make their masters even more suspicious about what was happening inside the wreck?

Chudleigh Pomeroy told him not to fret. "Those birds have seen nothing that would make the Storm think we're anything but a rabble of squatters. Even if they had, the Storm have bigger worries than us. By the time they get around to sending airships over, New London will be gone."

Tom surreptitiously touched wood. He knew the Engineers were working as hard as they could to perfect the Childermass engines, but he could not help thinking of the failed test yesterday. What if the next test was a failure, too?

He wished he could do more to help. He had been moved when Chudleigh Pomeroy asked him to become Head Historian, and he took his relic-collecting seriously, but he knew that it was a made-up job, not really necessary. New London was about the future, not the past.

With lunch over, Pomeroy announced that he was going to the Womb, and Tom volunteered to go with him. He had repaired the *Jenny Haniver* often enough, after all; he was sure the Engineers could find some small welding or wiring task to entrust him with aboard their new city. But they had not gone more than twenty yards from Crouch End when the danger bell began to ring again.

"Merciful Quirke!" exclaimed Pomeroy, turning back towards the entrance. "How are we supposed to get anything done at all with these incessant interruptions? I've a good mind to write a stiff letter to General Naga and tell him it just ain't neighbourly. . ."

Tom had grown quite used to the sight of distant Stalker-birds, but those new carcasses strung up outside the canteen made him uneasy. He glanced at the sky as he hurried Pomeroy towards shelter, and he was glad he had. The birds had returned in force, and they were not circling dots this time, but hurtling black shapes, dropping like missiles out of the sun.

"Get down!" he shouted, shoving Pomeroy to the ground just as a bird swept over, its steel claws whisking past a fraction of an inch above the old man's head. The danger bell was jangling again, and on the road to the Womb people were scattering and shouting. Saab Peabody, who'd downed a spy-bird earlier, came running out of Crouch End with his lightning gun at the ready, keen to add another to his tally. A bird came down on him, flailing its razor claws at his face, and he dropped the gun and fell blinded and screaming. Other birds were crashing through the beanpoles in the vegetable gardens, harrying a small, terrified group of children as their teachers tried to herd them into the safety of Crouch End. Even in there, among the cosy huts, the dead wings flapped.

Tom watched it all, trembling, doing his best to shelter Pomeroy. Saab seemed to have passed out; his lightning gun had fallen only a few feet away, and in his younger days Tom might have tried to reach it and do something heroic, but he was terrified of having another seizure, and so scared of the birds that he could barely move.

Wren, Theo and Cat had just emerged out of the rust-hills west of Crouch End when the attack began. They all heard the bell clanging, and the two girls stared without really understanding as the people below them scattered before the swift, swooping shapes of the birds.

"That's Dad!" said Wren, seeing Tom pinned to the ground beside Pomeroy, about thirty feet away. She turned to Theo, but Theo had already seen Tom for himself, and he was sprinting towards him through the bird-scoured sunlight.

Cat started to sob with panic. Wren snatched her crossbow and clicked the safety-catch off. They acted very military, these young Londoners, but it had always been a game for them till now; they'd never seen real violence before. Wren had, and although she knew she would shake like a jelly later, for the moment she was very calm. She took aim at a bird as it plunged towards Theo, and put a bolt through its body just before it reached him. One crossbow bolt would not rekill a Stalker-bird, but the blow was enough to throw it off-course, and Theo ran on without even knowing the danger he had been in.

The bird's attention had been drawn to Wren. It swerved towards her. She grabbed another bolt from Cat's quiver, but the bird would be upon her long before she could reload. She dropped the bow, snatched up a twisted length of iron drainpipe from the mounds of wreckage beside the path and smashed it out of the air as its claws came reaching for her. Then Cat grabbed a shard of metal too, and together they beat the thrashing bird to pieces.

Theo was halfway to Tom before he realized that he hadn't a plan. He had only started running because he wanted Wren to see that he was brave, and because he had always thought that Mr Natsworthy really couldn't look after himself. Bird shadows whisked across the ground; the reflections of wings flashed up at him from puddles. He wasn't even armed. . .

A little way beyond Tom and the old man a silvery gun lay on the ground. Theo threw himself at it, feeling claws rip the air above him as he dived. He rolled over, fumbling with the gun, feeling for a trigger among its complicated array of wires and tubes. He wished it had been something simpler – all soldiers knew that you couldn't rely on that sort of back-engineered Old-Tech garbage – but he told himself that beggars can't be choosers, and pointed the gun at a passing bird. When he squeezed what he hoped was the trigger a bolt of pure lightning dropped the bird limp and smouldering at his feet. Startled, he stood up, swinging the gun towards another bird. When he had brought down four of them the others started to notice him, but by then Londoners were shooting at them too – gaudy crackles of energy leaping from other guns like his, smoking birds and showers of feathers falling all around.

And then, quite suddenly, the attack was over. A lone bird soared eastward, too high to be touched by the bolts of lightning that crackled up at it. The danger bell clanged on and on and on until someone went to tell the girl who was ringing it that she could stop now. People appeared nervously from the holes and clefts where they had been hiding, brushing rust-flakes from their clothes, silent and pale with shock. The injured moaned; their friends shouted for help. . .

"Why did they attack?" people were asking. "Why now? After all these years. . ."

"That wasn't a real attack," said Theo, starting to shiver a little as he imagined what could have happened to him if those had been heavy assault birds instead of a reconnaissance flock. "That was a probe; they want to test your strength. . ." He stared about, getting his first real look at this unlikely settlement.

The Londoners stared back at him, wondering where he had sprung from, this young man in the uniform of their enemy.

Tom stood slowly, and started to help Chudleigh Pomeroy stand too. His heart was beating very hard, but he did not feel ill; his only worrying symptom was a hallucination that would not fade; he seemed to see Theo Ngoni standing before him, clutching a lightning gun.

"Hello, Mr Natsworthy," said the hallucination, with a nervous wave.

And then Wren came running – dirty, and with a cut on her forehead, but otherwise unharmed, thank

Quirke – running to hug him and ask was he all right? and say, "It's Theo, Daddy; Theo's here; you remember Theo; Theo's come all the way from Africa to find us."

37

LOVE AMONG THE RUINS

It was not a good time for a young Anti-Tractionist in a Green Storm greatcoat to arrive in London. People were frightened and angry, shaking their fists towards Shan Guo and asking what they had ever done to make the Mossies attack them. Things might have gone badly for Theo, if it had not been for the fact that he had shot down five of the nightmare birds. "That don't signify anything," insisted Mr Garamond. "That could all be part of their plan, to make us accept him so he can murder us all in our beds!" But Pomeroy told him to put a sock in it; the young man had saved him, and a lot of other people besides, and he, for one, was ready to welcome him.

Tom and Wren joined in, explaining how Theo had flown with them for a time aboard the *Jenny*, and visited the Traction City of Kom Ombo without showing any desire to murder anyone. And slowly, grudgingly, people started to admit that Theo might not be an agent of the Storm after all; only a lost stranger who should be offered hospitality.

The injured were treated, the lookouts redoubled, the lightning guns recharged. Chudleigh Pomeroy, who looked badly shaken but insisted that he was quite all right, asked Theo a lot of questions about how the war was going, very few of which Theo could answer, because Chudleigh Pomeroy had a Historian's notion of battles, all about tactics and the plans and decisions of generals, none of which Theo had really noticed while he was fleeing through the mud.

In the late afternoon, when the slanting sunlight shone right into Crouch End and through the windows of their little shack, Tom and Wren were finally able to get Theo to themselves. Over cake and nettle tea which Wren scrounged from the kitchens, they told him the story of their adventures, and listened to his own. And it was there that Tom first learned of Theo's meeting with Hester; of how she had rescued him in the sand-sea, and of what had followed, right up to the moment when she boarded that corvette with Lady Naga.

Wren took her father's hand as they listened. There were tears in his eyes. But all he said was, "Where is Hester now?"

Theo shook his head. "It was such chaos on the line. I think her ship got away safely. But wherever she is, she'll be all right. I've never met anyone as brave or as tough as her. And Mr Shrike will look after her. . ."

"Shrike," said Tom, and shook his head. "So it *was* him you two met on Cloud 9. I thought I'd finished him for ever on the Black Island. I hate to think of the old brute up and about again."

"I wouldn't be here now if he wasn't, Mr Natsworthy," said Theo. "He's changed since Oenone re-Resurrected him."

Tom didn't doubt what Theo said, but he still couldn't shake off his memories of the old Shrike, vicious and insane, who had hunted him through the Rustwater Marshes twenty years before. And now Shrike and Hester were together again, just as they'd been when she was a young girl. A rare, bitter feeling filled him. He was jealous of the ancient Stalker.

In the evening, when the sun had gone down into the haze of the west and the sky above the debris fields was turning lilac, Wren took Theo up to the Womb so that he could see for himself what the Londoners were doing there. She felt nervous, for although he was a moderate, civilized sort of Anti-Tractionist he was still an Anti-Tractionist, and had been brought up to hate and fear all moving cities. But New London had become so important to her that she had to show him; she had to know what he felt about it.

When they reached the hangar he stood looking up for a long time at the new city, while Wren nervously explained how it had come to be, and what those funny mirror-things were supposed to do. She couldn't tell what he thought, or whether he was even listening.

"But it hasn't got any wheels," he said at last.

"I told you, it doesn't need any," said Wren. "So you needn't look so old-fashioned at it; it isn't going to churn up your precious green earth or squash any flowers or bunnies. It's barely a Traction City at all. Think of it as a very large, low-flying airship."

They walked through the shadows under New London. Above their heads Engineers clambered about like spiders on the city's belly, making adjustments and repairs. All around them, on the hangar floor, kegs of water and crates of salted meat were waiting to be loaded aboard, along with coops filled with clucking poultry, and stacks of tinned food unearthed by salvage-teams from lost groceries and storerooms deep in the debris fields. Even the shacks where the people of

London had lived for so long were being dismantled and loaded on handcarts and scrap-metal sledges for transport to the holds of the new suburb. As Wren led Theo outside they met a whole line of them coming up the track from Crouch End, filling the twilight with dust and rust-flakes. From the northern end of the Womb came the voices of Len Peabody and his mates, busy clearing wreckage from in front of the hangar entrance and setting the demolition charges which would blast the doors off when the time came for New London to depart.

"So what do you think?" asked Wren, worried by Theo's silence. She drew him off the track into a narrow cleft of the wreckage where apple trees grew. She thought a Mossie might feel more at ease there, amid the gentle whisper of the leaves. She thought he would be heartened by the way nature was reclaiming the ruins of London. "Tell me," she said.

"You are set on going with them?" Theo asked.

"Yes," said Wren. "Dad wants to. I want to, too. I want to stand aboard New London and feel it moving, racing off to new places. . ."

"Hunting?"

"Trading, the way Anchorage used to."

"Bigger cities will hunt you."

"They won't catch us."

A bird fluttered in the undergrowth. Only a blackbird, but it made them both flinch, and they moved closer together.

"The thing is," he said, "I didn't expect any of this. I thought you were just exploring here. . ."

"That's Pennyroyal's fault," said Wren, who always talked too much when she felt nervous. "If he hadn't let my letter get all soggy you'd have known about Wolf's theory. . ."

"Hush. . ." Theo touched his finger to her lips to quiet her. He said, "I thought you'd be in danger now the barbarians are driving east again. I hoped I might find you and take you and your father home with me somehow, to Zagwa."

Oh, bother! thought Wren, because she had been pretty sure that he was about to kiss her again, and now she saw it wasn't going to work. He was a Mossie, and she was a city-girl. He was never going to approve of New London. And then she thought, *Well, what does it matter?* The way things were going, they might both be eaten by Harrowbarrow or pecked to bits by Stalker-birds before tomorrow night.

So she kissed him instead.

A single, electronic eye focused for an instant on Wren and Theo; zooming in on the smudge of their body-heat amid the cold sprawl of the wreck. A computer-brain considered them for a fraction of a fraction a second, then forgot them. ODIN swung its gaze westward, pulling back, struggling to make sense of the incomprehensible world it had awoken to. Where were the sprawling cities of its masters, New York and San Angeles, that it had been put in orbit to defend? Where had the new mountain ranges come from? All those new seas? And what were those huge vehicles creeping across Europe, trailing their long sooty smears of exhaust smoke behind them?

The old weapon clung to the one familiar thing that this changed world could offer it; the stream of coded data rising like a silken thread from somewhere in the uplands of central Asia.

38

THE MILLION VOICES OF THE WIND

The cities' war was going well. Panzerstadt Winterthur had been lost and Darmstadt and the Dortmund Conurbation were bogged down in the Rustwater somewhere, but the rest had found resistance surprisingly light. Up in the smoky skies their flying machines wheeled and swerved, harrying the withdrawing shoals of Green Storm airships, while their own ships, airborne gun-platforms hung from armoured gas-bags, lured flocks of Stalker-birds in close and hammered them into tornadoes of slime and feathers.

When it was quite clear that the Storm's armies had been shattered, Adlai Browne decided that the time had come for Manchester to do its bit. Within a few weeks the good old days of Municipal Darwinism would return, and he meant to see to it that Manchester was at the top of the food-chain when they did. His city gathered a guard of harvester-suburbs around it and rolled eastward with its jaws open, filling its gut with the rubble of watchtowers and fortresses, barns and farms and wind turbines.

By the time Wren kissed Theo in the ruins of London, Manchester was shoving its way through mile upon mile of lately-planted forest towards the static settlement called Forward Command. Around it swooped the Flying Ferrets, strafing Mossie rocket-nests. The armoured suburbs of Werwolf and Evercreech raced ahead of their mother-city like well-trained dogs.

A flight of Fox Spirits rose from somewhere in the Mossie citadel and tore towards Manchester. Orla

Twombley signalled the rest of her squadron and the Ferrets pulled together, rising in a howling flock towards the ships, which broke right and left, scattering air-to-air rockets. Orla cursed as a machine on her starboard wing (the wicker gyrocopter *Big Blue Plymouth*) ran into an oncoming rocket and blew apart, blinding her with its smoke. She got on to the tail of the Fox Spirit that had fired the rocket and chased it westward, tearing chunks out of its steering vanes with the *Combat Wombat*'s cannon. She stitched incendiary bullets along its flank and watched as the gas-cells started to burn. White escape balloons blossomed around the gondola as the crew bailed out. Some aviators regarded escape balloons as good target practice, but Orla had always insisted that the Ferrets shoot down ships, not people, so she swung around the collapsing airship and started back to help her comrades deal with the rest.

She was about three miles from Manchester when the sky split open. There was a shriek and a roar. Struggling to keep the *Wombat*'s nose up as it dropped towards the ground, she watched a lance of white fire lean across the sky. The *Wombat*'s canvas wings began to smoulder. Orla called on various gods and goddesses, and trained her fire extinguisher on the burning patches. The sky was filled with smoke and light. She thought she saw the fire-lance sweep northward, swerving towards one of Manchester's suburbs. As it moved away and the shrieking, roaring sound faded she realized that the *Wombat*'s engines had failed, and she could not restart them.

Surfing on the thermals above the burning forests she turned towards Manchester, but Manchester was motionless, its armour holed, its tracks destroyed, tier upon ruined tier leaking flame into the scorched sky. Orla had never imagined that there could be so much fire in the world. She circled the carcass once, weeping, aghast at the thought of so many dead and dying. There was nothing she could do to help them. She steered north-west, searching for somewhere to set down. The light in the sky had gone out, but it had drawn a sweeping line of brush-fires across the plains, and at points along the line great pyres were burning where suburbs and cities had stood.

At last, as the *Combat Wombat* began to lose height in the cooler air, an armoured city loomed ahead. It was Murnau, motionless but whole, and its lookouts recognized Orla's machine and opened a portal in the top tier armour to let her inside. As the *Wombat* touched down on the Über-den-Linden she felt the wheels buckle, and then the whole undercarriage gave way; she slewed to a standstill in a storm of splintering wood and snapped string, a flapping of seared canvas. She hadn't realized how badly the poor old kite had been burned. Hadn't realized how badly *she'd* been burned, until she saw the men who ran to help her staring. Her pink flying suit was charred black; her face black too, except for the patches around her eyes where her goggles had protected her.

Smoke trailed from her gauntlets as she waved the medical crew aside and staggered coughing towards the Rathaus. She had to tell someone what she had seen; for all she knew she was the only one who had escaped alive. "I must see the Kriegsmarshal. . ." she spluttered.

Von Kobold met her on the Rathaus steps. "Ms Twombley? That light – Those fires – We have lost contact with Manchester, Breslau, Moloch-Maschinenstadt. . . What the devil is going on out there?"

"Manchester's gone," said Orla Twombley. She collapsed, and von Kobold caught her, smudging his white tunic with soot and blood. "They're all gone," she said. "Turn your city about. Retreat! Run! The Storm have a new weapon, and it destroys everything. . ."

"A messenger, sir! A messenger from the front!"

The voice of Naga's aide booms and echoes round the inside of the war-room in the Jade Pagoda, echoes and booms around the inside of the general's head. He can't imagine what the man is so excited about. All week long there have been nothing but messengers from the front, and they have brought nothing but bad news. Naga isn't even certain where the front *is* any longer. Whatever luck he had has deserted him. Maybe it died with Oenone.

"General Naga!"

Well, here he is, this famous messenger, and nothing much to look at; a moon-faced sub-officer from one of the listening posts in the western mountains.

"Well?"

The boy bows so low that pencils shower out of his tunic pockets and rattle on the floor. "A thousand apologies, General Naga. I had to come in person. All our Stalker-birds have been reassigned to the front, and there is something interfering with radio signals. . ."

"What is it?" barks Naga. At least, he tries to bark it; it comes out as a tetchy sigh.

"The Lady Naga, sir!" (How bright his eyes are, this

boy. Was he even born when the wars began?) "She is alive, sir! A Stalker-bird came in from General Xao's division. It was badly damaged, but we deciphered the message. Lady Naga is on her way home."

The boy, who seemed so porridge-featured and uninteresting a few moments ago, is actually remarkably handsome; brave; intelligent. What is the Storm thinking of, making a young man of his calibre carry messages for outlandish listening posts? Naga lurches to his feet and lets his armour carry him towards the map-table. "Promote this man to lieutenant. No, captain." He feels almost young again. Oenone is alive! A hundred new strategies bloom in his head like paper flowers dropped into water. Surely one of them will halt the townie advance?

She is alive! She is alive! She is alive!

He is so overjoyed that it is almost a whole minute before he stops to wonder about the young woman who came to him out of the desert with such graphic stories of Oenone's death.

He snatches a sword from one of his generals. Officers and Stalkers scatter before him as his armour marches him out of the war-room, up the stairs. "General Naga, sir?" shouts one of the men behind him.

"The girl Rohini, you fool!" he yells – or tries to yell. (The truth is starting to dawn; *What has she done to me?*) "Fetch the guard!" But he doesn't really want the guard to deal with her; he wants to deal with her himself, with this good sword; he wants to split her head like a melon.

He doesn't bother knocking when he reaches the door of her chamber, way out in the western wing. His armour carries him through it, and shards and splinters of antique wood rattle off him as he climbs the five stairs to her living-space. She is rising from her seat to greet him as he reaches the top step, lovely and demure as ever, a big window behind her opening on to a moonlit balcony.

"My wife is alive," says Naga. "She is flying home. Are you going to keep up the mute act, or do you have any final words?"

For a moment she stares at him, hurt, frightened, confused. Then, realizing it just won't wash any more, she laughs. "You old fool! I'm glad she's alive. Now she'll see where her peace has brought us! To the edge of destruction! Not even you will listen to her Tractionist lies now."

"What do you mean?"

"You still don't understand?" Rohini laughs again, a little wildly. "She's working for them! She's always been working for them! Why do you think she married you? You're not exactly the answer to a young girl's dream, Naga. Half a man, wrapped up in clanking armour. Not even that, soon. I'm going to kill you, general, and your people will rise up and kill your traitor-wife. Then they will be ready to welcome their *real* leader back, when she reveals herself."

"What are you –" Naga starts to say. (And pauses, because at this point Rohini pulls off her hair, which turns out to be a wig, beneath which two things are concealed: short, blonde hair, which clashes oddly with her umber face, and a small gas-pistol, with which she shoots him. Naga's breastplate saves him from the bullet, but the impact makes him take a step backwards and he goes crashing and slithering down the stairs.)

"– talking about?" he asks the ceiling, as he lies in the splinters of the wrecked door, dazed.

Rohini – or whoever she is – appears at the top of the stairs. The gun is still in her hand. This time she aims at his face, not his armour. She is still smiling. She says, "Cynthia Twite, of the Stalker Fang's special intelligence group. A few of us kept the faith, General. We knew she would rise again."

"You've been poisoning me! The tea! You—"

"That's right!" says the girl chirpily. "And now I'm going to finish the j—"

Except she doesn't even finish the sentence, because just at that moment a shaft of light stabs in through the window, so bright that it looks solid, so hot that it sets Cynthia and everything else in the room instantly on fire. A roaring, shrieking noise drowns out her screams. In the shadows of the stairwell, Naga feels the heat on his face like the breath from an open furnace. Above him, Cynthia Twite is a black branch, burning. There is a sound of crashing masonry. The Jade Pagoda heaves sideways, as if it's having second thoughts about perching here on the mountainside. Naga tries to stand, but his armour won't obey him. Cinders of Cynthia rattle down around him as the light fades. "Help!" he yells into the smoke. "Help!"

Behind him, an ancient stone wall is tugged aside like a curtain. The main part of the Jade Pagoda is gone. He is looking down into the valley where Tienjing has stood, the capital of Anti-Tractionism, for a thousand years. There is nothing there but fire, and the million mournful voices of the wind.

39

FIRELIGHT

Wren began to feel embarrassed as she and Theo walked down to Crouch End. They had been alone in that nook in the wreckage for much longer than she'd intended. She was pretty sure she had finally got the hang of this kissing business, but she couldn't help but feel that everyone would know what she had been doing. Even when she let go of Theo's hand there was a sort of electric feeling in the air between them, and they couldn't stop glancing at each other.

But although half of London seemed to be standing about in the open space outside Crouch End, none of them so much as looked at Theo or Wren. They were all staring westward. And as Wren joined them she saw that the sky above the dinosaur-spines of the wreckage was glowing red, as if a huge fire were burning just beyond the horizon.

"What is it, Mr Luperini?" asked Wren, spotting Cat's father standing nearby. "Is it the war?"

Luperini shook his head; shrugged. Faint, eerie noises blew in on the wind; shriekings and roarings. A ghostly wing of light lit up the western half of the sky, blanching the stars. Wren took Theo's hand again.

"Reminds me of the night we zapped old Bayreuth," someone said.

"Wren!" Tom came hurrying over to them. "I was wondering where you'd got to. What do you make of this, Theo?"

Theo shook his head. "How long has it been going on?"

"About a half-hour – surely you must have noticed that first flash?"

"Um. . ." said Wren.

Theo frowned at the sky. "If it's gunfire, it's not like any I've seen before."

Dr Abrol came hurrying down the track from the listening post on the edge of the debris field where he spied on the Green Storm's radio messages and on those of the approaching cities. Londoners gathered round him, calling out to ask what he had heard on the airwaves.

"It's hard to be sure," he said nervously, his spectacles flickering with reflections of the sky. "Something keeps interfering with the signals. But it seems. . . It sounds as if. . ." ("What? What?" the people round him urged.) He swallowed hard, his Adam's apple making a neat little bob. "Whole cities have been destroyed," he said, and had to raise his voice to make himself heard over the cries, the curses, the hisses of indrawn breath. "Manchester. All sorts of *Traktionstadts* and suburbs. . ."

"Old-Tech!" cried Chudleigh Pomeroy, who had come wandering out in his dressing gown to see what all the fuss was about. "It has to be. The Green Storm have some sort of Old-Tech weapon. . ."

"But why wait until now to use it?" wondered Clytie.

"Who knows. Perhaps even they are scared of it. It must be horribly powerful."

"But where did they find it?" other voices asked. "What on earth is it?"

Lurpak Flint stood behind Clytie, his arms wrapped round her. "Perhaps it is not anything on earth at all. Remember, the Ancients left weapons in orbit. What if the Green Storm have found a way to wake one?"

"There are distress calls on the Green Storm's airwaves, too," Dr Abrol said. "Reports of an explosion at Tienjing. It's very confused. Sorry."

"Maybe the *Traktionstadts* have sent airships to Tienjing to try and blow up the transmitter that controls this weapon," Pomeroy suggested.

Another pulse of arctic light lit the sky. "Doesn't look like they hit it," said Len Peabody. "This is bad, ain't it? I mean, what's to stop the Mossies turning their toy on New London as soon as they see us leaving the debris field?"

Pomeroy sighed; shrugged. "Why, nothing," he said. "It is a problem, as you say. But it is not one we can do anything about. All we can do is pray to Quirke and Clio and all the other gods that the Green Storm will not think us worth wasting a blast of their spiffy new super-weapon on. New London is small, after all. Quirke willing, we may yet slip away. Go north, out of this horrible world the cities and the Storm have made. I fancy seeing the Ice Wastes before I die. . ."

He raised his voice a little, so that everyone else stopped staring at the sky and turned to listen. "This does not alter our plans. It may even help us, in a dreadful way; it may delay Harrowbarrow's arrival. So go to your beds, and try and rest. There's nothing to be gained by watching this fireworks party, and we have hard work ahead of us tomorrow. I, for one, could do with a snooze."

The clumps of Londoners began to disperse, wandering away in ones and twos to their homes. Tom recognized the look on the faces of those who passed him. He had seen it at Batmunkh Gompa; nineteen years ago. It was the look of people who have just learned that a civilization quite opposed to their own has just become the most powerful on Earth. Despite Pomeroy's brave words, they were afraid.

Only Wren and Theo, walking with heads together and their arms writhed around each other's waists, looked calm. They did not believe that some ancient weapon could come between them; they imagined the feelings they shared were stronger than the Storm and the cities and all the Old-Tech in the world. Tom let them go past him and watched them as they walked on ahead, remembering how he had once felt like that, with Hester.

He walked towards Crouch End beside Chudleigh Pomeroy. The old man was moving slowly, as if the Stalker-birds had shaken him more badly than he was admitting, but when Tom offered him an arm to lean on he waved it away. "I'm not quite incapable yet, Apprentice Natsworthy. Though I must say, things have been getting jolly exciting since you and your daughter arrived. Birds and 'burbs and doomsday weapons. . . There's barely a minute's peace."

Another pallid flicker of light came from the western sky. It seemed brighter this time, and Tom thought he saw a white blade of light slice across the stars, striking down at the earth from some immeasurable height. Again, faintly, he heard that roaring, shrieking sound. "Great Quirke!" he whispered.

"They didn't muck about, those Ancients."

"Was Lurpak right? Is it really up in orbit somewhere?"

"It's possible," said Pomeroy. "There is all sorts of stuff still circling up there. The old records list a few weapons which the Ancients were supposed to have hung in heaven. The Diamond Bat, Jinju 14, the Nine Sisters, ODIN. Most of them must have been destroyed in the Sixty Minute War, or fallen out of the sky in all the millennia since. But I suppose it's possible that one's still up there, and Naga's people have managed to awaken it."

"ODIN," said Tom. "I've heard that name somewhere. . ."

"Quirke preserve us! You must have actually been paying attention during one of my lectures, Natsworthy!" chuckled Pomeroy, but he sounded weary, and Tom started walking again, thinking that it could not be good for the old Historian to be hanging about here in the chill air. The white light had gone now, anyway; there was nothing to see but a sinister, reddish glow in the west.

"The name stood for Orbital Defence Initiative," Pomeroy said, as they strolled on together. "It was part of the American Empire's last, furious arms-race with Greater China. I wonder where on earth our Mossie friends dug up the access codes."

"Quirke Almighty!" Tom said suddenly, with such concern in his voice that Pomeroy stopped again and turned to peer at him.

"Everything all right, Natsworthy?"

"Yes," said Tom, but he was lying. He had remembered why the name ODIN sounded familiar. That had been the only legible word among the thousands of numbers and symbols scratched on the pages of the Tin Book of Anchorage, the relic which Wren had helped the Lost Boys steal from Vineland. Tom had almost forgotten about the book; he had assumed it was destroyed when Cloud 9 fell. Naga's people must have taken it with them to Shan Guo, and used it to arouse the dreadful weapon in the sky.

"Please," he said, "don't mention any of this to Wren."

Pomeroy chuckled again, and nudged him. "Don't want to spoil her romance, eh? Don't blame you, Natsworthy. It's good to see that our young people are getting on with the serious business of falling in love with each other, despite all these trivial distractions. And I like that Theo Ngoni. They'll be good for each other."

"If they live through this," said Tom. "If any of us do."

"The forces of History will decide that," said Pomeroy. "I've studied History all my life, and the one thing I've learned for certain is that you can't stand against it. It's like a river in flood, and we are just swept along in it. The big people, like Naga, or those *Traktionstadt* fellows, may try to swim against the current for a time, but little people like us, the best we can hope for is to keep our heads above water for as long as we can."

"And when we go under?" asked Tom. "What then?"

Pomeroy laughed. "Then it's someone else's turn. Your daughter and her young man, for instance. A London Historian's daughter and an Anti-Tractionist. Maybe they're the future."

They were drawing close to his comfortable little book-lined hut. As he turned and took Tom's hand, Tom said suddenly, "Mr Pomeroy, if anything happened to me, you would look after Wren, wouldn't you?"

Pomeroy frowned. He seemed about to say something flippant, but then realized how serious Tom was, and nodded instead. "Wren has Theo to look after her," he said. "But, yes, I'd do my bit, if she needed me. So would

Clytie; so would every other Londoner. You needn't worry about her, Tom."

"Thank you."

They stood for a moment side by side. Then Pomeroy said, "Well, good night, Apprentice Natsworthy."

"Good night, Lord Mayor. You're sure. . ."

"Don't fuss," said Pomeroy amiably. "I'm perfectly capable of putting myself to bed. And don't worry too much about the Storm, or Harrowbarrow, or any of the rest of it. London can take it."

He shambled off, and Tom went slowly home to his own hut, where Theo was to be staying now as well. But as he reached the door he heard Wren's and Theo's voices from inside, where they must be waiting for him to return. They were talking too softly to make out any words, but he knew what they were saying. They were telling each other all the things he and Hester had told each other once; all the things that lovers had always said to one another, imagining that they were the first people ever to say them.

Not wanting to interrupt, Tom turned away and went out into the open air again. He walked up into the rust-hills, going slowly to spare his heart. The western sky looked bruised. *I ought to do something,* he thought. *I have done so little for New London; just brought trouble, really. I should try to do something about this. It's my responsibility in a way; a family matter. But how could I hope to stop ODIN? I don't even know where the Storm control it from. . .*

And then he thought, *I might not be able to stop ODIN, but perhaps I could stop them using it on New London.*

General Naga was a good man, Wren had often

spoken about how he had treated her on Cloud 9; how fair and civilized he'd been. Perhaps he was only using the weapon because he was scared, and desperate. Perhaps he was the sort of man who would listen to reason. If he could meet a Londoner, and hear first hand about New London, surely he would understand that the Storm had no cause to fear it?

Tom was shaking so much that he had to sit down. Could it be done? He supposed it could. There was fuel enough in the *Jenny Haniver*'s tanks to reach Batmunkh Gompa. And then he remembered Theo telling him how Hester had rescued Lady Naga. Was *she* in Shan Guo, even now? Might she be able to help persuade General Naga to listen to what Tom had to tell him?

He walked back to Crouch End. He had been gone far longer than he'd realized; Wren and Theo had fallen asleep waiting for him. Tom went quietly past them to his pack, found paper and a pencil and wrote a letter for his daughter. He left it beside her, and stood looking down at her for a while, listening to her breathe, watching the small, sleeping movements of her fingers, just as he used to when she was a baby. He kissed her forehead, and she smiled in her sleep and snuggled closer to Theo.

"Night night, little Wren," Tom said. "Sleep tight. Sleep tight."

Then he went out of the hut and shouldered his pack and left Crouch End, heading for the Holloway Road and the place where the *Jenny Haniver* was moored.

On the plains west of London, Wolf Kobold stood on his favourite observation post, up on Harrowbarrow's armoured spine. The harvester was stationary, buried in a long hill of loose shale with just a few well-camouflaged gun emplacements and watchtowers protruding. It had travelled only by night since it broke away from the Murnau pack, for although the Green Storm's armies were collapsing these lands were still enemy territory: Wolf did not want his trip to London interrupted by any foolish battles.

But tonight, as the suburb prepared to move, a different sort of interruption had occurred.

Wolf swung his field-glasses and counted seven . . . nine . . . twelve immense bonfires blazing in the west. He was too young to remember MEDUSA, but that was the name that came into his mind. His lookouts – trusted men – had reported a blade of light striking down from the sky and setting off those fire-storms. He tilted his head, staring at the stars. They looked innocent enough now.

A nearby hatch squeaked open. Hausdorfer emerged. "Well?"

"Talked to the radio boys," said Hausdorfer. "They've been trying Manchester, Winterthur, Coblenz. Nothing. Some kind of distress signal from Dortmund, then they went dead too."

Wolf stared at the burning horizon. "What of Murnau?"

"Can't say. There's interference on every frequency now. But it looks like the Mossies have found themselves a new toy." He waited for an order. None came. "Do you want us to turn back, or what?"

"Turn back?" The notion was mildly surprising to

Wolf. He considered it for a while, then shook his head. "You know what survived best after the Sixty Minute War, Hausdorfer? Rats and roaches. It's true. I read it in a history book. Cockroaches and rats. So let the old cities burn. It's Harrowbarrow's time now. A time for cunning, creeping things. Fire up the engines. Steer straight on to London."

PART FOUR

40

WHAT HAVE THEY DONE TO THE SKY?

Hester and her companions had watched from the gun-slits of General Xao's new headquarters as the fire from the sky reached down and touched the cities which were closing in on Forward Command, turning them one by one into plumes of blazing fuel and incandescent gas. Shrike was with them, but saw nothing. The pulses of energy from the mysterious weapon upset the equally mysterious machines inside his head, making his eyes go blank and his armoured body shudder helplessly. Lesser Stalkers, who did not have Shrike's strength, or Oenone Zero on hand to tend to them, fared even worse. At dawn the defenders of Forward Command found their battle-Stalkers scattered in the trenches like fallen lead soldiers. But by then it did not matter, for on the western plains, where cities and suburbs and flocks of airships had been massed, there was now nothing but smoke.

"What have they done to the sky?" asked Hester, looking from the window at breakfast time. She was still feeling weak from her head-wound. She thought at first that the marbled haze which hung over the rooftops was the first sign of a relapse; something gone wrong with her eye or her brain. But a glance at the frightened faces of Oenone and Pennyroyal told her that they could see it too.

The sun rose, pink and shrunken. Flakes that looked like snow were drifting down everywhere. "Snow?" Pennyroyal complained. "In summertime?"

"IT IS ASH," announced Shrike. "THE SKY IS FULL OF ASH."

General Xao took advantage of the lull in the fighting to have the *Fury* repaired. "We cannot make contact with Shan Guo," she told her guests. "The new weapon seems to have interfered with our radio sets. So I am sending you home to Naga with a message. We need orders. Are we to advance? Recapture the ground they took from us? Or do we simply wait for them to surrender?"

Oenone looked at the columns of smoke rising from the dead Traction Cities. She said, "I can't believe Naga had such a thing and never told me of it. I can't believe he used it. All those lives gone. It's horrible!"

Xao bowed. "Personally, I agree. But let's not say it too loudly, Excellency. My people are most impressed with the new weapon."

And it was true; as they walked to the docking pan where the *Fury* lay, the four companions could hear the cheers and songs of victory rising from the lower levels of Forward Command and from all the trenches and fortifications round about. Gunshots popped like champagne corks as relieved Green Storm soldiers loosed off some of the ammunition they had been saving for the cities at the sky instead. When a bullet skipped off the metal pavement a few feet ahead of them they assumed at first it was a spent round falling. "Sweet Poskitt!" cried Pennyroyal indignantly. "They'll have somebody's eye out in a minute!"

Only when a flushed, furious-looking soldier lurched out into their path, working another round into the chamber of his carbine, did they understand that the bullet had been aimed at Oenone.

"Aleutian!" the soldier shouted. He pointed her out to his comrades, who were hurrying up behind him.

"There she is, friends! The Aleutian traitor who tried to destroy the Wind-Flower and set up Naga in her place!"

Shrike stepped in front of Oenone and unsheathed his finger-glaives. The soldier's companions drew back hastily, but he held his ground, still shouting. "Your time is over, Aleutian! She is risen! We have all heard the stories! A Stalker killing a thousand townies aboard Brighton! An amphibious limpet found on the sacred mountain! The Stalker Fang has returned!"

Hester pulled out her gun, but Oenone caught her wrist before she could shoot the angry soldier. "No. Leave him. Who knows what he's been through?"

Already some of General Xao's men were hurrying from the docking pans to pull the troublemaker away. As they seized him the man screamed, "Naga could not have made the cities burn like this! This is *her* victory! The Stalker Fang has returned to Tienjing and killed the crippled coward! Fly home, Aleutian, so she can kill you, too!"

Xao's men bundled him away. Oenone was shaking. Hester took her arm and guided her quickly towards the docking pan. "Don't worry. He's mad. Or drunk."

"I HAVE HEARD THE SAME RUMOURS FROM OTHER ONCE-BORN HERE," said Shrike. "THE IDEA THAT THEIR OLD LEADER HAD RETURNED WAS A COMFORT TO THEM WHEN DEFEAT SEEMED INEVITABLE."

"But Fang is dead, isn't she?" Pennyroyal said, trying to shield himself behind the Stalker. "You smashed her."

"She is dead," said Oenone. "She *must* be. . ."

But she was still trembling slightly half an hour later as the *Fury* carried her into the stained sky and began the journey homeward to Tienjing.

London. The night giving way to lightless dawn. Fog everywhere. Fog on the edge of the wreck, where the debris merges into green scrub-country; fog in the wreck's heart, where it rolls among the steep mounds of corroded deckplate. Fog on the Womb road, fog on the rust-hills. Fog creeping into the cabins and huts of Crouch End, fog hovering around blind lookout-posts and lifeless windmills, fog drooping on the steering-vanes and rigging of the *Archaeopteryx* in her secret hangar. Fog piled so deep over the plain that Stalker-birds on watch above can see nothing of London beyond a few tall spires of debris which rise out of the vapour like jagged islands breaking from a white sea.

Wren woke from unsettling dreams to the drip, drip, drip of moisture falling from the eaves; Theo beside her (so at least *he* hadn't been a dream); her father still not home. She slipped reluctantly away from Theo's warmth and roamed through the chilly hut, peeking into each room. "Dad? Daddy?"

His letter crunkled beneath her feet as she came back to Theo. Her head was still stuffed with sleep; she had to read his short message twice before she started to understand.

Her cry woke Theo, and she thrust the letter at him.

My dear Wren,
By the time you read this I shall already be in the
air. I'm sorry to leave without saying goodbye,
but, as you wrote once to me, "you would only try
to stop me". I don't want to be stopped, and I

don't want to remember you crying and upset, or angry at me. I will remember you always as I saw you tonight, safe with Theo.

I am going to try and explain to the Green Storm that New London is not a threat to them. This new weapon has changed everything, but I believe General Naga is a good man, and perhaps if I can make him understand that we Londoners are not so very different to his own people, he will let us go in peace. Perhaps I can even persuade him to stop using the weapon. I have to try.

I hope I shall be back in a few days, to see New London leave, but if I die, it really doesn't matter; the truth is, Wren, I am dying anyway. The doctor I saw in Peripatetiapolis told me that. I have been dying for a long time, and I shall soon be dead, with or without any help from the Green Storm.

The strange thing is, I don't mind too much, because I know that you will live on, and see marvellous things, and one day I hope have children of your own, who will be just as much of a worry and a joy to you as you were to me. That's what History teaches us, I think, that life goes on, even though individuals die and whole civilizations crumble away; the simple things last; they are repeated over and over by each generation. Well, I've had my turn, and now it's yours, and I mean to try and make sure that you live in a world that is free of at least one threat –

Wren had her coat on and was halfway to the door before Theo even finished reading. He was glad of an excuse to stop; the letter was private, and he felt wrong for looking at it. "Where are you going?" he asked.

"The hangar, of course!"

"He'll be gone. . . He says. . ."

"I *know* what he *says*, but we don't know when he wrote that, do we? He's ill; it probably took him longer than he allowed for, going all along the Holloway Road." She wasn't tearful, just very angry at Tom for keeping such secrets from her. And how on earth did he hope to fly all the way to Shan Guo without her to help?

She and Theo ran off together, stopping only to cadge a flask of water from the kitchens. Angie was helping make breakfast. Wren pushed the letter at her and said, "Wake Mr Pomeroy and show him this!" and ran off before the other girl started asking questions.

The day was grey and cheerless. It seemed to Wren to smell of ash, as if the immense pall of smoke from all those slaughtered cities had drifted east overnight to blanket London. As they ran on the murk grew thicker; fog hid the deeper parts of the debris field, and the spires and blades of wreckage that towered on either side of the trackway took on a ghostly look.

"Is what your father said true?" asked Theo as they ran. "Is he really that sick?"

"Of course not!" Wren replied. "He's just saying that because he thinks I won't feel so bad then about him going off to Shan Guo. His heart hurts him sometimes, but he's got pills for it. Green ones."

The fog grew deeper. By the time they reached the terminus at the eastern end of the Holloway Road they could not see ten feet in front of them, and when they finally emerged from the old duct they found themselves in a white world where they could barely see each others' faces even though they stood side-by-side, holding hands.

At first they thought both airships were gone, but when Theo collided with the *Archaeopteryx*'s underside tail-fin they realized that only the *Jenny Haniver* was missing.

"Who goes there?" shouted a nervous voice.

"It's me! Wren!"

A greyish stain appeared in the fog and condensed into Will Hallsworth and Jake Henson.

"It is, you know," said Jake.

"Pass, friend," said Will.

"Where's my dad?" demanded Wren, who didn't have time for games of soldiers.

"He came by early this morning," said Jake.

"Very early," agreed Will. "Said Mr Pomeroy had asked him to take the *Jenny* on a reconnaissance trip and he'd be back soon. I 'spect he's circling up there now, delayed by all this fog."

"It's a real London particular!" said Jake.

"Why didn't you stop him, you idiots!" screamed Wren.

"Steady on!"

"He said it was orders from the committee. We couldn't argue with that."

"Was he armed?" asked Theo.

Will and Jake looked sheepish. "Not when he got here, no."

"But he made us give him one of our lightning guns. He said he might need it if he ran into any of those Stalker-birds up above all this pea-soup."

Wren turned to Theo, almost fell against him. She was tired by their journey along the Holloway Road, and she felt that she would never see her father again. She was ready to cry. "He's gone. He's gone for ever!"

Echoey sounds came out of the dank throat of Holloway Road. Footsteps and voices. Someone was approaching, and the sound of their coming was rolling ahead of them down the tunnel. Theo held Wren and tried to comfort her while they all waited for the newcomers to emerge. The hard beams of electric lanterns poked through the fog, lighting up all the little individual water droplets without illuminating anything.

"Zagwan?" said a tetchy voice, from behind the torch-glow.

"Me?" asked Theo.

"Put your hands up! Step away from the airship!"

"I'm nowhere near it," protested Theo.

"No, that's me," said Will Hallsworth.

"Is it?" A shape blurred out of the fog. It was Garamond, holding the revolver he had taken from Wolf Kobold. "Where's Wren?"

"Here," said Wren. "What is all this about?"

"We caught you just in time, I see," said Garamond.

"Just in time for what?"

Other figures were appearing behind Garamond; they surrounded Wren and Theo in the fog like a circle of stones. Wren thought she recognized Ron Hodge and Cat Luperini among them.

"They were going to steal the *Archaeopteryx*!" said Garamond, loud and triumphant. "Natsworthy has taken his own airship east, and now he sends his daughter and their Green Storm accomplice to take the *Archie*. They planned to leave us with no way of escape when the Storm's Stalkers march in."

"What are you talking about, you silly little man?" shouted Wren. "My dad's gone to try and talk to Naga..."

"Exactly! To betray us to his Green Storm paymasters; yes; we have read the letter. I *thought* it was a little too neat, your African friend turning up at the very moment the birds struck! You arranged that attack just so that he could appear to save us, thinking it would make us trust him. Well, Wren Natsworthy, I have news for you; I don't trust him; I don't trust you, and I don't trust your traitor father!"

Wren's fist caught him full on the nose. He went backwards into the fog with a muffled squeal ("Ow! By doze! By doze!"). Theo held Wren back as she tried to fling herself upon him, though she couldn't even see him any more. Sobbing, she screamed at the fog that hid him. "What were you doing, reading my letter? That was private! From my father! I told Angie to show it to Mr Pomeroy, nobody else!"

"Wren," said Cat, coming to help Theo restrain her. "Wren, Wren..."

"It's Garamond who's the real traitor! When Mr Pomeroy hears you tried to arrest Theo he'll—"

"Wren..."

"What?"

Cat hung her head, fog-water dripping from her hair. "Mr Pomeroy is dead."

"*What?*"

"Angie found him when she took your father's letter to his hut. All yesterday's excitement must have been too much for him. He died last night, in his sleep."

Garamond lurched out of the fog, one hand clutching his nose, blood dribbling down his chin. "Take theb both!" he ordered nasally. "Tie their hands. Brig theb to Crouch Ed. The Ebergency Cobbittee can decide what to do with theb."

41

BACK IN BATMUNKH GOMPA

The *Jenny Haniver* purred eastward through the poisoned sky, towards the wall of mountains which marked the eastern borders of Shan Guo, and the broad pass through them which was barred and guarded by Batmunkh Gompa. As he drew close to the fortress-city Tom opened the general channel on his radio set and sent out again the message he had been repeating ever since he left London, explaining that he came in peace. There was still no reply. He turned the knobs on the front of the set, scrolling up and down the airwaves. Static spat and popped like a fir-cone fire, and some kind of interference shrilled. Faintly, behind the gales of white noise, someone was speaking Shan Guonese, fast and panicky.

Ten miles more to the mountains. Tom had flown through these skies before, with Hester, flying from Batmunkh Gompa to London in an attempt to stop another Ancient weapon. He tried not to think about how that voyage had ended, but he could not keep the memories from welling up. Doubts started to gnaw at him. He had failed then, and he would fail again. His scheme of pleading with Naga, which had seemed so promising to him last night, began to feel more and more like madness. He should not be here! He should have stayed with Wren. . .

He started to put the *Jenny* about, but as he did so he saw three arrowheads of dark shapes waiting for him in the sky astern. He felt his heart clench like a fist. Memories of yesterday's attack and the birds on the long stair at Rogues' Roost wheeled round him. He snatched Jake Henson's lightning gun from the co-pilot's seat, trying to ready himself for the attack. The birds would make short work of the *Jenny,* but at least he would take a few dozen of them with him.

The birds held their position. He started to realize that they were not attacking, just keeping watch on him. Perhaps they had been there ever since he rose out of the fog-banks over London. It was so hard to see anything in this hazy, tar-brown light. . .

And then, at last, the voice he had been waiting for came rustling out of the radio set; a stern voice, speaking in Shan Guonese. He looked eastward, and saw the white envelopes of two Fox Spirits glowing in the gloomy sky. The voice translated its order into Anglish. "Barbarian airship, cut your engines. Prepare to be boarded. We are the Green Storm."

Tom had just time to stow the lightning gun in a hiding place high in the envelope before they came aboard. They were as unfriendly as the Green Storm soldiers he remembered from Rogues' Roost, but they were not arrogant any more; they seemed afraid. "How did you know General Naga is at Batmunkh Gompa?" they demanded angrily, when Tom tried to explain what he was doing here in the air-approaches of their city.

"I didn't. Is he? I thought he'd be in Tienjing. That's your capital, isn't it? I thought from Batmunkh Gompa you would be able to take me to Tienjing."

"Tienjing is gone," said the leader of the Storm patrol, pacing about nervously on the *Jenny*'s flight-deck.

"Gone? What do you mean, gone?"

The young officer didn't answer. Then she said, "Anna Fang's ship was called the *Jenny Haniver*. I saw a film about her life in basic training."

"This is the same ship," said Tom eagerly. "Anna was a friend of mine. I inherited the *Jenny* when she was, when she. . ."

"Quiet!" screamed the officer in Shan Guonese, wheeling round to quell the outburst of whispering that had broken out among her men. They seemed to come from half a dozen different countries, and were busy translating Tom's words for each other. The officer barked more orders, and two of them came forward to hold Tom and manacle his hands. "You will come with us to Batmunkh Gompa," she said.

"I just want a chance to talk to General Naga," said Tom hopefully. "I have something important to tell him."

"About the new weapon?"

"Well, partly, I suppose. . ."

More whispering, more orders, none in any language that Tom could understand. Some of the men returned to their own ship and reeled in their spidery boarding-bridge. The officer took control of the *Jenny Haniver*, and Tom peered over her shoulder as they flew on towards Batmunkh Gompa, remembering how he had first come here with Anna and Hester all those years ago. The Wall was as sheer and black as before, and still armoured with the deckplates of dead cities, vast discs of metal like the shields of ancient warriors. But on the summit, where the oak-leaf banners of the League had blown, long lightning-bolt flags hung limply in the reddish sun, and between them an immense statue of Anna Fang stood pointing westward, summoning the people of the mountains to battle against the Traction Cities. As the *Jenny* descended past her Tom noticed that she was a lot prettier than the real Anna Fang had been, and that a lot of bird-droppings had drizzled down her face.

Then they were over the wall, and sinking past the vertical city on its eastern side, the pretty laddered streets and swallow's-nest houses all just as Tom remembered them, except that extra docking pans had been constructed on the lower levels, and hundreds of concrete barrack blocks now covered the valley floor at the western end of the lake. The *Jenny* flew over them, making for a cluster of buildings outside the city proper, on a crag which jutted out from the northern wall of the pass. Tom saw an old nunnery perched on the flat summit surrounded by what looked like an encampment of tents. The lightning-bolt flags were everywhere, interspersed with giant-sized portraits of General Naga. On the pan at the crag's foot where the *Jenny* set down someone had scrawled big Chinese letters in whitewash, and then underneath, in shaky Anglish ones, SHE IS RISEN!

"What does that mean?" asked Tom.

"It means nothing," snapped his captor. "The lies of Anti-Naga troublemakers." She was a grim young woman, and not in any mood to chat, but she did at least allow Tom to keep his green heart-pills when her men hustled him across the pan to one of the squat blockhouses behind it, and then into a tiny, limewashed, concrete cell.

All the time he was being ordered about, or marched around; all the time someone else was in charge of him, Tom had felt quite fearless; what happened next was not up to him, and barely seemed to matter. But as soon as the iron-bound door slammed shut on him and he was left alone his fears came crowding in. What was he doing here? How was Wren coping, back in London? And what had that Green Storm girl meant when she said Tienjing had *gone*? Had he misheard her? Had she used the wrong word?

It was very quiet in the cell. Strangely so, for when he was last in Batmunkh Gompa one of the things which had hooked in his memory were the sounds; the puttering motors of the balloon taxis, the cries of street vendors, the music from the open-fronted teahouses and bars. He stood on the bunk in the corner of his cell and looked out of the small, barred window. The city stretched away from him, a scarp of stairs and houses where nothing moved but the flags. No smoke rose from the chimneys; no airships waited in the harbour, only a few scurrying figures could be seen on the steep streets. It was as if the city had been abandoned, and the people who remained had all pitched tents on the crag above. A mystery. . .

Footsteps, voices, out in the narrow entryway beyond his door. He jumped down, surprised. He had expected to wait hours or days for the Storm to deal with him. But the door opened, armed guards in white uniforms took up positions on either side of it, training their guns on Tom, and with a clank of armour a tall, yellowish man whom he recognized as General Naga came in, stooping as his exoskeleton carried him through the low doorway. Tom was relieved that his request for an audience had been taken seriously, but astonished by the speed; panicked, too, for he had not quite finished working out what he was going to say to this fierce-looking soldier.

Naga's narrow eyes narrowed even more as he looked Tom slowly up and down, taking in his travel-stained clothes and unkempt hair. His armour looked scraped and battered and servomotors inside it whined and crunched unhealthily when he moved. There was a wound on his face, freshly dressed with lint and sticking-plaster.

"You are the barbarians' envoy?"

Tom was taken aback. What was the man talking about?

"You came in the Wind-Flower's old ship, and claim to bring word of the weapon. But you look like a sky-tramp. Not even in uniform. Are the *Traktionstadts* so certain of victory now that they expect me to surrender to a buffoon?"

"Surrender? But the new weapon. . ."

"Yes, yes!" shouted Naga. "The new weapon! You have destroyed Tienjing, you have destroyed Batmunkh Tsaka; you almost destroyed me!"

Tom felt as if a chart which had been guiding him through treacherous territory had suddenly turned out to be upside-down all along. A bad-dream feeling. If Naga did not control the ODIN weapon, who did? The cities? But those fires in the west last night. . . Had the Storm not *seen* those cities burn? Had the news not reached them?

He closed his eyes and breathed deeply for a moment. This was all beyond him. But he could still do what he had come here for. "I'm nothing to do with the *Traktionstadts*," he said. "I come from London."

"London?"

"I came to ask you . . . to beg you. . . The survivors there – I know you know of them – they are building something; have been building something for many years. . . They are making a new city; a city that hovers, and will not harm the earth, and has no wish to eat any static city of yours. I'm here to tell you that they – we – mean you no harm; we have no quarrel with the Storm. If you could call off your birds, and let us go in peace when we leave the debris fields. . ."

Naga was frowning. "A hovering city?"

"It's called magnetic levitation," said Tom. "It sort of floats. . ." He waved his hands about, trying to demonstrate, and then remembered something Lavinia Childermass had said. "It's not really a city at all, more a very large, low-flying airship. . . My daughter is there. . ."

Naga turned to one of the officers behind him and barked out something in Shan Guonese. Tom didn't know many of the words, but he recognized the tone. The general was asking, "Is this fellow mad? Why are you wasting my time with him?" A moment later, without another look at Tom, he stalked out of the cell, his guards behind him.

"Please," Tom shouted, "your wife will vouch for me! Is she here? Are her companions here?" (It had suddenly occurred to him that if Tienjing had been destroyed, Hester might have been destroyed with it.) He said, "Please, I am a friend of Theo Ngoni and Hester. . ."

"My wife?" Naga turned, glaring at him. "She is on her way home. I will certainly tell her all about you when she arrives." But he made it sound like a threat, not a promise.

The door slammed shut. Tom was left alone again.

Outside, Naga stopped for a moment to think. His men clustered together, glancing fearfully towards the misty heights of Batmunkh Gompa. He knew what they feared. It seemed inconceivable that after destroying Tienjing the barbarians had not turned their devil-weapon on the Shield-Wall and opened a path for themselves into the mountain kingdoms. And yet, when the few airships he had managed to salvage from the disaster at Tienjing flew here at dawn they found the place untouched, although the populace and half the garrison had already fled into the hills. What were the townies waiting for? (Naga had already discounted the reports which said that Traction Cities had been destroyed last night, too. They must be mistakes, or lies put out by the enemy to add to the Storm's confusion.)

And what did the appearance of this madman Natsworthy mean, aboard the Flower's old ship?

"London," he muttered. "Poor Dzhu told me something about London."

One of his officers, a captain from the Batmunkh Gompa garrison, saluted smartly and said, "There has been increased activity among the squatters there, Excellency. We have been watching them with spy-birds."

"You have records?"

"There is a file in the Intelligence office on Thousand Stair Avenue."

"Hurry there, and fetch it."

The captain saluted and ran off, grey-faced with fear and clearly expecting the fire from the sky to fall on Batmunkh Gompa at any instant. Naga watched him go. He thought wistfully for a moment of Oenone and then crushed the thought and muttered, "London. . ."

He remembered the night after the Wind-Flower died; how he had stood on the top of the Shield-Wall while the smoke of the burnt northern air-fleet drifted up from the hangars below him, and faint and far away the lights of London glittered. It seemed to General Naga that all the troubles of the world began with London.

42

THE FUNERAL DRUM

That afternoon, as the fog thinned and dirty sunlight broke over the debris fields, the people of London buried their Lord Mayor. Bareheaded, and with black mourning-bands tied around their sleeves, eight members of the Emergency Committee carried the shrouded body of the old Historian along a winding, little-used path between the rust-hills, while the rest of London followed, and Timex Grout beat out a solemn, steady rhythm on a drum made from an old oil-can. *Boom, boom, boom*, the echoes rolled away, across the wreckage, out across the plains beyond, up into the mottled sky where a few Stalker-birds still circled, very high, watched all the time by lookouts with charged lightning guns.

In Putney Vale, a mossy space between the masses of debris, where trees grew thickly and shaded the graves of all the other Londoners who had died since MEDUSA-night, they laid him to rest, and piled the earth over him, and marked the place with a metal marker, carved with the symbol of his Guild, the eye which gazes backwards into time. Lavinia Childermass offered up a prayer to Quirke, asking London's creator to welcome the old man when his soul reached the Sunless Country. (She did not believe in gods or afterlives, being an Engineer, but she had been Pomeroy's friend as well as his deputy, and she understood the need for this ritual.) Then Clytie Potts stepped forward and sang in a thin, uncertain voice a paean to the goddess Clio.

"He should have been here to steer New London out

of the debris fields," said Len Peabody, angry at the unfairness of it all.

"Now," said Mr Garamond. "It's time we elected a new Lord Mayor."

"Lavinia will be the new Mayor," said Clytie Potts. "That's what Mr Pomeroy wanted."

"Mr Pomeroy is dead," said Garamond. "The Committee must decide. And then we must discuss what's to be done with the prisoners."

Wren had not been allowed to attend the funeral. Other Londoners had pleaded her case, but Garamond, his nose swollen to twice its usual size and the colour of an aubergine, stood firm; she and Theo were dangerous agents of the Green Storm, and he insisted that they should be locked up. And so they were put in two old cages, salvaged from the wreck many years ago, which had once held animals in the zoological gardens in Circle Park, and were now kept in a dank corner of Crouch End to confine intruders, murderers and lunatics whom Garamond imagined might threaten the security of London. They had never been used before, and he looked very pleased with himself as his apologetic warriors shoved Wren and Theo inside, padlocking the barred gates behind them.

There, in the shadows, on the mattress which was her only furniture, Wren said her own prayers for Chudleigh Pomeroy as the muffled *boom, boom, doom* of the funeral drum came echoing across the debris like a heartbeat.

"What now?" asked Theo, from his cage. Dark as it

was in this part of the End, Wren could see him looking out at her through the bars. If they both reached out they could touch; just their fingertips. "What will happen to us now?"

Wren didn't know. It was hurtful to be accused and imprisoned like this, but she found it hard to be scared of silly old Garamond and all her London friends. Sooner or later it would all be sorted out, she felt sure. She barely had the strength to think about it though; she was too busy mourning Mr Pomeroy and worrying about her father.

They slept a little; talked a little; Wren made patterns with the straw on the floor of her cage. The day crept by. At evening time, when the dinner-gong was summoning everyone to the communal canteen, Angie Peabody arrived with food and fresh water for them. She poked the tin bowls in through the bars of the cage, and would not meet Wren's eye.

"Angie?" Wren asked. "*You* don't believe what Garamond says about us, do you? You know I'm not any sort of spy."

"Don't know what to believe any more," the girl replied gruffly. "There's been nothing but trouble ever since you got here, I know that. Them birds coming yesterday, and your friend turning up. . . Saab got hurt badly, Wren; we don't even know if he'll see again, and he'll always have the scars, and you don't care a bit; you just went off yesterday evening with your boyfriend or whatever he is. . . It don't look good, does it?"

Wren felt dazed with shame. It was true she hadn't spared much thought for Saab or the others hurt in the attack; she'd been too taken up with thoughts of Theo. "That was wrong of me," she admitted. "But it hardly makes me a Green Storm spy. Angie, a week ago Garamond was saying we were in league with Harrowbarrow; it was me and my dad who brought Wolf Kobold here? Remember?"

"How do we even know Kobold was what he said he was?" Angie retorted. "You say he went off to find this Harrowbarrow place. *He* might be Green Storm too, and safe in Batmunkh Gompa or somewhere now."

That made Wren think of her father. She reached out through the bars, trying to touch Angie, who backed quickly away. "Angie, you've got to get me out of here! I have to find a way of going after Dad. . ."

Angie took another step backwards, disappearing into the shadows. "Mr Garamond said we ain't to talk to you," she said.

Wren threw herself down on her mattress, which rewarded her by bursting and poking her in the side with a sharp, rusty spring. "I'm sorry, Theo," she said.

"It's not your fault."

"It is. If I hadn't written you that letter you'd have stayed with your own people. You'd never have come here."

"And if you hadn't talked to me that afternoon by Pennyroyal's swimming pool on Cloud 9 I'd have been killed or captured when the Storm attacked, and you wouldn't have to worry about me at all."

Wren reached out of her cage and touched his fingers. She traced the hard, warm curves of his nails, the little rough bits of skin beside them, the whorls of his fingertips like contour-lines on a tiny, Braille map.

Late that night they were awoken by the last person Wren had expected to come visiting them. "Wren?" a voice asked, and she opened her eyes to see Lavinia Childermass hunkered down outside the gate of her cage. The Engineer had an electric lantern with a blue glass shade. In its dim light her bald head shone like an alien moon. Wren scrambled up, spearing herself on the mattress-spring again, and heard Theo moving in the neighbouring cage.

"Wren, my dear, are you awake?"

"Sort of. What's happening? Is it Dad?"

"He has not returned, child."

"Then. . ."

"We have a new Lord Mayor," said the Engineer. "The Committee elected him this evening."

"But I thought you were Mr Pomeroy's deputy? I thought. . ."

"The Committee decided that it would be unwise to have an Engineer as mayor," Dr Childermass said calmly. "They still remember Crome's regime. And with the war drawing closer they thought it wiser to elect someone with a *security* background. . ."

"You can't mean—"

"Mr Garamond is Lord Mayor of London now, Wren. He played on the fears of the committee to make them support him. I am sorry to say that he has turned a lot of people against you. I think most of London believes that you and Theo and your father had something to do with those birds and the death of poor Chudleigh."

"But. . ."

"Shhh! I think they will forgive you, Wren; you are a Londoner's daughter, after all. But Garamond is going to propose that Theo be killed, and from the talk at the canteen this evening I think a majority of the Committee will side with him. He argues that we cannot allow an Anti-Tractionist to live here, learning our secrets."

"He's mad!"

"Perhaps he is, a little. Paranoid, certainly. Poor Garamond; he was no older than you on MEDUSA night. He survived because he was in one of the deep Gut prisons, where Magnus Crome had sent him for being an Anti-Tractionist sympathizer. The day after the disaster he led a band of survivors east, imagining that the Anti-Tractionists he had always admired would help them. But the soldiers they met upon the plains just gunned them down; poor Garamond only escaped by playing dead, hidden under the bodies of his friends."

"You can see why he wouldn't trust Anti-Tractionists," said Theo.

"But it doesn't give him an excuse to start killing people!" Wren complained. "And it *certainly* doesn't give everyone else an excuse to *let* him!"

"I agree," said the old Engineer. "But they are scared; the birds, the war, the new weapon. Even the prospect of leaving the debris fields is enough to unsettle them after so many years. And when people are scared, it can bring out the worst in them. That is why I am going to let you go. I am sure that Theo will be able to find you shelter at one of the Storm's settlements. I don't imagine the war will last much longer now that the Storm have this orbital terror-weapon, so you will be in far less danger there than with us."

She reached inside her rubber coat and brought out some sort of Old-Tech device; the type of thing Engineers presumably kept in their pockets all the time. It looked like a can-opener and buzzed like a horsefly, and made the padlock on Wren's cage clack open. "I brought your pack with me, Wren," Dr Childermass said, as she moved across to Theo's cage, and Wren, still not quite believing that they were going, fitted her arms through the shoulder-straps and heaved it on.

"I should carry that," said Theo, scrambling out of his cage.

"I can manage. We'll take turns."

Lavinia Childermass led them to a small back way out of Crouch End; a hole in the roof-plate at its lowest point where it sloped down to touch the ground. Scrambled out with them and stood watching them as they set off together into the wreckage, moving closer as they went away from her, as if they thought an old Engineer would not approve of people holding hands and wanted to be safely hidden in the shadows before they finally touched.

Lavinia smiled. She had had a child of her own, once, but in those days the Guild of Engineers had taken all infants straight to the communal nurseries, and she had never known her little Bevis. *Dead long ago*, she thought, and the sudden sadness made her remember the funeral drum, and Chudleigh Pomeroy lying cold under the earth in Putney Vale. If she had not been a logical, disciplined Engineer she would have found the world too sad a place to live in.

She watched Wren and Theo until the shadows and the wreckage swallowed them. *Well*, she thought, *that is one less thing to worry about*. And she went quickly through Crouch End and up the Womb road, returning to her work aboard New London.

43
HOMECOMING

he *Fury* reached Batmunkh Gompa shortly after sundown, crossing the Shield-Wall by the light of a smudged and bloodstained moon. She had been heading for Tienjing when the master of a passing freighter advised her captain to reroute. "Tienjing is burning! The barbarians have a new weapon! A lance of fire that strikes from the sky! Batmunkh Tsaka is gone, too! Naga has fled to Batmunkh Gompa, but not even Batmunkh Gompa can stand against the fire from heaven! Save yourselves!"

"What's happening?" grumbled Hester, tired and crotchety after the long flight, one hand pressed to her aching head. "Surely the cities can't have a super-weapon too?"

"Typical!" said Pennyroyal. "You wait years for an all-powerful orbital heat-ray thingy, and then two come along at once. . ."

"PERHAPS THE STORM DO NOT CONTROL THE NEW WEAPON," said Shrike.

"But it blew up cities! We watched it! Who else would want to do that?"

"A THIRD FORCE," suggested Shrike. "SOMEONE WHO HATES THE CITIES *AND* THE STORM AND WANTS TO SOW CONFUSION."

"Like who?" asked Hester.

"THE STALKER FANG."

"But she's dead!" said Pennyroyal. "Isn't she?"

"PERHAPS THE RUMOURS WE HEARD FROM THE ONCE-BORN AT FORWARD COMMAND ARE CORRECT," said Shrike. "I WAS RE-RESURRECTED. WHAT IF SOMEONE HAS RE-RESURRECTED HER?"

"And you think she is behind these calamities?" asked Oenone. She sounded afraid, but faintly hopeful too, as if it would be a relief to learn that her husband was not responsible.

Shrike said, "WHEN THE NEW WEAPON STRUCK, I REMEMBERED SOMETHING WHICH THE STALKER FANG SAID BEFORE I DISABLED HER. SHE SPOKE OF A THING CALLED ODIN. 'THE GREATEST OF THE WEAPONS WHICH THE ANCIENTS HUNG IN HEAVEN.' I BELIEVE SHE HAS AWOKEN IT JUST AS SHE PLANNED. SHE STRUCK AT TIENJING BECAUSE NAGA WOULD BE THERE, AND AT BATMUNKH TSAKA IN THE HOPE OF KILLING YOU, OENONE ZERO."

"But she's *dead*," insisted Pennyroyal.

"He's got a point, for once," Hester agreed. "You pulled her head off, Shrike. Threw the rest of her off Cloud 9. That should have done the trick."

But Oenone looked troubled. She had looked troubled all the way from Forward Command, and now she said, "Maybe not. She was a very advanced model. Dr Popjoy had put in experimental systems that even I may not have understood. It's possible that if someone had gathered the body parts they might have been able to. . ."

Her voice faded away. She shrugged unhappily.

"Oh, fantastic," said Hester.

"I might be wrong. . ." Oenone went to the window, looking south into the haze of dirty smoke from Tienjing. "I hope I'm wrong. We must ask Dr Popjoy. As soon as we dock at Batmunkh Gompa I'll send for him. Popjoy will know."

The city behind the Shield-Wall lay in silence, only a few dozen lamps burning in its dark streets. More lights shone on the valley floor; a river of lanterns pouring eastward, reflecting in the waters of Batmunkh Nor. The population was fleeing, just as they had fled the threat of MEDUSA the last time Hester was there. She thought what an odd place it must be to live if you had to keep packing all your belongings into carts and running away, and then reminded herself that MEDUSA had been nearly twenty years ago, and that a whole generation had grown up since she and Tom left this city in the *Jenny Haniver*.

"Gods," she said grumpily, rubbing her head again. "I'm getting too old for this. . ."

Fox Spirits guided the *Fury* to a temporary airfield below an old nunnery on a crag. The ancient building was surrounded by what looked at first like giant lichen; a shapeless mass of grey and brown and white. It was people. Refugees from the city, and survivors of Tienjing brought in aboard the ragtag fleet of freighters and military transports that was moored along the edges of the field. They huddled together against the cold, wrapped in furs and blankets, sheltering under awnings and tents. As Hester, still limping slightly, led her companions past them they started to stand up and shuffle aside, forming an avenue of staring faces. A whispering, like the wind in trees, ran through the crowd, as people pointed out the Lady Naga and her Stalker to their neighbours and their children.

Maybe they were saying that she was to blame for their disaster; that if she had not destroyed the Stalker Fang it would be the townies suffering instead. Maybe they had heard she was dead. Maybe, seeing Shrike and Hester walking beside her they thought she was a phantom come here from the Halls of Shadow with two demons to guard her.

Oenone barely noticed the stir that she was causing. She kept thinking of the Stalker Fang. *I must speak to Popjoy*, she thought, and looked east towards the lakeshore, where the old Stalker-builder had his retirement villa – but the evening mist lay thick above the lake, and she was not even certain that Popjoy's place could be seen from here.

At the door of the nunnery a tired-looking sub-officer greeted them. "Lady Naga! You are safe! Gods be thanked!"

Safe, thought Oenone. Yes; even if Fang had returned, Naga would sort everything out. She was safe at last. She returned the boy's salute, remembering him from her husband's staff at Tienjing; a friendly boy with a flop of black hair always falling across his eyes. She was glad he had survived. She said, "My husband is here?"

"The general will be overjoyed! I shall take you to him!"

Oenone followed him through the tall, carved doorway. Hester, Shrike and Pennyroyal went with her, not knowing what else to do.

"I shall need to see the scientist Popjoy," Oenone told their guide. "Can you find him for me?"

The sub-officer seemed nervous. "He is dead, Lady Naga. Murdered at his house by the lake, about three weeks ago. We think one of his Stalkers went wrong and. . . " He shrugged. "I heard what had been done to him. No human being could have had such strength. . ."

Oenone looked at Hester. Shrike said, "DID YOU FIND THE STALKER THAT KILLED HIM?"

The boy looked startled at being spoken to by a Stalker, but he recovered, and said, "No. But Popjoy's sky-yacht was stolen. Perhaps if the killer was an experimental model it might have had the wit to escape. Apparently Popjoy's house was full of . . . horrible things."

He addressed his words to Oenone, but he was looking past her at her companions, as if wondering for the first time who they were and whether he had been right to admit them to Naga's emergency headquarters.

"These are my friends," said Oenone hastily, and introduced them: "Mr Shrike; Professor Pennyroyal; Mrs Natsworthy."

The boy frowned. "Natsworthy?"

He took Oenone aside and they spoke for a moment in Shan Guonese. Hester heard the name Natsworthy mentioned several more times. She reached for the big gun on her shoulder and eased the safety catch off; asked Shrike, "What are they saying?"

Before the Stalker could translate, Oenone came back to join them, smiling. "Hester," she said, "your husband is here."

She might as well have carried on talking in her own funny language, Hester thought, for what she said made no sense at all.

"Tom Natsworthy," said Oenone. She took Hester's hands in hers and smiled into her face. "He arrived this morning, aboard Anna Fang's old ship. . ."

"No," said Hester, not believing it; not wanting to.

"He is being held in a cell down by the docking pans at the foot of this crag. But don't worry; I shall

417

tell Naga to free him at once. You should go to him, Hester."

"Me? No."

"Go to him." Oenone pulled off the ring she wore and pressed it into Hester's hand, folding Hester's fingers over it. "Take this; tell the guards I sent you. Mr Shrike can translate for you. They will let you talk to him. Tell him that orders will soon be coming from my husband to let him go."

"But he won't want to see me. Send someone else."

"You are still his wife."

"You don't know about the things I've done."

Oenone stood on tiptoes and kissed her. "Nothing that can't be forgiven. Now go, while I talk to Naga."

Hester turned and went, Shrike at her side, everyone in the passage turning to stare, wondering who she could be.

Pennyroyal lingered. "So Tom's here, eh?" he said. "These Natsworthys do pop up in the most unlikely spots. But I'll stay with you if I may, Empress. There's the small matter of the reward you mentioned. . ."

"Of course, Professor," said Oenone, and let him go with her as she followed the sub-officer through the maze-like corridors. The god that was worshipped in this place went by a different name to hers, but she still felt calmed by the old incense smells and the centuries of prayers that had sunk into the carved ceilings and lime-washed walls. Nuns in nasturtium-coloured robes clustered in doorways, watching. Green Storm officers hurried by, staring at her. Most of them did not look happy to see her, but she did not care. Thank God she had been able to come here! She felt glad that she had been able to reunite Hester with her husband, and looked forward happily now to her own reunion with Naga.

Up three stairs to an ancient door. The sub-officer knocked, then held the door open for Oenone to walk through. Pennyroyal went with her. In his grey cloak he looked the part of a high-ranking Green Storm officer, and the guards inside saluted him smartly as he followed Oenone into General Naga's makeshift war-room.

Around a big table covered in charts stood several dozen people, the ragged remnant of Naga's government. Some of them looked pleased to see Oenone. Naga, raising his eyes from his charts, just gazed at her. There were bruises and cuts on his face, and dents in his armour, and his good hand was mittened in dirty bandages. But he was alive.

"Thank God!" Oenone said happily. She wanted to hug him. But it would not be seemly for the leader of the Storm to be embraced, in public, in front of his captains and his councillors, so she controlled herself and lowered her eyes from his and bowed low and said, "Your Excellency."

Naga said nothing. Around him, wise people who knew how much he had longed for her nudged their moonstruck, staring comrades and started gathering up charts and swords and helmets and edging towards the chamber's various doors, but Naga called them back. He still had not spoken to his wife.

"I heard about Tienjing," said Oenone.

"It came from the sky," said her husband, watching her face. "From one of those old devil-weapons in high orbit, we think. A finger of light . . . of energy . . . it destroys all it touches. . . I am not the man to ask. When it struck Tienjing I was flat on my back at the foot of a staircase." He tried to gesture, but the gears in the shoulder of his battered exoskeleton grated and seized. "Damn it!" he muttered.

"Let me," said Oenone, glad of an excuse to touch him. The watchful officers drew aside to let her go to him, but when she reached out to unscrew the bolts which held his shoulder-piece in place his bandaged fist caught her across the side of the head. She fell sideways, hit the table, and crashed to the floor amid a rattle of fallen teacups and compass-dividers. Some of Naga's officers cried out, and she heard one say, "General! Please!"

"Naga. . ." Oenone said. She could barely believe what was happening. She thought his exoskeleton must have gone wrong and made him lash out without meaning to. But when she looked up at him she saw that the blow had been deliberate.

"This is all your fault!" he shouted. His mechanical hand swept down and grabbed a handful of her hair. He heaved her upright like a sack. "Look what your peace has led to! You told me to treat the barbarians like human beings, and now they are destroying us!"

Oenone had never imagined this. She did not know how to cope with his anger. "No, no, no, no," she said, "Traction Cities have been destroyed too; I saw them burning. You must have heard reports. . ."

"Lies!"

"Naga, the Stalker Fang is back! She controls this thing!"

A murmuring in the room; cries of alarm; of disbelief.

"Think," begged Oenone. "The reports from Brighton. The limpet found in Snow Fan Province. . . She wants us to think the townies have the weapon, so that she can use it against us all! She is insane! We have to find the transmitter she uses to speak with it and. . ."

"Lies!" said Naga. "I have already discovered where the thing is controlled from. It is the London Engineers again, just like MEDUSA. Those harmless squatters we have ignored for so long started busying themselves like ants a few weeks ago, and now this happens." He snatched a photograph from the piles on the table, an aerial view of London taken by a spy-bird. "Look! You can see their bald heads! They infest that wreck like maggots in a corpse! And today a Londoner came here with some wild tale to try and put us off the scent. It is MEDUSA all over again! It all begins and ends with London!"

"Then what about Dr Popjoy?" babbled Oenone. "Fang must have needed him to repair her, and when he had done it she killed him. . ."

"Popjoy was another Engineer! We thought he had come over to our side, but he was working for his old Guild all along! That body they found in his villa was so mangled it could have been anyone! Your former master faked his death and escaped to London to help his old Engineer friends deploy the weapon."

"No," whispered Oenone. But his theory made a sort of sense. How could she hope to show him he was wrong?

Naga stared at her, breathing hard. "And you were part of their plan too, weren't you Zero?" he said. His voice had grown softer and colder. "You were their creature all along, you Aleutian sorceress. It was Popjoy who first brought you to the Jade Pagoda. How shy and sweet you seemed! But you destroyed Fang and then

421

distracted me, whispering about peace, about love. . ."
He drew his sword. "And all along you were just buying
time for the townies until their new weapon was ready!"

Oenone tried to control her helpless trembling. She
stretched out her hands towards her husband. "Please
believe me. I would never betray you. All I ever wanted
was peace."

Naga struck her again, a stunning blow from his
mechanical fist. She went down on her knees, keening,
her hands cupped to catch the blood from her nose. He
shoved her head down and drew his sword. But the thin
stalk of her neck, bared in the lantern-light, looked so
fragile and ivory-pale that he could not bring himself to
sever it. She had a scurf of grime along her hair-line, dirt
behind her small ears, like a child.

Naga slammed his sword down, burying the blade
deep in the wood of the chart table. As Oenone dropped
sobbing at his feet he wheeled round and bellowed at his
officers, "Take her away! Lock her up! I'll hear no more
talk of peace!"

He tried not to watch as they dragged her to the door.
A few hardliners, old opponents of the truce, shouted
out, "Kill her!" One drew his own sword, and would
have butchered Oenone there and then if his friends had
not restrained him.

"No!" Naga shouted. The heavy door swung shut
behind his wife. It was easier to be strong now that he
could not see her frightened face. "I will behead the
traitor Zero myself, in public, in the main square of
Batmunkh Gompa!"

A few of his listeners looked almost as woeful
as Oenone had, but most were pleased by his
announcement; some even cheered.

"First," Naga told them, "we must gather what ships we can, and fly to London. We shall capture the barbarians' transmitter, and turn the new weapon upon their own cities! This war is not lost! Follow me, and we shall make the world green again!"

44

PILLAR OF FIRE

"Nothing that cannot be forgiven," Oenone had said, but it seemed to Hester, as she went in the cold wind down those long stairways to the docking pans, that she had done things that no one could forgive. She did not know what she could say to Tom; and did not like to think what he might say to her. But she hated to think of him cooped up in one of those little buildings, whose roofs she could see below her in the glow from the big lamps around the pans. There was a lot of activity down there; airships were being fuelled and filled, and one of them was the *Jenny*; a familiar, rusty-red envelope among the white of the Storm's warships.

Everything went blurry, and Hester had to wipe her sleeve across her eye. She was glad Oenone and Pennyroyal weren't there to see her snivelling. Only Shrike was with her (she could hear the heavy, comforting tramp of his feet on the stairs behind her) and Shrike had seen her weep before.

The narrow alleys behind the pans were full of loud confusion; the Storm seemed punch-drunk, and the simple business of preparing ships was leading to squabbles and rows between the remnants of different units who spoke different languages and dialects. Pushing through them, Hester felt a tightness in her chest and throat, a building panic at the thought of seeing Tom.

She stopped a passing aviator to ask the way to the cells, and was pleased at how he started bowing and saluting when she showed him Lady Naga's oak-leaf ring. But as she climbed the stone steps to the building he indicated, she heard running footsteps behind her.

"IT IS THE ONCE-BORN PENNYROYAL," announced Shrike.

"What does *he* want?" grumbled Hester, though secretly she was glad of a reason to delay her reunion with Tom.

Pennyroyal came panting up the steps to her. She knew as soon as she saw him that something had gone badly wrong. "Hester! Shrike!" he gasped. "Thank Poskitt! We've got to flee! I mean fly! That villain Naga. . .!"

"What's happened?" demanded Hester.

Pennyroyal waved his arms about, trying to find a gesture big enough to express the disaster. "I didn't know what was happening; don't know the lingo; but some of the men in there were speaking Anglish to each other, and they were saying she was a traitor. . ."

"Who's a traitor?" Hester grabbed him by the collar of his cloak and shook him. "What's happened, Pennyroyal? Where's Oenone?"

"That's what I'm telling you! She's in prison! He broke her little nose, the brute! He blames her for this terror-weapon. They're saying he's vowed to cut off her head once the cities are defeated. Oh, the poor child! Oh, Merciful Clio. . ."

Pennyroyal was genuinely upset, and Hester felt a pang of grief and pity too as she began to understand what he was saying. She hid it in her usual way, by growing angry. "You mean it was all for nothing? All that trouble and travelling? Losing Theo? We just got her out of one prison and into another? Can't the silly cow be left alone for a minute without getting herself locked up?" She looked at Shrike, who was staring silently at the buildings above. "Reckon we can do something? Get her out?"

"No way!" said Pennyroyal instantly. "He's locked her in some high turret. Stalkers and men with hand-cannon to guard her."

"THERE ARE MANY ONCE-BORN THERE," agreed Shrike. "I WOULD HAVE TO KILL DOZENS OF THEM. I COULD NOT DO THAT, AND DR ZERO WOULD NOT WANT ME TO."

"She'd want us to save our own skins!" Pennyroyal said firmly. "What if someone seeks us out? They're running about like mad bees up there, getting ready to fly off and attack some poor city or other. And they're hardly going to leave us on the loose, are they? If they think Oenone is a traitor they must think we are too, and they'll want *our* heads to complete the set. . ." He pawed at Hester's back, snivelling with terror as she turned away from him. "Hester, your ship's here; you've got to get me away. . ."

Hester turned and shoved him. He went backwards with an indignant yelp, rolling down the steps. "We've travelled far enough together," she shouted. "I told you in Airhaven; I don't want you on my ship. You can make your own arrangements."

Pennyroyal shouted something after her, but she did not look back. Above the noise from the docking pans she could hear other sounds; cheering and trumpet-blasts coming down from somewhere above her as the remnants of the Storm celebrated Oenone's arrest. The guard on the cell-block door heard it too, and Hester was relieved to see that he looked puzzled by it. Communications were ropey in this ramshackle harbour;

no sign of telephones or speaking tubes, just small boys running to and fro with messages. It might be some minutes before word of Oenone's fall from favour reached down here, and longer still before descriptions of her companions started to circulate.

Sure enough, the oak-leaf ring elicited more bowing and saluting from the cell-block staff. Hester was welcomed inside, while Shrike explained her business in a language she didn't know. A man ran and unlocked a heavy door, beckoning Hester through. "Wait here," she told Shrike, and stepped inside. An oil lamp had been lit, and in the slow flaring of the light she saw the prisoner sit up on his bunk and turn his face towards her.

The guard said something in his own language, but neither of them noticed.

"Tom?" said Hester.

Tom rose and came towards her. He did not speak, which Hester guessed was because he was so surprised to see her; she imagined that he could not believe it was really her.

She didn't know that Tom already knew she was in Shan Guo; indeed, from what Theo had said, Tom believed she'd been here for some days. It was a surprise to him when the cell door opened and she came in, but not a total one; surprise was not the reason why he did not speak. Hester had hurt him very badly, and when he thought of her he still felt angry. But now that she was here, standing a few feet from him, her familiar smell blowing towards him on the draught from the open door, he found that he still loved her, too. If he could not speak, it was simply because he had too many different things to say.

"Well," said Hester lamely. "Here we are again!"

"I left Wren in London," he said, guessing what her first question would be.

"In *London*?"

"She's with Theo; it's all right; she's safe, but. . ."

"Theo Ngoni? You mean he's alive?"

"He found his way to London. Told us he'd seen you. How brave you'd been. . . Saving Lady Naga. . ."

The guard was staring at them. Hester swung her gun down from her shoulder and pointed it in Tom's direction, saying to the guard in her creaky Airsperanto, "Unchain the prisoner; he's coming with me."

The guard shrugged; she couldn't tell if he understood what she had said, but he seemed to get the general idea, and he quickly unlocked the shackles that chained Tom to the wall. Hester grabbed Tom by the arm and led him quickly away, nodding at the other guards. Tom wondered if he should refuse to go with her; tell her that he didn't trust her any more, after what she had done before. But this did not seem the moment, and besides, a part of him was glad to have her in charge again.

Outside, Shrike was waiting. Tom flinched backwards when the Stalker's dead face turned to stare at him.

"It's all right," said Hester. "He's a friend now."

"Right," said Tom, remembering what Theo had told him about the old Stalker, but finding it hard to believe. "Hello, Mr Shrike. Sorry I killed you."

Shrike bowed faintly and said, "I DID NOT TAKE IT PERSONALLY."

Above their heads, with a shriek and a roar, the sky ripped open down a long seam. Light drenched them, bright as day and white as death. The ground lurched. Shrike gripped his head and his eyes flared and flickered.

The shouts of the soldiers and stevedores on the docking pans changed to frightened screams, and Hester screamed too and flung her arms around Tom, tugging him close. But the sword of light that blazed above them was not aimed at Batmunkh Gompa. It stood upon the mountains further south, blazing and shrieking, too bright to look at and too tall to comprehend. The sky filled with vapour, and blue threads of lightning crackled and flashed.

"What is it doing?" shouted Tom. "There are no cities there. . ."

The glare faded; the shrieking ended in a thunderclap, and then the night returned. The ground still shuddered. Hester still held Tom tight. Shrike hissed and shook himself, recovering. A pillar of cloud marked the place where the light had been, and at its foot a red glow gathered, a brazier brightening among the mountains.

"Zhan Shan!" Tom heard people saying. "Zhan Shan!" he said himself. He was very frightened. Hester's embrace was comforting for a moment, until he remembered and pushed her away. "They have turned it on Zhan Shan! The holy mountain is erupting!"

"Who'd want to blow up a volcano?" asked Hester, angry at herself for having hugged him. Around them bells were ringing, whistles blowing, white ships rising into the night. Who could say when the weapon would strike again?

"Come on," she said.

They wove through the busy harbour to the pan where the *Jenny* was moored. A group of Green Storm aviators were running towards her. Hester shouted at them that she was taking this ship. A hatch at the stern of the envelope hung open; she barked at the startled ground-crew to close it and stand clear. The men shrugged and saluted, but as they drifted away a harbour officer came hurrying over, shouting in Airsperanto. "Where are your orders? What's your unit? All ships have been commandeered for General Naga's strike against the barbarians!"

"No." Hester held out her hand, showing him Oenone's ring. "I'm taking her out myself; Lady Naga commands it."

The man had started to salute when he saw the ring, but stopped when he heard whose it was. "Lady Naga is a lackey of the Municipal Darwinist conspiracy!" he shouted, turning. "Friends! Here! The traitor Zero's accomplices are—"

Hester made her hand into a fist and the ring flashed as she punched the man hard in the stomach and again in the head as he curled over. She thought of killing him, but she did not want to with Tom watching. Leaving him gasping in the shadows at the edge of the pan she hurried the others up the gangplank. Other ships were taking off from the neighbouring pans; big transports going to collect troops from the plateau above. Nobody noticed the *Jenny* rise among them, and her red envelope faded quickly into the night as she veered away across the lake of Batmunkh Nor. By the time the harbour officer recovered enough to start shouting for help there was nothing to be seen of her but a wreath of exhaust smoke dissolving into the air above the pan.

They flew without lights, but the light of the eruption on faraway Zhan Shan came in through the gondola windows, red and unhealthy and bright enough to read by. While Hester steered, Tom stood at the window and looked out at the crescent-shaped gash which had been torn in the volcano's north-eastern side. The mountain itself was hidden in the darkness and the distance, so the gash seemed to hang in the sky like a burning moon.

"I still don't understand," Tom muttered to himself. "Why attack a mountain?"

Shrike heard him. "ZHAN SHAN COULD GO ON ERUPTING FOR WEEKS," the Stalker said. "THE PUMICE-CLOUDS WILL DISRUPT AIR TRAFFIC OVER THOUSANDS OF MILES. WHOLE PROVINCES WILL BE SMOTHERED. IT IS A BLOW FROM WHICH THE GREEN STORM CANNOT RECOVER."

"Then the cities *do* control ODIN. . ."

"THE STALKER FANG CONTROLS IT."

"The Stalker Fang's *alive*?"

Shrike nodded.

Hester, who had been intent on steering the airship past a rearing pinnacle of rock, relaxed a little as they flew into clear air beyond it, and looked back at her passengers. "We'll circle round and head west," she said. "I can set you down at London, Tom."

"What about your friend Lady Naga?" asked Tom. He had never met the unfortunate young woman, but he felt guilty at leaving her locked up. "Perhaps when Naga's ships have flown off we could. . ."

"SHE IS UNDER GUARD," said Shrike. "THEY WOULD NOT LET US TAKE HER ALIVE. IF NAGA BLAMES HER FOR ODIN, THERE IS A SIMPLER WAY TO SAVE HER: I WILL FIND ODIN'S GROUND STATION, AND PROVE WHO IS REALLY RESPONSIBLE."

"But the ground station could be anywhere," protested Hester.

"THE STALKER FANG HAS RETURNED TO SHAN GUO," said Shrike, turning, sniffing the musty air as if he hoped to pick up the other Stalker's scent. He found a map of the Heavenly Mountains and spread it on the chart-table. He stabbed his finger down on Snow Fan Province, then Batmunkh Gompa. "SHE ABANDONED THE LIMPET HERE. SHE KILLED POPJOY HERE. SHE IS IN THESE MOUNTAINS SOMEWHERE. SET ME DOWN, AND I SHALL FIND HER."

"Anna Fang had a house at a place called Erdene Tezh," said Tom. "We found the deeds to it among her things when we took over the *Jenny*." He pointed to the place on the chart. "Maybe she's gone home."

"IT IS POSSIBLE. THE STALKER FANG CLAIMED TO HAVE MEMORIES OF HER FORMER LIFE. PERHAPS THEY HAVE DRAWN HER BACK."

Tom felt pleased that the Stalker liked his suggestion. "Do you think we should go back to Batmunkh Gompa and tell somebody?" he asked.

"Definitely not!" said Hester.

"THEY WOULD NOT BELIEVE US," said Shrike. "THEY THINK WE ARE PAWNS OF THEIR ENEMIES. I MUST GO TO ERDENE TEZH AND SEARCH FOR HER MYSELF."

"Is that your own idea?" asked Hester suspiciously. "Or is one of Oenone's secret programmes still running in that brain of yours?"

Shrike turned to look at her. "I DO NOT KNOW. BUT DR ZERO REBUILT ME FOR A PURPOSE. I AM THE ONLY ONE WHO CAN DESTROY THE STALKER FANG. I MUST SEEK HER OUT AND REASSASSINATE HER."

"Thought you couldn't kill anybody."

"STALKERS ARE NOT ALIVE, SO IT WILL NOT BE KILLING," Shrike said patiently. "EVEN IF IT WERE, IT WOULD HAVE TO BE DONE." He waved one massive hand at the windows, at the mountain burning in the south. "IF SHE IS ALLOWED TO CONTINUE THIS DESTRUCTION, MILLIONS OF ONCE-BORN WILL PERISH."

Tom swallowed, and said nervously, "I can fly you to Erdene Tezh."

"It's not our business, Tom," Hester warned him.

"It is," Tom told her. "Because if you're right, we're the only people who really know who's responsible for all this. What sort of world will be left for Wren if we let it keep happening? We have to do something." He was about to explain the connection between ODIN and the Tin Book, but that would only make Hester think it was Wren's fault, which wasn't what he meant at all. "*I* have to do something," he said weakly.

"All right," said Hester. He was as lovely and infuriating as ever. She'd never been able to resist his stupid bravery. "All right. Let's go to this Erdene Thingy place. It's not as if I've got anything better to do. Only when we get there you're not going to do anything heroic; you're not going to risk your life, or try and talk to the Stalker Fang. You're going to stay safe in the airship and let Shrike go and kill her. And this time he'd better do it properly."

45

HARVEST

Wren, awakening, wondered for a moment where she was, remembered what had happened, felt afraid, and then decided that she did not care, because Theo was there with her, breathing softly, his face pressed into the curve of her neck, the heavy, comforting weight of his arm thrown across her.

They had gone west when they left Crouch End, because all the roads and paths Wren knew through the wreckage led west. They had walked for hours, listening out all the time for sounds of pursuit. They had seen the pulse of fire plunge into the mountains and stood in silence, hand in hand, watching the red glow gather in the sky behind Zhan Shan, throwing the summit of the giant volcano into silhouette. At last they had settled down to rest on the very westernmost edge of the debris field, where it petered out into a rash of smaller fields, scattered chunks of track and deckplate, towering wheels. They had taken shelter inside one of the wheels, in a cylindrical cave about twelve feet high where a crank must once have been attached. (Or a connecting rod, or a gubbins of some other kind; neither of them knew enough about the wheels of cities to say for certain.) It was, at least, dry, and not too cold, and they had cuddled together there with Wren's pack as a pillow and fallen quickly asleep.

Now a half-hearted daylight filled the circle of the cave-mouth. Wren woke Theo as gently as she could, and scrambled round him to the entrance. Peeking out, she saw the deserted margins of the wreck stretching away in hazy sunlight. She craned out further. It was too misty to make out Zhan Shan, but she could see the tower of smoke that stood above it, wet-slate grey, and as tall as the sky. The ground seemed to shake faintly, and she thought she heard a distant rumbling.

"Well, it wasn't a dream," she said. "Why would the Storm turn the weapon on their own land?"

"It must be another civil war," said Theo. He poured some water for them from the canteen Lavinia Childermass had given them. "Naga's probably zapping his rivals."

"Charming," said Wren. "And these are the people whose mercy we're going to be throwing ourselves on?"

"Either that or go back to Mr Garamond."

"Fair point. What's for breakfast?"

"Gravel," said Theo, opening a box that Lavinia Childermass had put inside Wren's pack. "I think it started out as some kind of flapjack. It's probably very nutritious. . ."

"Shhhh!"

The rumbling sound was growing louder. The ground was definitely shaking, vibrations flaking small scales of rust off the old wheel.

"The volcano?" said Wren.

Theo shook his head.

They scrambled down out of their shelter and stood on the wheel's rim, staring westward. The rumblings came and went, gusting on the wind. A ridge bulged and shivered, its profile altering as they watched. A gleam of metal showed beneath the scrub, and a fist of exhaust smoke rose triumphantly into the air.

"Oh, Quirke!" said Wren.

"Harrowbarrow," whispered Theo.

Wren nodded. She had almost forgotten the existence of Wolf Kobold. Her first thought was, *Thank Quirke we got out of the debris field before he arrived*, but it was drowned out immediately by another thought coming close behind it: *What about the others?*

"We've got to warn them!" she said.

"Why?" asked Theo. "They'll know soon enough. If it moves as fast as it did when I saw it tear through the line, they'll hear the engines in London before long."

"But they might not," said Wren. "The lookouts are young, they've never heard town engines; they'll think it's the volcano, like we did. . ." She tried to tell herself that it served the Londoners right for accusing people and locking them in cages, but all she could think of were her friends; Angie and Saab, Clytie, Dr Childermass. Even Mr Garamond didn't deserve to be eaten by Harrowbarrow. The waste of it appalled her; those years of thought and effort and hard work –

"We've got to delay it," she said. "I'll go aboard and divert them somehow. Even if it only buys an extra half hour, it might help. Don't you see? New London has to move today; now, ready or not! Once it's out of the fields it should be able to outrun Harrowbarrow."

"Oh, not on your own," said Theo.

"Yes, because I can't take you, because you're the mossiest Mossie in the whole world and a terrible liar and Wolf Kobold doesn't believe people like you even deserve to be alive. So you're going to go and be safe somewhere."

"Wren," he protested. She hugged him, tight, tight. It would be so easy to just keep out of Harrowbarrow's way and pretend that none of this had anything to do

436

with her, but it had; what would her father think of her if he knew she'd had a chance to save his city and she'd fluffed it? What would she think of herself? She kissed Theo. "Go," she said. "Harrowbarrow sends scouts out ahead sometimes, on foot. If they catch you they won't ask questions. Please go."

"How will I find you again?"

"I don't know," said Wren, pulling away from him. Harrowbarrow's engines snarled. "I'll think of something," she promised. She couldn't quite bring herself to let go of his hands. "Look, the gods went to all this trouble to bring us together; you don't think they'd let a silly little enormously dangerous armoured suburb come between us, do you?" She checked herself, because she was starting to babble. It had been the same on that air-quay at Kom Ombo. She seemed to be able to say anything except the thing she wanted to say.

In the end, Theo said it instead. "I love you."

"Gosh, really? Me too! You, I mean. I, I love you." She started to move back towards him, then pulled herself away. *There*, she thought, *I've told him; now I'll have one less regret when I get down to the Sunless Country.* She turned and started to stumble away through the brambles and the gobbets of rusting wreckage, northwards into Harrowbarrow's path. "Hide!" she shouted at him, seeing him standing there watching helplessly from the shadow of the abandoned wheel. "Go and hide!" She pressed on, half-afraid and half-hoping that he would insist on coming with her.

When she looked back again, she could no longer see him.

Theo ran a little way into the thickets of alder which filled the scooped-out hollow of an old track-mark nearby. There he stopped. He wanted to be with Wren, but he knew that if the Harrowbarrovians were as bad as she'd described he would only be going to his death, and bringing more danger down on her by making Kobold wonder why she was with an Anti-Tractionist.

Yet he could not just hide.

He turned east and started loping towards the debris field. The Londoners were not bad people. They deserved all the warning he could give them. He would run to the hangar at the west end of Holloway Road and tell the lads on guard there what was coming for them.

Wren waded through the waist-high weeds. The day was dimming as the pall of smoke from the distant volcano spread across the sky. End-of-the-world weather. Harrowbarrow's engines had fallen silent. She wondered if Wolf Kobold was on his bridge, watching the land ahead through his periscope. She pulled off her jacket and turned it inside out. The red silk lining was tatty and faded after all her adventures, but it was still the brightest thing about. She climbed up on a nameless chunk of wreckage and started to wave the jacket above her head, shouting, "Wolf! Wolf! It's me! It's Wren!"

After a few minutes she jumped down and started plodding on again. She could feel the ground stirring underfoot as the harvester-suburb drew nearer. From time to time she waved the jacket and shouted, but she couldn't even see Harrowbarrow any more; it had squirrelled down into a deep trench. Wren glanced at the sky. No Stalker-birds. Honestly, she thought, where were the Green Storm and their city-zapping super-weapon when you needed them? It was sheer incompetence, letting Harrowbarrow drive so far behind their lines.

A hummock of greyish earth ahead of her suddenly proved that it wasn't a hummock after all, by standing up and pointing a gun at her and shouting "Stop!" Wren screamed and dropped her jacket. All around her, more grey-clad men were appearing from the undergrowth. She didn't recognize their faces, but she knew by their get-ups and their tinted goggles that they were one of Harrowbarrow's scouting parties. She raised her hands and tried not to let her voice wobble as she said, "I'm Wren Natsworthy. I'm a friend of your mayor."

One of the men searched her for weapons, more thoroughly than Wren felt was really necessary (surely they must know that you couldn't hide anything *very* dangerous inside your bra?). Their leader said, "You come," and they were off, running quickly through the rough, stumbly country, squeezing through crannies in the walls of track-marks and wading across their flooded floors. The men moved fast and easily, and shoved Wren when she showed any sign of flagging. She was exhausted by the time the armoured flank of Harrowbarrow came in sight, half submerged in mud and torn-up bushes.

A hatchway opened. The scouts led Wren inside, and slammed the hatch-cover shut behind her. Then

Harrowbarrow went grinding on its way towards the debris fields.

It felt very strange to be back in the streets of the burrowing suburb after all that had happened; very strange indeed to stand in Wolf Kobold's Town Hall, on soft carpets, among velvet curtains and fine paintings and the gentle glow of argon up-lighters. Wren stared at herself in a mirror, and barely recognized the dishevelled, weather-beaten young Londoner who looked out at her.

"Wren!"

They must have called him up from the bridge. He wore boots and breeches and a collarless shirt with big fans of sweat spreading down from the armpits. He looked thinner than she remembered, and she wondered if it had been very hard for him, that journey alone across the Out-Country. Just for an instant she felt pleased and relieved to see him, and she seized on the feeling and used it to make a smile; a shy, warm smile. "Herr Kobold. . ."

"Why so formal, Wren?" He came to her and took both her hands in his. "I'm so happy you came to meet us. What brings you here? You are alone? Where is your father?"

"He is still in London," she lied.

"Do the Londoners know of our arrival?"

"Not yet," Wren told him.

"Then what are you doing here?"

"I've been waiting for you. I knew you'd come. . ." She let her smile fade; looked as if she were about to cry, to faint. Kobold helped her to a chair. "Oh, Wolf," she said, "Dad's a prisoner! After you left, the Londoners thought we must have been in league with you. They locked us in horrible cages, old animal cages from the zoo. Dad's not well, but they won't let him out. So I escaped, and I've been living in the debris at the edge of the field, waiting and waiting, and I thought you'd never come!"

Kobold's arms went around her, pulling her face against his chest. Wren managed to squeeze out a few tears, and then found that if she thought hard about Theo and Dad it made her cry for real. She said shakily, "Harrowbarrow is my only hope. You'll keep Daddy safe, won't you, when you eat New London?"

"Of course, of course," said Kobold, stroking her hair. "By this evening we will be at Crouch End; the Londoners and all they have will be our prize; your father will be safe."

Wren pulled away from him, looking horrified. "This evening? But you'll be too late! They are to leave this afternoon! The launch date has been brought forward because of all the fighting. . . Oh, you must go faster!"

Wolf shook his head. "Impossible. It will take us that long to skirt the debris fields. . ."

"Show me," said Wren, wiping her face with the back of her grubby hand.

She followed him along the fuggy walkways and across the dismantling yards, where gangs of men were preparing heavy cutting and rending engines. They climbed the ladder to the bridge and found Hausdorfer at the helm, his peculiar spectacles flashing as he nodded a greeting to Wren. He started to say something in German to Kobold, but the young mayor waved him away and led Wren across to the chart table, where a

441

map of the debris fields had been spread out. Wolf must have drawn it from memory after he returned to Harrowbarrow; Wren instantly saw several errors, as well as big blank spaces in the heart of the field, where Wolf had never been.

He pointed at the map with a pair of dividers, tracing a line that wriggled around the northern edge of the main field and then struck in towards Crouch End. "That's my plan. . ."

"Why not go straight across the middle?" asked Wren.

"I don't know what lies there. The wreckage might be impassable. And there are those electrical discharges the Londoners tell stories of. . ."

"Fairy stories," said Wren dismissively. "It's just as you suspected. The sprites are a tale they told us to keep us from nosing about. That one we saw the first day was faked by one of Garamond's boys hiding in the debris with a lightning gun." She smiled at him. "Look. If you want to be sure of reaching Crouch End before they get their new city moving, go this way. There's a sort of valley stretching through the wreckage that will take you almost all the way there. There are no lookouts in that part, either, so you'll stay undetected longer."

She picked up a pencil that hung on a piece of frayed string from the corner of the table, and drew a line on the chart for Harrowbarrow to follow; west to east through the debris field; straight along Electric Lane.

The lads on watch beside the *Archaeopteryx* had heard the muffled engines in the west by the time Theo arrived.

They were standing on a high promontory of wreckage outside the hangar, squinting into the murk. As he scrambled towards them he heard one say, "I can't see anything. It's the volcano," and the other reply, "Or maybe it's an airship engine. Maybe there's an airship circling above all this smog. . ."

"It's not an airship!" Theo shouted, and ducked as they turned towards him, afraid that they would fire their crossbows at him. But they only stared. The same boys he'd talked to yesterday. He tried to remember their names; Will Hallsworth, and Jake Henson.

"Will," he said, walking towards them with his hands outstretched to show he was not armed. "Jake, there's a suburb coming. Harrowbarrow. You've got to warn the others. Your new city has to move out now."

"Don't listen to him," Jake warned his companion. "He's a Mossie! Mr Garamond said—"

"Mr Garamond is wrong," Theo insisted. "If I was a Mossie, what would I be doing coming to warn you about Harrowbarrow?"

"Maybe there *is* no Harrowbarrow," said Will, thinking hard. "Maybe it's a Mossie trick."

A snarl of engines drowned out his voice, coming from somewhere to the south-west. A crash and clang of falling debris, too. The Londoners stared. Smoke and clouds of dust and rust-flakes drifted across the southern sky.

"It's surfacing!" shouted Theo. "It's reached the edge of the wreck! Come on!"

"What about the *Archy*?" asked Jake. "We can't just leave her here!"

"We'll have to fetch Lurpak or Clytie. . ."

"There's no time!" shouted Theo, as the rusty deck-plate beneath them shook and shifted, dislodged by the vibrations from the hungry suburb that was shouldering its way through the wreck a mile to the south.

"Well, *we* can't fly her!" wailed Will.

"I can."

"Yes, home to your stinking Mossie friends; we're not falling for that one!"

"Will," shouted Theo, "I'm not with the Green Storm! Trust me!" He scrambled into the hangar, staring at the *Archaeopteryx*. "Is she fuelled?"

"I think so. Lurpak Flint was down here yesterday working on her."

Theo rattled the gondola door. It was locked, and when he asked for the keys Will and Jake looked blank. He picked up a hunk of metal and smashed the door in, then grabbed a knife from Will's belt and started to hack at the ropes which anchored the airship. "Her controls will probably be locked," he shouted as he worked. "But that doesn't matter. The wind's with us; even if I can't get the engines on it'll still be quicker than running to Crouch End."

Will and Jake started to object, then gave up and joined him. The airship shivered as the ropes fell away. Theo noticed two rockets resting in racks beneath the forward engine pods. If he could get to Crouch End and persuade the *Archaeopteryx*'s crew to return with him, there was a chance they could slow or stop Harrow-barrow; he'd heard stories of how a well-aimed rocket, shot down an exhaust-stack or into a track-support, could bring a whole city to a halt. Then New London would have time to escape, and perhaps Theo could find his way aboard the crippled harvester and reach Wren.

The three boys scrambled into the gondola as the untethered airship began to rise. On the flight-deck,

Theo found that he could work the elevator and rudder wheels, although he had no way to turn on the engines. Sunlight poked in through the gondola windows as the *Archaeopteryx* rose out of the top of the hangar, trailing camouflage netting and uprooted trees. The brisk wind boomed against the envelope, already pushing her westward, and Theo spun the rudder-wheel so that her nose began to swing towards Crouch End.

The first rocket punched through the prow of the envelope and tore the whole length of the ship, exploding in the central gas-cell and sending a spume of fire out through her stern. Theo heard Jake and Will scream as the gondola lurched sideways. Struggling with the useless controls, he saw another ship go sliding past behind the sheets of smoke billowing from the *Archaeopteryx*'s envelope; a small armed freighter in the white livery and green lightning-bolt insignia of the Storm. Machine guns opened up from a nest on her tailfins as she sped by, and bullets came slamming into the *Archaeopteryx*'s listing gondola, and into Will, smashing him backwards through a shattering window. "Will!" screamed Jake, as Theo dragged him to the deck.

Peering through the smoke, he had a brief, dizzy view of the debris field. Above it, low and menacing, a shoal of white ships circled. The Green Storm had arrived.

46

THE SHORT CUT

The warships circled low over Crouch End; low enough that everyone could see the rockets glinting in their racks and the Divine Wind machine-cannon twitching in the swivelling turrets. A few of the braver Londoners ran for crossbows and lightning guns, but Mr Garamond shouted at them not to be so daft. He hated the Storm, but he knew that trying to fight them would be madness.

Someone tied a white bed-sheet to an old broom-handle, and Len Peabody waved it frantically as the leading ship came down. She was the *Fury,* the only real warship in the fleet, but none of the Londoners noticed how tatty the other ships looked; they were too busy staring at the soldiers and battle-Stalkers who spilled from the *Fury*'s hatches as she descended.

General Naga was the first to jump down, relying on his armour to absorb the shock of landing. Straightening up, sword in hand, he breathed in the rusty, earthy air of the debris field, and heard his troops disembarking behind him. He glanced to his right. Two of his ships had landed on top of the big wedge of wreckage there, and others were circling it. A party of his men were herding more Londoners down the track that led from it.

"The site is secure, Excellency," announced his second-in-command, Sub-General Thien, running to his side and dropping on one knee to salute.

"Resistance?"

"One of our armed freighters shot down a ship that

rose from the western edge of the ruins. And the gunship *Avenge the Wind-Flower* was struck by some sort of electrical discharge and destroyed with all hands. She reported movements in the western part of the wreck before she was hit. I've sent the *Hungry Ghost* to investigate."

Naga strode towards the waiting Londoners. His feet sank into the deep drifts of rust-flakes with crunching sounds, each footstep unpleasantly like the noise Oenone's nose had made when his fist struck it. He tried again to stop thinking of her. She was a traitor, he told himself sternly. Half the men in this fleet would have mutinied if he had not dealt firmly with her. He had to be strong if he were to save the good earth from these barbarians and their new weapon.

But the barbarians were something of a disappointment. Ragged, unkempt, unarmed except for a few home-made guns and bows which they had dropped when they saw Naga's force landing. They had *vegetable gardens*, for the gods' sake, just like real people! Their leader was a frightened little man with a scrap-metal chain-of-office round his neck. "Chesney Garamond," he said, in Anglish. "Lord Mayor of London. I'm here to negotiate on behalf of my people."

"Where is the transmitter?" barked Naga.

"The what?" Garamond gaped fearfully at him.

Naga raised his sword, but the man's bruised face and swollen nose reminded him suddenly of Oenone, and he lowered it again. His armour grated and hummed as it tried to compensate for the quick shivering of his sword-arm. "Where are you hiding it?" he demanded. "We know the ground station is in London. Why else have you lurked here all these years? Why else did you destroy one of our ships just now with your electric gun?"

"That weren't us," said another man earnestly. "That was just power discharging from the dead metal. Your skyboys got too close to Electric Lane. I'm sorry."

"And the movements the crew reported in the wreckage over there?"

"There's nothing there except our youngsters on lookout," said Garamond. "Please don't hurt them; they're just kids—"

Naga swung to address his waiting troops. "This savage knows nothing! Find me Engineers!"

"Coming, sir!" A sub-officer ran up at the head of a squad of Stalkers, each carrying a struggling, bald-headed prisoner. An old woman was dumped on the ground at Naga's feet. He waved his men back and watched her scramble up.

"Where is the transmitter?"

The Engineer looked curiously at him. Naga had the uneasy feeling that she could sense the swirl of guilt and fear behind the stern face he wore. She said, "There is no transmitter here, sir."

"Then how do you talk to your orbital weapon?"

The way her eyes widened made Naga wonder, just for a moment, if he had been wrong. The Londoners started to murmur together, until his men cuffed and threatened them into silence.

The Engineer said, "They are surprised, General, because they all believed it was you who controlled this new weapon. Certainly we do not. We have no quarrel with anybody; we are simply building a new city for ourselves."

"Ah, yes, your floating city! I did not believe that story when your agent came babbling of it at Batmunkh Gompa, and I do not believe it now. Shut those barbarians up!" he bellowed, rounding on his men. The barbarians stared fearfully at him. A little boy started to cry, and was quickly hushed by his mother. Naga felt ashamed.

When he turned back to the lady Engineer, she was holding out a thin, lilac-veined hand to him. "Come and see for yourself. . ."

The attack ship *Hungry Ghost* hovered over the smouldering wreck of the *Archaeopteryx* and made certain there were no survivors, then veered away towards the south-west to investigate the movements that the crew of *Avenge the Wind-Flower* had reported before that lasso of electricity jumped out of the debris field to snare them. The *Hungry Ghost*'s captain took his ship higher, not wanting to meet the same end. Almost at once he saw the mounds of wreckage below him shifting and slithering. He stared down at the movements, not really understanding, until an old track tumbled sideways to reveal the scarred, armoured carapace shoving along beneath it.

The suburb's lookouts saw the ship above them at the same instant. Silos yawned open in its armour and a flight of rockets tore through the *Hungry Ghost*, blasting her engine pods off, smashing the gondola in half, ripping off a tail-fin. Smouldering, sagging, she drifted downwind, while Harrowbarrow ploughed onwards below her.

"Damn it! That's all we need!"

Wolf Kobold's angry shout made Wren cringe. She was sure that Harrowbarrow must be near the western end of Electric Lane by now, and she had been waiting and waiting for the first sprite to strike. When it did, Wolf would know that she had betrayed him. But for the moment, it seemed, she was still safe. He saw her flinch and came to stand with her, in the corner of the bridge where she had gone to get out of the way of his men.

"Nothing to worry about, Wren," he said. "It seems my forward rocket batteries just shot down a Green Storm warship. The savages are in London already."

"Oh!"

"Don't worry!" He laughed at the look of dismay upon her face. "We have dealt with the Green Storm before. My lookouts say that these ships are old; a ragbag of freighters and transports. Naga clearly doesn't think your London friends are worth sending a real unit to deal with. We shall crush them easily."

He shouted instructions at Hausdorfer, and the navigator shouted in turn down the speaking-tubes beside the helm. The suburb increased its speed, and shocks came trembling through the deck and walls of the bridge as it butted massive chunks of rusting metal aside and track-plates and sections of old building went tumbling over the hull or were crunched and crushed beneath the heavy tracks. Wren braced herself against the chart table. Wolf Kobold put his arm around her. "It will be all right," he promised. "Another hour, we'll be there. Thank you for this short cut, Wren. I won't forget it."

Maybe there would be no sprites, thought Wren. Or maybe they were striking Harrowbarrow's hull already, dozens of them, doing no harm at all against its thick armour. Maybe all she had achieved by her ruse was to ensure that New London would be devoured even sooner.

And would it really be so bad if it was? It would serve the Londoners right for what they'd done to her. And good might come of it. She imagined Harrowbarrow growing strong and glorious on Dr Childermass's technology; a hovering city many tiers high. And she could be chatelaine of it all. Perhaps Wolf would make her Frau Kobold, Lady Mayoress of his new city. After her time in the debris fields the thought of a life surrounded by his tasteful furnishings and books seemed quite attractive. And she would tame him, make him treat his workers and his captives fairly. . .

"We're entering your valley, Wren," said Wolf warmly, listening to another report from Hausdorfer, who was taking a turn at the periscope. "The way is clear ahead, just as you promised."

Theo and Jake ran through some trackless tangle of debris, pushing past wires and hawsers, girders, fallen tier-supports like felled redwoods. Their clothes were singed and charred by the fires they had escaped from as the *Archaeopteryx* came down. They did not know where they were, or where they were going, and they could not hear each other speak because of the immense din of engines and scraping, grinding, tearing, squealing metal, which seemed to come from all around them, and from the sky above them, and up through the ground beneath their running feet.

A cleft between two rubble heaps ahead. A sort of path – or more likely just a stream-bed, where water sluiced down off the heights of the wreckage when it rained. Jake ran towards it, shouting something. Theo started to hurry after him, and then glimpsed a sign in the debris, half hidden by the scales of rust which were avalanching down the sides of the heaps as they shook and shifted under the weight of the nearby suburb. A crude skull and crossbones. DANGER.

Theo remembered something Wren had told him about Electric Lane.

"Jake!"

Ahead of him Jake was stumbling out through the cleft into a broad, fire-stained valley. "Watch out!" Theo hollered, over the noise which made it impossible to hear even his own thoughts. "Come back! The lightning will get you!"

"What?"

Something got Jake, but it wasn't lightning. An immense steel snout burst out from the steep wall of wreckage that formed the far side of the valley. Jake started to run back towards Theo, and a segment of clawed steel track came down on him like a giant's foot; a wheel two storeys tall rolled over him and on, and then another and another. The suburb's engines whinnied and growled as it dragged itself free of the wreckage and started to turn, making ready to speed east along the valley. Only a small suburb, but from where Theo stood it seemed world-filling; an armoured escarpment pocked and pitted with tiny windows, gun-slits, air-vents, hatch-covers and a stitchwork of rivets; people inside it somewhere all unaware of the boy they had just squashed beneath their tracks.

Theo scrambled backwards as the wreckage he stood on began to slide and toss, churned into restless waves. He tried running, but the broad, flat fragment of deck-plate he chose to run across began to tilt steeper and steeper, until he was climbing a hill, crawling up a cliff, struggling to keep a finger-hold upon a sheer wall. He fell, struck some other piece of wreckage, windmilled, tumbled down the valley's side and landed hard in mud and water at the bottom.

He lay there shivering, glad of the brackish water seeping through his clothes because its cold touch told him he was still alive. "Thank God!" he whispered. "Thank God!" And then, opening his eyes, realized that there was not as much to be thankful for as he had thought.

The stunted trees which grew around the edges of the pool he lay in were charcoal statues. Beyond them was Harrowbarrow. A steel tsunami, rolling straight towards him, tumbled debris foaming and frothing ahead of it. Theo pushed himself up and started to run, but from the wreckage ahead of him an immense brightness burst, crackling overhead, flinging his jittery shadow on the rust-flakes at the edge of the pool.

Electricity, in blinding skeins, tied Harrowbarrow to the valley walls. Lightning tiptoed across its metal hide, licked in through windows and silo-mouths, set fire to scraps of vegetation clinging to the tracks and bow-shield. The engine roar faltered and failed and in its place was a crackling, crinkling, cellophane noise, like God crumpling His toffee-wrappers.

In the dancing blue light Theo splashed through the shallows and flung himself at the only thing that was not made of metal – a boulder, dredged from the earth by London's tracks. He scrambled on to its dry top, praying that his movements and his wet clothes would not draw the surging electricity down on him. Above his head the sky was hidden by a cage of blue fire; Harrowbarrow was scrawled with scribbles of light. Sparks chased through the debris around the boulder's foot, and the wet mud fizzed. A tree caught fire with a woof, and burned like a match.

Then, abruptly, the storm ceased. A few last sparks, yelping like ricochets, arced across the gaps between Harrowbarrow and the valley walls. Wreckage slithered down around the suburb's tracks with a sliding clatter. Smoke shifted slowly, smelling of ozone. Theo remembered to breathe.

Harrowbarrow lay silent, motionless, its armour scarred by smouldering wounds where the sprites had touched.

"Wren?" said Theo, into the silence. "Wren?"

47

THE BATTLE OF CROUCH END

General Naga stood on the sloping floor of the Womb and looked up at New London. He could see himself reflected in the long curve of the tiny city's underside, and again in one of those strange, dull mirrors that hung beneath it. Why would anyone build such a thing? Could Natsworthy have been telling the truth? Did the Londoners believe that this contraption would actually *fly*?

He tried to force his doubts aside. He was a soldier; he was used to doing that; but today, for some reason, the doubts stayed, nagging. If this mad city was really all that London's Engineers had been building, then where was the transmitter which controlled the new weapon? Had Oenone been telling him the truth too? Had he shamed and struck her for no reason?

The soldiers he had sent aboard New London were returning, climbing down one of the steep boarding ladders. The young signals officer he had put in charge of the search ran across the oily floor and saluted. "Excellency, we have found no sign of a transmitter. Certainly nothing powerful enough to reach the orbital weapon."

Naga turned away. He shut his eyes and saw Oenone smile her small, shy smile and say, "I told you so." *What now?* he thought. *What now?*

"Should we destroy the barbarian suburb?" asked the signals officer.

Naga looked at it. All mobile cities were an abomination; the world must be made green again. But today, for some reason, he could not bring himself to give the order. He was glad of the distraction when another man came racing into the Womb, shouting, "General Naga! The *Hungry Ghost* has been shot down! There is something approaching from the west!"

Naga unsheathed his sword and strode outside into the glum, grey daylight, soldiers and frightened Londoners crowding out behind him. Faintly, over the rust-hills and the rubble-heaps, he heard the screel of C50 Super-Stirling land-engines. *Thank gods*, he thought. *A harvester-suburb!* At last; something he could destroy without a qualm. He turned to the waiting officer to order an air attack, but before he could speak the engine sounds cut off abruptly, and in their place there rose a crackling, a lashing. . . He turned and shaded his eyes, and saw the western skyline fizz with lightning.

"Sprites!" one of the Londoners shouted. "They must have come straight through Electric Lane, the poor devils! They've been struck!"

On Harrowbarrow's bridge the smoke stirred slowly, tying itself into gentle knots. Wren lay on her back on the floor and watched it. The dull red emergency lights flickered. Someone groaned. She began to hear other voices; cries and angry shouts coming from other parts of the suburb. No engine noise now to drown them out.

She tried to work out if she had been injured. She didn't think she had. Someone had crashed into her and she had fallen to the floor; perhaps she had been unconscious for a few seconds. She was shaking, and her head was full of memories of the things she had just seen – the sparks spewing from failing instruments and exploding control-panels; the helmsman screaming as the metal wheel he was gripping became a mandala of blue light.

She supposed her plan had worked. She supposed she should feel pleased with herself.

Wolf Kobold stumbled to his feet. There was blood on his face; black in the red light. "Up!" he shouted hoarsely. "Everybody up! Get up! I want the emergency engines on line at once! Hausdorfer, get down to the engine districts and bring me a damage report! Lorcas, pull us out of this damned lightning-swamp. . . Zbigniew, organize scouting teams; get them out *now, now*!"

"But the lightning. . ."

"Whatever it was, it's gone; spent for the moment. We mustn't let this delay give the Londoners time to escape."

Zbigniew started shouting orders into the speaking tubes, while Lorcas dragged the dead helmsman's body from the wheel and flung it to the floor. Wren started to edge towards the companion-ladder amid the sounds of Kobold's dazed men stirring; groans and frightened questions; curses. Someone asked, in Anglish, "What in the name of the Thatcher has happened?"

"Her," said Hausdorfer. He was on his feet, gripping the back of Kobold's chair for support. He was pointing at Wren, his hands shaking almost as much as hers. "She led us here!"

Kobold looked at her. "No."

"It was her, Wolf!" growled Hausdorfer, unbuttoning the holster on his belt. "Think with your head, not your heart. She knew this would happen! She hoped to fry us and protect her friends!"

"No," said Wolf again, but Wren saw his face change as he struggled to keep on believing she was innocent, and failed.

She ran. A man standing near the top of the ladder reached out to grab her, but she kicked him hard between the legs and writhed past him and down through the floor of the bridge. The steel rungs still tingled with electricity under her hands, sending little numbing shocks kicking up her arms. She heard Wolf shouting, "Catch her!" and his men scrambling to obey, but they were too sluggish for her and she was already climbing down into the smoke and shadows of the Dismantling Yards.

She jumped the last few feet, landed on something soft, peered through the smoke at it and realized that it was a dead man, burned by the currents which had surged through the suburb's deckplates. She felt sick for a moment, knowing that she was responsible. Was this how Mum felt, she wondered, when she killed the huntsmen?

"Wren!" shouted Wolf's voice, somewhere above her. "You don't think you can escape, do you?"

She forgot her guilt and fled. If anyone was to blame, she thought, as she pounded across the yards, it was Wolf Kobold for bringing his town here hunting in the first place. Ahead of her, stairs led up into the maze of Harrowbarrow's residential streets. As she ran towards them the metal beneath her feet began to judder, jerkily at first, then settling into a steady, pulsing rhythm.

"They're already starting the back-up engines, Wren!" called Wolf.

Ducking behind an abandoned town-grinder she peered through the gloom and saw him crossing the yards, calling out watchfully, like the seeker in a game of hide-and-seek. "Weren't expecting that, were you? Thought you could destroy the 'Barrow by luring us into that lightning, but the 'Barrow's stronger than you know, Wren. We'll be moving again soon, and we'll eat your precious London friends for supper. If you're *very* nice to me I'll keep you alive long enough to watch them die. . ."

A damaged power-coupling close to him spurted sparks, and she saw the sword in his hand flash. He went out of sight behind a support-strut and she took her chance and ran, up the stairs and into the smoky, dingy streets.

They were not quite as dingy as before; big rents had been torn in Harrowbarrow's hide, as if someone had gone to work on the armour with a colossal tin-opener. Bars and planks of smoky sunlight stuck down through the holes, and the shade-loving Harrobarrovians tried to avoid them as they hurried around making repairs. Squads of armed men ran past, but they were not looking for Wren. She kept to the shadows like everybody else and jogged towards the stern, looking for a way out. A few of the sally-ports were opened, but they were all clogged with scavengers hurrying out into the debris field. Wren tried not to think what they would do when they reached Crouch End. At least the Londoners would be warned of their coming; the noise of those sprites must have been heard halfway to Batmunkh Gompa. But even if they had time to prepare, how could they stand up for themselves against Harrowbarrow's ruthless scouts?

"Wren!" bellowed a voice behind her.

She turned on to a dingy, tubular street called Stack Seven Sluice. She was halfway down it when she heard the running feet coming up fast behind her. "Wren!" the voice was inhuman, distorted by echoes. She tried to run faster, but strong hands caught her, swung her round.

"Theo!"

"Are you hurt?" asked Theo.

Wren shook her head. She tried to speak but she could only croak. She hugged Theo.

"I came in through a hatch down near the bows," he said. "It came open when the lightning struck. I climbed in, and started looking around, and I heard people hunting for you. I came aft and I saw you, and I shouted. . ."

"I heard. I thought you were Wolf Kobold. I thought you were far away by now, safe. . ."

"I couldn't just *leave* you."

She hugged him tighter and said, "Theo, we can't stay here. We've got to find a way off this place. It's going to be moving again soon. It's all been for nothing. I thought I could stop them, but all I've done is made them angry. . ."

Naga ran down the track to Crouch End while his makeshift air-fleet launched itself into the skies above London again, the big shadows of the airships rushing across the huddled prisoners. He looked for Garamond, and found him sitting miserably on the edge of a raised vegetable bed. "Get your people under cover," he ordered. "There's a harvester out in the wreckage there somewhere. They'll probably have raiding parties closing in on us. Move everyone into that Womb place; we can defend that against them."

Garamond looked up at him, dazed and scared and not quite understanding. As if to convince him, quick puffs of smoke burst from a dozen points in the wreckage and something hummed over his head and clanged against Naga's breastplate, causing the general to stagger backwards a few paces before his armour compensated for the blow. Two of the Green Storm soldiers waiting nearby spun about and fell, flinging their limbs out so clownishly that several of the watching children laughed. The other soldiers began to run for cover, guns at the ready, shouting at panicking Londoners to get out of their way. Garamond started yelling, "Everybody into the Womb, please! Into the Womb, everyone! Quickly!"

Above the rust-hills one of Naga's airships burst suddenly into fans of smoke and belching scarlet flame. Another fired rockets down at some target on the ground and came to a shuddering halt as cannon-fire from below ripped off its engine pods and rudders. Whatever the suburb was it had clearly survived the electric trap it had blundered into. "Harrowbarrow", the Londoners had said. Naga recognized the name vaguely; a shadowy place which even the Storm's intelligence wing knew only from rumours. But Naga had come up against plenty of other harvesters in his time; Evercreech and Werwolf, Holt and Quirke-Le-Dieu. They were hard places; rip off their tracks and destroy their engines and they would still keep coming, extending spare wheels and firing up emergency motors. He shielded his eyes against the light and watched his airships burning – four of them now, a good crop of escape-balloons drifting downwind, thank gods. He knew he had a fight on his hands.

He looked behind him to check that the Londoners were doing as he'd ordered, and saw them hurrying up the track to the Womb. Some carried bundles of belongings, others clutched the hands of scared children, or helped the old and sick hobble along. Sub-General Thien was ordering squads of battle-stalkers into the rust heaps to stop any Harrobarrovians who tried to circle round and cut them off.

Naga took a carbine from one of his dead soldiers and threw it to the first Londoner he saw; a wide-eyed girl. "Covering fire," he ordered. For a moment he wondered if he had done the wrong thing and she was going to turn the gun on him, but she ran away to join his own troops, who were crouched among the heaps of scrap metal west of the vegetable gardens, taking potshots at any townies who moved up in the rust-hills.

"What about the Londoners' new city, Excellency?" asked Sub-General Thien, running over to crouch at his side. "Shall we destroy it?"

Naga stared at the long wedge of the Womb while bullets whirred past him like wasps. What would it be like to live all these years in a rubble-heap, to work so hard, only to see the thing you had built snatched away when it was almost finished?

Sub-General Thien was saying, "We can't risk the Engineer technology falling into the hands of these *Traktionstadt* vermin."

Naga patted him on the shoulder. "You're right. Find

that woman Engineer and tell her to start her engines. The new city must leave at once."

Thien gaped at him, eyes wide behind his visor. "You're letting it go? But it is a mobile city! We are sworn to destroy all mobile cities. . ."

"It's not a city, Sub-General," said Naga. "It's a very large, low-flying airship, and I intend to see that it comes to no harm."

Thien stared a moment longer, and seemed to understand. He nodded, saluted, and Naga saw him grinning as he hurried off, crouched low and zigzagging to avoid the bullets. Beneath his armour Naga felt himself trembling; it was not easy to go against everything he had believed for so many years. But Oenone had taught him that there sometimes came a time when beliefs had to be abandoned, or altered to suit new circumstances. He knew that she would approve of what he was doing.

He ran across open ground to the vegetable gardens and crouched down beside the young London girl he had given the gun to. "What's your name, child?'

"Angie, Mister. Angie Peabody."

He squeezed her shoulder with his mechanical hand, sharing his courage with her the way he had so many times with so many other frightened youngsters in tight corners like this. "Well, Angie, we're going to fall back to the Womb, and keep these devils at bay until your people can get their new city moving."

"You're 'elping us, Mister? Cor, ta!"

Her young face and bright, startled smile reminded Naga so strongly of Oenone that as he went running on to pass the same message to his own troops he had to pull his visor shut so that they wouldn't see his tears. He thanked his gods that the harvester had come, and that he had a battle to fight and people to defend; no politics to confuse him, no super-weapons to worry about, just a chance to die like a warrior, sword in hand, facing the barbarians.

48

A VOYAGE TO ERDENE TEZH

Above the white knives of the mountains the sky was full of memories. Tom and Hester didn't talk much as the *Jenny* flew away from Batmunkh Gompa, but they didn't have to: each knew what the other was thinking of. All the voyages they'd made in this little ship; all the castles of cloud they'd flown her round, the glittering seas they'd seen below, the tiny, toy-like cities, the convoys and the trading posts, the ice-mountains calving from Antarctic glaciers. . . The memories linked them together, drawing them closer, but they were all stained and spoiled by the things Hester had done.

So they did not talk. They took turns to sleep; to eat; and when they were together on the flight-deck they only spoke about the mountains, the wind, the sinking pressure in number three gas-cell. Tom fetched the lightning gun from its hiding place, and explained how it worked. They flew over small towns, high, sparse pasture-land and ribbons of road. They saw no other ships. Tom kept the radio switched on, but all they heard were a few confused scrabblings of battle-code; garbled distress calls on elusive frequencies, interspersed with pulses of interference, like breakers on a pebble shore. The sunlight faded. The sky was veiled with volcanic ash and city-smoke. The *Jenny* crossed a high plateau. Ahead rose the snow-spires of the Erdene Shan.

A sad, unwelcome thought came into Tom's head: this was the last journey of his life.

And as if she guessed what he was thinking, Hester

took his hand. "Don't worry, Tom. We'll be all right. Hopeless missions are what we do best, remember?"

He looked at her. She was watching him solemnly, waiting for a smile, some sign of forgiveness or approval. But why should he forgive her? He snatched his hand away. "How could you do it?" he shouted. All the stored-up anger he had been nursing since she left came out of him in a rush that sent her reeling back as if he'd hit her. "You sold Anchorage! You betrayed us all to the Huntsmen!"

"For you!" Hester's face was flushed, her scar dark and angry-looking. Her voice slurred the way it always did when she was upset, making it hard to hear what she said next. "For your sake, that's why I did it, because I was afraid you'd go off with Freya Rasmussen. . ."

"I should have done! Freya doesn't kill people, and enjoy doing it, and lie about it afterwards! How could you *lie* to me, all those years? And in Brighton, too. . . Abandoning that little Lost Boy. . . How *could* you?"

Hester raised one hand to shield her face. "I'm Valentine's daughter," she said.

"What?" Tom thought he'd misheard.

"Valentine was my father."

Tom was still angry. He thought this was another lie. "*David Shaw* was your father. . ."

"No." Hester shook her head, her face hidden now by both her hands. "My mum and Valentine were lovers before she married. Valentine was my father. I found out a long time ago, at Rogues' Roost, only I never told you, 'cos I thought if you knew then you'd hate me. But now you hate me anyway so you might as well know the truth. Valentine was my dad. His blood's in me, Tom; that's why I can lie and steal and kill people and it doesn't feel wrong to me; I *know* it's wrong, but I don't *feel* it. I'm Valentine's daughter. I take after him."

Her one, grey eye peered out at him between her fingers, as if she had turned back into the shy, broken girl he had fallen in love with all those years before. A memory came to him, clear as sunlight, from Wren's thirteenth summer, when she and Hester had just been starting to fight; Hester standing at the bottom of the staircase in their house at Dog Star Court and shouting up at her sulky daughter, "You take after your grandfather!" At the time he'd thought she'd been talking about David Shaw, and he'd thought it surprising, because she'd always said that David Shaw had been a quiet, kind man. But of course she had been thinking of her *real* father.

He felt the last of his anger drain away, leaving him shaky and ashamed. What must it have been like for her, keeping such a secret for so long?

"And Wren, too," she snuffled, weeping now. "He's in her too, why else would she steal that Tin Book thing? Why else run out on us? That's why I had to go, Tom. Maybe if she just has you she'll be all right, maybe the Valentine in her won't come out. . ."

"It's not *Thaddeus* Valentine who Wren takes after," Tom said gently. He went to her and took her hands, pulling them aside and down so that he could see her face. "If you could see her now, Het; she's so brave and beautiful. She's just like Katherine."

He had thought that he didn't want to kiss her, but all of a sudden he realized that he had wanted nothing else, ever since they'd parted. The things she had done which had made him so angry, the lies she'd told him and the men she'd killed, only made him want her more. He had loved Valentine when he was a boy, and now he loved

Valentine's daughter. He kissed her face; her jaw, her damaged, tear-wet mouth. "I don't hate you," he said.

From his station high in the envelope, where he had been keeping watch for pursuers, Shrike heard the sounds from the flight-deck; their rustling movements and the things they whispered to each other. Hester's constant weakness for the other once-born saddened him. Scared him too, for he could tell from the sick, arrhythmic stutter of Tom's heart that Tom would not live long. What would Hester do without him? How could she have invested all her hopes in something so fragile? And yet her small voice, audible only to a Stalker's ears, still drifted up the companionway, murmuring, "I love you I love you I always loved you Tom oh only you and always. . ."

Embarrassed, Shrike tried not to listen to her, concentrating hard upon the other noises around him. And faintly, faintly, beneath the noise of engines and envelope fabric and the wind in the rigging he sensed a third heartbeat, another pair of lungs filling and emptying; the familiar chattering of frightened teeth.

A few empty crates stood between the air-frame struts. A heap of tarpaulins quivered in a corner. Shrike ripped them aside, and stared down at the once-born huddled underneath.

It was hard for a flat, mechanical voice like his to sound weary, but he managed it.

"SO, PROFESSOR; WE MEET AGAIN."

"THERE IS A STOWAWAY ON BOARD," the old Stalker announced, climbing down the companionway with his captive. Tom and Hester sprang apart, straightening their clothes and their ruffled hair, turning their attention reluctantly to Nimrod Pennyroyal as Shrike shoved him on to the flight-deck.

"Please, please, please, forgive me!" he was begging, pausing to add, "Oh, hello Natsworthy!"

Tom nodded awkwardly, but did not say anything. He knew that there would be no more time for him to be alone with Hester, for the plateau below was narrowing and rising, and the steep buttresses of the Erdene Shan were only a few miles ahead.

"Throw him out the hatch!" said Hester angrily, fumbling with the buttons of her shirt. "Give him to me; I'll do it myself!" She felt that dropping Pennyroyal thousands of feet on to some nice pointy rocks would help her regain her dignity. But she knew that Tom would not want that, so she restrained herself, and asked, "How in the gods' names did you slip aboard?"

"I couldn't just let you leave me in Batmunkh Gompa, could I?" Pennyroyal started babbling. "I mean, for Poskitt's sake, I wasn't going to hang around and let Naga chop my head off or something. Authors lose all their appeal to the public if they are only available in kit form. So I sneaked aboard while those Green Storm chappies were fuelling her, and hid in the hold. If Mr Shrike hadn't come poking about I'd still be there, being no trouble to you at all. Where are we going anyway? Airhaven? Peripatetiapolis? Somewhere nice and safe, I trust?"

"Nowhere's safe any more," said Tom. "We're going to Erdene Tezh."

"*Where?* And, indeed, *why?*"

"Because we think the Stalker Fang is there."

Pennyroyal's eyes bulged; he writhed in Shrike's grip. "But she'll kill us all! She'll have airships, soldiers, Stalkers. . ."

"I don't think so," said Tom. "I think she's quite alone. How else would she have been able to return without Naga's intelligence people suspecting anything?" He grunted and clutched his chest, feeling his heart straining in the thin, high-altitude air. For a moment he felt an absolute hatred of Pennyroyal. What was the old man doing here? Why was he haunting them? He wondered if he should tell Hester about his failing heart. When she learned that the old wound was going to kill him she would murder Pennyroyal out of hand. . .

But he still did not want to tell Hester how ill he was. He wanted to cling for as long as possible to the pretence that he was going to survive, and sleep in her arms tonight, and fly on with her in the morning to fresh adventures in other skies.

"Tie him up in the stern cabin," he said.

"But Tom, be reasonable!" Pennyroyal wailed.

"Tie him nice and tight. We can't risk having him on the loose."

Shrike dragged the spluttering explorer away; Hester touched Tom's face with her fingertips and followed, promising to tie the knots herself and leave Shrike to guard him. Alone on the flight-deck, Tom steered the *Jenny* between the snow-spires of the Erdene Shan, up and up until the topmost peaks were sliding past the windows like vast, blind ships, snow-fields ghostly in that ashen light.

When Hester came back to the flight-deck he said,

"We'll be over the valley in another half-hour if Anna's old charts are right."

"They should be," said Hester, hugging him from behind. "Erdene Tezh was her house, wasn't it?"

Tom nodded, wishing he could kiss her again, but too wary of the spines and spikes of rock he was flying through to even glance at her. "Anna told me once she planned to retire here."

Hester hugged him tighter. "Tom, when we get there, if it *is* her, we're just going to let Shrike kill her, aren't we? You're not going to try to talk to her, or argue with her, or appeal to her better nature, are you?"

Tom looked sheepish. Hester knew him too well; she had already guessed the half-formed plans he had been turning over in his mind all day. He said, "At Rogues' Roost that time, she seemed to know me. She let us go."

"She isn't Anna," Hester warned him. "Just remember that." She kissed the hollow of his neck beneath his ear, where the swift pulse beat. "What I told you that night on Cloud 9, about you being boring; I didn't mean it. You're not boring. Or maybe you are, but in a lovely way. You never bored me."

They crossed a high pass. On the eastern side the ground fell steeply, down, down, down, a valley opening, white and then green, a wriggle of river in its deep cleft, a lake at the far end, and, on an island there, the house of the Wind-Flower. Tom, through the *Jenny's* old field-glasses, saw a saucer-shaped antennae poking from its roof. Then the sky filled with wings.

Hester had just enough time to push him to the floor before the first wave of Stalker-birds shattered the *Jenny's* front windows. Two of them came into the cabin, filling it with their flapping, the idiot flailing of their green-eyed heads. Hester snatched the lightning gun and shot the first before it saw her. The other came shrieking at her, its knife of a beak aimed straight at her eye. She fired the lightning gun at it and it exploded, filling the flight-deck with gunge and feathers. She looked down at Tom. "Are you all right?"

"Yes. . ." He looked scared and white. Hester squirmed upright, hissing with pain as the movement wrenched strained muscles. She peered out of the windows. More birds were circling the *Jenny*, and she could see a couple tearing at the starboard engine pod. She aimed the lightning gun through the side window and shot them both, then tossed it down to Tom and snatched her own gun down from an overhead locker. She started aft along the gondola's central corridor. Pennyroyal was screeching in the stern-cabin, and through the half-open door Hester saw the flap of wings and the gleam of Shrike's armour as he beat the birds back. "HESTER!" the Stalker shouted.

"I'm fine," she promised. She heard wings and claws inside the little medical bay where Anna Fang had once treated her for a crossbow-wound. Kicked the door open and turned her gun on the birds that had torn their way in through the roof there. The gun was a good one – the steam-powered Weltschmerz 60 with the underslung grenade-launcher that she'd picked up for a song in El Houl – but it made more of a mess of the medical bay than the birds had, shredding the outer wall till it looked like a doily. Through the holes she could see more birds going for the engine pod, and heard it choke and die, the propeller slowing. "Oh, damn it," she said, and pumped a grenade through the pod's cowling, blowing it to pieces along with the birds.

472

Back out in the corridor she shouted, "Tom? You all right?"

"Of course! Don't keep asking!"

"Put us down then."

"*Down* isn't a problem," said Tom, checking the row of gas-pressure gauges on the instrument panel and seeing all the needles whirling towards zero. Unbalanced by the loss of the starboard pod, the gondola was tilting steeply sideways. Scary shapes flapped by outside, but Tom tried to ignore them, saving the lightning gun in case more got in. Gaudy, yellowish light licked in through the larboard windows. The envelope was burning.

Hester kicked open the stern-cabin door. Shrike was in the process of ripping a resurrected eagle to pieces. He looked like a scarecrow, coated with slime and feathers, and he swung his dead face towards her and said, "THIS SHIP IS FINISHED."

"Not the *Jenny*," said Hester loyally. "Tom'll get her down all right. Go forward. Keep him safe."

She stood aside to let him go past her. She'd been hoping the birds would have killed Pennyroyal, but they'd been too busy with Shrike. The explorer lay on the floor where she'd left him, bound and gagged, looking up at her with round, pleading eyes. She considered shooting him, then shouldered her gun and pulled her knife out, stooping. Pennyroyal gave a squeal of fright, but she was only cutting the ropes on his feet and his wrists.

As she stood up again the remains of the long stern-window disintegrated in an ice-fall of smashed glass and the wide black wings of a Resurrected condor filled the cabin. Its claws raked Pennyroyal's head as it came

473

flapping at Hester. She dropped the knife and tried to bring her gun to bear, but there was no time. She heard herself scream; a terrible, thin, little-girl scream, and suddenly Shrike was back in the cabin with her, pulling her out of the way of the driving beak, grabbing the bird, its blades striking sparks from his armour as he crushed it to his body.

The *Jenny Haniver* lurched as another of her gas-cells exploded; her nose tipped up, her stern down. Hester was flung on top of Pennyroyal, who clung to a bulkhead. She saw Shrike stumble towards the stern, where the mountains glowed in the twilight beyond the smashed window. The bird was strong; half-crushed, it still flapped and clawed. The spasmic beating of its wings over-balanced Shrike. He smashed the bunk and crashed against the stern wall, which started to give way beneath him with a splintering sound.

"Shrike!" screamed Hester, scrambling down the hill of the deck to help him.

"Hester, no!" yelled Pennyroyal through his gag, pulling her back.

The wall collapsed. Shrike turned his face for a second towards Hester. Still clutching the condor, he fell. "Shrike!" she shrieked again, as the gondola tilted back to the horizontal. She kicked herself free of Pennyroyal and scrabbled as close as she dared to that gaping rent where the wall had been. "Shrike!"

No answer. Nothing to see in the smoke and the wind and the rain of burning fragments from her dying ship. Only the echoes of Shrike's last cry bouncing up at her from the abyss where he had fallen: "HESTER!"

From the wall of the Stalker's garden, Fishcake watched the burning airship draw a long, bright trail down the sky, deep into the shadows of the valley. The wind was carrying the sound away, or maybe burning airships made no sound; at any rate, it all seemed to be happening in silence. It was very beautiful. The igniting gas-cells were like fountains, showering out golden fragments which twinkled and faded as they fell. Blazing birds tried to flutter away from it, and they fell too, their bright reflections rising towards them in the waters of the lake until they met in a white kiss of steam.

A footfall in the snow behind him made Fishcake look round. The Stalker stood there, watching. "It is the *Jenny Haniver*," she whispered calmly. "How sweet of somebody to bring her home. . ."

The airship settled in marshy ground on the lake's far shore. As the smoke of its burning spread across the reed-beds Fishcake was almost sure he saw people running away from it. *Mr Natsworthy,* he thought, *and Hester.* And he felt suddenly afraid, because he remembered what he had sworn to do to Hester, and was not sure that he had the courage to do it.

His Stalker's hand rested on his shoulder. "They are no threat to us," she whispered. "We will not hurt them."

But Fishcake gripped the knife inside his jacket and thought about the last time he had seen the *Jenny Haniver*, flying away without him into the skies of Brighton.

Tom splashed through ankle-deep water and dropped into wet grass, hugging the precious lightning gun. Hester was close behind him, flinging down Pennyroyal. Survivors of the Stalker-bird flock clawed and shrieked around the blazing envelope, still trying to worry it to death. Hester lifted her gun and emptied the last of its grenades into the inferno. The explosion lit up the lake, the slopes and cliffs around it, the lonely house on its island. The *Jenny*'s rockets went up too, with orange flashes. Then there was only the swirling smoke, and the flames dancing in the smashed birdcage that had been their little airship; twenty years of memories burning away to charcoal and sooty metal.

"Tom?" asked Hester.

"Yes," he said. His chest ached, but not badly. Perhaps being with Hester again had healed his broken heart. He hoped so, because his green pills had been in the *Jenny*'s stern-cabin.

"Our *Jenny Haniver*," she said.

"She was only a thing," said Tom, wiping at his eyes with a singed cuff, looking around. "We're all right; that's all that matters. Where's Shrike?"

"He's gone. He fell. Up there somewhere. . ." She pointed towards the enormous silence of the mountains.

"Will he come after us?"

Hester shrugged uneasily. "He fell a long way, Tom. He saved me, and he fell. He might be damaged. He might be dead, and there's no one to bring him back this time."

"Just us then," said Tom, and he took her in his arms

again, and kissed her. She smelled just as she had on the night they first kissed, of ash and smoke and her own sharp sweat. He loved her very badly, and he was glad they were alone again, in danger and the wilds, where nothing that she had done mattered.

Not quite alone, of course. He had forgotten Pennyroyal, who knelt up in the bog and said in an irritable, gag-muffled voice, "Do you *mind*?"

Hester pulled away from Tom reluctantly and nodded towards the house. "This must be the place."

"We'd better get on with it, then." Tom took the lightning gun from his shoulder and checked it while Hester tied Pennyroyal's hands and feet again, reknotting the ends of the cords she'd cut earlier.

"You can't leave me here, bound and helpless!" Pennyroyal complained, through his gag.

"We can't have you running around free," said Hester. "You'd sell us out to the Stalker for a handful of copper."

"But what if you don't come back?"

"Pray we do," she suggested.

Tom felt unhappy about leaving the old man behind, but he knew she was right. They were already in enough danger, without a Pennyroyal on the loose behind them.

"How are you proposing to get out of this place?" Pennyroyal howled, as they started to leave, but they had no answer to that, so Hester just tied his gag tighter.

It was hard, rocky country, that valley of Erdene Tezh. Hester liked it. She could hear the grass singing, and smell the earth, and it reminded her of Oak Island. She took Tom's hand and they walked together through the gloomy light, looking over their shoulders from time to time at the burning brazier that had been the *Jenny Haniver*. The ground rose in a steep, grassy slope to a docking pan behind a windbreak of pines. The trees made a steady sighing sound as their needles combed the wind. The same wind boomed against the taut silicon-silk envelope of an air-yacht. It was locked and abandoned-looking, but knowing it was there made them feel more hopeful. They moved on, dropping down towards the lake again, towards the causeway.

Hester took the lightning gun from Tom. He was breathing hard, sounding winded. "Stay here with the airship," she said. "Let me go."

He shook his head. She touched his face with the tips of her fingers; his mouth, warm in the cold. They started together across the causeway. Tom was slow, but she was glad of that, because it meant that she could draw ahead of him, ready to deal with whatever was waiting for them in that house. There was a creaking noise, but when she swung towards it was only plates of ice grinding and grating together at the edge of the lake. Further out, clear water shone grey and still. She looked ahead again, towards the house.

There was someone standing on the causeway.

"Tom!" she yelled, raising the lightning gun. But she didn't pull the trigger. It was not a Stalker that stood there watching her. Just a child. A pinched white face and shabby clothes and a lot of filthy hair. She took another few steps, and recognized him. How had he come here? But it didn't matter. She lowered the gun completely and turned to Tom. "It's Fishcake!"

Running feet behind her. She heard the boy grunt and, turning, saw the knife flash as he slashed it at her throat.

478

She dropped the lightning gun and grabbed his thin wrist, bending the knife away, twisting his arm until he cried out and let it go. She caught it as it fell and stuffed it through her belt, like a stern teacher confiscating a catapult. She pushed Fishcake away and he fell down and started to cry.

"Tom," said a whispering voice from above them. "Hester. How nice of you to drop in."

The Stalker. She had been standing in the shadows at the causeway's end where ten worn stone steps led up to a gate. She came carefully down the steps, limping, the grey light shining faintly on her bronze face.

"She's my Stalker!" shouted Fishcake. "I found her after you left me behind. She's been good to me. She's going to help me kill you!"

Hester looked for the lightning gun, but it had fallen down among the rocks at the waterside. She started to scramble down to fetch it, but steel hands caught her, lifting her, dragging her, gripping her face; a metal arm went across her chest, pulling her back hard against an armoured breastplate.

"No!" shouted Tom, running for the fallen gun.

"Please don't be disagreeable, Tom," whispered the Stalker, "or I shall break her neck. I could do it very easily. You wouldn't want that, would you?"

Tom stopped running. He could not speak. He felt as if someone had jammed a rusty skewer through his left arm-pit, deep into his chest. Pain ran down his arm, too, and up his neck, along his jaw. He fell to his knees, gasping.

"Poor Tom," the Stalker said. "Your heart. Poor thing."

Crouched by her feet, Fishcake watched hungrily. "Kill them!" he shouted, in his thin, angry voice. "Her first, then him!"

"They were Anna's friends, Fishcake," said the Stalker.

"But they left me behind!" sobbed Fishcake. "She murdered 'Mora and Gargle! I swore I'd kill her!"

"They will both die soon enough."

"But I swore it!"

"No," whispered the Stalker.

Fishcake shouted something and groped for the knife in Hester's belt, but the Stalker swiped him aside, so hard that he was thrown right off the causeway, down on to the ice, which starred and moaned beneath him but did not give way. Howling with pain and betrayal, Fishcake crept back to the causeway. Sobbing, slithering over the wet stones, he ran away from the house.

The Stalker Fang let Hester go and stooped over Tom. Her steel hand rested on his chest, and her eyes flared as she sensed the erratic, stumbling beats of his heart. "Poor Tom," she whispered. "Not long now."

"What's wrong with him?" asked Hester.

"He's going to die," said the Stalker.

"He can't! Oh, he can't! Please!"

"It doesn't matter," whispered the Stalker. "Soon everyone is going to die."

She lifted Tom in her arms, and Hester followed her as she carried him up the steps and through her frozen garden, into her tomb of a house.

49

NEWBORN

Pell-mell along Stack Seven Sluice, the thick air full of the snattering of dynamos and clang of running repairs down in the District. Up rusty rungs that rose for ever, trembling with vibrations as the engines came on line. Wren exhausted, scared, hurting, each lungful of air a stabbing ache in the strained muscles of her chest and back, and the only thing that drove her on the fact that Theo was with her now. He reached out sometimes to touch her, encouraging her, but they could not speak, for it was too loud in these dank ladderways, these iron throats that filled with hot breath and angry bellowings as the wounded suburb struggled back to life.

They were soon lost. They wanted to go forward and down, but the tubular streets twisted round on themselves and looped blindly about, leading them up and aft instead. At last they emerged on to a catwalk high above some open square at the heart of the engine district, looking down past lighted windows and giant ducts into a space where a hundred fat brass pistons were pumping up and down in sprays of steam, their speed increasing as Theo and Wren leaned over the handrail to watch.

The handrail trembling; the whole suburb lurching forwards. "It's moving!" shouted Wren, but Theo couldn't hear her, and there was no need to repeat it for it was quite obvious by then that Harrowbarrow was under way again. No time to repeat it anyway, for just then an engine-worker in greasy overalls popped up through a hatchway in the catwalk and stared at them, mouth opening wide as he shouted down to his mates below.

Theo and Wren fled, and found a spindly ladder leading up through the sousaphone maze of ducts and tubes which coiled above their heads. Condensation fell on them like warm rain as they dragged themselves up under the curve of the suburb's armour. At the top of the ladder was a hatch; it took both of them to twist the heavy handles and heave it open. Daylight came pouring in, and fresh, cold wind. Wren looked down the ladder, and saw torches moving on the catwalk below; men gathering to stare at her and point. Then Theo, who was already through the hatch, reached back to pull her up into the open air.

At least I'll die in daylight, she thought, lying panting on the filthy armoured back of Harrowbarrow. A narrow walkway ran along the suburb's spine, without handrails. On either side of it a few hundred feet of battered armour sloped down to the suburb's edges, where the tracks ground by; clogged with earth and hunks of rust. Beyond them, the spires and spikes of ruined London sped past.

Theo slammed the hatch shut behind them and started to drag Wren away from it, shouting something about Kobold's men following them up, but before they had gone very far the metal around them suddenly erupted in sparks and little spurts of smoke and dust, and she realized they were being machine-gunned – not very accurately, thank Quirke.

Theo flung himself down half on top of her as a plump white shape soared above the wreckage to larboard. Through the spray of rust and soil flung up by

Harrowbarrow's tracks Wren saw that it was a rather elderly-looking airship with the markings of the Green Storm, gun turrets swivelling to squirt fire at the racing suburb.

"The Storm are here!" she shouted.

"We're friends!" Theo yelled. Wren held on to him to save him from being thrown off Harrowbarrow's back as he waved his arms and shouted, "Help! Help!" But to the aviators in that ship he was just another flea-sized shape creeping about on the suburb they'd been ordered to destroy; they swung their guns towards him again and Wren heard the bullets swishing overhead as she pulled him down beside her.

A few yards from where they lay a circular hatch-cover slid open in the suburb's armour, and a revolving gun-emplacement popped up like a jack-in-the-box. It had been built on the turntable of an old fairground roundabout from a coastal pleasure town that Harrowbarrow had eaten long ago, and as it spun around and around cheerful calliope music came from it, along with puffs of gunsmoke and streamers of white steam. The barrels of its four long guns recoiled rhythmically into their armoured housing as they fired, lacing the sky above the suburb with cannon-shells. The airship which had shot at Wren and Theo burst into flames and was left quickly behind as the suburb went thundering on. Overhead, two other ships veered away, envelopes and tailfins filling with ragged holes.

The coming of Harrowbarrow could be heard in the Womb by that time. As the Londoners struggled aboard their new city with whatever possessions they had managed to save the scrap-metal clangour of the approaching suburb filled the sky outside and echoed around the central hangar.

A Green Storm runner came to find Naga, who was waiting on the open stretch of deckplate at New London's stern. "Our airships can't hold her, sir. The *Belligerent Peony* has just been downed. Only the *Fury* and the *Protecting Veil* are left."

"Pull them clear," ordered Naga. "Tell the ground-troops to get aboard this . . . machine." He turned as Lavinia Childermass came running out of the stairwell that led down to her engine districts. "Well, Londoner?"

"We are ready, I think," the old Engineer said.

"Good. The harvester-suburb is nearly upon us. I am going aboard my airship, I shall try to hold it off as long as I can, but it is strong. Best pray that your new London is fast."

"It is fast," promised Dr Childermass as Naga turned away, his stomping armour carrying him towards the boarding ladders up which squads of Green Storm troopers were hurrying. She ran after him, jostled by passing soldiers. "You should stay, General! The birth of a town is a great event!"

Naga turned, and bowed, and hurried on. "Good luck, Engineer!" she heard him shout. She watched him go, thinking how strange it was that he should turn out to be New London's midwife. Then, remembering her position, she went haring back to her own post. The deckplates were trembling as, one by one, her assistants threw the starting-levers of the Childermass engines. By the time she reached her command-room in the heart of the underdeck the faint whine of the repellors had risen to a pitch beyond her hearing, and there was an odd, bobbing movement in the floor. New London was airborne.

She reached for the speaking tube that linked her to the Lord Mayor's navigation room, high in the new Town Hall. "Hello! Ready?"

"Ready," came Garamond's voice, muffled and peevish. Lavinia Childermass hung the tube in its cradle and looked at the scared, expectant, grimy faces of her crew. Even down here she could hear the crash and rattle as Harrowbarrow shouldered its way towards her through the debris fields. She nodded, and her people sprang to their controls.

Outside the Womb, Naga watched Harrowbarrow's scouts scurry aside as the noise of their suburb's approach grew louder. He fired his pistol at a couple of them, to speed them on their way. The sky above those rust-hills west of Crouch End was filling with dust and debris, as if a scrap-metal geyser had erupted there. And suddenly the hills themselves shifted, slithered, bulged and burst apart, and tearing through them came Harrowbarrow's brutal snout.

The Womb lurched and seemed to settle. At its northern end Peabody's men had set off their explosive charges, and with a dreamy slowness the tall, corroded doors at the hangar mouth fell forward, crashing down into the rust and rubble outside.

Harrowbarrow ground its way over the ruins of Crouch End; bright rags of curtains and carpet snagging on its clawed tracks. The cruiser *Protecting Veil* fired a flight of rockets at it and rose out of range before the one remaining swivel-gun on Harrowbarrow's back could swing around to target her. The *Fury* swooped towards the Womb, and Naga ran forward and leaped aboard as she hovered for a moment just above the ground. By the time his armour had hauled him through the hatch and on to the flight-deck the ship was high again. An aviatrix came running to him with reports, but Naga waved her away, tense as an expectant father. He went to a gun-slit and peered down at the mouth of the Womb.

"Come on!" he muttered. "Come on!"

Crouching on Harrowbarrow's spine, Wren and Theo tried to shield each other as the rust-hills broke over the suburb like a wave. Giant fists and fangs of metal came clattering and scraping over the armour, some tumbling high into the air, some caroming over the hull so close that Wren felt the wind of them as they whisked past her. Then they were gone, Crouch End was being crushed beneath the tracks, and ahead, on the crest of the next ridge, the Womb lay waiting.

"Look!" she shouted. "Theo! Look!"

From the open doorway of the old hangar New London was emerging, the magnetic mirrors on its flanks shining like sovereigns. It hovered outside the Womb for a moment, dipping a little, uncertain of itself. *A newborn city*, thought Wren, *like something from the olden days*, and she wished and wished that her father could be here with her to see it.

Righting itself, New London started to move, the heat-haze shimmer beneath its hull increasing as it put on speed, hovering away northwards across the debris field. And Harrowbarrow swung northwards too, the jolt of its snarling engines throwing Wren off her balance as it began powering in pursuit of the new city. She sprawled awkwardly backwards, afraid for a moment that she would roll down the slope into the endlessly grinding teeth of the suburb's tracks, but she managed to find a handhold. As she clawed her way back to Theo she saw the hatch they had come through heave open again and Wolf Kobold climb out.

He looked pleased to see them, but not in a good way.

50

THE STALKER'S HOUSE

There were some blue squares. Dusty blue, against a background of black. Tom, who had not expected to wake at all, woke slowly, from half-remembered dreams. The squares were sky, showing through holes in a crumbling roof. The clouds had cleared; there was a patch of evening sunlight coming and going on the mildewed wall. He lay on something soft, and there were smells of must and damp around him. His hands and feet felt miles away; his head was too heavy to lift; someone had crammed a big, square slab of stone inside his chest. Faint jabs of pins and needles in his limbs let him know that he was still alive.

"Tom?" A whisper. He moved his head. Hester bent over him. "Tom, my dearest. . . You blacked out. The Stalker said it was your heart. She said you were dying but I knew you wouldn't. . ."

"The Stalker. . ." Tom began to understand where he was. The Stalker Fang had scooped him up and taken him inside with her. She had laid him on a bed; an old, worm-eaten, weed-grown bed whose draperies had been nibbled thin by moths, but still a bed; the place you put someone you meant to take care of.

"She let us live," he said.

Hester nodded. "She's tied my hands and feet, but not yours. She didn't bother with yours. If you can reach the knife in my belt. . ."

She fell silent as the Stalker Fang limped into the room and sat down on the end of the bed, watching Tom with her cold, green eyes.

"Anna?" he asked weakly.

"I am not Anna," whispered the Stalker. "Just a bundle of Anna's memories. But I'm pleased you're here, Tom. Anna was very fond of you. You were her very last memory. Lying in the snow, and you looking down and calling her name."

"I remember," said Tom faintly. "I thought she was already dead."

"Nearly," whispered the Stalker. "Not quite. You'll understand. Soon you'll make the same journey."

"But I'm not ready."

"Nor was Anna. Perhaps no one ever is."

Behind her, through the open doorway, Tom could see a room stuffed with machines; lights and screens and bits of kit too complicated for his tired, shocked brain to fathom. He said, "ODIN. . ."

"I talk to it from here."

"Why did you turn it on your own people?"

The Stalker watched him with her head tipped a little to one side. "An overture, before the symphony begins," she whispered. "By attacking both sides I made each think the other was to blame; they will be too busy with each other to come looking for me, and that will give me the time I need."

"To do what?"

"I have been preparing a sequence of commands; a long and complicated sequence. I shall begin transmitting them soon, when ODIN comes clear of the mountains again. They will divert it on to new orbits, give it new targets to strike at."

"What targets?"

"Volcanoes," said the Stalker. She reached out gently and stroked Tom's hair. "Tonight ODIN will strike at forty points along the Tannhäuser chain. Then on across the world; the Deccan volcano-maze; the Hundred Islands. . ."

"But why?" asked Hester. "Why volcanoes?"

"I am making the world green again."

"What," cried Tom, "by smothering it in smoke and ash, and killing thousands of people. . ."

"Millions of people. Don't get excited, Tom; your poor heart might not take it, and I am so looking forward to having someone sensible to talk to."

"And what about me?" asked Hester, as if she was afraid the Stalker were trying to steal Tom away from her.

"As long as you don't try to be foolish or destructive, you are safe. I suppose you will starve in a week or so – there is no food left here. But until then I shall enjoy your company. Anna always felt our destinies were linked, from that first night aboard Stayns. . ."

The Stalker stopped talking and looked behind her, where a light had begun to flash among the thickets of cabling in the next room; red, red, red.

"No rest for the wicked," she whispered.

Outside, Fishcake blundered sobbing along the lakeshore. His Stalker had *hit* him. She could have *killed* him. She had cast him out. She didn't care about little Fishcake any more. She had never cared, not really. He snivelled and whimpered, stumbling over rocks and shingle until he missed his footing and splashed into the shallows. The cold water startled him into silence.

Away across the water the furnace that had been the *Jenny Haniver* was dying down into a comforting red bonfire. Fishcake tramped along the curve of the shoreline to the wreck-site. There was nothing left of the airship now but struts and ribs and one buckled, glowing engine pod, but the explosion had showered the contents of her holds across the reed-beds, and among the debris Fishcake found a few food-cans. Their labels were burnt off, of course, but they made encouraging sloshing noises when he shook them, and one of them (Tricky Dicky be praised!) was a square tin of fish – sardines, or pilchards – with a key fixed to the lid. Fishcake twisted it open and ate greedily, scooping the fish and the delicious, salty juice into his mouth.

He felt better with some food inside him, and started to nose around among the reeds for other scraps. It wasn't long before he heard the plaintive noises coming from among the rocks uphill. "Mmmmm! Mmmmm!"

Fishcake crept closer, thinking that Tom and Hester must have had a companion aboard their ship who'd been wounded in the crash and whom they'd abandoned (how like them!). But when he reached the place he found it was a poor old man, trussed up and gagged; another of Tom and Hester's victims.

"Great Poskitt!" the man gasped, when Fishcake pulled the gag off, and "Brave boy! Thank you!" as Fishcake used the sharp edge of the sardine tin to saw through his ropes.

"They're inside," said Fishcake.

"Who?"

"Hester and her man. The Stalker took 'em inside. Says they're her friends. How could anybody think Hester was her friend? That face – enough to put you off your breakfast. If you'd had any breakfast. I haven't had none for weeks. Help me open this tin, Mister."

He was asking the right man, said Pennyroyal, and as soon as the ropes parted he reached inside his coat and fetched out an explorer's pocket-knife, a miraculous object which unfolded to reveal a tin-opener, a corkscrew, a small pair of scissors and a device for getting stones out of airship's docking-clamps, as well as an array of blades which made brisk work of the ropes on his feet. It occurred to Fishcake to wonder why he had not mentioned the existence of the knife before Fishcake went to the trouble of cutting his hands free with a sardine-tin, but he wanted to like his new friend, so he decided he was probably concussed. There were some gashes on his head, and blood had run down his face like jam down a steamed pudding. (Fishcake was still much preoccupied with thoughts of food.)

They opened three tins. There was algae stew in one, rice pudding in another, and condensed milk in the third. It was the best meal that Fishcake ever tasted.

"I say," ventured Pennyroyal, watching him eat. "You seem a bright lad. Would you know a way out of here, at all?"

"Popjoy's sky-yacht," muttered Fishcake, wiping milk from his chin. "Over there near the house. I don't know how to fly it."

"I do! Could we snaffle it, do you think?"

Fishcake licked the lid of the rice pudding tin, and shook his head. "Need keys. Can't start the engines without keys and you'd need engines among all these mountains, wouldn't you?"

Pennyroyal nodded. "Where are the keys? Just out of interest?"

"She's got them. Round her neck. On a string. But I'm not going up there again. Not after what she did! After all I went through for her!"

The boy started to cry. Pennyroyal was unused to children. He patted his shoulder and said, "There, there," and "That's women for you!" He thought about keys and air-yachts and glanced nervously at the house on the crag. Some sort of antennae thing on the roof was turning, glinting blood-red in the rays of the sinking sun.

Ten miles away, in frozen silt on the bed of a mountain lake, Shrike stirred. His eyes switched on, lighting up constellations of drifting matter. He remembered falling. He had fallen past crags and cliffs, and punched through the crust of ice on this lake, leaving an amusing hole the shape of a spread-eagled man. He could not see the hole above him, so he guessed the lake was deep, and that night was falling in the world above.

He prised himself out of the silt and started walking. The water grew shallower as he neared the shore. Thick ice formed a rippled ceiling twenty feet over head, then ten. Soon he was able to reach up with his fists and punch his way through it. He dragged himself free, an ugly hatchling breaking out of a cold egg.

The moon was rising. Shards of the *Jenny Haniver*'s fallen engine pod shone on the screes high above him. He climbed towards them, sniffing for Hester's scent.

51

THE CHASE

The Londoners had always imagined themselves leaving the debris fields in a leisurely way, perhaps moving at no more than walking speed until they grew used to New London's controls. Instead, here they were, barrelling north through the wreck of old London as fast as the new city could go, slaloming around tumbles of old tier-supports and giant, corroded heaps of tracks and wheels. Down in the engine rooms the Engineers heaved desperately on the levers which angled the magnetic repellors, while up in the steering chamber at the top of the Town Hall Mr Garamond and his navigators peered out through unglazed, unfinished viewing-windows and shouted to the helmsmen, "Left a bit! Right a bit! Right a bit! Oh, I mean, left, left, LEFT!"

Harrowbarrow raced after them, only half a mile behind, steam fuming from its blunt snout as it readied its mouth-parts for the kill. It did not have to swerve and wriggle as New London did; tall heaps of wreckage that the new city had to avoid Harrowbarrow simply butted its way through. The constant crunch and shudder of these collisions kept threatening to jolt Wren and Theo off the precarious handholds they were clinging to, high on the harvester's spine. But Wolf Kobold, who was well-used to his suburb's movements, never lost his footing, and barely paused as he came towards them, except to glance sometimes at the view ahead, and grin when he saw the gap narrowing between Harrowbarrow and its prey.

"You see?" he shouted. "It was all for nothing, Wren! Another ten minutes and that precious place of yours will be in the 'Barrow's gut. And you; you and your black boyfriend – I'm going to string your bowels off the yard roof like paper chains, and nail up your carcasses in the slave hold so your London friends can see what comes to those who try to make a fool of me!"

He was close enough by then to swipe at them with his sword. They scrambled backwards, away from him. The swivelling gun emplacement behind them let out another stuttering roar as a white airship soared past astern, but Kobold only laughed. "Don't think the Mossies can save you! They won't dare come in range of that gun. . ."

He lunged forward, and the point of his sword struck sparks from the suburb's armour inches from Theo's foot. Theo looked at Wren. Near her, where one of the chunky rivets that held Harrowbarrow's armour in place stood slightly proud of the plating, a shard of wreckage had snagged. Theo threw himself down and pulled it free. It was an old length of half-inch pipe, rusty and sharp at the ends. It was too long and heavy to use for a sword, but Theo had nothing better, so he turned with a cry, swinging it at Kobold. Kobold jumped back, raising his blade to deflect the blow. He looked surprised; even pleased. "That's the spirit!" he shouted.

Aboard the *Fury*, Naga said, "We have to silence that swivel-gun. There is no other way we can get within range. . ."

"Sir!" one of his aviators interrupted. "On the suburb's back –"

Naga swung his telescope along the woodlouse curve of Harrowbarrow's spine. Twenty yards behind the gun-emplacement two figures seemed to be dancing – no, fighting; he saw the flash of sparks as their swords met. "One of our men?"

"Can't tell, sir. But if we fire on the gun we may kill whoever it is. . ."

"That can't be helped, Commander. Let their gods look after them; we have work to do."

A flight of rockets sprang from the airship, and Wren ducked as one sizzled past her, close enough for her to glimpse the snarling dragon-face painted on its nose-cone and the Chinese characters chalked along its flank. It burst on the armour close to the gun turret, but not close enough to do more than rattle shrapnel against it. The other rockets went wide, exploding harmlessly on spikes of wreckage. Harrowbarrow was speeding through a region where long, jagged shards from London's upper tiers lay heaped on top of each other, forming a lattice through which the westering sun poked its unhealthy crimson beams. Clinging to the armour with both hands, Wren looked up at the sharp spines flicking past. It was like rushing through an enormous, untidy cutlery drawer. *If we run ourselves upon one of those*, she thought, *it will put an end to all our problems. . .*

The blades did not seem to trouble Wolf Kobold. He waved his sword, shouting something to the gun-crew, and the gun turned with a swirl of fairground music and filled the air astern with black puff-balls, so that the airship yawed hastily and vanished for a while behind the wreckage. Then he renewed his attack on Theo, more earnest and less playful now, as if Wren and her boyfriend were a distraction he wanted to be rid of before the serious business began.

Theo did his best, grunting and shouting out with effort as he swung the rusty pipe to and fro, trying to parry Wolf's blows, but he was no swordsman, and he found it harder than Wolf to keep his footing on the lurching, lumbering armour. After little more than a minute, during which Theo was driven steadily back towards the housing of the swivel-gun, Wolf made a sudden feint, and Theo, lurching sideways to avoid his blade, lost his footing. He fell awkwardly, his head cracking against the armour underfoot. The pipe flew out of his sweaty hands. Wren caught it as it clattered past her. Wolf was already standing over Theo, sword raised to finish him.

She threw herself forward, not knowing what she meant to do, just determined that Wolf should not have it all his own way. She heard somebody scream, and it was her; a hard, ragged scream of terror and rage and panic which seemed to give her the strength she needed as she swung the pipe to fend off Wolf's descending sword.

More sparks; a shock that jarred her arms in their sockets. For a comical moment Wolf stood amazed, staring at the sword-hilt in his hand, the blade broken off halfway along its length. He looked at Wren. He shrugged and threw the broken sword away. He flipped his coat open and pulled a shiny new revolver from its holster.

Despite all the noise, the relentless speed, it seemed to grow very quiet and still on the back of Harrowbarrow in those last moments. Even the swivel-gun had stopped firing. When Wren glanced round in the hope of spotting some miraculous escape she saw the gunners gawping at her out of their little window.

"Goodbye, Wren," said Wolf.

He hadn't noticed that white, persistent airship swinging into range again above his suburb's stern. The rockets tore past him as he pulled the trigger, and the shot he fired went wide, flicking through Wren's hair without touching her. The shock-wave from the exploding swivel gun kicked him backwards; he struggled to save himself, slipped, fell forward, and the sharp end of the pipe that Wren was still clutching went through him just beneath his breastbone. The impact knocked her down, and the other end of the pipe wedged against a seam in the armour, driving it clean through Wolf's body.

"Oh!" he shouted, looking down at it.

"I'm sorry," said Wren.

Wolf raised his head and stared at her. His eyes were very blue and wide, and oddly innocent. He looked as if he were about to cry. When Wren pulled at the pipe, with some idea of tugging it out of him, he lurched sideways, pipe and all, and went tumbling away from her like a broken doll down the long slope of the suburb's flank until he hit the tracks.

Later, she would pray that he had been dead by the time those sliding slabs of machinery caught him. She would tell herself that it had not been his screams she heard as he was snatched and mangled and ploughed down into the earth, only the shrieking of stressed metal somewhere, some shard of long-dead London crying out as Harrowbarrow ground over it.

But by then they were on the outer edge of the debris field. A wide plain stretched ahead of them, empty as an ocean, except for the lights of New London which was a quarter mile ahead and racing northwards, crossing open country now, the wreck of its mother city left behind it like a sloughed-off skin.

"Girl!" someone was shouting, and in her shocked state Wren could not work out who it was; not Wolf, for sure; not his gunners, who had vanished with their swivelling turret; not Theo, who was struggling to his feet, his face streaked with blood from where he'd struck his head. She looked up. The Storm's white ship hung low above her, keeping pace with her by some miracle of stunt-flying which only an aviator could properly appreciate. Reaching down to her from a hatch in the gondola was something that she took at first to be a Stalker, until he shouted again, "Girl!" and beckoned irritably for her to take his hand, and she recognized General Naga.

The *Fury*'s gondola smelled of gun smoke and air-fuel. Naga strode around issuing orders to his aviators, glancing at Wren just long enough to say, "You are Londoners? Captured by the harvester?"

Wren just nodded, clinging tight to Theo and finding it hard to believe that they were both still alive. It did not seem like the moment to try and explain that she and General Naga had met before. She could not stop shaking, or thinking about Wolf Kobold. As the *Fury* veered away from Harrowbarrow and flew towards New London, she let Theo go and went to crouch in a corner, where she was sick till her stomach was empty.

They touched down on New London's stern, where a crowd of Londoners and Green Storm soldiers were waiting. "Wren!" cried Angie happily, waving, forgetting that Wren had ever been a suspected spy.

"Miss Natsworthy! Mr Ngoni! Thank Quirke you're safe!" shouted Mr Garamond, helping them from the gondola. *No thanks to you*, Wren felt like saying, but then she realized that he already knew that, and that his clumsy hug was his way of saying sorry, and she hugged him back.

The new city had a curious feel; there were none of the tremors and half-muffled shocks and lurches that you felt aboard a Traction City, just a sense of dreamlike movement, and of speed. But perhaps not quite *enough* speed, for Harrowbarrow filled the view astern, its mouthparts opening to reveal a hot gleam of furnaces and factories inside.

"You'd have thought they'd stop when Kobold died," said Theo.

"They don't know," Wren replied. "Or maybe they do, and they don't care. Mr Hausdorfer and the others can handle a simple chase without their master. Harrowbarrow never cared about Wolf the way Wolf cared about Harrowbarrow. . ."

She didn't want to talk about Wolf. The way he had looked at her when he realized she'd killed him would stay with her always. She tried to tell herself that it was good she felt so guilty and so soiled by what she'd done. Better that than to be like her mother, and not care. But it did not feel good.

She took Theo's hand, and together they went to stand among the other Londoners at the stern-rail. Behind them, Naga was giving orders to his surviving officers, telling Sub-General Thien, "You will return to Batmunkh Gompa with the *Protecting Veil*. My wife believes that the Stalker Fang controls the new terror weapon. Help her find it and destroy it."

"Yes, Excellency. . ."

"And New London is to be granted safe passage through our territories."

"Yes, Excellency. . ."

"Now, I want everybody off the *Fury* before I take her up."

"But Excellency, you cannot fly alone!"

"Why not? I flew alone at Xanne-Sandansky and Khamchatka. I flew alone against Panzerstadt Breslau. I should be able to handle a filthy little barbarian harvester like this."

Thien understood; he bowed and saluted and started shouting orders. Wren, looking round to see what all the excitement was about, saw the *Fury*'s crew jumping down on to the deckplates, saw Naga heaving himself aboard. She looked away. What was happening astern was far more interesting than anything the Storm could do. She barely noticed when the *Fury* took off again.

Harrowbarrow was driving towards them through sprays of wet earth. Its armour was holed, there were fires on its upper decks, and one of its tracks was grinding, but Hausdorfer didn't care. He'd been sceptical about this place his master had brought them so far to eat, but now he'd seen it move, seen it *fly,* he understood what young Kobold had been on about. "More power!" he screamed into his speaking tubes. "Open the jaws! They are defenceless! They are ours!"

Naga turned the *Fury* towards the oncoming suburb and took her down almost to ground-level. She was a good ship; he enjoyed the way she answered to his touch on the wheels and levers, and the purr of her powerful engines when he switched them to ramming speed. As Harrowbarrow's jaws opened he aimed straight at the red glow of the furnaces in her dismantling yards.

When the Harrobarrovians started to understand what he was planning, guns began firing from inside the jaws, shattering glass in the gondola windows, starting fires. A shell from a hand-cannon punched through Naga's breastplate, but his armour kept him upright, and his mechanized gauntlets gripped the helm, keeping the blazing ship on course. The suburb was closing its jaws, but not quickly enough. Naga fired all the *Fury*'s remaining rockets, and watched them streak ahead of him into its maw. "Oenone," he said, and her name, and the thought of her, went with him into the light.

The blast was brief; a sunflower blossoming in the dusk, stuffed with shrapnel seeds. There was a blunt, muffled boom and then other sounds; thuds and squelches as large fragments of wreckage rained down into the

Out-Country. Aboard New London, no one cheered. Even the soldiers of the Storm, who had grown up singing jolly songs about the destruction of whole cities, looked appalled. One or two small pieces of debris landed on the deck, plinking like dropped coins. Wren stooped to pick up one which fell near her. It was a rivet-head from Harrowbarrow's hull, still warm with the heat of the explosion. She put it in her pocket, thinking that it would make a good exhibit for the New London Museum.

What was left of Harrowbarrow – the broken stern-section, half filled with fires – settled into the Out-Country mud. It would be part of the landscape soon, like old London. The survivors, stumbling clear, stared about in bewilderment. Some looked towards the debris fields which filled the southern horizon, wondering what sort of life they would be able to make there. Others ran after New London, shouting out for help, begging their fellow Tractionists not to leave them here defenceless in the lands of the Storm. But New London was beyond earshot, pulling away from them quickly across the vast, dark plain, smaller and smaller; until it was only a fleck; a gleam of amber windows dwindling in that enormous twilight.

52

LAST WORDS

The Stalker Fang limped around her chamber. Her bronze face was lit by the winking lights on the heap of machinery, by the green numbers which flicked and squiggled on her goggle screens. Through the open doorway Tom and Hester watched, and each time her eyes were turned away from him Tom made another little movement, easing himself closer to Hester, until he was able to reach out and touch the knife in her belt.

"Not long now," the Stalker whispered, glad of this audience to whom she could explain her work

Tom was thinking of Wren, hoping that New London would go nowhere near the Tannhäusers or any of the other mountains ODIN was to target. "Why volcanoes?" he asked "I still don't see how that can make the world green. . ."

The Stalker's fingers spidered over ivory keyboards. "You have to take the long view, Tom. It isn't only Traction Cities which poison the air and tear up the earth. All cities do that, static or mobile. It's human beings that are the problem. Everything that they do pollutes and destroys. The Green Storm would never have understood that, which is why I didn't tell them about my plans for ODIN. If we are really to protect the good earth we must first cleanse it of human beings."

"That's insane!" cried Tom.

"Inhuman, perhaps," the Stalker admitted. "The ash of volcanoes will choke the sky and shroud the Earth in darkness. Winter will reign for hundreds of years.

Mankind will perish. But life will survive. Life always does. When the skies clear at last, the world will grow green again. Lichens, ferns, grasses, forests, insects; higher animals eventually. But no more people. They only spoil things."

"Anna would not want that," said Tom.

"I am not Anna. I just use her memories to understand the world. And I understand that humanity is a plague; a swarm of clever monkeys which the good earth cannot support. All human civilizations fall, Tom, and all for the same reason; humans are too greedy. It is time to put an end to them for ever."

Tom struggled to rise, wondering if he could reach the machine, smash it, and pull out all those complicated flexes and ducts. The Stalker Fang seemed to read his thoughts; the long blades slid out of her fingertips.

"Do be sensible, Tom," she whispered. "You're very ill, and I'm a Stalker. You'd never make it, and Hester wants you to stay alive for as long as you can. She loves you very much, you know."

She moved behind her pile of machinery, making some adjustment to the cables which trailed up through the ceiling to the aerial on the roof. Tom tugged the knife out of Hester's belt and she fumbled it from him and clasped it between her hands, sawing awkwardly at the old ropes the Stalker had used to tie her wrists.

As he crept across the causeway, Pennyroyal tried to keep calm by imagining how he would describe all these adventures to his enthralled readership. *Caution urged that I should stay away from that dreadful house, but*

the fate of whole cities hung in the balance, and my poor companions were prisoners within. I knew that to run would leave an irredeemable blot on the honour of the Pennyroyals! (And I do need that key, Poskitt-damn-it!) *My faithful native companion, Fishcake* (can that be his *real* name?) *led me to the end of the fatal causeway and would go no further. I would not have allowed it anyway, for I could never let one so young risk his life in mortal combat with the Stalker.* (Stalkeress? Stalkerine? Gods, I hope it doesn't come to actual combat! I wish that lad had had the nerve to come instead of me; the beastly little coward. . .) *It was a little unsettling, I confess, but as I went on alone through the gathering darkness I began to feel curiously nerveless. I have found myself in a lot of dicey situations over the years, and what I've learned is that it's always best to remain cool, collected and* GREAT POSKITT'S HAIRY ARSE WHAT'S THAT?

Only an owl!

Only an owl. . .

Shuddering, Pennyroyal took a nip of brandy from his secret hip flask and started hunting along the water's edge for Tom's anti-Stalker gun. The boy had said that Hester dropped it here somewhere. Pennyroyal didn't mean to go any closer to that damned house without it. Ah! There it was. Still humming. Looked undamaged. *A dashed odd-looking weapon, but they don't call me Dead-eye Pennyroyal for nothing! Setting the stock of the strange gun firmly against my shoulder* (is that where it's supposed to go?) *I resumed my cat-like progress. . .*

The Stalker Fang was busy with her machinery. From time to time the words and numbers crawling across the goggle screen were replaced with a furry, greyish picture. Tom realized that he was seeing what no human being had seen for millennia; the world from space, viewed through the eye of ODIN. Oddly, it was not very impressive.

Could ODIN really destroy humanity? Surely it would break, or run out of power, or something in that crazy stack of old machinery that the Stalker was using to talk to it would go wrong, and that would be the end of her plans. It made him angry that he and Hester had come so far and sacrificed so much to avert such a tatty effort. At least MEDUSA had looked worth dying for; its entrails had filled a cathedral, and its cobra-hood had towered over London. This new weapon was just space-junk, controlled by a mad old Stalker from a place that looked and smelled like a teenager's bedroom. . .

Beside him, Hester gave a little grunt of triumph as the knife severed the rope on her wrists. She stooped to start work on the one which bound her ankles.

The Stalker Fang was talking to ODIN again, tapping at her ivory keys, whispering the codes to herself as she conducted her bargain-basement apocalypse. Sometimes she whispered something to Tom and Hester, too: "Just think, my dears; all that pretty lava. . ." Anna Fang had liked having someone to talk to, and the Stalker she had become had inherited the taste. When Hester whispered, "Now!" and Tom rolled off the bed and stood up she said, "Where are you going?"

"Come on!" hissed Hester, her arm around him, supporting him, dragging him towards the nearest window. She hadn't Tom's education, and she hadn't really followed the Stalker's rambling talk. All she cared about was saving Tom. She refused to believe that there was no hope at all.

But Tom knew there was little point in trying to outrun the Stalker Fang, who turned and came towards them as they neared the window. He twisted round to face her. Hester was still trying to drag him to the window, but Tom shook free of her. He had come to Shan Guo to talk, not to fight; if Naga wouldn't listen to him, perhaps this Stalker might. *I am not Anna*, she had said, *just a bundle of Anna's memories. . .* But what was *anyone* but a bundle of memories?

Tom reached out to her. "We can't stay," he said. "We have a daughter. She'll need us."

The Stalker's eyes flickered. "A daughter. . ."

"Her name's Wren."

"A daughter. . ." She clapped her hands together with a clang. "Tom, Hester. . . How wonderful! When I, when Anna first saw you together she, I knew you were meant for each other! And now you have a baby girl. . ."

"She's not a baby girl any more," said Hester. "She's a great big stroppy young woman."

"We brought her up," said Tom, "we kept her safe; we taught her things; she learned to fly the *Jenny Haniver*. . . And now you want to kill her along with everybody else."

The Stalker shrugged – an odd movement for a Stalker; it made her armour grate. "You can't break eggs without making an omelette, Tom. Or is it the other way around? Where is she, this daughter of yours?"

"In London," said Tom. "In the wreck of London. The people there are building a new city, a floating city. . ." He wished now that he had paid more attention to Dr Childermass's technical explanations. "It doesn't claw up the ground, it doesn't eat other cities, it doesn't even use up much fuel. Why can't it have a place in your green world? Why can't Wren?"

The Stalker hissed and turned away, going back to her machines.

Tom stumbled after her, and Hester, who had resigned herself to listening to the two of them chat, came with him.

The Stalker's fingers were rattling at her keyboards again. The grey image on the central screen changed, from a view of Zhan Shan's blazing wound to a more distant panorama of the clouded limb of the earth. Then it began to close in again, the machinery behind the screen wheezing and clicking, the images flicking past like shuffled cards. A charcoal-grey patch expanded to become the wreck of London, then filled the screen. Tom recognized Putney Vale and the Womb as ODIN's gaze slid eastward, then north.

"Nothing moving. . ." whispered the Stalker.

"What are those bright patches?" asked Tom.

"Those are burning airships."

"*What?*" Tom stared as more specks of white fire slid past; then, just off the northern edge of the wreck, a burning sprawl like a hole torn in the screen. What had happened in the debris fields since he'd been gone? What had happened to Wren? His heart clenched into a fist and began to batter at his ribs.

"Ah!" hissed the Stalker. "That must be your floating city. . ."

She was quicker at reading the grainy pictures than Tom. It took him a moment to understand that he was looking down at New London. It was well outside the debris fields, moving north. And still the machinery whirred and nattered and the image on the screen kept flicking, changing, pulling closer and closer to the new city until he could make out people milling about on its stern. Dozens of people, lining the handrails, staring back towards the debris fields as New London bore them safe away. And he could make out faces now; the faces of his friends; Clytie and her husband, Mr Garamond laughing for once, looking happy – And there was Wren; dishevelled, smeared with what looked like soot, but Wren for sure; he cried out as her face slipped across the screen, and the Stalker swung ODIN's gaze to focus on her, still zooming in and in.

"It's Wren! She's all right!"

Tom felt Hester's hands tighten on his arm as she watched their daughter's face swim up towards them out of the grey fuzz of the picture. "Wren," she said. Her voice sounded shaky. "What's she done to her hair? It's all lopsided. . . And there, behind her, look! It's Theo!"

ODIN zoomed again and there was nothing on the screen except their daughter's face. Tom went closer, pushing past the Stalker Fang, reaching out to touch the glass. At such close range the image started to grow vague; Wren's face broke down into lines and specks and flares of light; this smudge of shadow an eye, that white smear her nose. He traced with his hands the curve of her cheek, wishing he could push through the screen somehow and touch her, speak to her. Surely she must be able to feel him watching her? But she only smiled and turned her head to say something to the boy behind her. Tom felt as if he were already a ghost.

The Stalker hissed like a kettle coming slowly to the boil.

"Please don't hurt her," said Tom.

"She will die," the Stalker whispered. "They will all die. For the good of the earth. Your child will have a few years more, if she is lucky. . ."

"And what use will a few more years be if she's starving and scared, watching the sky fill with ash?" asked Tom. He took another step towards the Stalker, excited by a sense that he was getting through to her, or to some weird, mechanized remnant of Anna Fang that nested within her. "Wren deserves to live a long time, in peace, and have children of her own, and see their children. . ."

"Sentimentality!" the Stalker sneered. "The life of a single child means nothing, compared with the future of all life."

"But she is the future!" Tom cried. "Look at her! At her and Theo –"

"It is for the good of the earth," the Stalker repeated coldly. "They will all die."

"You don't believe that," Tom insisted. "The Anna bit of you doesn't. Anna cared about people. You cared about me and Hester enough to rescue us. Anna, don't use the machine. Switch it off. Break it. Smash ODIN."

He crumpled at the knees and would have fallen if Hester had not supported him. The Stalker was hissing angrily. Hester, thinking that she was about to attack, pulled Tom backwards and turned so that her own body was between them. But the creature had swung away, flailing with one hand at its own skull. "Where is Popjoy?"

"Dead," said Hester grimly. "You killed him. It's the talk of Batmunkh Gompa."

"*Sathya, I...*" the Stalker said. "They must be exterminated. It is for the good of... *Tom, Tom, Hester...*"

That bony sound again; steel fingers on ivory keys. Green letters flicking up. "What is she doing?" asked Hester, afraid that the maddened Stalker was telling ODIN to drop fire on New London. Tom shook his head, as lost as her. The Stalker paused, studied a ribbon of green light that scrolled down another of her screens, typed again, hit a final key and turned to them. She was trembling; a quick, mechanical vibration, like an engine pod on full power. Her marsh-gas eyes flared and flickered. She reached out to her guests with her long, shining hands.

"What have you done?" asked Tom.

"*I have...* She has... We have..."

From the far side of the room, through another doorway, they heard a crunch and slither of feet on broken tiles. The Stalker spun to face the noises, her finger-glaives sliding out, and Pennyroyal shouted out in terror as he stepped into the chamber and her green eyes lit up his face. He was holding the lightning gun in front of him, and as the Stalker tensed to spring at him he squeezed the trigger. A vein of fire opened in the air, juddering between the gun's blunt muzzle and the Stalker's chest. The Stalker hissed and bared her claws and Pennyroyal backed away from her wailing, "Argh! Poskitt! Please! Spare me! Help! Stay away!" and never taking his fingers off the triggers. The Stalker's robes began to burn. Lightning was crawling across her calm bronze face, St Elmo's fire pouring from her finger-glaives. She fell heavily against the ODIN machinery and the lightning wrapped that too. Stalker-brains and goggle screens exploded, broken keyboards sent anagrams of ivory keys rattling across the floor like punched-out teeth, flames ran up the cables and set fire to the ceiling, and still Pennyroyal kept firing, and shouting, and firing, until the gun faltered and failed.

After a while, when they had started to grow used to the silence, he said, "I did it! I killed it! Me! You wouldn't have a camera about you, I suppose?"

The Stalker Fang lay on her pyre of machinery. Tom waved away the smoke and went closer, watching her cautiously. Things were on fire inside her; he could smell the gamey stench, and see the firelight flicker beneath her armour. Her bronze mask had come off, baring the grey face beneath, shrivelled and grinning. Tom tried not to feel disgusted as he looked at it; after all, he would soon be taking the same journey himself.

The dead mouth moved. "*Tom*," sighed the Stalker. "*Tom*." Nothing more. The green glow in those headlamp eyes died to a pinprick, and went out.

Pennyroyal was staring at the spent gun in his hands, as if wondering how it came to be there. He dropped it, and said, "There's an air-yacht moored down below. The keys are round that thing's neck."

It never occurred to Tom to ask him how he knew. He reached out and took the keys. They came away easily, for the cord they were threaded on had almost burned through.

"She *is* dead this time, isn't she?" asked Pennyroyal nervously.

Tom nodded. "She's been dead a long time. Poor Anna." And then the pain came in his chest again and he couldn't speak; he doubled over, groaning, while Hester clung to him and tried to soothe him.

"I say!" said Pennyroyal. "Is he all right?"

"His heart. . ." Hester's voice was tiny; trembly; she'd not felt as helpless or as scared as this since she was a little girl watching her mother die. "Don't die, Tom." She grovelled on the floor with him, holding him as tight as she could. "Don't leave me, I don't want to lose you again. . ." She looked up through her tears at Pennyroyal. "What shall we do?"

Pennyroyal looked as scared as her. Then he said, "Doctor. We've got to get him to a doctor."

"No use," said Tom weakly. The worst of the pain had passed, leaving him white and frightened, shining with sweat in the light of the rising flames. He shook his head and said, "I saw a doctor in Peripatetiapolis and he said it was hopeless. . ."

"Oh, oh. . ." wept Hester.

"Great Poskitt!" cried Pennyroyal. "If this doctor of yours had been any good he'd hardly have been working in a little place like Peripatetiapolis, would he? Come on, we'll find you the best medicos money and fame can buy. I'm not having you die on me, Tom; you and Hester are the only witnesses I have to the fact that I've just killed the Stalker Fang! Wait until the world hears about this! I'll be back at the top of the best-seller lists in a flash!" He held out his hand. "Give me the key. He'll never make it across the causeway. I'll bring the sky-yacht down in the garden."

Hester glowered at him.

"Well, all right," said Pennyroyal, "you go and fetch the yacht, and I'll stay here with Tom."

"Please stay, Het," Tom said weakly.

Hester passed the key to Pennyroyal, who said, "Hold

on, Tom. Back in a jiffy. You might want to wait outside," he added, as he hurried away. "This building's on fire."

Carefully, Hester began to drag Tom after him, along the villa's mouldering halls and out into the cold of the garden. They heard Pennyroyal's footsteps crunching off along the causeway, then silence, broken only by the rush of the flames inside the house. Firelight lapped across the gardens, gleaming on frosted grass and the ice-hung branches of bare trees. Beside a frozen fountain Hester laid Tom down, pulling off her coat to make a pillow for him. "We're going to get you to Batmunkh Gompa," she promised. "Oenone will sort you out. She's a brilliant surgeon; saved Theo's life; mine too, probably. She'll make you well again." She held his face between her hands. "You're not to die," she said. "I don't ever want to be parted from you again: I couldn't bear it. You're going to be well. We'll take the Bird Roads again. . ."

"Look!" said Tom.

Above the mountains, a new star had appeared. It was very bright, and it seemed to be growing larger. Tom managed to stand, walking a few paces away from the fountain for a better view.

"Tom, be careful. . . What is it?"

He looked back at her, his eyes shining. "It's ODIN! It must have . . . blown up! That's what she was doing, before Pennyroyal appeared. She ordered it to destroy itself. . ."

The new star twinkled like a Quirkemas decoration, and then began to fade. At the same instant the roof of the house collapsed with a roar and a rush of sparks, and a spear of pain went through Tom's side, so much worse than before that even as he fell he knew this was the end of him.

Hester ran to him, her arms around him; he heard her screaming at the top of her lungs, "Pennyroyal! Pennyroyal!"

Pennyroyal reached the docking pan, and saw the boy creep out of the pines to meet him. Even here the ground was lit by the glow of the fire on the island; the sky-yacht's silvery envelope shone cheerfully with orange reflections. Pennyroyal waved the key as he hurried towards it. "Nothing to fear now, young Fishpaste! I sorted your Stalker out. All it took was a bit of good, old-fashioned pluck."

He unlocked the gondola and climbed inside, the boy following. The yacht was a Serapis Sunbeam, rather like the one Pennyroyal had owned in Brighton. He squeezed into the pilot's seat and quickly found the key-slot under the main control-wheel. Lights began coming on. The fuel and gas gauges all showed half full, and the engines worked after a couple of attempts. "First I must collect my young friends," Pennyroyal said. After what they had just endured together he felt Tom and Hester really *were* his friends; his comrades. He was determined that he would save young Tom.

"No," said Fishcake coldly, from just behind him.

"Eh? But it's all right, child; there's no danger now. . ."

"Go now," said Fishcake, and he reached around from behind the pilot's seat and pressed one of the blades of Pennyroyal's own pocket-knife against his throat.

"They left me behind," he said.

In the garden Hester heard the engines rumble and rise, and said, "He's coming, Tom, the airship's coming!"

Tom wasn't listening. All he heard was the word "airship", and as all pain and feeling began to leave him he saw again the bright ships lifting from Salthook on the afternoon that London ate it, long ago.

The sky-yacht rose and hung above the garden. The downdraft from its engine pods whipped Hester's hair about and made the burning house behind her roar like a furnace. She looked up. Fishcake was staring down at her through one of the gondola windows. She recognized the look on his face, solemn and triumphant all at once, and she felt sorry for him, for all the things he must have seen and been through, and all the long miles he had had to come for his revenge. Then he turned from the window and shouted something at Pennyroyal and the yacht rose, curving away towards the mountains, the drone of its engines whispering into silence.

There's no way out this time, Hester thought. And then she thought, *There is always a way out*. She pulled Fishcake's long, thin-bladed knife out of her belt again and laid it down in the shadows beside her, where it gleamed with reflections from the fire; a narrow doorway leading out of the world.

She kissed Tom's face, and for a moment he half woke, although he still didn't quite know where he was; memories and real life were all tangled up inside his mind, and he thought that he was lying on the bare earth, on that first day, fresh-fallen out of London. But he didn't care, because Hester was with him, holding him tight, watching him, and he thought how lucky he was to be loved by someone so strong, and brave, and beautiful.

And the last thing he felt was the touch of her mouth as she kissed him goodbye, and the last thing he heard was her gruff, gentle voice saying, "It will be all right, Tom. Wherever we go now, whatever becomes of us, we'll be together, and it will all be all right."

53

THE AFTERGLOW

When they came for Oenone it was still dark, and the breeze that blew in through the small window of the room where they'd been holding her smelled of ash. Faint earth-tremors shivered the floor. She had been feeling them all night in her sleep. Her dreams had been filled with the crash of falling masonry echoing across the valley from Batmunkh Gompa.

She washed her aching face in cold water and said her prayers, assuming they were taking her to be killed. But when they led her down the stairs she found Sub-General Thien waiting for her. He looked weary and slightly dazed and his uniform was streaked with dirt.

"Naga is dead," he said.

Oenone saw him staring at her broken nose and the bruises that had spread around her eyes. If Naga was dead then Thien was the most senior officer in Batmunkh Gompa, she thought. He would try to seize power for himself, and he would not want her around to remind people of the man he was replacing.

"Come with me, please," he said.

She followed him outside, on to a balcony where the cold wind tugged at her clothes. The southern sky was a wall of shadow, lit faintly from behind by the red flaring of the volcano. The voices of the nuns chanted steadily somewhere inside the building, the chant rising in volume for a while each time the ground shook. In the courtyard below the balcony Oenone saw hundreds of faces looking up expectantly; Green Storm soldiers and aviators; refugees from Tienjing.

She felt nervous in front of such an audience, but not afraid of dying. She knew that poor Naga would be waiting for her in Heaven, and her mother and father too, and her brother Eno; all those whom she had loved and lost, who had gone ahead of her.

"What do you make of it?" asked Thien. He was looking upward too, and she realized that it was not at her the people in the courtyard were staring, but at something above her head; above the roofs of the nunnery; above the mountains. Across the few patches of the sky which were still clear hundreds of shooting stars were streaking, white and green and icy blue.

"What do you make of it?" asked Thien again.

He wanted her scientific opinion, Oenone realized. She licked her lips, which had grown very dry. "I would say that something – some *things* – are falling into the upper atmosphere."

"More weapons?" Thien sounded very scared.

Oenone watched for a moment, thinking. "No. No, I think it's a good thing. I think something big has exploded in orbit, and those stars are some of the fragments, burning up."

"The cities' weapon?" asked Thien. "You think it is destroyed?"

"It was not theirs," Oenone said. She was about to explain her theory about the Stalker Fang, and tell him that Shrike must have found the ground station and destroyed it, but it would be better kept a secret; if the cities learned who had turned ODIN on them it would lead to more fighting. "It was all an accident," she said. "Some old orbital, gone mad. Let's pray it's over."

Thien nodded, and reached for his sword. She had told him what he wanted to know, thought Oenone, and now she was no more use to him. She could not help squeezing her bruised eyes shut. She heard the ringing rasp of the long blade sliding from its scabbard. She heard the chink of metal against stone. She opened one eye, then the other. Thien was kneeling in front of her, laying his sword on the pavement at her feet. Down in the courtyard everyone else was kneeling too. Soldiers bowed their heads, saluting her, fist-to-palm.

"What are they doing?" she asked, bewildered. "What are *you* doing?"

"Our armies are smashed," said Thien. "The barbarians' cities are broken. The world is in turmoil. We need someone to lead us down new roads. I'm not the man for that."

He rose, and took Oenone by the arm, bringing her gently to the front of the balcony so that all the people waiting below could see their new leader.

The engines of the air-yacht failed a few miles from Batmunkh Gompa, and Fishcake abandoned her there and set off walking, leaving Pennyroyal behind. Pennyroyal spent a while trying to restart the yacht, but ash had clogged its air-intakes and it would not work. Reluctantly, finding his way by the light of the meteor showers streaking across the northern sky, he set off on foot through the ash-drifts to the nearest Green Storm base. There he attempted to surrender, but the Storm were in such a state of confusion that nobody wanted to be saddled with a townie prisoner. "At least send ships to Erdene Tezh!" he begged. "My friends may still be there! It was the ground station! The Stalker Fang was controlling the weapon from there. . ."

"No one was controlling the weapon," said the base commander, waving a communiqué she'd just received from Batmunkh Gompa. "Naga's widow says that one of the Ancients' orbital devices malfunctioned, and destroyed targets at random."

"But. . ."

"You are free to go, Professor."

It was months before Pennyroyal found his way back to Murnau. He used the time well, making use of the long waits at provincial air-harbours and caravanserais to write his greatest work; *Ignorant Armies*. It was surprisingly truthful by Pennyroyal's standards. He confessed all his previous lies in Chapter One, and kept as close as he could to the facts when he described what he had seen and done at Erdene Tezh.

But when he finally reached the Hunting Ground he found himself in a world that was changing quickly. The predators were growing so savage and the prey so scarce that even the staunchest of Municipal Darwinists were starting to wonder how much longer the system could keep going. People were looking for new ways to live, and Murnau had shocked everyone by settling down on a hilltop west of the Rustwater and going static. Refugees from Zhan Shan were moving there, helping the Murnauers lay out fields and plant crops. Old von Kobold had kept on a few of his harvester-suburbs, and an air-force, led by Orla Twombley, which whizzed around the margins of his pale of farmland and scared off any predator that came too close.

Undaunted, Pennyroyal went in search of his

publishers, but Werederobe and Spoor wouldn't touch his new book. After Spiney's exposé, said those gentlemen, nobody would believe any more wild yarns from Nimrod Pennyroyal. Least of all them. Anyway, the Mossies were friendly now; had he not heard about the treaty von Kobold had signed with the Widow Naga? And, incidentally, what *had* happened to the advance they'd paid him for his previous book?

Pennyroyal spent ten months in debtors' prison, boring his fellow inmates with endless stories of his wonderful adventures. When some of his old friends from Moon's clubbed together and paid his debts he slunk away to Peripatetiapolis where one of his former girlfriends, Minty Bapsnack, still had a soft spot for him. He lived out his final years in her house, and they were not unhappy. But even Minty took his story with a pinch of salt, and she never lent him the money he needed to publish *Ignorant Armies*.

Fishcake did not see the shooting stars. By the time the wreckage from ODIN began to streak across the sky he was beneath the lid of smoke from Zhan Shan. He bypassed Batmunkh Gompa in the dark and walked on for days, up roads clogged with ash and refugees.

He was the only person travelling towards the volcano, not away. The eastern flank of the mountain had been ripped open, and the people who had lived beneath it were fleeing in ragged columns, with tales of whole towns being buried, whole cities swept away. But the western slopes, though shaken and dusted with ash, had not suffered so badly. When Fishcake came over the ridge above the hermitage he saw the little house still standing, the cattle in their pasture eating bales of hay brought up from the lowlands, fresh prayer-flags flapping on the shrine at the head of the pass. He shuffled towards the door on bare, bloody feet, and collapsed on the step, where Sathya found him next morning when she came out to milk the cow. In his frost-bitten hand he was still clutching the little horse that his Stalker had made for him.

He would stay there with Sathya for many years, growing into a strong, handsome young man of the mountain kingdoms. He would come to forget a lot of the awful things he had been through, but he never forgot what he had done at Erdene Tezh. That was his secret, and at first it made him feel strong and proud, because he'd carried out his promise to the gods and sent Hester Natsworthy and her husband to the Sunless Country. But later, when he was grown up and married, watching his own children play with Anna's little horse in the dust outside his foster-mother's hermitage, he came to feel less certain about it. Those were the years when the Widow Naga was pushing hard for peace, preaching her policy of forgiveness towards old enemies. Sometimes Fishcake wished he had shown a little more forgiveness himself, and let the Natsworthys aboard that sky-yacht after all. But at least (he told himself), he hadn't *killed* Hester and Tom; he'd just taught them a lesson by abandoning them as they'd once abandoned him. They were tough and resourceful, and he was sure they had survived.

Dear Angie,
It's hard to believe that it's four whole months
since we left you at that cluster in the Frost
Barrens! And that it's nearly a year since New
London was born!! I wish Theo and I could be
there with you to join in the birthday celebrations,
but we shan't be ready to leave Zagwa for a few
weeks yet. I hope trade is going well up there in
the Ice Wastes; that you are selling lots of
levitating armchairs to the people of the ice cities,
and the Childermass engines are keeping you out
of the jaws of predators!

I'm writing this in the garden at Theo's parents'
house, sitting on a lovely terrace overlooking the
gorge, in the afterglow of sunset. It's beautiful
here, and Mr and Mrs Ngoni and Kaelo and
Miriam are all very sweet and welcoming, and
seem to have got used to the idea that their Theo
is going to marry a townie girl and live in the sky.

The merchantman that brought us here put in at
Airhaven on the way south for fuel and gas. When I
dropped in to the bank there I found that – guess
what? – I'm rich! I had quite forgot the five
thousand which Wolf Kobold had paid us for his
trip to London, but there it all was, still safe in the
Jenny Haniver's account. I felt a little bit guilty
about keeping it, but I suppose we earned it fairly;
after all, we took Wolf to London as he asked, and

*it's no fault of ours he tried to eat it. Anyway, I
have spent some of the money already, on an
airship of my own, and she is being overhauled
at Zagwa harbour as I write. She's a converted
Achebe 1000, and we plan to call her Jenny
Haniver II. So when we come home we shall be
traders in our own right; Ngoni & Natsworthy of
New London, purveyors of Mag-Lev furniture to
the gentry. . . Trade is opening up again with the
east now that the Green Storm has gone and the
new League has made peace with the cities. We
may even cross the ocean to America, and see
my old friends and my old home at Anchorage-
in-Vineland, and tell them about everything
that's happened. And of course we shall often
come to Zagwa.*

*Theo had a letter back from the Widow Naga,
which was very nice of her when you consider that
she's got the whole of the new Anti-Traction League
to run, and half the mountain kingdoms still knee-
deep in ash. She told him that Mum and Mr Shrike
reached Batmunkh Gompa with her on the evening
before Zhan Shan got zapped, and they rescued
Daddy and flew off in the Jenny Haniver. She
doesn't seem to know where they went, or why,
but the burnt-out wreck of a ship with Jeunet Carot
pods was found later at a valley in the Erdene
Shan. She says that, if I want to, I could go there,
and pay my respects in the place where they died.*

*It's thoughtful of her, but I don't want to go. I feel
certain Dad and Mum are dead, but even if that is*

the Jenny's wreck at Erdene Shan, that's not where they are. They've gone. Nobody knows where, and no one ever will. But I like to think that they've taken the Bird Roads, west of the sun, beyond the moon, flying off together into wild skies and wonderful adventures. Sometimes, without quite meaning to, I find myself looking up, as if there's still a part of me that expects to see the Jenny Haniver come out from behind a cloud or the shoulder of a mountain, bringing them home. . .

And now the light has gone, and the moon is rising, and here comes Theo, running down the stairs from the house to tell me that the evening meal is ready. So I will close now, and hope this finds you soon.

With love to all of London,

Wren

54

SHRIKE IN THE WORLD TO COME

Shrike had arrived too late. He ran like a ghost through the mountains, and came to Erdene Tezh just before dawn, when the sky above the lake was scratched with the trails of shooting stars.

The house was a ruin by then; grey ash; charred beams; a few trickles of white smoke still drifting across the garden. In a chamber full of carbonized machinery he found the remains of the Stalker Fang, and knelt beside her. The gimcrack Engineer-built part of her brain had stopped working, but he sensed faint electrical flutterings fading in the other, older part. He unplugged one of the flexes from his skull and fitted it into a port on hers. Her memories whispered to him, and his mind drank them.

The sun rose. Shrike went back out into the garden, and in the gathering light he saw Tom and Hester waiting for him by the fountain. He had not noticed them in the dark, for they were as cold as the stones they lay upon.

Shrike went down on his knees beside them, and gently drew out the knife which Hester had driven through her own heart. At first he thought that if he were quick he could still carry her to Batmunkh Gompa and make Oenone Zero Resurrect her. But when he started to lift her he found that she had clutched Tom's hand as she died, and she was still clinging tightly to it.

If Stalkers could cry, he would have cried then, for he knew all at once that this was the right end for her, and that she would not want him to take her from this quiet valley, or from the once-born she had loved.

So he lifted them together, and carried them away from the house. As he crossed the causeway the slack weight of their bodies shook a faint memory loose in him. He checked to see if it was one of those he had just absorbed from Anna Fang, but it was his own. Long ago, before he was a Stalker, he had had children, and when they were sleepy and he had carried them to their beds, they had lain just as limp and heavy in his arms as Tom and Hester lay now.

The memory was a fragment; a gift; a down-payment on that knowledge of his past which Oenone Zero had promised would come to him when he died. But that would not be for a long time. He had been made to last.

He found a place at the head of the valley where a river tumbled down in white cataracts past a rocky outcrop; where a stunted oak tree grew. It reminded him of things Hester had told him about the lost island of her childhood. There he laid her down with Tom, side by side, still holding hands, their faces almost touching. Unsheathing his claws for the last time, he cut away their soggy clothes, the belts and boots they would no longer need. There was a shallow cave at the foot of the rocks nearby, and he went and sat down in it, watching and waiting, wondering what he would find to do in a world that no longer held Hester.

That evening airships buzzed down to land at the ruin on the lake. After a while they went away again.

Days flew over the valley of Erdene Tezh. In the fitful sunlight Tom and Hester began to swell and darken beneath their shroud of flies. Worms and beetles fed on them, and birds flew down to take their eyes and tongues. Soon their smell attracted small mammals, who had been going hungry in that cheerless summer.

Shrike did not move. He shut down his systems one by one until only his eyes and his mind were awake. He watched the graceful architecture of Tom and Hester's skeletons emerge, their bare skulls leaning together like two eggs in a nest of wet hair. Winter heaped snow over them; the rains of spring washed them clean. Next summer's grass grew thick and green beneath them, and an oak sapling sprouted in the white basket of Hester's ribs.

Shrike watched it all while the years fell past him, green and white, green and white. The small bones of their hands and feet scattered into the grass like dice; larger ones were tumbled and gnawed by foxes; they turned grey and crumbly and it became hard to tell whose had been whose.

The oak sapling grew into a tree, spread out a canopy that blushed green in summer and threw dancing shadows over Shrike; shed acorns that became new saplings, grew old, trailed beards of lichen, died and fell and rotted, giving up its goodness to the roots of younger trees which were spreading down the hillside to the lake.

Shrike sank deeper into his fugue. Stars blurred over him; seasons blinked at him. The trees became a wood. Bare branches breathed in, exhaled green leaves, turned golden, bare, breathed in.

At last a human figure began to flash in front of him, stooping again and again to place something around his neck. With a deep effort he began to rouse himself; the flicker of day and night becoming less frantic as the whirl of seasons and centuries slowed.

A summer morning. Green light shining through the leaves of an ancient oak wood. Garlands of flowers decked Shrike's torso, and the remnants of older garlands lay dried and crumbling in his mossy lap. His shoulders were shaggy with ferns. A bird had nested in the crook of his arm. Of Tom and Hester nothing remained but a little dust blowing between the gnarled roots of the trees.

Goats were moving through the wood. The bells on their necks chimed softly. A small once-born boy came and stood looking at Shrike, and was joined by a girl, still smaller. They had ochre skin, brown eyes, dusty black hair.

"HELLO," said Shrike. His voice was rustier and more screechy than ever. The boy fled, but the girl stayed, speaking to him in a language which he did not know. After a while she went and picked some small blue flowers among the oak-trees and made a crown for him. Her brother came back, cautious, wide-eyed. The little girl brought some fat and rubbed it into Shrike's joints. He moved. He stood up. Gravel and owl-pellets cascaded off him; he shook himself free of cobwebs and birds' nests and moss.

The girl took his hand, and her brother led them down the valley amid a bleating, chiming crowd of goats. They stopped at a village, where adult once-born came to stare at Shrike, and poke him with sticks and the handles of simple farm tools. Listening to their excited chatter, he started to decipher their language. They'd thought him nothing but an old statue, sitting there in his cave. They had hung flowers about his neck for luck each summer when they brought their goats up to the high pastures. They had been doing it since their mothers' mothers' time.

Down a track to a paved road, riding on a cart now, the children beside him. The sun was redder than Shrike recalled, the air clearer, the mountain climate kinder. A town lay cupped in a wooded vale. Shrike wondered if his new friends realized that its ancient metal walls were made from the tracks of a mobile city, and that some of its round, rust-brown watchtowers had once been wheels. They seemed simple people, and he imagined that their society had no machines at all, but as they brought him through the town gates he saw delicate airborne ships of wood and glass rising like dragonflies from tall stone mooring-towers. Silvery discs, like misty mirrors, swivelled and pivoted on their undersides, and the air beneath them rippled like a heat-haze.

They took him to a meeting place, a big hall in the city's heart. People crowded round him to ask questions. What kind of being was he? How long had he been asleep? Was he one of the machine-men out of the old stories?

Shrike had no answers. He asked questions of his own. He asked if there were any places in the world where cities still moved and hunted and ate each other. The once-born laughed. Of course there weren't; cities only moved in fairy tales; who would want to live in a moving city? It was a mad idea!

"What are you *for*?" asked one boy at last, pushing to the front of the crowd. Shrike looked down at him. He pondered a while, thinking of something Dr Popjoy had told Anna.

"I AM A REMEMBERING MACHINE," he said.

"What do you remember?"

"I REMEMBER THE AGE OF THE TRACTION CITIES. I REMEMBER LONDON AND ARKANGEL; THADDEUS VALENTINE AND ANNA FANG. I REMEMBER HESTER AND TOM."

His listeners looked blank. Someone said, "Who were they?"

"THEY LIVED LONG AGO. IT SEEMS ONLY YESTERDAY TO ME."

The little girl who'd found Shrike looked up at him and said, "Tell us!" Around her, people smiled, and nodded, settling down cross-legged, waiting to see what stories he had brought for them out of the lost past. They liked stories. Shrike felt, for a moment, almost afraid. He didn't know how to begin.

He sat down on the chair they brought for him. He took the little girl on his lap. He watched dust-motes dancing in the ancient sunlight that poured like honey through the hall's long windows. And then he turned his face towards the expectant faces of the once-born, and began.

"IT WAS A DARK, BLUSTERY DAY IN SPRING," he said, "AND THE CITY OF LONDON WAS CHASING A SMALL MINING TOWN ACROSS THE DRIED-UP BED OF THE OLD NORTH SEA. . ."